WHAT *Hope*
REMEMBERS

Books by Johnnie Alexander

MISTY WILLOW

Where She Belongs
When Love Arrives
What Hope Remembers

MISTY WILLOW · BOOK THREE

WHAT *Hope* REMEMBERS

A NOVEL

JOHNNIE ALEXANDER

Revell

a division of Baker Publishing Group
Grand Rapids, Michigan

Published by Revell
a division of Baker Publishing Group
P.O. Box 6287, Grand Rapids, MI 49516-6287
www.revellbooks.com

Printed in the United States of America

Library of Congress Cataloging-in-Publication Data
Names: Alexander, Johnnie, author.
Title: What hope remembers / Johnnie Alexander.
Description: Grand Rapids, MI : Revell, a division of Baker Publishing Group, [2017] | Series: Misty Willow ; 3
Identifiers: LCCN 2016056151| ISBN 9780800726423 (softcover) | ISBN 9780800728939 (print on demand)
Subjects: LCSH: Man-woman relationships—Fiction. | First loves—Fiction. | GSAFD: Christian fiction. | Love stories.
Classification: LCC PS3601.L35383 W46 2017 | DDC 813/.6—dc23
LC record available at https://lccn.loc.gov/2016056151

This book is a work of fiction. Names, characters, places, and incidents are the product of the author's imagination or are used fictitiously.

17 18 19 20 21 22 23   7 6 5 4 3 2 1

For Carol Anne and Joy

My treasured friends in the Sunland

For thus said the Lord GOD, the Holy One of Israel,
"In returning and rest you shall be saved;
in quietness and in trust shall be your strength."

Isaiah 30:15

- 1 -

The June sun beat on Gabe Kendall's bare head and tapped into his childhood memories of the horse farm. He leaned his arms on the weathered fence and let his mind bask in the remembrance of long summer days under tranquil blue skies.

The pastures, lush and green. The paddock with its packed dirt circuit. The stables, once alive with the soft snuffles of contented horses and the familiar smells of oiled leather, fresh hay, and honest sweat.

Except for the glow of memory, nothing was the same.

The horse barn, the machine shed, even the nearby house were smaller than he remembered. Perhaps a consequence of seeing his uncle's place for the first time with grown-up eyes. Or maybe his imagination had tricked him into thinking everything about the place was bigger. God knew he'd experienced too many nights when the only way he could lull himself to sleep was to conjure up happier times.

That long-ago summer, the summer after Mom's last illness, he'd cut hay, filled the silo with the yellow kernels of newly harvested corn, and ridden horseback every chance he got. When the chores were done, he dozed beneath the old sycamore back by the pond. And he prayed for a return to *before*. The same prayer he wanted to pray now.

Not that it would do any good.

Praying wouldn't erase the cracked paint on the fence and the buildings, the clumps of weeds overtaking the grass. Wouldn't transform the land into the paradise he remembered. Ugly facts taunted him with their stark reality.

A forlorn air hung over the place, heavy with regret and heartache. But the silent emptiness wasn't because of his adult perspective or the glow of childhood memory.

Whisper Lane Stables might be a thriving business if Rusty were still alive. Except then he'd know how low Gabe had fallen . . .

His muscles tensed at the *thwack* of the house's screen door, and he jerked toward the noise. Aunt Tess strode toward him, and he breathed out the adrenaline pulsing through his body. His fisted hands slowly opened, and he swiped his palms against his jeans.

"It's not how you remembered." Tess stood next to him and stared into the distance. Her jet black hair, plaited into one thick braid that nearly reached her waist and evidence of her great-grandmother's Native American heritage, held streaks of gray that hadn't been there before.

"I should have been here." Gabe put his arm around her, pulling her into a sideways hug and breathing in her familiar scent. Charlie cologne. At least one thing hadn't changed.

"You're here now." Her voice caught, but she quickly regained control. "I'd have visited you. If you'd let me."

"I couldn't."

"You're too full of pride. Just like your uncle."

"I miss him."

"So do I." She flashed a smile. "But it's nice having you here again. Just like old times."

He pressed his lips together and slowly inhaled. In the past several years, he'd steeled himself against showing weakness, but a few kind words from his uncle's widow could turn him into a blubbering idiot if he wasn't careful.

Time to change the subject.

"See you still have the old pickup." He nodded toward the dusty two-tone Ford F-150 parked beside the detached garage. The once-vivid red had faded, and the tan sides hadn't fared much better. The dent where Gabe had accidentally hit a fence post still marred the rust-spotted fender. But hey, he'd only been twelve at the time.

"I kept it for you," Tess said.

"You should have sold it."

"Wasn't mine to sell. Besides, it's not worth much to anyone but you and me."

"Rusty taught me to drive in that heap."

"I remember. Your mom wasn't too happy."

"She sure gave me a tongue-lashing," Gabe said. "But I overheard her telling Dad about it later. They were laughing."

"She could never stay mad at you for long." Tess gazed up at him, then squeezed his arm. "Look at you. So like Rusty when he was your age."

"Except he never disgraced the family."

"Neither have you."

Gabe snorted. "You haven't talked to my dad lately, have you?"

She looked away for a moment, then turned toward him again, a warm smile brightening her face. "Come inside, and we'll get you settled. I have a batch of snickerdoodles cooling on the counter. Are those still your favorite cookies?"

"Anything you bake is my favorite."

"Let's go, then."

"Would it be okay if I didn't take you up on that offer right away?"

"Is something wrong?"

"It's been a while since I've been on a horse." He trusted her to understand that the longing inside him ran deeper than his need to be in a saddle again. He craved the freedom, the solitude, of a long ride in fresh air and sunshine.

Her concern changed to empathy, and she pointed toward one of the pens. "Take Daisy. It'll do her good to stretch her legs."

"You're still naming horses after flowers?"

"Only that line. She was Marigold's last foal." Sadness flickered in Tess's dark eyes. "Looks just like her. Same sweet disposition too."

"I remember Marigold. What happened to her?"

"I sold her."

"Without telling me?" he asked, then wished he hadn't. The answer, any answer, only added another loss to his pile of guilt.

"At first it was too hard to write about. And later, well, I guess by then it was old news." She pressed her lips into a tight smile. "Are you riding back to the Hearth?"

"Not today." Probably not ever. The stone fireplace, all that remained of a nameless pioneer's cabin, was best left alone. "Does that land on the north side of Glade Creek still belong to you?"

"For now. I lease it to one of the locals for his Angus herd. Which reminds me. I have this thing to go to tonight."

"What thing?"

"An appreciation reception at the old Misty Willow homestead."

"Appreciation for what?"

"It's been named to the National Register of Historic Places. I'm on the committee that put together the application. We're also planning a huge celebration in a couple of weeks."

Something niggled at Gabe's memory. A scandal of some sort. "Do the Sullivans still own that place?"

"No. And yes." She chuckled. "Promise you'll go with me, and I'll catch you up on the local news after your ride."

"You've got a date." He headed for the tack room for a saddle, then turned and jogged backward. "I don't have to wear a tie, do I?"

"You are so like your uncle."

He'd always wanted to be. If only his life hadn't taken a different turn.

~

So this was the place.

Amy Somers clambered on top of the rustic picnic table and drank from her sports bottle. Normally she didn't care for the taste of the vitamin-enriched water, but the long hike from the cottage had made her thirsty.

The sun glinted on the creek's broad surface, and long-stemmed cattails gathered in clumps along the bank. Wild daisies, purple clover, and Queen Anne's lace rose from the grassy field. The ancient willow balanced on the edge of the creek, its elegant fronds dipping their ends into the sparkling water.

Family picnics took place here. Burgers and hot dogs, potato salad and baked beans, followed by exhilarating games of tag, mostly futile attempts to catch fish, and restful catnaps.

At least that was what she'd been told. She'd never been here before today.

Not because she hadn't been invited. Staying away had simply been easier.

She sipped more water, then propped her slightly pink arms across her knees. Sunburn. Another joy of country living. A summer-scented breeze momentarily cooled her skin, and she added sunscreen to her mental shopping list.

The same breeze lifted the willow's fronds so they appeared to dance beside the creek.

The misty willow. The engagement tree.

First AJ and then Brett had proposed to their respective brides in this quiet, peaceful, bug-ridden place. Her cousin, she understood. Like Gran, AJ preferred the rural community over the hustle and bustle of life in the big city.

But her brother had her flummoxed. About ten months ago,

Brett had been honored as one of Columbus's up-and-coming young professionals. His thriving business, inherited from their grandfather, was poised to become a major regional development firm. His future seemed golden.

Until he turned his back on all of it—the lucrative investment opportunities, his luxury apartment, Monday nights with the guys—and settled into a four-bedroom ranch down the road from the cottage. True, it had the most elegant upgrades of any ranch-style house in Glade County. Amy made sure of that, steering her sister-in-law to only the finest granite countertops, deluxe appliances, and high-end cabinetry during the rehab.

But it was still a house in the middle of nowhere among people who weren't like the Somerses. People who didn't know the difference between a dessert spoon and a soup spoon. Who'd rather have barbecue and beer than filet mignon and a fine wine.

She swiped angrily at the tears that unexpectedly dampened her cheeks.

Brett and AJ were the only family she had, and now she'd lost them. They'd fallen in love, married, and lived within two miles of each other.

They thought she'd moved from Columbus to be closer to them. One big happy family. Didn't they know her at all?

The truth . . . She could hardly bear to face the truth herself, let alone tell her brother and cousin. She'd already had her fill of their pity.

Enough!

She scooted off the picnic table, suddenly anxious to do what she'd come to do—find the plaques Brett and AJ had hung on the engagement tree. To trace the initials engraved into its trunk, the initials of couples who believed in "till death do us part."

To wallow in the pain of being left alone. Abandoned again.

But instead of slipping between the willow's draping fronds, she veered toward the creek and plopped onto the bank. She picked a white daisy from a nearby clump and twirled its rough stem between her finger and thumb.

He loves me. He loves me not.

No need to pull the satiny petals from the golden center. She had no *he*.

She tossed the daisy in the creek. It drifted with the gentle current, floating lazily, carelessly.

Once it disappeared behind a partially submerged boulder, Amy rose, then hesitated as the sound of a welcoming nicker came from across the creek. A buckskin horse ambled toward the bank, and the rider lifted his hand in a friendly wave.

Amy took several steps backward, her gaze never wavering from the intruder and his horse. Another foot or so and he would be trespassing. Though there was little she could do about that.

Besides, she had no idea what arrangements AJ had with the neighbors. For all she knew, this guy was allowed to come and go as he pleased. The stranger reached her side of the creek, then dismounted. He ambled toward her, allowing plenty of slack in the reins, while the mare nibbled at the lush grass near the shore.

"Howdy," he said with an exaggerated twang. She waited for the expected appraising look, idly wondering what form it would take. The quick up-and-down or the lingering once-over?

But his eyes, shaded by the brim of a well-worn Stetson, never left her face. Not knowing whether to be intrigued or insulted, she maintained the poker face she'd perfected during her lobbying career and did her own appraisal. Light brown hair, worn a little too long, poked from beneath the beige hat. A tan tee fit tight against muscles used to exercise. Despite the summer heat, he wore jeans and low-cut work boots.

Handsome enough for a lark, perhaps even for a night on the town. If he let her choose his wardrobe.

His lips curled as she finished her inspection. The slight smile was like a spark to her temper's short fuse.

"You're trespassing."

"Am I?"

"As soon as you crossed to this side of the creek."

"I'm Gabe Kendall. Maybe you know my aunt. Tess Marshall."

He can't be.

Amy stared at him, then blinked and looked away. Even though the stables were located across the road from the cottage, she hadn't allowed herself to indulge in those memories. Now they hovered at the edge of her mind.

She took another step backward.

"Are you all right?" His voice held genuine concern, but Amy didn't want his sympathy. Or to renew their acquaintance. That would only lead to an awkward walk down memory lane.

She slid onto the edge of the picnic table's seat and took a sip of water. "Just a little tired. The hike back here was longer than I expected."

He scanned the horizon, first one direction then the other. "You live at the Sullivan hideaway?"

"If you mean the cottage, yes. I moved in earlier this week."

"My uncle Rusty always called it the hideaway. Said if you didn't know it was there, you wouldn't know it was there."

"Isn't that true of anything?"

"It was his strange sense of humor. Guess you had to have known him."

I did know him.

Rusty and Tess were characters in her canopy world, a secluded place where people didn't break dishes and throw sharpened words at each other. A place where parents didn't promise to be back soon but never came home.

After the plane accident, she'd wrapped her canopy world of too few happy moments and pushed it to a place so deep inside of her that even months of her recent therapy hadn't touched it.

14

"Are you married to . . . what's his name? Goes by initials, doesn't he? Last I knew, he lived in the hideaway."

"You mean AJ? He's my cousin."

The stranger's gaze deepened and his mouth slightly opened. Amy could almost see the wheels in his mind turning as he looked for any resemblance to the girl she used to be.

"I remember you. We—"

"I doubt it." Amy turned her head and stared, unseeing, at the surrounding fields. Moving to the cottage had been a mistake. In her haste to escape from the present, she'd never expected that living here would push her into the past.

"You're Amy."

Still avoiding his gaze, she bit the inside of her mouth, pressing her teeth into the tender flesh. Physical pain she could handle. But not the anguish churning inside.

If only she'd had other options. Though the truth was, she had hoped to find the same peace here that Gran had found. Despite her protests of hating the country, Amy wanted to be near Brett so he wouldn't forget the little sister he'd promised never to leave. And she wanted to be near Jonah.

Never had she expected to run into Gabe Kendall.

He stepped into her peripheral vision and tilted his head to catch her gaze. "You're Amy Somers."

"I am." *Only because it's too late to be anyone else.*

"We rode together sometimes. When you took lessons from my aunt."

His words floated along the breeze between them as the memories slipped from the canopy into her consciousness. She glanced at the buckskin. With her creamy coat and black stockings, her ebony mane and tail, the mare could be Marigold. But that was impossible. Too many years had gone by. Too many to indulge in a childhood crush.

"I don't remember you," she said, her tone clipped and even.

"I guess I shouldn't be surprised." He gave a sheepish shrug. She'd have found it endearing if her heart wasn't made of stone.

She stood, pushing away from the table and the nostalgic scent of horse sweat and leather. "I should be going. It was nice meeting you." *Again.*

"Do you want to ride?" he asked hurriedly.

"Excuse me?"

"You said you were tired. Daisy and I can take you back to the hide—the cottage."

Panic gripped her throat, and she clutched the neckline of her top.

"I'll walk alongside if that's what's got your rope in a tangle. Though it looks to me like you could use a good gallop. May be just the thing to set the world right again."

She grasped the table edge and dug her fingernails into the wood. "You know nothing about me," she finally said. Her voice rasped with harshness.

"Maybe I should take my own advice, then." He tipped his hat and gathered the reins. With a fluidity that took Amy's breath away, he was astride the mare. Daisy took a few steps forward, and Amy shrank against the table.

"You're not afraid of Daisy, are you?" The concern in his voice also shone in his eyes. "She's as gentle as they come."

"I'm not afraid of anything," Amy retorted. But her voice wavered, and her breath seemed to strangle in her throat.

He held his gaze steady, and it took all her practiced skill not to wither into a heap. But he couldn't know she cared anything about what he said or what he thought. Nor could she show weakness. That only led to pain.

– 2 –

*G*abe pulled out of his aunt's driveway, expertly engaging the gears of Tess's Dodge Ram pickup. The vehicle had seen better days, and he doubted she was holding on to it for the same sentimental reason she kept the Ford. When it came to feeding the horses or buying new wheels, Tess fed the horses. She'd lived that philosophy for so long it was as natural to her as breathing.

The horses weren't the only ones benefitting from his aunt's generosity. Despite her insistence he take some time for himself, he needed to find a job as soon as possible. But it wouldn't be easy given his record. Besides, the local farming community wasn't exactly in an economic upswing.

"I still can't get over you running into Amy Somers like that," Tess said as they drove past the hideaway's entrance. Except for the drive and the gate, the rest of the property was almost completely hidden from the road by its tall, thick hedge. "I had no idea she'd moved here. It's so odd."

"Why's that?"

"She's a city girl. Too high and mighty for us country folk. And how could she not remember you?"

"No reason why she should." He said it lightly, as if it didn't matter. But truth be told, he'd been stung by her words. He could understand her forgetting the arrowhead he'd given her, though even that seemed unlikely. But who didn't remember their first kiss?

Tess settled back in her seat, a slight smile brightening her features. "I can picture her so clearly as a young girl. All dressed up in her fancy riding habit. Her boots polished to a brilliant shine. She had such an instinct for seating a horse."

"You'd never know it from seeing her now."

"What do you mean?"

"She seemed scared of Daisy. I thought she was going to have a panic attack when I offered to let her ride back to the hideaway. Or, as she so quickly corrected me, the 'cottage.'"

"Amy scared of a horse? That does sound strange. All I know is that she quit her lessons after her parents were killed." Tess sighed heavily. "Such a tragedy."

"Yeah," Gabe murmured.

"Riding seemed to help you after your mom died." Tess gently squeezed his arm in a comforting gesture. "I thought being in the saddle would ease Amy's grief too. Her grandmother tried to persuade her to come back, but she refused."

Gabe eased the truck to a rolling stop, checked both directions, then made the left turn. Aunt Tess was right—living with her and Uncle Rusty had patched up the broken pieces of his heart after Mom lost her last battle with cancer. They allowed him to grieve, to get angry, when all Dad wanted him to do was suck it up like a man. A fourteen-year-old man.

But it had been Amy, with her long golden hair, calm blue eyes, and mercurial demeanor who showed him it was okay to laugh again.

The memory he'd been holding at arm's length pushed through, and he blinked against the pain of the last time he'd touched her hand.

They rode in silence for several minutes before Tess broke into his thoughts. "The driveway is just around this bend," she said.

He startled, then focused on navigating the deep curve. The imposing brick house, set back from the road among several huge trees, looked completely different than he remembered.

"The last time I was here, I was trespassing."

"You didn't."

"An empty house is a great place to pass around a bottle of whiskey. Especially when you're underage."

"It was that Nate Donley, wasn't it? He never was a good influence on you."

"I think his mother said the same thing about me."

"She was oh so wrong. You were perfect. Still are."

"Thanks for believing that. Especially when we both know it's not true."

"We're going to a party, Gabe. No gloomy thoughts allowed. You hear me?"

He chuckled at her reprimanding tone, as if he were a kid again. "Yes, ma'am," he said smartly.

"Though I confess, if I'd known you were sneaking in there, I might have joined you."

"You wanted to drink whiskey with Nate and me?" Gabe teased.

She gave him a reproving look. "I only wanted to see inside. All those years the house stood empty, I just thought it was such a shame. But unlike you and your miscreant friend, I resisted the temptation."

"How come?"

"Because I wasn't a teenager without any sense. Besides, it wouldn't have been right. I'd never been inside when the Lassiters lived there. Why should I after they were gone?"

"They wouldn't have known."

"But I would have."

Gabe turned into the drive and stopped the car. Through the

windshield, the restored house, lush lawn, and well-tended land-scaping welcomed them. The front porch had been rebuilt since the last time he'd stood on it, and the windows gleamed in the light of the early-evening sun.

"It sure looks different than it used to."

"It's just as lovely inside too."

"So you did go exploring," he teased.

"Only after Shelby—that's AJ's wife—invited me to join the committee." She pointed straight ahead. "You can park beyond that gate."

Gabe continued up the drive. Several cars had parked in the graveled loop that circled the grassy area beside the house, but Tess directed him farther up the lane. He drove through the gate and past a hedged fence on his right. About fifty feet farther on was a paved parking lot.

Once they were out of the car, he pointed toward the hedge. "Isn't that where the barn used to be?"

Tess nodded. "Now it's the archaeological dig."

"Any chance of seeing the tunnel?"

"They're still digging it out, but I can ask AJ to show you around."

"I haven't seen AJ in years." Even then, they'd only been ac-quaintances. Never close friends. "I'd be surprised if he remem-bered me."

"Do you think I haven't talked his ear off about my favorite nephew?"

"Your only nephew." They smiled at the old familiar joke, then Gabe frowned. "I guess that means he knows . . ."

"He does. But he won't hold the past against you."

Gabe wasn't so sure, but this wasn't the time to discuss the issue. He took her arm and escorted her along the graveled drive. After walking through the gate, they passed a weathered wheelbarrow with a white chicken statue perched near the front wheel. Tiny colorful flowers on thick green vines cascaded over the sides while purple and gold irises, yellow and white daisies, and flowering vines lined the fencerow.

"What's Shelby's story again?" Gabe asked. "The condensed version."

"Her ancestors settled Misty Willow a couple hundred years ago. But shortly before her grandparents died, AJ's grandfather, Sully Sullivan, somehow ended up with the property. When Sully died, he left it to AJ."

"Who didn't do anything with it."

"Not until Shelby showed up a year ago, wanting to buy it. She turned it into a home again and moved in with her two daughters."

"And now it's a museum."

"The Lassiter Family Underground Railroad and Civil War Research Center."

"That's a mouthful."

"Which is why we still call it Misty Willow." Tess stopped to wave at a couple who slowly drove by on their way to the parking area. "At least no one will be able to take it away from the Lassiters again."

"Who would want to?"

Tess gave him a strange look, as if she wanted to say something but didn't know how.

"What is it?" he asked.

"I was just thinking how much you remind me of Rusty." She placed her hand along his cheek. "And I want to thank you for coming with me tonight."

"Did I have a choice?" he teased.

"Not really. Let's go in, shall we?"

Gabe followed Tess up the stairs of the concrete patio. Apparently there was more to the Misty Willow story, something she was hesitant to tell him. He had a vague memory of the long-ago feud between the Lassiters and the Sullivans. But none of it had anything to do with him, so why had Tess suddenly become so secretive?

She knocked on the doorframe, and Gabe took a long look around the serene countryside before he reluctantly followed Tess inside the huge brick house.

- 3 -

*B*alancing a plate of hors d'oeuvres and a glass of punch, Gabe stood in the doorway to what had probably been the family's living room. Folding chairs filled in the gaps between a couple of seating areas and various displays. All he had to do was claim one.

He noted the room's exits—an open door leading to the outside patio, a set of closed double doors, and the entrance from the hallway he'd just walked through. None of the unoccupied chairs gave him a line of sight to all three.

He shifted toward the sound of a childish laugh. A small sofa sat at an angle to the fireplace, the hearth graced with a large bouquet of flowers. Amy Somers sat beside a young boy bent over an electronic tablet. The two seemed lost in their own world.

In this unguarded moment, Amy's expression showed none of the wary defensiveness she'd worn at the creek. Before he could stop himself, he glanced at her left hand. The same surreptitious peek he'd managed earlier when she'd clutched the picnic table. No wedding band then and none now.

Yet the boy's blond hair matched hers almost exactly. Their family resemblance was unmistakable.

Just then Amy glanced up and caught him staring. He tried to hide his embarrassment with a broad smile. "Mind if I join you? I never quite got the trick of handling a plate and a glass at the same time."

"If you wish," she said distantly.

He set his plate and glass on the coffee table, then situated a folding chair so his back was to the double doors. Under the circumstances, it was the best he could do. Not that he expected any trouble here.

Once he was seated, he focused on the boy. "Who's this young man?"

Amy playfully poked the boy with her elbow.

"I'm Jonah," he said as he looked up from the screen. "Jonah Jensen."

"Glad to meet you. I'm Gabe Kendall."

"Are you a friend of Aunt Amy's?"

An odd sense of relief buoyed Gabe's spirits. So Jonah was her nephew, not her son. Not that it should matter.

"He's an acquaintance," Amy said.

Gabe started to say something about them knowing each other when they were teenagers but changed his mind. "We met earlier today back at the creek."

"By the engagement tree?" Jonah asked.

"What's the engagement tree?"

"It's a nickname for the weeping willow," Amy answered.

"We go fishing there sometimes," Jonah chimed in.

"Do you catch anything?"

"Naw," the boy said. "Uncle AJ says we're just drowning worms. But it's still fun."

"Sure is. Guess I'll have to take my fishing gear with me next time I ride out there."

"Ride?" Jonah's eyes widened. "Like on a motorcycle?"

"Like on a horse."

"I've never ridden a horse before." His voice was filled with awe. "Have you, Aunt Amy?"

She pasted on a smile and gazed at Gabe. "I'm surprised to see you here."

"I tagged along with Tess. She's on a committee for the Lassiter foundation. Though I guess you already know that."

"Actually, I don't. I haven't been involved with the heritage project. Or anything else to do with this place."

"I'm glad that didn't keep you from coming tonight."

"Dad made her," Jonah said.

"He did not," Amy protested.

"He said—"

"Never mind what he said." She straightened her shoulders and gave Gabe a smile that didn't reach her eyes. "Are you interested in local history?"

"Not sure I ever gave it much thought."

"Then you'll want to avoid our hostess. It's about the only thing she talks about."

"Shelby? I talked to her and AJ when we got here." He focused on Amy's facial expression while keeping his tone nonchalant. "Though it turns out Shelby and I met a couple of times when we were kids. We actually remember each other. AJ remembered me too."

"How interesting," Amy said drily.

"Do you know about the hidden room?" Jonah asked.

Amy immediately squeezed Jonah's knee and whispered, "You're not supposed to talk about that."

"You just said not to tell Elizabeth and Tabby," he whispered back. "And Dad."

"But I meant no one. Their mom doesn't want them to know where it is."

"You won't say anything, will you?" Jonah said, a tentative expression in his clear blue eyes as he looked at Gabe.

"Who are Elizabeth and Tabby?"

"They're just girls. We're kinda cousins."

"Don't worry. It'll be our secret." Gabe leaned forward to whisper conspiratorially. "Any chance of seeing this hidden room?"

"It's under the floor." Jonah tilted his head toward the wall behind him with a knowing look. "In the hall closet."

"Don't you dare go near it," Amy said. "Not with all these people around. And never without me. Promise?"

"I promise." Jonah's tone clearly said "enough already."

The kid's impudence gave Gabe a mischievous urge to pursue the topic despite Amy's irritation.

"Have you been in it?" he asked.

"Once." Jonah pretended to flinch as Amy shot him a "would you be quiet" look.

"If you must know," she said, bending forward so no one else could hear, "Jonah and I explored the room when no one else was here." She put her arm around the boy and gave him a little shake. "It's supposed to be *our* secret."

"What's it like?" Gabe tensed as a blond man entered the door from the hallway. He carried a snack plate and smiled when he noticed Jonah and Amy.

Jonah's face lit up. "Hi, Dad."

"Hey there, buddy." The man tousled Jonah's hair as he settled onto the couch beside Amy. He nodded at Gabe. "I don't think we've met. I'm Brett Somers."

Of course. Amy's brother. "Gabe Kendall."

"Nice to meet you, Gabe. Amy didn't tell me she was bringing a date."

Amy's eyes shot daggers at her brother. "He's not my date."

Brett leaned back in exaggerated response to her vehemence, almost exactly mirroring Jonah when he'd done the same. "I didn't recognize you as one of the locals," he said to Gabe, "so I thought she dragged you here. Sorry."

"Tess Marshall was married to my uncle," Gabe said. "I stayed with them sometimes as a kid."

"I thought you looked vaguely familiar." Brett's congenial tone was welcoming. Certainly more than Amy's had been. "I remember going to the stables a couple times. That was years ago."

"I don't recall you spending much time in the saddle."

"Riding was Amy's hobby, not mine."

Gabe glanced at Amy. She stared at the game Jonah was playing, but her thoughts were obviously somewhere else. Sitting beside her brother, she looked even slighter than she had before. A fragility surrounded her as an adult that he didn't remember seeing in her when they were younger. But of course, he'd been a kid then himself. Kids didn't notice such things.

"Aunt Amy, do you know how to ride a horse?"

"I used to."

"Can you teach me? Please."

Emotions cascaded across Amy's face, there and gone before Gabe could catch any of them. She seemed to be drowning right before his eyes. He wanted to pull her from whatever turmoil held her in its grasp, but he didn't know how.

"I want to ride," Jonah said. "Can I, Dad?"

"Maybe when you're older, son." Brett gently touched Amy's arm, and the cascade stilled.

If not for Amy's reaction, Gabe would have volunteered to give Jonah a couple of lessons. But he sensed an undercurrent between her and Brett, and the last thing he wanted was to get sucked into it. Or to think too much about why the people he barely knew—AJ, Shelby, and Brett—remembered him. But Amy, who'd gone riding with him every chance she could, claimed she didn't.

"I never get to do anything." Jonah put the game on the table, then crossed his arms. "How old were you when you rode a horse?"

Gabe wasn't sure who the question was directed to, but before he could decide whether or not to answer, Amy spoke. "It doesn't matter." Her quiet voice was steadier than Gabe would have expected. "Our circumstances are different."

"Is that why you don't ride anymore?" Jonah asked. "Because now we're the same?"

"It's more than that."

Suddenly Gabe felt like an intruder. He didn't belong in this private place Jonah and Amy had entered, a place where only the two of them understood the conversation.

"What do you mean, you're the same?" Brett asked. Even he seemed confused.

"We both stayed in a hosp—" Jonah began.

"Hotel," Amy broke in. "We both stayed in a hotel when we . . . when we went on vacation. Didn't we, Jonah?"

Amy stared at the boy and he stared back, then he nodded his head slowly. "Yeah. That's what we did."

"Always fun staying at a hotel," Gabe said lamely.

The eddy beneath the conversation swirled around and between them. Brett, engrossed with the shrimp on his plate, seemed to regret asking the question, and it didn't take a rocket scientist to know what Jonah had intended to say.

Not *hotel* but *hospital*.

So why had he and Amy both been in the hospital? And why didn't she want Gabe to know?

Not that it was any of his business. He wasn't here to get entangled in the lives of these people. Especially not Amy's, since she'd made it clear she wanted nothing to do with him.

He only wanted to help Tess spruce up her property while he figured out the next chapter in his life. For now, God alone knew what the future held, and he wasn't telling. All Gabe could do was pray that this time he made the right decisions, did the right things.

In quietness and trust is my strength.

His paraphrase of the Isaiah verse gave him hope that the answers would eventually come.

Gabe's own plan for his life certainly hadn't worked out. One reckless moment, and the path he'd been on had been destroyed.

Now he wished he'd stayed at Tess's this evening. Sprawling on the sofa with a remote in one hand and a sports drink in the other was preferable to maneuvering around the Somers family landmines.

"Gabe?" Amy said softly.

"Beg your pardon."

"I just asked what you do," Brett said.

"You don't know?"

"How would I?"

"Guess you wouldn't." Gabe forced a tight smile. "I'm kind of between jobs right now. So it seemed a good time to visit Tess. Help out around her place. What about you?"

"Property development. Investments. That kind of thing."

"Don't let Brett mislead you," Amy said. "He's put his company on autopilot. Who knows what will be left of it by the time he returns. If he ever does."

"I talk to my assistant every day," Brett said, then looked sheepish. "Almost every day. Nothing's on autopilot."

"It's not the way Sully did things."

"I'm not Sully. And I don't want to be."

Gabe shifted in his seat. Maybe he should make an excuse and leave the siblings to their spat. Besides, he'd been sitting too long.

Brett must have noticed his discomfort. "Sorry," he said. "We're having a difference of opinion on my current management style."

"I'll leave you to it," Gabe said. "I need to stretch my legs a bit anyway." He nodded, then left the living room. As he entered the hall, a young woman asked if she could take his plate. He handed it to her, then looked around the hallway. A stairway to his right led up to the second floor. He rubbed his hand against the banister's polished wood.

He and Nate had slid down this banister a few times during

their furtive hijinks all those years ago. The house had been broken then, debris covering the floors and strange haunting noises coming from the attic. Probably nothing more dangerous than a few squirrels, but boys being boys, they'd concocted a couple of eerie ghost stories.

The murmur of multiple conversations came from the room across the hall, but Gabe had no desire to chitchat with anyone. As he stood in the foyer, undecided what to do, two young girls followed by a yellow retriever entered through the front door, and a cool breeze wafted through the hall.

That was where he wanted to be. Outside. Breathing fresh air. He couldn't get enough of it.

– 4 –

Amy's mind swirled with conflicting thoughts as Gabe left the room. He was only a year older than she was, so he should be on some kind of career ladder. Yet he'd neatly dodged Brett's question about his profession. Evasiveness always piqued her interest. Every experienced lobbyist knew the benefit of ferreting out hidden information. One never knew when it might come in handy.

Her curiosity had nothing to do with Gabe personally. Only with what he was hiding.

"Did you try these jalapeño poppers?" Brett asked, his voice a little too disinterested. The family therapist had advised him not to nag, but he couldn't seem to help himself.

"I didn't," she said pointedly. "But I ate three garlic chicken puffs and two spinach roll-ups. Plus I had a fruit cup. Didn't I, Jonah?"

"Yep," he said. "I counted."

"You counted?" Amy asked in disbelief. "Et tu, Brute?"

"Huh?"

"Never mind."

Brett tapped Jonah's leg. "You wouldn't lie to me, would you, son? Like you just lied to our new friend?"

Jonah's face turned red. "I didn't want to lie. But—"

"Don't blame him for backing me up," Amy said.

Brett took a bite of the cheesy popper. Amy could practically see the wheels turning as he weighed his possible responses. He was new to all this dad stuff. Just like she was new to all this aunt stuff. Neither of them wanted to make any mistakes.

"I didn't want a stranger knowing my business," she said.

"He's not exactly a stranger. Didn't you have a crush on him once?"

Brett couldn't have known that. Could he? If so, she needed to distract him, to keep his focus on Jonah. Besides, even she had to admit it was wrong to encourage her nephew to lie.

"I'm sorry, Jonah," she said. "I shouldn't have said what I did. There was no need to."

"No, it was my fault," Brett said. "I put you on the spot. But no more lying, okay, buddy?"

"Okay, Dad."

"Later you can tell Mr. Kendall you're sorry." Brett elbowed Amy. "Don't you think he should?"

"You think I should apologize to him, don't you?"

"Don't you want to set a good example?"

She resisted the urge to throttle him, but it wasn't easy. Were all big brothers this annoying? "You've become too honest," she whispered.

"What can I say? It's the new me."

She gave an exasperated sigh, then stood. For Jonah's sake, she'd confess one of the two lies she'd told Gabe today.

"I'm going to mingle," she said. "Don't leave without telling me good-bye."

"I won't," Jonah promised.

"See you later, gator."

"After while, 'dile."

Amy squeezed Jonah's knee. Their version of the silly farewell began the first time they'd met. Feeling ill-at-ease and wanting to appear cool, she'd gotten it wrong. Jonah teased her about the goof, and now it was their thing. Just hers and Jonah's.

She reached the doorway, then looked back. Brett and his mini-me son sat side-by-side on the sofa, heads bent over Jonah's game.

In a moment like this, seeing her brother with his son, Amy could forgive Brett for wanting a different life than the one he'd been leading. And because he was Brett, he'd gotten what he wanted. He always got what he wanted.

He had Jonah for several weeks while his mom was away. And Brett had married Dani, the only woman who'd been able to capture his heart. They were deeply in love, and he adored her.

But Amy's luck was never as good as her brother's. Not in life. Not in love.

She stepped into the hall as Gabe went outside. She smoothed her dress, straightened her shoulders, and followed him onto the porch.

He turned at the sound of the door opening behind him and leaned casually against the wooden column.

"Mind if I join you?" she asked.

"Please do."

She perched on the railing and smiled up at him. "I haven't been honest with you."

"About what?" He gave her a quizzical look, but both his expression and his voice told Amy that he knew exactly "about what." At least he thought he did. She'd been dishonest about two things, but she'd confess the minor one. The other one could wait. Maybe forever.

"Jonah was going to say hospital."

"So I guessed."

"He was in a car accident last year. A serious one. The injuries were severe, and he was in a coma for about three months."

"I'm sorry to hear that. I wouldn't have known from seeing him just now."

"He's made a great recovery. But it hasn't been easy. And now his parents are a little overprotective."

"Understandable."

"They fuss over him all the time. It's annoying."

"Were you driving?"

"Driving what?"

"The car. Jonah's accident."

"No, no." She shook her head. "We didn't even know Jonah then."

"You didn't know . . . but I thought . . ."

"I see your aunt hasn't filled you in on our dirty laundry."

"She's not one to do that."

"Short version. After Jonah's accident, Brett found out he was the dad. He and Meghan—that's Jonah's mom—are doing their best to co-parent despite their past history."

"I take it the history isn't pleasant."

"It's not. But they've put it behind them. It hasn't hurt that Brett is a newlywed and Meghan is working again. Jonah is living with Brett while his mom is in New York at an artist's retreat."

"So you weren't involved in the accident?"

"No."

"But you've been in the hospital too?"

"More like a clinic." Amy gauged his expression, knowing the thoughts running through his mind. *Rehab. Alcohol. Drugs. Maybe both.* His eyes studied hers, but she didn't glance away. She needed to know how he judged her.

"You don't owe me any explanations," he said. "I just hope you're better."

His noncommittal statement held a clear message—he wasn't interested in prying into her past. Perhaps his own reserve cooled his curiosity, or maybe he just didn't care. Though her finely honed people instincts told her that wasn't true.

"Thank you," she said, hoping he knew how much she meant it. "I am."

A comfortable silence surrounded them for a few moments. A curiously comfortable silence given how ill at ease she'd been with him at the creek. His showing up like that, seemingly out of nowhere, had stunned her.

The teen she'd known was no longer a boy, but a man whose hazel eyes, in this moment, held her captive.

Inexplicably, she wanted to take his hand. To relive the memory of their only kiss while sharing another.

She blew out a soft breath, releasing the longing into the evening breeze.

"Why are you really here?" she asked.

"Tess invited me."

"I don't mean *here*. I mean"—she waved her hands to encompass the countryside—"here. Visiting your aunt."

"She needs me."

"Why?"

"Apparently you haven't been to the stables in a while."

Not since I was thirteen. Dad was there too, that long-ago day, talking to Rusty. As Amy had ridden around the paddock for her lesson, hope soared within her. Dad had promised to buy her a horse, and she was certain he was making an offer on Marigold. Soon she would have her very own horse.

But then Dad had unexpectedly gone on that trip with Mom. Their plane crashed. No one survived.

And she'd never gone back to the stables.

She gave an involuntary shudder.

"Are you cold?" Gabe's tone held more surprise than concern. No wonder. The sun hung low in the sky, but its heat still warmed the summer air.

"I'm fine," she said.

"You seemed lost there for a minute."

"Maybe I was. You said something about the stables."

"Only that the place is a little run-down." He snorted a strange sound. "A lot run-down. It's so different than I remembered, than I imagined it when . . . I guess I've been away too long."

Amy nodded in understanding, allowing her thoughts to briefly touch the canopy memories. The lessons at the stables had been her refuge, the bright spot of her childhood. She could be most herself while riding, could whisper her heartaches into silky ears while brushing out a long mane.

Those were good days, days too precious to be exposed to remembrance. So she skirted the edges, recalling the whitewashed fencing, pristine and gleaming. The lovely flowerbeds that Gran admired. The irises—yes—Gran had taken irises to Tess. The women had planted them together while Amy sat on the fence and gazed over the pasture. Wishing with all her heart that this was her home, here, with the horses and the sun-scented breezes. How she longed to be with the horses every day instead of when it was convenient.

Mom's life held too much flurry, too many other appointments or plans for shopping and meeting friends for lunch, to drive Amy "all the way out to those smelly stables." But Dad and Gran tried to get her there as often as they could.

Dad because he loved his daughter. And to assuage his guilt.

Gran because she loved her granddaughter. And pitied her.

She sensed their feelings, but their guilt and pity didn't matter. Nothing did once she crossed beneath that arched iron entryway into Whisper Lane Stables. This was her magical world. All the anger, the stomach upset, the turmoil of her home life was forgotten. For a few hours, she could pretend nothing existed except this reality of horses and Tess's homemade cookies.

She pushed the memories beneath the canopy where they belonged. Safe and hidden.

"I'm surprised you didn't notice," Gabe said. "You have to see it every time you leave your driveway."

"I avoid looking." She didn't want to talk about the stables anymore, didn't want to know the place she'd loved so much was no longer perfect.

A pang unexpectedly struck her. Was that how Shelby felt when she returned to Misty Willow and saw her grandparents' house in such disrepair?

Amy tried to shake the thought away. The situations were totally different.

Shelby's was worse.

No wonder she'd been angry with the Sullivans. With AJ. Her grandparents' home was taken away from them and then abandoned until Shelby reclaimed it. She had wanted nothing more than to raise her children in that house. But then she turned it over to a nonprofit foundation rather than take a chance on losing it again.

Amy's plan was to develop the property into an upscale retreat, and she still smarted from being outwitted by a goody-two-shoes mom.

If AJ hadn't fallen in love with Shelby, Amy might not have given up so easily.

How different things would be if the events of the past year had turned out the way Amy wanted instead of how they did.

She'd still be in her Columbus high-rise apartment. Still plotting and scheming as part of her high-profile lobbyist job. She'd have her sights set on Washington and how she could become part of that glittering society.

But after her collapse, she never returned to the firm. All her plans had been ruined, leaving her alone and lonelier than she'd ever been in her life.

-5-

She avoids looking?

Gabe turned away, biting his lip so he wouldn't say something he might regret. Must be nice to put on blinders and ignore what's going on right across the road. Spoiled and over-indulged, Amy Somers probably didn't know or care that military personnel fought every day to protect her from threats she'd never know about. Or that some people were so desperate they risked everything for the sake of their families.

He glanced back at her and immediately checked his rising anger. With her blonde hair flowing past her shoulders and backlit by the sun's low rays, she resembled a golden statue. Her arms were clasped around her slender body—her expression stoic yet sad.

It was how she'd stood at her parents' memorial in the moments before he stepped beside her and reached for her hand.

The same impulse that had gripped him then gripped him now. But in his childish innocence, the boy could offer solace for her heartbreak. The man could no longer do that. Not when she claimed to have forgotten the memories that meant so much to him. Not when she'd grown up to be more beautiful than he could ever have imagined.

A city girl, Tess had called her. Definitely not the gal for a guy who'd traveled the road he had.

She abruptly faced him. "What happened to the stables?"

He could think of no reason to downplay the truth. "After Rusty died, the upkeep was more than Tess could do on her own."

"Then why didn't you come back sooner?"

"The Marine Corps wouldn't let me." Not exactly a lie. He'd been stationed in Afghanistan when he received news of Rusty's death. His leave had been too short to do much more than attend the funeral and help Tess with the most immediate matters.

"You're a Marine?"

"Why do you sound so surprised?" Maybe because his dream had been to have a horse farm of his own one day. Or maybe because his dad was career Air Force. Since she didn't remember him, she wouldn't know either of those things. And yet his heart told him she did.

"I shouldn't be surprised. You have the look of a soldier." Her lips curved into a teasing smile, and she gently tugged his hair. "Except for this."

Tantalized by her intoxicating perfume, he wanted to take her hand and caress her scented wrist. He stuck his hands in his pockets.

"Not a soldier—a Marine. I guess, after my discharge, I got a little scraggly."

"Scraggly looks good on you."

"You're not flirting with me, are you, ma'am?" he said in an exaggerated drawl. He couldn't help giving her the once-over. Her stylish dress, a vibrant blue that enhanced her eyes, skimmed her body then slightly flared above her knees. "Not that I mind."

She gave him another teasing smile, then by silent agreement they walked toward the graveled drive.

"When were you discharged?" she asked.

"A while ago."

"Couldn't have been that long ago."

"Why do you say that?" he asked, keeping his tone light. He should tell her, get the ugly truth that he'd endured the humiliation of a dishonorable discharge out in the open. But he didn't want to spoil this moment. It might be his only chance to talk to her. Once she learned of his record, she'd stay as far away from him as she could.

The truth could wait.

"Like I said, you look like a—a Marine."

"What does a Marine look like?" he asked.

"It's the way you stand, the way you walk. Even inside the house, you were scanning the room. Watching everyone."

"Didn't know I did that."

"You can relax. We don't have terrorists in Glade County. Nothing ever happens out here."

He gave a polite chuckle. "Guess some habits are hard to break." The wariness may have started while he was on tour, but his senses had sharpened even more in prison. Maybe Tess was right about him needing time to acclimate to the world beyond the iron bars.

They reached the graveled drive, then headed back toward the front porch.

"What about you?" Gabe asked. "What do you do?"

"I used to be a lobbyist-slash-consultant in Columbus. But circumstances changed." She sighed, then gave a wry smile. "Now I'm painting the cottage. Hanging around with Jonah."

"Did you like it, being a lobbyist?"

"Most of the time."

"What were your favorite causes?"

"The ones that paid the most money."

"So you're a mercenary."

"Just being honest." She caught his gaze as if to assess his reaction. Maybe she already knew his recent history. AJ could have told her.

This could be her way of challenging him to come clean with where he'd spent the past few years.

Later. He'd tell her later.

"Most of my projects were land developments," she said. "Which was helpful since that's Brett's area of expertise. He usually knows what's available, the zoning and all that."

"Sounds interesting, I guess. Nothing I'd ever want to do."

"Why not?"

"Politicians." He tugged at his open collar. "Having to wear a tie."

"You sound like AJ. Our grandfather wanted him to go into politics. Instead, he teaches school and coaches football. Such a waste."

"I doubt he thinks so."

"Think of the power he gave up."

"Is that what you want? Power?"

"Not enough to run for office myself. But to be a hidden influence behind the public face can be exciting."

"Then why did you give it up?"

"It was time." She paused on the sunny side of a hickory tree. "I guess I'm in a kind of limbo right now."

"I guess I am too."

"You don't have any plans for the future?"

"Only to help Tess fix up her place."

"It's not easy, is it? Being grown up. Responsible."

"At least I have a chance to ride again. I missed that."

Amy's expression hardened and she turned away. As she did, her shadow was swallowed by the long shadow cast by the tree. She slid a strand of her hair through her fingers, an unconscious gesture she'd had even as a kid.

What had happened to the girl who could ride for hours? Who never wanted the day to end when she was at the stables?

He should say good-bye. Walk away and leave her be. But his

heart wouldn't let him. The worst she could do was say no. He took a deep breath.

"How about we ride together sometime? Maybe go back to the Hearth."

See if that triggers your forgotten memories.

~

Amy froze as her mind raced. If Gabe went to the Hearth, he'd retrieve the tin box they'd hidden within the chimney's loose stones. He'd find the letter she'd written him before she left for college, and he'd find the arrowhead.

Hiding the items in the box had been her way of saying a final good-bye to her childhood dreams. But if he found them, he'd know she remembered every moment they'd spent together.

Maybe she should try to get there first. If she could even find the place again. It'd been hard enough last time, and that had been over ten years ago.

Her heart cried to say yes. To go riding with him, to be with him when he retrieved the box. But she couldn't. Those memories had to stay tucked inside her hidden canopy. Protected and unsullied from who she'd become.

"It's sweet of you to ask. But I haven't ridden since—"

"Aunt Amy," Jonah shouted as he raced across the lawn. When he reached her, he bent over, hands on his knees, and panted to catch his breath.

"You okay there?" she asked.

"Yeah. Daddy said it's time to go. I have to get a good night's sleep because of my appointment."

"What time do you need to be there?" Amy asked.

"I don't know." He lifted his shoulders so they almost touched his earlobes. "Daddy said we have to get up before the rooster crows. But we don't have a rooster."

"Give it time." The way Brett was embracing country life, he'd have an entire flock of chickens and probably a few ducks before the summer was over.

She glanced at Gabe, sensing he was curious about the appointment but was too polite to ask. "It's routine, a few tests to be sure he's healing the way he should."

"I get to pick where we go to lunch," Jonah said.

"Pick someplace good," Amy said. "If you stop by on your way home, I'll have a special treat for you."

"What kind of treat?"

"I haven't decided yet. But it'll be yummy."

"You're not going to make cookies again, are you?"

"What's wrong with my cookies?"

"They're gross." Jonah covered his mouth with both hands. "I wasn't supposed to tell you that."

"They weren't that bad. Only a little burnt."

Beside her, Gabe chuckled, and she shot him a dirty look.

"At least she tried," Jonah said, obviously parroting one of the adults in his life.

"My aunt Tess baked snickerdoodles for me today," Gabe said. "They're delicious."

"Snickerdoodles are my favorite."

"Mine too."

"My mom makes them." Jonah pulled at a blade of grass, then studied it intently. "Seems like she hasn't made them in a long time."

At his plaintive tone, Amy rested her hand on the back of his neck. "She'll be home before you know it. And I bet she'll bake you all the cookies you can eat."

"I guess so."

Amy wrestled with what else she could say to brighten Jonah's mood. He missed his mom—she understood that—but she didn't know how to cheer him up. If only Shelby were here. She always knew what to say. Amy glanced at Gabe, a silent plea for help.

He bent to Jonah's level, his hands above his knees. "I've got an idea. What if I share my snickerdoodles with you? They might not be as good as your mom's, but you still might like them."

"You'd do that?"

"I can bring them to you tomorrow."

"We'll be gone all day."

"Not a problem. I'll leave them on your doorstep."

"Do you know where I live?"

"Two or three miles down the road from me."

"I think that's a great idea."

Gabe held up his palm for a high five, and Jonah smacked it.

"Thank you," Amy mouthed over Jonah's head.

"Any time," Gabe mouthed back.

They returned to the house, and Gabe held the door open for Amy and Jonah to precede him into the hallway. Brett and Dani, sitting together on one of the stairsteps, greeted them. Jonah made a beeline for the couple and fell playfully against Brett's shins.

"Whoa there, buddy," Brett said as he grabbed his son around the waist and sat him on a lower step. "You ready to go home?"

"Do I have to?"

"I think we do."

Amy touched Gabe's arm. "Have you met Brett's wife?"

"Didn't have the pleasure."

"Dani Somers." Amy gestured from one to the other. "Gabe Kendall."

"He's Tess's nephew," Brett added.

"It's nice to meet you," Dani said. "I don't know what we'd do without Tess's help."

"Thanks, I'll pass that on to her." He gestured toward the expensive camera Dani held in her hands. "I take it you're a photographer."

"One of the best," Brett said.

Dani blushed and slightly shook her head. "He's biased. But

I'm the official historian for events like this one." She raised the camera. "Would you mind?"

Gabe tapped Amy's arm. "How about it? Will you join me for a photo?"

"Amy doesn't like her picture taken," Brett cut in.

"I wish you'd quit that," Amy snapped.

"Quit what?"

Brett thought he knew so much. Why couldn't he just leave her alone? She took a calming breath, then smiled at Gabe. "I'd love to have my photo taken with you."

"Sitting or standing?" Dani asked.

"Standing, I guess," Amy said, and Gabe nodded.

Dani posed them against a screen she'd set up in another room. Amy stiffened when Gabe casually put his arm around her waist.

"Can you pretend you like me?" he whispered. "For the camera."

"I suppose," she whispered back. She consciously relaxed against him, nestling within his arm. The same feeling she'd had all those years ago returned, still as strong and powerful as it had been the day their lips first touched.

As Dani clicked the shutter, Amy couldn't help but raise her eyes to Gabe's. For this moment, but only this moment, she'd let her heart have its way.

"You two are so photogenic." Dani shot a few more photos, then lowered the camera. "These are going to be great."

Gabe leaned toward Amy's ear. "Thank you."

"For what?"

He grinned and dropped his arm. "Dani, do you think I could get a print of at least one of those?"

"Why do you want a print?" Amy asked. "They'll probably be on social media."

"It's not every day I get my picture taken with a beautiful woman. I might not get another chance."

Dani shifted her gaze from one to the other. "It's up to you, Amy."

"I want to see them first."

"You'll have to look at them another time," Brett said. He and Jonah were leaning against the doorframe. "We need to get this guy home."

"I'll email them to you," Dani said to Amy. "Just give me a couple days."

"Thanks." Amy smiled triumphantly at Gabe. Though she wasn't sure what she'd won.

– 6 –

Tess poured two cups of decaf and set a plate of snicker-doodles on the kitchen table. The evening had worn her out, but she didn't want Gabe to see how tired she was. At least she'd been able to talk to AJ about the mounting feed bill. He'd promised to cover it for her. She'd hated to ask, especially since it was a short-range solution to a long-range problem. Her creditors wouldn't hold off much longer. Then what would she do? And how could she explain it to Gabe?

Every morning, Tess thanked God that she was the one Gabe called about his release. But she dreaded telling him the drastic step she was considering. She'd have to tell him sometime, and soon, but first he needed time to get over the ordeal he'd been through. He couldn't do that if he was worrying about her or the future of the stables.

At least tonight they could bask in the warm feelings of being together for the first time in way too long and enjoy the companionable aftermath of a pleasant evening with the neighbors.

"Did you have a nice time?" she asked when Gabe joined her. He'd changed from his dress clothes into shorts and a T-shirt.

"Nicer than I expected."

"Because of Amy?"

"We took a short walk. Chatted a little."

"I guess it's not surprising. You and Seth Norris were the only single men there, and he just graduated high school a year ago."

"It sounds like you don't think much of her."

Tess hadn't meant to sound like anything, but Gabe was probably right. The news that Amy was living at the cottage had nettled, though Tess couldn't explain why.

"Amy is . . ." She paused, then shrugged. "She's Amy."

"What does that mean?"

"Nothing really." She slowly stirred a packet of Splenda into her decaf. "To tell you the truth, I didn't expect her to be there."

"Why not?"

"She hasn't shown much interest in the foundation. Though I suppose she has better things to do."

Gabe reached for another snickerdoodle, and Tess picked at a loose thread on the yellow-and-blue tablecloth.

"You were fond of her when we were kids," he said.

"True. But then she grew up and, oh, I don't know. She no longer has time for those who were fond of her when she was younger."

"She seems troubled to me," Gabe said. "Did you know she was in some kind of clinic?"

Tess straightened, trying to remember if she'd heard anything about that. "When?"

"She didn't say. But she told me about Jonah—you know, her nephew?"

"I know Jonah. We've been praying for him for a long time." She shook her head, thinking about the weeks he'd spent in the children's hospital. "Thankfully, he seems as healthy as any boy his age."

"You didn't pray for Amy?"

"I would have if I'd known she was ill. But no one said anything." She picked up a cookie she didn't really want just to have something to do with her hands. "I haven't seen Amy in over a year. At her grandmother's funeral. No, wait. She was at Richard's funeral too."

"Who's Richard?"

"Richard Grayson. Remember the old banker?"

"Not really."

Tess debated whether to fill him in on Richard's part in the Misty Willow saga, then decided against it. Nothing could be gained by gossiping about the past.

"You were talking about Amy. What's wrong with her?" she asked, then inwardly chuckled. Apparently her qualms didn't include gossiping about the present.

"She didn't say that either."

"Sounds like she didn't say much."

"I guess we both have our secrets."

Once again, Tess wished she could take away the burden Gabe carried. Or at least help him to see he had nothing to be ashamed of. "You didn't tell her?"

"She might not like living across the road from a convicted felon."

"Don't call yourself that. It's not who you are. The circumstances—"

"The law doesn't make exceptions for circumstances."

"Sometimes they should."

"It doesn't matter. Not anymore."

Tess's heart ached at the resignation in his voice. She longed to remove the sting of the past few years. And the sting of how it could affect his future. All because Gabe was in the wrong place at the wrong time.

No one in their right mind could blame Gabe for what happened. Except his father. Steve Kendall didn't care about circumstances, only the stigma of having a prison inmate for a son. She'd love to know how many times Steve had visited Gabe. Certain she'd hate the answer, she refused to ask the question.

"Why doesn't she ride anymore?" Gabe asked, breaking through Tess's muddled thoughts. "If I remember right, she was a promising student."

"Um, she was." Tess allowed her thoughts to drift into the past. Images flashed in her mind. Amy sitting on the fence, looking out over the pasture. She and Gabe riding into the woods behind the pond. The conversations with Joyanna Sullivan about having Amy return to the stables.

"It was like her love for horses died when her parents did."

"Riding makes me feel whole. Free."

"People grieve in different ways." Tess rose from the table and retrieved a glass container from the counter for the cookies. "Her dad was so supportive of her riding. I suppose in a strange way the two are connected in her mind. Without him, riding lost its appeal."

"I could never give up riding." He grimaced. "Except when I was forced to. I think it's what I missed most."

"Not my home cooking?" Tess teased.

"That's a given. I meant in general. I can tell you one thing, galloping across a field is something I'll never take for granted again."

"You can ride every day now if you want to."

"When I'm not looking for a job."

"I thought we weren't going to talk about that for a while. You need time. Relax. Enjoy yourself." She placed her hand on his. "Figure out what you want to do."

"That's the problem, isn't it? I don't know."

"There must be something."

"I wanted to be a Marine. But I can't go back to that, can I? And there's not much need for my skills around here. Even if someone would hire me."

"People around here will understand. You just need to give them a chance."

"That means telling people. Not something I'm eager to do."

"Something will come up. I know it will."

"Always wearing the rose-colored glasses, aren't you?"

"Worries are always with us. I choose to be as optimistic about them as I can." Brave words firmly spoken. Harder to believe if she couldn't hold on to the land she loved. Losing Whisper Lane would be like losing Rusty all over again—everything they'd built together gone with the stroke of a pen on a sales contract.

How could she do it? What would happen if she didn't?

In the silence that followed, the peaceful hum of the refrigerator was interrupted only by the whir of the ice maker. The open kitchen windows welcomed a gardenia-scented breeze that toyed with the muslin curtains. Tess barely registered the faint nocturnal chorus that whispered comfort to her soul.

Optimism.

Sometimes she wearied of always being the one who looked on the bright side. But what choice did she have? To do anything else would be to give in to despair.

~

Gabe downed the rest of his decaf, then carried his dishes to the sink.

"Don't you want another cookie before I put them away?" Tess asked.

He patted his stomach. "I think I've had enough. Though that reminds me. I promised some to Jonah. He told me snickerdoodles are his favorite too."

"Then we'll make sure he gets at least a dozen," Tess said lightly. She carried the cookie plate to the counter. "I'll pack them up right now."

"I told him I'd drop them off at his house tomorrow. He's got some kind of doctor's appointment."

"Anything serious?"

"Routine, according to Amy. Though I doubt she would have told me even if it were something serious. She's not very open."

"She never was." Tess placed a baker's dozen of the cookies in a plastic container, separating the layers with parchment paper. "Looks like the two of you have something in common."

"Meaning?"

"There's nothing you can't tell me, Gabe. Whether it's about when you were in Afghanistan or that prison. You've had it rough, and it's not healthy to keep it all bottled up inside."

"Look who's talking."

"I wrote you every week."

He stifled a sigh, then jammed the drainer into the sink. "So you did."

Bright and cheery letters that gave no hint of how hard things had gotten for her since Rusty's death. He could do nothing to help her while he was behind bars, so she didn't tell him anything that would cause him to worry.

"Your letters meant a lot," Gabe said. "Just knowing I'd have mail from you helped me make it through the days. I should have written back. I started to, countless times."

He'd sent her birthday cards, Christmas cards, with short notes inside. But the letters he tried to write ended up in the trash. Living the dull routine of prison life, ashamed that this *was* his life, he'd had nothing to say.

"All that matters is that you're here now. And I'm glad of it."

"Me too." He turned on the hot water tap and squirted soap in the sink. Bubbles erupted beneath the spurting stream.

"Let me do those."

"Already got them started. In the morning, I'll take a look at the dishwasher. See what's wrong with it for you."

"Now don't be making yourself a honey-do list. That dishwasher has been broken for two or three months now, and I'm getting along fine without it."

"I only want to help." He gave her a teasing smile. "Gotta earn my room and board."

"One day at a time, Gabe. There's no rush."

Later that night, he lay in his bed and let her words wash over him. *There's no rush.* But he couldn't hang around here forever. He needed a plan, a direction for his life instead of this aimlessness. If only he could figure out somewhere for a former Marine and ex-con to fit in. Something legal. Where no one shot at you or threatened to blow you up.

He was starving for purpose, for a home of his own, for meaningful work. And someday, some far-in-the-future day, a woman to love with as much respect and passion as Rusty had loved Tess.

While serving his sentence, he'd read the New Testament accounts of Paul's imprisonments. The great apostle never wavered in his trust that he was running the course God had laid out for him. Gabe ached for that same assurance, that someday all this would make sense. That he could change his plea from "Why me?" to "Thy will be done" and wholeheartedly mean it.

But he wasn't there yet. For now, the future looked bleak, and his only hope was that somehow, somewhere, he'd hear God's still small voice.

Instead, other niggling thoughts drove away sleep. How could he get Amy back on a horse? And what wasn't Tess telling him?

– 7 –

*G*abe tossed back the covers and planted his feet on the wooden floor. The red numbers glowed on the clock radio, the same one that had been on that same nightstand when he was a boy: 5:45.

Of course it was.

In less than twenty minutes, he showered, shaved, dressed, and made his bed so tautly not even his father could have found a flaw to complain about.

He flipped on the kitchen light, then started the coffeemaker. After pulling on his work shoes, he quietly unlocked the outside door and stepped into the early-morning sunrise. Dew moistened the grass, and birds scolded each other from the limbs of the nearby trees. A peacefulness blanketed the horse farm, the calm before the hustle of a new day.

Once inside the stable, he greeted Daisy first and slipped her an apple-flavored treat. Then he said hello to the other horses while pouring grain into their bins and stroking their noses. After letting the horses loose, he mucked out the stalls, a job he never minded despite the odor and mess. Replacing the dirty straw, inhaling the freshness of the flat golden strands—he wasn't sure why, but clean stalls held a wholesomeness he found appealing.

No rush, Tess had said.

Too bad he couldn't spend the rest of his life doing this. But that would be taking advantage of her kindness, and while he appreciated having a place to live while he sorted things out, he needed to get back on his own two feet.

After a hearty breakfast of scrambled eggs, hash browns, and sausage links, he headed to the garage to find the tools he needed to fix the dishwasher. As he crossed the graveled drive, a Jeep Cherokee swung alongside him. The window lowered, and AJ Sullivan propped his elbow on the frame.

"Hey, Gabe," he said. "How's it going?"

"Can't complain."

"Has Tess told you about the big Heritage Celebration we're having at Misty Willow in a couple of weeks? That's when we're making the official announcement about it being listed on the historical registry."

"She mentioned it."

"We still have a lot to do to get ready, and I could use some help. It's a temporary job, but if you're interested . . ."

"I am."

"Appreciate your enthusiasm, but don't you want to know the details first?"

"I'll do just about anything that needs doing."

"Glad to hear it. I have a teacher's training thing at the high school tomorrow, so can you start on Thursday?"

He'd start that very minute if AJ wanted him to. "Just tell me what time and where to be."

"Come to my place. Say around nine." AJ grinned. "I know the farmers around here consider that a late start, but I like to have breakfast with my girls."

"Can't blame you for that. Besides, then I can help Tess with the morning chores around here."

"There's one other condition."

"What's that?" Gabe asked warily.

"Tess told me you played baseball in high school. I want you on our church softball team."

Gabe chuckled. "Whatever I was expecting, it sure wasn't that."

"Does that mean you're in?"

"I haven't played in a long time."

"It'll come back to you. Besides, it's mostly for fun."

"Yeah, right." Gabe chuckled again, enjoying the long-lost feeling of being included in something good. "I'm in."

"Great. First game is tomorrow night. Tess can tell you how to find the ballfields."

"What about practice?"

"Meet me there an hour early. We'll get you warmed up."

"You're the boss." Gabe gestured toward the house. "You want to come in? There's still coffee in the pot."

"Thanks for the offer, but I've got to get going." AJ pulled an envelope from the Jeep's console. "Could you give this to Tess for me?"

"Sure." Gabe glanced at her name on the envelope. "I am grateful for the job, AJ. For the chance."

"We're glad to have you for a neighbor. Glad, too, that Tess has someone here. It's been lonely for her since Rusty died."

"I know she misses him."

"We all do." AJ gripped the steering wheel with one hand and shifted gears with the other. "I'll see you in a couple of days. Come early if you want pancakes."

"I'll do that."

Gabe stepped to the side while AJ backed up and headed down the drive. No wonder Tess thought so highly of the Sullivans.

He peered toward the sky, squinting against the sun's cheery brightness. *It's a start. Thank you.*

~

Amy pressed the slender roller into the painting tray and applied the luscious shade of dark teal to the top of the cabinetry beneath the cottage's long row of windows. She'd already painted the shelving and sides of the lengthy built-in. Though most of the cabinets had open shelves, four had doors, which she'd taken outside. They were next on her to-do list.

For now, she delighted in the smooth movement of the roller across the cabinet as the rich paint covered the faded ivory. As fanciful as it sounded, giving the cottage a makeover was like a healing balm to her restless spirit.

Besides, the rooms probably hadn't been painted since before AJ moved into the place. That must have been, what, at least six or seven years ago? He probably thought once was enough. He was oh so wrong.

Amy doubted he'd have repainted Gran's bungalow before his wedding if Shelby hadn't insisted. Men!

Though, to be honest, Amy had behaved badly when she heard about that project. She understood it—the bungalow was Shelby's home now. And she'd made terrific color and fabric choices. But it stung to see Gran's home transformed from a serene showplace to a lively kid-friendly jamboree.

Surely AJ felt it too, at least a little. He'd spent the most time there with Gran. Going to church, treating her to lunch, and watching all those silly Cary Grant movies.

Amy pressed the roller too hard onto the cabinet, and paint splatted onto her shirt and the window.

"Great," she muttered. She hurriedly wiped the paint off the glass, then smoothed the splotch on the cabinet.

She could have done all those things with Gran too, if she'd lived as close to her as AJ did. It wasn't Amy's fault she had to work ten-hour days or that she was obligated to attend more social functions in a week than AJ attended all year.

After finishing the final section, she stood back to admire her work. The gleaming color was a perfect complement to the pale teal walls and the glossy white baseboards and window frames. No longer a worn-out man cave, the entire room now had an air of sophisticated tranquility.

Her conscience panged as she balanced the roller's handle onto the tray. What if AJ felt the same way about the cottage as she did about the bungalow? That by repainting the room, she had erased his presence from it?

He had once sought refuge from hurt and loneliness in this place, just like she was doing now.

Her cell rang, interrupting her gloomy thoughts. Ignoring it, she washed her hands at the kitchen sink. After the voicemail alert sounded, she accessed the message.

"Hi, Amy. This is Logan Cassidy. Been a long time since we chatted. When you get a moment, I'd like to talk to you about one of your former clients. Call me. Thanks."

She smiled to herself, pleased to know her prior employer had lost at least one client when she hadn't returned. Hopefully more than that. Sometimes she missed the rumor-shooting gallery, though she was glad the bull's-eye was no longer on her own back. She'd had enough of that last year after abruptly walking away from her prestigious position.

Not that she'd exactly *walked*.

No, she'd danced the hours away and ended up in a hospital emergency room. Abandoned and alone until Brett arrived. These past months, including two stints at the clinic, had been grueling. She never wanted to go through that again.

A day at a time. She only had to get through one long, lonely day at a time.

As she poured a glass of juice and dutifully recorded it in her notebook, she chased away her gloomy thoughts by mentally flipping through the clients she'd left behind. Who was most likely to turn to Logan Cassidy for assistance?

A rap sounded on the front door, and Gabe smiled at her through the window screen.

"Hey, there." He held up a container. "I brought Jonah's cookies."

"I thought you were dropping them off at Brett's house."

"I'm without wheels and you live closer."

The annoyance she wanted to feel wasn't cooperating. Probably because he'd kept his promise to Jonah.

"Come on in," she said. "Door's unlocked."

As Gabe entered, he eyed the canvas-covered furniture she'd pulled willy-nilly into the center of the room and wrinkled his nose at the smell of fresh paint.

"You've been a busy girl."

"Woman."

"Excuse me?"

"I'm not a girl. Or hadn't you noticed?" She added only the merest hint of suggestiveness to her tone.

"I noticed," he said flatly. "I didn't mean any offense."

So much for teasing the grown-up stable boy. "None taken."

There was a moment of awkward silence, but Amy didn't feel the need to end it.

Finally Gabe did. "Have you heard from Jonah? Or his dad?"

"Not yet."

"I was just wondering how his appointment went."

"It's nice of you to be concerned."

"Aunt Tess told me something about the accident. Said her church had been praying for Jonah."

"I think a lot of people were doing that." *But not me.* Amy had been so wrapped up in her own life, she'd given little thought to Jonah during the long weeks he'd been in a coma. At that time, the boy had been Brett's problem, a mistake they all thought had been dealt with when Meghan discovered she was pregnant. Sully paid her to disappear, but last year AJ had found her and Jonah too. A child none of them knew existed.

If Amy could go back to that time, to when Jonah was unconscious and Meghan needed all the support she could get . . . But that was useless thinking. The past couldn't be relived, only discarded.

"Are there enough cookies in there for me to try one?" she asked with more enthusiasm than she felt. Habit calculated the calories before she could stop the number from flashing in her brain. Dread filled the empty spaces inside her and knotted her stomach. She pressed her hand against her abdomen. If he said yes, she'd have to eat one. She couldn't.

A smile started at one corner of Gabe's mouth and gradually spread to the opposite side. A noncommittal, lazy smile that caught her breath and quickened her pulse.

"I'm sure there is, but only if you promise not to eat them all." He popped open the lid and tilted the container toward her.

"Maybe I better not."

"Not even a small one?"

He didn't mean it. She knew he didn't mean it. But the placating words sounded so much like something Brett would say. They echoed in her head until she couldn't stand them anymore.

"Who told you?" she asked, then stepped backward and closed her eyes. She was overreacting, but she couldn't stop herself.

"Told me what?"

She took a couple of deep breaths and let other words flow inside. *I am fearfully and wonderfully made. My soul knows it very well.* The self-talk calmed her breathing.

"Amy, are you okay?"

She opened her eyes but didn't meet his gaze. "I'm fine," she said.

"Can I get you something?" he asked. "Maybe a glass of water?"

Before she could answer, he grasped her elbow and led her to a chair. She perched on the canvas-covered arm, and he knelt beside her. "What just happened?"

"Nothing." She stared at her bare feet and toes polished a vibrant and glittery violet. So appropriate for summer, she'd thought, when the pedicurist offered her a choice of colors. Flecks of teal paint dotted her flesh.

"I thought for a minute there you were going to pass out," Gabe said.

She met his gaze and felt self-consciously warmed by the worry in his hazel eyes. The same hazel eyes that had looked into hers a lifetime ago before he slipped the jagged arrowhead into her hand. The simple gesture had given her more comfort, more strength than he could possibly know. That was the last time she'd seen him.

Did he remember that moment as clearly as she did? Did he remember it at all?

~

Gabe shifted his weight as he knelt by the chair, his hand temptingly close to Amy's bare leg. He closed his fingers into his palm. "What can I do?"

"I'm fine, really. I think I forgot to eat lunch. What time is it?"

"Around 2:30 or so."

"That late?"

"Sure you don't want a cookie?"

"I'll have a salad instead. How about you? I have plenty." She stood, and he rose beside her to be sure she didn't keel over.

"I've already eaten." He pushed the container into her hands. "I'll leave these with you and get going. Let you eat in peace."

"Please don't go. I mean, I wouldn't mind a bit of company."

"Are you sure?"

"I have sandwich stuff too if the salad doesn't do it for you."

"If you insist. I never turn down a home-cooked meal." He

chuckled. It was a lame attempt at humor considering all the institutional meals he'd eaten over the past several years.

"It's not really home-cooked," Amy said.

"Close enough." Definitely better than prison food. He followed her to the step leading to the tiny kitchen. As she walked around the counter, she closed the notebook lying there and stuck it inside a drawer.

"Anything I can do to help?" he asked.

"I can handle it."

"Know your way around the kitchen, huh?"

She gave him an enigmatic smile, then pulled a container of meat and cheese and another of mixed greens from the fridge.

"We'll have to eat standing up. As you can see, things are a mess right now."

"I can help you put things back where they belong. If you want me to." *Please say yes.*

"That'd be nice. But first I have four cabinet doors to paint."

"The ones outside? I can give you a hand with those." *Cool it, Kendall. No need to act like an overeager puppy.*

"I won't say no." She retrieved plates and bowls from a nearby cabinet. "Sure you don't want a salad too? The radishes and cucumbers came straight from Shelby's garden."

"If you insist." He put together a sandwich while Amy topped their salads with sunflower seeds. "Did you do all this painting today?"

"The walls yesterday. The woodwork today." She handed him a glass of iced lemonade. "It wasn't that hard now that the pool table is gone."

"You had a pool table in here?"

"Not me, AJ. It sat right there." She gestured at the empty space beyond the kitchen counter. "Took up that entire corner. He and some of his students moved it out last weekend."

"Where did they put it?"

"In an outbuilding at Gran's. I mean at AJ's. Where he lives now."

"Your grandmother hired me to mow her yard when I stayed with Rusty and Tess." He hoped to see a flicker in her eyes, something, anything, to indicate she remembered those days. But her expression remained downcast.

"It's not the same," she said wistfully. "Not with Gran gone."

"Places never are like we remember them." He bit into his sandwich, then sipped his drink. "How long did you say you'd been here?"

"Only a week. The lease ended on my apartment, and I decided not to renew. It seemed like a good time to take a break from the city."

"How do you like living in the country?"

"I'm still adjusting. Just wish I'd gotten the painting done before I moved."

"Are you planning any other improvements?"

"Depends on how long I stay." She toyed with her lettuce, moving the leaves around the bowl. "What about you? Any plans?"

"I got a job offer today."

Her eyes brightened with polite interest. "That's great," she said. "Doing what?"

"Not sure. AJ came by this morning. Said he needed help getting ready for some big shindig at Misty Willow. You probably know all about it."

"I've heard talk."

"You're not involved?"

"So far I've managed to stay away from the planning meetings. But I've been asked to play emcee for the formal presentation so I'll be onstage with all the local dignitaries."

"Wow. I'm impressed."

"It's not that big of a deal, really. Though, all things considered, it was nice to be asked."

"Considering what things?" He immediately held up his hand. "Sorry, didn't mean to be nosy."

"No, it's okay." She focused on her salad, seeming to choose her words with care. "I haven't always gotten along with Shelby. AJ either, to be honest. Surely your aunt told you about the lawsuit."

"What lawsuit?"

"Tess really didn't tell you?"

"No."

Amy put down her fork, though she hadn't eaten more than a bite or two.

"Everyone else around here knows, so you may as well too. Before Misty Willow was protected by the foundation, AJ leased it to Shelby. I had other plans for the property so"—she bit her lip and looked him square in the eyes—"I sued them."

Gabe stared at her in disbelief. "You sued your cousin? And his wife?"

"She wasn't his wife then. Anyway, all has been forgiven, and to show that to the world, we'll all be onstage together. One big happy family."

At least now he knew what Tess wasn't telling him. She probably hadn't wanted to say anything else negative about Amy.

"What about you?" she asked. "Will you be at the 'big shindig'?"

"Looks that way. Tess has an old stagecoach stored in one of the barns. If it's in good enough shape, we'll use it to take guests from the house back to the creek." He proudly poked his chest with his thumb. "You're looking at the driver."

"You're kidding." This time, her interest appeared genuine, and her bemused smile revealed a slight dimple near her jaw. "A real stagecoach?"

"Are you interested in riding shotgun?" he teased, then held his breath waiting for her answer. Fear and doubt flickered across her face. The doubt he could understand. She probably didn't want him to think she was interested in him. But what was she afraid of?

- 8 -

*A*my glanced out the corner window. The freshly painted frame gleamed, but she barely noticed. Why hadn't she taken the cookies and sent Gabe on his way? Instead, she'd accepted his offer to help her paint the doors, even invited him to a late lunch. Her second one of the day, though he didn't need to know that.

She'd panicked when he'd offered her a cookie. If he'd offered her poison, she couldn't have been more repulsed. Instead of being in control, she'd let fear control her.

Face it, she was lonely. Quiet country living wasn't what she was used to. As much as she wanted to be—needed to be—away from her previous life, she'd gotten used to the hubbub of busy people doing important things.

Nothing important happened out here.

She missed her apartment. The choice to leave it hadn't been easy, only unavoidable. Poor investments, a party-girl lifestyle, and those months in the clinic had taken their toll on her financial reserves. She wasn't exactly broke—at least not by most people's standards—but the luxury apartment was an expense she could no longer afford. Not when she needed time to regroup. To recover.

Gabe cleared his throat and looked at her expectantly.

"Sorry," she said. "I got lost there for a moment."

"I shouldn't have put you on the spot." He finished his sandwich, eating quickly with no wasted motions. "That was good. I'll have to return the favor sometime."

"Do you cook?"

"I make the best chili you've ever eaten."

"Seriously? Chili?"

"Seriously."

"This isn't exactly chili weather, so I guess I'll have to take your word for it."

"Just wait till the next rainy day."

"It'll have to be an all-day thunderstorm, the kind where no one wants to leave their house."

"Next time we have one of those, I'll be over."

"Honestly?" She tilted her head, unsure whether to believe him. He sounded serious, but his eyes twinkled with mischief.

"Wait and see." He didn't come out and say it, but his tone made it clear this was a kind of dare.

Two could play that game. "You bring the chili, and I'll make dessert."

"What kind of dessert?"

"My famous homemade lemon meringue pie."

"Homemade?"

"My gran's secret recipe. She won several ribbons at the county fair with her pies, so you know it's a good one."

"Makes my mouth water just thinking about it."

"Then I guess you better hope for a thunderstorm."

"I'll pray for one."

Amy couldn't help but laugh. If nothing else, the teasing banter had lightened her mood. Though she'd have to remember to check Gran's recipe and stock up on all the ingredients next time she went into town.

She started to clean up the dishes but then her phone rang. Logan again.

"Do you need to take that?" Gabe asked. "I can step outside."

"It's nothing important. Besides, I want to get those doors painted."

"Like I said before, I'm glad to help."

"If you really want to." She finished stacking the dishes, then slipped canvas shoes on her bare feet.

Together they carried the paint and supplies outside. Gabe helped spread a plastic tarp beneath the shade of a trio of silver birches, and they set to work. He'd almost finished his first door before he broke the silence.

"What did you mean earlier?"

"When?"

"You asked me who told me. Told me what?"

She gave a dismissive shrug. "I overreacted. It was nothing."

"It must be something."

Amy leaned back on her heels and let the silence of the day surround her. What little traffic traveled this road had its noise masked by the dense hedges that had grown up around the front fence. Hedges so thick and tall that only the locals knew the cottage existed behind the tightly woven branches.

The trees along the lower fence line separating this property from the bungalow rustled in the sun-warmed breeze. Songbirds flitted from branches to electric poles and back again. All was at peace here. Quiet and serene.

She wished her life was the same.

"If you don't want to tell me," Gabe said, "I understand. Guess I shouldn't have asked."

She let another moment pass, following his movements as he rolled the paint over the paneled door. The luxurious teal glistened with purity and freshness, and his movements were steady and unrushed.

Until he'd spoken, the silence between them had been comfortable and relaxed. She couldn't remember the last time she'd been so at ease with anyone outside her family. And she wasn't always congenial with them. Especially since she'd returned from the clinic. Sometimes it seemed they guarded every word, afraid to say the wrong thing at the wrong time. Or, like Brett, too often said something to irritate her then wouldn't stop apologizing. They bent over backward not to upset her, which in itself was so maddening.

Was she really that difficult to be around? That sensitive to every word they spoke to her?

Yes, she was. But she was trying hard not to be. And she'd prove it.

"I have this thing with food," she said finally, her body tensing as she waited for his reaction.

He rested the roller on the pan. "What kind of thing?"

"The official diagnosis is EDNOS. It means Eating Disorder Not Otherwise Specified."

"I'm sorry."

She studied his face. "I don't want your sympathy. That's not why I told you."

He held her gaze, his eyes soft and gentle but without that pity she hated.

"I'm not starving myself to death. I never even came close." She hugged one leg close to her chest and rested her chin on her knee. "Closer than a normal person would, I suppose. But I got help before it got too bad."

"That's why you were in the clinic?"

"More of a treatment center. In Virginia."

He barely nodded. She sighed heavily, knowing he said nothing because he didn't know what to say.

"When I refused a cookie and you said, 'Not even a small one,' you sounded so much like Brett." She shook her head in aggra-

68

vation. "I thought you were urging me to eat. And I hate when people do that."

"I was only teasing."

"I know. I knew it then. But I lost control for a moment."

"Being at the treatment center has helped, then?"

"I've been there twice. I don't want to ever go back."

"Is that a possibility?"

"I hope not." She didn't think she could endure going through all the protocols and therapies again. Neither did she want to pay for it. A few more weeks at the facility would take the last of her savings.

But even more than that, she longed to be well and healthy.

"We talked a lot about food during lunch," Gabe said. "If I'd known—"

"You wouldn't have promised to make me your famous chili?" She forced a lightness she didn't feel into her tone, then exhaled and turned away. "That's why I don't like people to know. They watch what they say and then everyone's uncomfortable."

"Only because they care about you."

"So they say. It's still annoying."

"I can imagine."

"I doubt it."

"It's true I don't know what it's like to have people monitoring everything I eat. But I know what it's like for people to be afraid of saying the wrong thing around me."

"What wrong thing?"

"You really don't know?"

"If I did, I wouldn't have asked."

"I should finish this other door first because when I tell you, you'll want me to leave."

"Because that's what everyone else does?"

He shrugged and ran his roller through the tray.

"I'm not like everyone else," Amy said quietly.

"If there's only one thing I know about you, it's that."

"Is that a compliment or a way to change the subject?"

The lazy smile began its slow movement, as if he knew a secret he held close to his chest. Before it had time to reach the opposite corner of his mouth, he spoke. "Not going to work, huh?"

She leaned forward and turned his face toward hers. She held his gaze, or perhaps he held hers. She wasn't sure.

"The word people don't like to say around me is *food*. What's your word?"

~

Without taking his eyes from hers, Gabe rested the roller on the edge of the pan.

"Prison."

Amy drew back, as if to give space for the word to expand between them. Her fingers slipped from his jaw to her lap.

"Not you." The words were almost a whisper, spoken quietly but with conviction.

"That's where I've spent the last few years."

His eyes, alert for each nuance of her expression, never left her face. But she kept her features still as if she meant to prove her claim that she wasn't like everyone else. Most people asked him why, and for that very reason, he knew she wouldn't.

She leaned forward, tucking her knee into her chest again. He could still feel the gentle touch of her fingers on his jaw, soft as a butterfly's wing. Another token to hide away in his heart.

"I'll finish this door and then I'll be going."

"There's no need to leave."

"You sure about that? Maybe I'm a serial killer."

"Serial killers don't get to leave prison. Do they?"

"Not usually." He should tell her, get it out in the open. But all criminals claimed their innocence, and no one ever believed them. Besides, he didn't want to talk about the past. Not on this perfect summer day. He didn't want to overstay his welcome either.

"All done," he said as he finished painting the door.

He stood, then reached for Amy. She took his hands without the slightest hesitation, and he pulled her to her feet. They stood, inches apart, as they had that long-ago day at the Hearth. He stared into her eyes, willing her to recall the same memory he did. But all he saw were unasked questions. He gently squeezed her fingers, then let them go.

"Thanks for the second lunch," he said. "And the company. I enjoyed both."

"Then why are you leaving?"

"I've already stayed longer than I intended."

"You're still in prison, aren't you? One you've created for yourself." A crestfallen expression appeared on her face. "I didn't mean to say that out loud."

"Maybe you're right," he said. "Guess I hadn't thought of it that way."

"Gabe, I need to . . ."

A light tap from a car horn sounded from the gate. The door opened, and Jonah jumped out. He waved to them, then unlatched the gate and swung it open. After the vehicle pulled through, Jonah closed the gate and ran up the slope toward them.

Whatever Amy intended to say was lost in her obvious delight at Jonah's arrival.

Couldn't we have had one more minute, God?

– 9 –

*A*my's heart warmed as Jonah raced toward her. Somehow his joyful exuberance took her back to the sweetest memories of her childhood, when she and Brett played tag and hide-and-seek here on long summer nights. In their innocence, they'd been unprepared for the ugliness they'd be facing as their parents' arguments led to divorce, shared custody, and manipulative maneuverings. Even as bad as that was, it didn't compare to the devastating loss they experienced when the plane crash left them, and AJ too, orphaned and alone. The Tragic Trio, the press dubbed them. Ohio's own poor little rich kids.

But she also wished she'd had more time alone with Gabe. The news that he had been in prison should have shocked her. Instead, she felt a strange conviction he had a good explanation. If they hadn't been interrupted, he'd have told her everything and she'd have told him the truth—that she had never forgotten that long-ago day at the Hearth. The words they'd said to each other. Their only kiss.

But perhaps it was best she'd been denied the chance by Brett's arrival. Gabe might have thought she was interested in rekindling their teenage romance. Maybe she was, if only to escape her

72

loneliness. But she doubted he was the type of man to engage in a summer dalliance, and she wasn't willing to commit to anything long-term. Not when her life was such a mess.

"Hey, Aunt Amy." Jonah practically tackled her, and she had to brace herself to keep from falling.

"Whoa there, buddy," Gabe said, helping to steady her. "You gotta be careful with the ladies."

"Did you bring the cookies, Mr. Gabe?"

"Sure did. They're inside."

Without another word, Jonah hurried through the door.

Brett sauntered toward them, and Amy welcomed him with a quick hug. She stood back while he and Gabe greeted each other, and then gestured toward the cottage. "You want to come on in?"

"Sure," Brett said.

"It's nice seeing you again, Brett," Gabe said. "But I should be going."

"Let me transfer the cookies to another plate first," Amy said. "Then you can take Tess's container with you."

"Okay," he agreed. But he sounded uncomfortable. Perhaps he felt he was intruding on a family moment. True, Amy wanted to talk to Brett about Jonah's doctor's appointment. But she didn't want Gabe to leave. Not yet.

When they got inside, she busied herself pouring a glass of milk for Jonah and giving him a plate for his snack. "Things are a bit of a mess," she said. "You can sit on the floor, I guess. But don't touch the cabinets. Or anything else that might be wet."

"Would it be okay if I go outside?" Jonah asked.

"That's a great idea."

Jonah glanced at Brett, who nodded assent, then he headed out the door.

"How did his appointment go?" Amy asked once Jonah was out of earshot.

"You know how it is," Brett said. "Go to one place and wait, then another place and wait. But it's all good news so far. They did a CAT scan, and the preliminary look was promising. We'll know more in a few days."

"Did you talk to Meghan?"

"Yeah. She was a wreck not being here."

"I'm still surprised she went to New York."

"I'm glad she did. She needed a break, and it was too good an opportunity for her to pass up. And Dani and I need this time with Jonah."

"One little happy family?"

"Scoff all you want, but yes. We are." Brett broke one of the cookies in half but paused before taking a bite. "We really are."

"Just remember this moment when he's a teenager," Amy teased.

"Remind me of it."

Gabe chuckled and glanced toward the doorway where they could see Jonah through the pane. "Looks like he's enjoying those cookies. Tess will be glad."

"Tess can bake him all the cookies she wants as long as he shares with the rest of us," Brett said. "These are good."

"She'll be glad to know you all enjoyed them." Gabe took the container Amy handed him. "Thanks again for lunch. Maybe we can do it again sometime."

"Whenever that day-long thunderstorm comes along," Amy said. "I'll walk you to the gate."

"Afraid he'll get lost?" Brett teased.

She gave him a withering look. "Just being neighborly." Behind her, Brett made a harrumphing noise, but she ignored him.

Once they were outside, Gabe paused by Jonah.

"What did you think of those snickerdoodles?" he asked.

Jonah appeared deep in thought for a moment. "They're as good as Mom's," he said decidedly, then wrinkled his nose. "But I like Mom's better."

"As you should."

"Good answer." Amy tousled Jonah's hair. "I'll be right back."

When she and Gabe reached the gate, she self-consciously rubbed her arms as if feeling a sudden chill. "We didn't get to finish our talk," she said.

"Maybe that's a good thing."

"It's just . . . I told you about my eating disorder because I wanted you to hear it from me. It goes the other way too."

"What do you mean?"

"I want to know your story from you. No one else."

"There's no story."

"I don't believe that."

He shifted his weight uncomfortably from one foot to the other. "Don't feel sorry for me. I don't like that any more than you like pity."

"I won't," she stammered. "I don't."

He gripped her elbow, and for a lingering second she thought he was going to kiss her. Instead, he let her go, slipped through the gate, and was gone.

~

Amy walked up the slope to the cottage with an ache in her heart she never expected to experience. She wished that when she went back inside, somehow Gran would be there. She yearned to pour out her heart, to tell her what she'd said to Gabe and what he'd said to her. Maybe Gran's wisdom and her unconditional love could help Amy sort out the tangled mess she'd made of her life.

She also wanted to tell Gran how sorry she was for not spending more time with her. For not listening to her stories.

Brett walked out of the house as she neared the porch. "You okay? You look a little sad."

"I'm fine." She pasted on a smile, more for Jonah's sake than Brett's. Her brother wouldn't be fooled.

"Are there any more cookies?" Jonah asked.

"Only for you to take home," Amy said. "Your dad might get mad at me if I let you spoil your supper."

Jonah made a face, then brightened. "I asked Dr. Marc if I could ride a horse."

"What did he say?" Amy glanced at Brett's stony expression. "Or shouldn't I ask?"

"Let's just say I won't be donating to any more of his favorite charities for a while," Brett said.

"First he said yes," Jonah said. "Then later he said he wanted to think about it. But he only said that because Daddy talked to him."

"Why don't you run a lap around the cottage?" Brett suggested. "Stretch your legs."

"You mean so you can talk without me hearing?"

Brett looked over Jonah's head at Amy. "He's a smart one."

Jonah snorted and slowly walked around the corner. Once he was out of sight, Brett blew out air.

"I started riding when I was younger than he is," Amy said quietly.

"You hadn't spent weeks in a coma."

"I know. But—"

"Don't push it, Amy. If anything happened to him . . ." Brett's jaw set in a hard line. "Meghan would never forgive me. I'd never forgive me."

"You can't protect him from everything. And if you try, he'll resent you for it."

"We're letting him take swimming lessons. Why can't that be enough?" He glanced at his watch. "We need to get home and change. There's a game tonight."

"What kind of game?"

"Church softball league."

"You're playing church softball?"

"Surprised?"

"Flabbergasted."

"Why don't you come with us?" He scrutinized her appearance. "Though you might want to wash your face first. Get rid of that paint."

"What paint?" She swiped at her cheeks. "Where?"

"There." He touched her chin then her cheek. "And there. Also there."

"You couldn't have told me this earlier? I am so embarrassed."

"Because Gabe saw you like that?" Brett flashed his dimples. "To him you looked adorable."

"I doubt that."

"Trust me, you did. AJ asked him to join the team too, you know."

"No, I didn't."

"So how about it? Softball game with the family? Not-so-fine dining afterward?"

"Sounds like the best time ever, but I think I'll pass."

"So what's on your menu for this evening?" He held up his hands before she could answer. "Just making conversation."

"Sure you were."

He looked apologetic, but why couldn't he understand she didn't like his overprotectiveness any more than Jonah did? His subtle and not-so-subtle questions only made her want to lash out at him. Even avoid him.

One of her counselors had said she was lucky to have someone in her life who cared enough to hover. But it still aggravated her. "I had a salad not that long ago. Just before Gabe and I painted the cabinet doors, in fact. So I'm not hungry for the simple reason I just ate. Plus I saved two"—she held up her fingers—"snickerdoodles for later." She hadn't, but he didn't need to know that.

Brett drew her into a spontaneous hug. "Just eat supper too. Okay?" She lightly punched him, and he doubled over in exaggerated pain.

"Hey, Jonah," he called. "We need to get out of here before Aunt Amy beats me up."

Jonah came running around the other side of the cottage, then raced Brett to the car. Once again, Amy made the trek down the slope to open and close the gate.

On her way back to the cottage, her phone buzzed. Logan. The guy sure was persistent. She frowned but accepted the call.

"Amy," he said enthusiastically. "How have you been?"

"Fine. You?"

"I'll be perfect if you say yes to my invitation."

"Invitation to what?" She entered the cottage and awkwardly plopped onto a canvas-covered chair.

"Only coffee."

"Why don't I believe that? Oh, I know. Because you said something in your message about one of my former clients."

"So I did." He chuckled softly. "But I'd rather not discuss it on the phone."

"I don't think I want to discuss it at all."

"It's important, Amy. Otherwise I wouldn't have called. Besides, I miss our secret strategy sessions. Don't you?"

No, she didn't.

Amy moved the phone away from her mouth so he wouldn't hear her resigned sigh. Those long chats that broke all the rules regarding client confidentiality seemed daring at the time and had been helpful to them both. But it was another part of her past she wished she could erase.

If this were anyone but Logan, she probably would have already hung up by now. If she'd even answered the call.

But he'd been her confidential sounding board more than once during her lobbying days. And an accommodating plus-one on the rare occasions she didn't have a steady escort.

"When and where?" she asked.

"That depends. Where are you living these days?"

"In Glade County outside Madison. At my cousin's cottage."

"I'm glad to know you're still in the state. How about tomorrow around 10:30? You name the place."

"There's a coffee shop on London Avenue. Can you find the address?"

"I'm sure I can."

"Then I'll see you in the morning."

"Great. See you then."

They hung up, and Amy leaned her head against the back of the chair. Logan obviously wanted information, but if he also hoped to lure her back into his world, he'd be disappointed with her answer. Those long days of scheming, plotting, and strategizing were over.

But not her painting days. The kitchen and bathroom were still on her list, but she'd tackle them another time. She cleaned the brushes and rollers, took a shower, and looked ahead to a lazy evening.

A lonely evening.

Unless she went to that game.

– 10 –

*A*my slipped a pink tailored jacket over her black pantsuit and scrutinized her reflection in the bank of full-length mirrors situated in a corner of the room. The lightweight jacket rested effortlessly on her hips, and the pant legs fitted around her ankles in a sleek version of harem pants. She placed a pink high-heeled shoe on one foot and a silver high-heeled sandal on the other. Which pair to wear?

"Knock knock," Shelby said from the front room.

"Come on in. I'm back here." Amy opted for the pink heels, then noticed Shelby's partial reflection in the mirror. She turned and consciously held in her stomach.

Both Shelby and Dani, dressed in shorts, tank tops, and sneakers, stood at the threshold leading into Amy's dressing room/closet combo. Dani's brunette hair was braided loosely across the top of her head. Wispy strands framed her face and crawled out of the loose bun at the nape of her neck.

Amy looked beyond them. "Where are the kids? Outside?"

"They went with the guys," Shelby said. "I'm so glad you called. Surprised but glad."

"Beats staying home alone." Amy rummaged beneath a pile

of clothes sprawled across a bureau for her black clutch. "Ready to go?"

"You look lovely," Shelby said with a smile meant to be gracious but that didn't quite make it.

Amy eyed her skeptically. "You mean I look overdressed."

"It really is a beautiful outfit," Shelby said. "But it's a softball game. The ground is dusty and the guys get all sweaty."

"Well, I hadn't quite made up my mind." Amy gestured at the tops, pants, and skirts thrown helter-skelter while she'd tried to find the perfect look of easy sophistication she wanted. "As you can see."

Dani looked at her own attire and giggled. "Maybe we're underdressed." She stepped into the room and picked up a violet tunic lying on a chair. Though the top was sleeveless, a swath of fabric formed an angled collar that flowed down one side. "This is so beautiful."

"You can try it on if you want," Amy said.

Dani's eyes rounded. "Are you sure you don't mind?"

"Go ahead." Amy examined her reflection again. She touched the smooth fabric of her jumpsuit with regret. The deep lace-covered V neck actually made her look voluptuous, and the small belt accentuated her waist. To be honest, she had wanted Gabe to see her in something dressier than hiking and painting clothes.

Dani held the tunic to her shoulders and sighed. "Times like this I wish I had your height."

Amy appraised her, then flipped through one of the wheeled wardrobe racks for something that wouldn't fall to Dani's knees. She found a sleeveless designer top in a coral geometric pattern and handed it to her sister-in-law. "Try this. The color complements your complexion. And I have the perfect necklace."

She rummaged through her jewelry chest and pulled out a multi-strand gold chain. "Ta-da."

"This is so much fun," Dani said as she peeled off her tank top.

"What about you, Shelby?" Amy asked.

"I don't know," she said doubtfully but with a wistful look on her face.

"But your eyes say yes," Amy teased. "Besides, if I have to change, we all have to change."

Before Shelby could protest, Amy gathered several tops, including a Vera Wang in navy blue with cutout shoulders, and piled them into her arms.

"If you insist," Shelby said gleefully.

Dani fastened the necklace over the coral top and struck a pose. She'd also managed to squeeze into a pair of Amy's capris. The hem practically reached her ankles and the pockets were squeezing out at the sides. "What do you think?"

Amy and Shelby appraised Dani, then exchanged glances with each other.

"I knew you'd look great in that color," Amy said. "The top looks beautiful."

"But maybe you should stick with your shorts," Shelby added.

Dani swiveled and twisted in the mirror to get a better look at the rear view. "I suppose you're right."

"You also need other shoes." Amy ran her eyes over her rows of heels, sandals, casual shoes, and boots. Dani probably wore a size six, six-and-a-half. Shelby maybe an eight. While she needed a massive size nine. The curse bestowed on the tall. "But none of mine unless you want to look like Big Foot."

"Not a prob," Shelby said. "We can stop by Dani's house on the way to the game. We're driving right past it. Speaking of, we better get moving or we'll miss the opening pitch."

Amy changed into a pale yellow shirt with a draped hemline over a matching camisole, beige shorts, and matching shoes. A simple gold pendant encircled her throat.

Despite her own prodding to get moving, Shelby was the last one to pull together an outfit. While she wavered between the Vera Wang top and a tailored taupe blouse with turquoise shorts and clunky accessories, Amy brushed Dani's hair and fastened it with a coral clip adorned with tiny diamond chips.

"I can't decide," Shelby moaned as she turned and twisted in front of the mirrors.

"The turquoise," Amy and Dani said together.

Finally, the three posed together and admired their reflections. Shelby had even managed to find a pair of taupe sandals with butterfly clips on the straps that she could tighten enough to almost fit.

"This is so much fun," Dani said. "And don't we look fabulous?"

"We'll be the best-dressed spectators there," Shelby said.

"Nothing wrong with that." Amy searched through her shelves of bags and pulled out three. "One last touch."

"Lovin' it." Dani practically bubbled with excitement as she examined the leather tote Amy handed her. "Look, my purse fits right inside it."

"I guess that works," Amy said while she transferred the items in her clutch to a brown leather bag. "Okay, I have to ask. You both are married to guys with exceedingly deep pockets. Haven't you ever gone on a blow-out shopping spree?"

"Not me," Shelby said. "We live on AJ's teaching salary. It's more than enough since we don't have a mortgage or car payments."

"Says the missionary kid," Amy said dismissively, then immediately regretted her retort. If she'd been better at budgeting, she wouldn't be in the financial mess she was in now. "I'm sorry, Shelby. That was mean, and I'm trying to not be mean. Sometimes things just pop out."

"I'm sorry too. I didn't mean to sound so pompous," Shelby said. "And you're not a mean girl. If you were, Dani and I wouldn't look like we just stepped out of a *Glamour* photo shoot."

Amy acknowledged the apology with a smile. She had to admit, the more time she spent around Shelby, the more she genuinely liked her. And the more she wanted them to be true friends. Dani too.

"We really need to go." Shelby herded them toward the doors.

"I'll drive," Amy said. "Sorry, Shelby, but we're dressed in style and we're going to arrive in style."

"Fine by me. I know my Camry's a bit on the blah side."

Once they were on their way, after a quick stop for Dani to change from her sneakers into a pair of gold flats, Amy glanced at her sister-in-law in the rearview mirror.

"What about you, Dani? No shopping sprees for you either?"

She shrugged uncomfortably. "Brett has tried to get me to go wild, but it doesn't feel right somehow. I never want him to think that—because it's so not true."

"Think what?" Amy asked.

When Dani didn't respond, Shelby answered for her. "That she's like some of the women he dated."

That only wanted his money. Amy nodded understanding.

Shelby turned around in her seat and smiled at Dani. "But he knows that isn't true. You should let him spoil you sometimes."

"You're probably right," Dani said. "But to never have to worry about money ever again? That takes some getting used to."

It goes the other way too. To never worry about money and then needing to watch every dollar. So not easy.

"Tell you what," Amy said. "The next time Brett suggests you go shopping, give me a call."

"Me too," Shelby chimed in.

"We should go to New York," Amy said. "A girls' weekend. Though more than a weekend because we'd have to drive." The fear of losing Dani might have gotten Brett onto a plane, but Amy planned to keep her feet safely on the ground. No matter what.

"We should do that," Shelby agreed. "I've never been there. Have you?"

"Not me," Dani said from the backseat.

"I went with Mom and Gran once," Amy said. "We went shopping, to the theater, way too many museums. But we had a good time."

"Tell us about it," Shelby urged.

At first Amy wasn't sure she could. Her images of the New York trip were tucked beneath her canopy world. But Shelby's gentle prodding and Dani's enthusiastic wonder coaxed the happy memories from that safe place, and Amy found herself talking about them without choking on unshed tears or feeling the need to vomit.

When they arrived at the softball fields, Shelby directed Amy where to park. As they got out of the car, a woman carrying a small box approached.

"Hi, Shelby," she said. "This is great timing. So glad I caught you. And look at you ladies all spiffied up. Aren't you a sight?"

"Hi, Louise," Shelby answered. "You probably know Dani, and this is Amy. She's AJ's cousin."

After the greetings, Louise held out the box. "Thank you so much for the casserole. Here's your dish and a little something special. Fudge nut brownies."

"Yummy," Shelby said. "How is Arnold?"

"Good enough to warm the bench, but he won't be playing for a while." She laughed merrily. "Not that he's needed much with all these young good-looking men we've rounded up for the team."

"I guess it's one way to evangelize," Shelby teased.

"Well, I'll let you all get to your seats. It's quite the game. Our new first baseman clears the bases every time he gets to bat. And it's only the fourth inning."

"The fourth inning?" Shelby exclaimed with a laugh. "AJ will think I got lost."

Louise laughed too, then left them, and Shelby placed the box in Amy's car.

"What was that all about?" Amy asked.

"Her husband had an operation last week, so I took over a casserole. She was returning the dish."

"With brownies?"

"Oh, you know, the whole 'never return a full dish empty' thing."

"The what?"

"It just means that when someone makes something for you, it's nice to return their dish along with something you've made."

"I didn't know that." Amy had simply returned the container of snickerdoodles Gabe brought over for Jonah. It never occurred to her to send anything back with it. "Dani, did you know that?"

"One of my foster mothers said it all the time. The one who taught me to play pool."

"Your foster mother taught you to play pool?" Amy turned to Shelby. "Did you know that?"

"Um, yeah. Dani almost always wins when we play. Unless Brett cheats."

"How come I didn't know that?"

"You know it now." Shelby laughed and grabbed Amy's arm. "Come on. We're already late."

Amy followed Shelby and Dani up the bleacher steps, her thoughts in a bit of a whirl. So many things she didn't know. The unwritten rules of neighborly living. Details about Dani's past. It made sense that Shelby and Dani were close. After all, they worked together at Misty Willow, and the two couples often socialized. But Amy couldn't help but feel like the odd one out once again.

Before taking her seat, she gazed at the field. AJ was on the pitcher's mound and Brett hovered near third base. The batter grounded the ball, the shortstop scooped it up and tossed it to first, where Gabe caught it and tagged the base. An easy out. As the team jogged in to the bench, he glanced her way and stopped in his tracks. Their gazes held, and his lazy smile tugged at his lips.

I hope he thinks I'm beautiful.

~

Gabe stared at the bleachers, unable to take his eyes off the gorgeous blonde looking his way. And his chest swelled with pride as Amy only had eyes for him.

AJ clapped him on the shoulder, pushing him toward the bench. "We're all going out after the game. Want to join us?"

"Do you think she'll mind?"

AJ glanced at Amy, then gave Gabe another push and laughed.

The rest of the game seemed to play out in slow motion. Gabe struck out every time he batted. Team hero the first four innings. Team goat the last five.

Somehow it didn't matter.

- 11 -

*G*abe pulled the thick tarpaulins off the stagecoach and coughed from the dust. He hadn't seen the contraption before except in a few photos Tess sent him when he was on his second tour. In one picture, Rusty stood beside his treasured find, his boot on the step. In another, he perched on the driver's seat, a broad grin spread across his face. With his beat-up Stetson, the one Gabe now wore, and the reins in his hand, Rusty could have been an extra in a John Wayne movie.

He'd have loved that.

Gabe had passed the photos around to the others in his unit along with the brownies and cookies Tess sent in her care packages. He sighed heavily as he rolled the tarp into a loose pile. After 9/11, he'd intended to spend his life as a Marine, and given the chance, he'd go on another tour. But that chance would never come.

His hand glided across the coach's finish until a splinter scraped his finger. The slivered wood cut into his flesh, and a drop of blood wet his skin. A brilliant red smear against his tanned complexion. Nowhere near as cute as Amy's paint-speckled face.

He wiped his finger on his jeans and climbed up to the driver's seat. The brittle leather creaked beneath his weight.

Amy.

No matter what he was doing, how much he tried to control his thoughts, he couldn't get her out of his mind. For the umpteenth time, he relived the moment she'd touched his jaw, her lovely blue eyes focused only on him.

The conversation played as he bowed his head and clasped his hands between his knees. Her voice was still as intoxicating as the day he fell in love with her.

"What's your word?"

"Prison."

"Not you."

He raised his head and stared unseeing at a spider-webbed corner of the barn, saw again the shock in her eyes that she tried to hide, heard her quiet response.

Not you.

Words a stranger wouldn't say. Which meant she'd slipped up. He gulped hay-scented, musty air.

His suspicion was right. She remembered him. She *knew* him. But for reasons he couldn't fathom, she didn't want him to know.

He could live with that.

"Gabe," Tess called as she entered the barn. "Are you in here?"

"Yeah." He climbed from the seat. "Checking out the stagecoach."

"How bad is it?"

"It's seen better days."

She frowned as she surveyed the coach. "Rusty always meant to restore it. Just another one of the many things he never got around to."

The unspoken words hung between them: *Because he died too soon.*

Gabe pulled her into a sideways hug. "Tell me why we're doing this again?"

"It seemed like a good idea when I suggested it," Tess said. "Though now I'm not so sure."

"How long has it been in storage?"

"Almost as long as we've had it."

Gabe ran his hand over one of the metal wheels. "It needs more work than we can get done in less than a couple of weeks."

"I guess we'll have to stick with the tried-and-true hay wagon instead." She looked over the stagecoach again. "It'd still be fun to have this at Misty Willow for the celebration."

"I can try to drive it over. Could be fun."

"It could be a disaster. Have you ever driven something like this?"

"Not by myself." On the occasions when Rusty had hitched a horse to a wagon, he'd sat beside Gabe, ready to lend a steadying hand if needed. "But I'm not a kid anymore. I think I can handle it."

"Do us both a favor and practice around here before you go out on the road. You can hitch up Abner and Casper. They make a good team."

Gabe nodded agreement. The two American Saddlebreds shouldn't have any trouble pulling the coach. As long as the wheels didn't fall off.

"I appreciate your volunteering to help at the celebration," Tess said.

"I think you're the one who did the volunteering."

Tess flashed him a guilty grin. "You could have said no."

"And disappoint my favorite aunt? Never."

"I hope you won't find it too boring."

"I'd rather take people to the creek and back than stand around and try to make small talk with them." He also wanted to have something to do in case Amy spent the day ignoring him. She never had responded to his invitation to ride shotgun.

~

Amy tapped her newly manicured nails on the table, then checked the time on her phone. Again. She'd give Logan five more minutes, no more, then she was leaving. She had better things to do than wait around for him to show up. Like painting her kitchen. Or shopping for furniture to fill up the space where the pool table had stood. Perhaps a round oak table like the one Gran used to have there.

Another minute passed, and the bell over the door dinged. Logan breezed in, spied Amy, then smiled broadly as he maneuvered his way to her table.

"Four minutes to spare," she said as he pulled out the chair across from her.

"You had me on a countdown?" he asked in disbelief. "I got lost."

"Don't you have a GPS?"

"What can I say? It led me astray."

Amused by his unintentional rhyme, Amy let her irritation fade. She'd forgotten how personable Logan could be. And how attractive with his dark hair and blue eyes.

"At least I'm here now." He folded his arms on the table, his warm smile melting the last of her put-upon attitude. "You're looking lovely."

"Flattery doesn't impress me," she said with a flirting lilt in her voice. "You should know that."

"It's not flattery when it's the truth." He gestured toward her to-go cup. "What are you drinking?"

"Iced mocha."

"I'll have the same."

Before Amy could stop him, he popped out of the chair and placed his order at the counter. She breathed out a puff of exasperated air, then grabbed her bag and joined him.

"Why did you want to meet me, Logan?"

He inserted his credit card into the reader and faced her. "Maybe I've missed you. Wanted to see how you were doing."

"Try again."

"You did quite the disappearing act. One day you're saying no to even the most lucrative clients in favor of your own select list; the next you're gone and your clients are left scrambling."

Amy stood quietly, her focus intent but revealing nothing. What could she say? At the back of her mind was the knowledge that everything about this meeting—what she was wearing, what she drank, what she said—could be tomorrow's white-hot topic. Not that Logan was known for gossiping. But it only took him telling one person who told one or two more, the details getting garbled in the retelling. Who could blame her for being guarded?

"Not that I minded when a couple of those clients put me on retainer." Logan returned his card to his wallet and took his drink from the barista with a smile. "It's a nice day. Why don't we walk around this charming town?"

In other words, he didn't want anyone eavesdropping on their conversation.

"I'd like that," Amy said. "Though I'm not sure how much charm you're going to find here."

His smile deepened. "I already have," he said meaningfully.

"Flattery again."

He leaned close as he steered her toward the door. "Truth."

Once outside, they wandered toward the town square. A monument to the community's World Wars I and II veterans, shaded by a pair of red maples, dominated the middle of the small park. Wrought-iron benches lined the pathways radiating from the center to the outer sidewalks.

Logan gestured at the nearest bench. Amy sat and crossed her legs toward him. Subtle, purposeful body language born from habit. And a need for casual masculine attention. Besides, she couldn't resist a little harmless flirting with an old friend.

Logan didn't disappoint. "Whoever you've got wrapped around your little finger these days is one lucky man. Anyone I know?"

Only a Stetson-wearing ex-con with a slow smile that pulled at her heart. Not that she had Gabe wrapped around her finger.

Far from it. He was too much his own man to be any woman's plaything.

"There's no one," she said.

Logan raised his eyebrows. "Seriously?"

"Why are you so surprised?"

"You always have a man in your life. Believe me, I've tried to catch you in between them."

"*Au contraire, mon chéri*," she said, playfully tapping him on the knee. "I recall a couple of times when I was free and you were not."

"I always got free as fast as I could." He rested his arm across the back of the bench and stroked her shoulder. "Never was fast enough."

"Who are you seeing now? Anyone I know?"

His eyes softened with meaning. "Only you."

"Really? That's the best line you've got?"

He drew her closer. "Admit it, Amy. Even when we were with other people, there was always an attraction between us. Isn't that why we were each other's standby dates to all those government functions we've been to? I don't think I need a line to catch your attention."

She studied his face, wanting to see behind the words. He was right about their mutual attraction, and they definitely made a fine-looking couple. Whenever she had an event her significant other couldn't attend, she called on Logan. And he did the same. Their evenings always ended with nothing more than a chaste goodnight kiss. It almost seemed like they took turns, by silent agreement, resisting temptation.

Maybe that's why she hadn't expected this come-on.

~

Gabe signed the signature card and slid it across the desk with a contented smile. Opening a checking account might be a small thing to most people, but for him it was a huge step on the road back to normalcy. The only blight was that the money for the deposit had come from his dad. Though it pained his pride to accept the check, and he'd been tempted to return it in little pieces, truth was, he needed it.

The bank officer, a cheerful woman with an attractive smile, organized the paperwork into a folder while he tucked his new debit card in his wallet. At least now he could buy the parts he needed to get the Ford up and running again. Also a new sander and varnish for the stagecoach. A few buckets of white paint for the fence.

But first, his errand for Aunt Tess.

"Could you tell me how to get to the library?" he asked.

"Go up to the corner and straight across the town square." She slipped her business card into a slot inside the folder. "Are you an avid reader?"

"I suppose I am." He'd certainly read plenty the past six years. "But I'm picking up a couple of books being held for my aunt."

"Who's your favorite author?"

"That's hard to say. I read a lot of history. Biographies, military nonfiction. What about you?"

"I go in spurts. If I find an author I love, I read everything they've written and then go on to someone else." She handed him the folder with another cheery smile. "If there's anything else we can help you with, please let us know." The smile deepened. "Let *me* know."

Gabe grinned. He'd forgotten what a boost a little flirtation could be to his ego. "I'll do that," he said.

He left the bank and drew the sun-warmed air into his lungs. The freedom of walking around town, any direction he wanted, wherever he wanted, called to him like a siren. He left Tess's truck parked on the street and headed for the library.

At the corner, he paused to check for traffic, then crossed the street into the square. Along one of the paths, a young couple sat on a bench. The man had his arm around the woman's shoulder as they gazed into each other's eyes. They seemed oblivious to the world around them, but Gabe recognized Amy's model-perfect profile, her silky blonde hair, and her long gorgeous legs.

Feeling as if he'd been sucker-punched, he jaywalked to the opposite sidewalk. Of course, she was seeing someone. He was a fool to think she didn't already have a man in her life. He stepped behind a parked SUV and looked toward the square. At this distance, it was even harder to make out the details, but one thing was certain. Whoever the man was, he and Amy were more than just friends.

– 12 –

Amy slid a strand of hair through her fingers. "You've surprised me, Logan," she said. "I thought you wanted to talk about a client."

"I do. At least, I did." Logan's fingers caressed the nape of her neck. "But since we're both unattached, maybe the timing is finally in our favor."

Confused thoughts whirled around her head, around her heart. If Gabe hadn't come back to Whisper Lane, she'd have agreed to going out with Logan. To exploring a potential relationship with him. Even now, circumstances being what they were, maybe she should. He could be exactly what she needed—a distraction from the man she wanted but her torrid past wouldn't allow her to have.

"I don't know," she said. "Life seems a bit too complicated right now to be involved with anyone."

"You want to talk about it?"

"Let's talk about why you called me."

He held her gaze, then slowly nodded. "Okay. I wanted to say thank you."

"For what?"

"I was a beneficiary of your, what shall we call it? Your sudden departure. A few of your clients weren't willing to stay with your old firm after you left, and they went knocking on other doors. Including mine."

"Who in particular?"

"Dylan Tapley."

"Um." She nodded slowly, dispassionately, while her stomach roiled at the mention of Dylan's name. He had blamed Amy when his grandiose plans for an upscale private retreat had failed, and they'd exchanged heated words the last time they spoke.

She forced a smile. "I wish you luck with him."

"I told him you'd done everything you could for him. That it wasn't your fault."

Maybe not. But neither was she entirely blameless. Dylan had hired her to get the necessary waivers and permits for his development before the passage of a controversial federal initiative to control runaway development in a geographical area southwest of Columbus. Dylan's property was in that zone.

Amy had taken Dylan's money even though she knew what few others did—a secret coalition had worked to fast-track the initiative and approval was imminent. Once it went through, governmental restrictions protected most of the acreage from the type of development Dylan had planned.

Neither Dylan nor Logan knew of Amy's deceit. She meant to keep it that way.

"He took a risk, and he lost money," she said. "Hopefully he learned from his mistakes." Just like she had. Or at least was trying to.

"He said that when the initiative passed, you wanted him to buy land around here."

"I tried to pull together two or three local landowners, but the whole thing fizzled." Not quite the whole truth, but close enough. Besides, Logan probably knew more details than he was letting on. "There's plenty of land in central Ohio for what Dylan wants. I'm surprised he hasn't already acquired something."

"He wants to build in Glade County. Not just a resort either, but a mixed-use development. Houses, condos, stores. Restaurants. Maybe even a movie theater."

"That is ambitious."

"It's the silver lining of the federal initiative," Logan said. "With all that land off-limits, developers need to look farther out. But this county is still within commuter distance to the capital. Dylan is getting a head start.

"If you want, I can ask Brett if he knows what's available. Though rural farmland isn't his specialty."

"Dylan has already selected the land he wants."

"Then what do you want from me?"

"A little history." Logan took a deep breath, as if reluctant to continue the conversation. Amy braced herself, certain she didn't want to either. "One of those local landowners you mentioned is your cousin, isn't it? AJ Sullivan."

"Yes." Her tone was brisk, professional. "But now that land is owned by a foundation with a name longer than your arm."

He chuckled. "I saw it in the public records. But here's what I don't understand. Since your cousin didn't want the land anymore, why didn't he let you take control of it? He'd have walked away with a lot more money than he got from that lease agreement he entered into."

"He wanted to protect it from people like Dylan."

"But you were the one who brought it to Dylan's attention."

Amy carefully considered her response, trying to calculate three steps ahead to what Logan truly wanted, what she could say, and what she should keep to herself.

Almost a year had passed since that whole debacle. Why couldn't the past stay in the past?

Finally she gave in to her exasperation. "If this was anyone but you, we would not be having this conversation."

"I know. But you have to understand how important this is to me. Having Dylan as a client is a game changer." Logan paused, took a deep breath, and smiled broadly. "I've gone out on my own."

Amy widened her eyes. "You're not with Kennedy and Gaines anymore?"

"I hung out my shingle about three months ago. Right now, Dylan is my most important client. He's ambitious, shrewd. Best of all, he has connections."

"You mean his uncle."

Logan nodded. "If Dylan pulls off the first phase, his uncle will help bankroll the rest. And probably give Dylan a vice-presidency in his company."

"And as Dylan rises, so do you."

"It never hurts to have a wealthy benefactor. I have a few dreams of my own, you know."

"Political office?"

"When the time is right."

Amy sipped her drink, her gaze focused on the opposite storefronts. An insurance company, a florist, a bakery. The staples of any small town.

Joseph Tapley, a bachelor with a handful of nephews, had a reputation for dangling his money and promises of power in front of each of them. The upscale resort had been Dylan's first major project, and his failure had infuriated his uncle.

"Why did you tell Tapley about your cousin's property?" Logan asked.

A straightforward question with a straightforward answer. "Dylan needed a Plan B. Property that could be quickly negotiated and settled. AJ had never wanted that land, so it should have been a win-win. But I was mistaken."

"He'd already signed the lease agreement?"

"That's right."

"But you thought the lease was illegal?"

"It was AJ's land. He could do what he wanted with it."

"Then why did you file the lawsuit?"

Her building frustration threatened to blow. She focused on breathing, willing herself to stay calm. Logan was a friend, not a rival nor an enemy. And she'd shut the door on this part of her past. No one could force it open again unless she let them.

"What I did was wrong, and AJ has forgiven me. It's over."

"I think you were right to file the lawsuit. Your mistake was in withdrawing it."

Amy stared at him. His words were like the ripping of a bandage from a wound that hadn't healed. During a family therapy session, she'd apologized to AJ and Shelby for what she'd done. They'd been gracious and forgiving. But Amy had threatened Shelby's dream of raising her children in her grandparents' home. Even though everything had worked out, could Shelby ever truly forgive Amy for making her life miserable during that time?

"Winning the lawsuit wouldn't have helped Dylan," she said. "The Misty Willow acreage wasn't enough for his project. The other owners wouldn't have sold their farms no matter how much Dylan offered them. People around here"—she gestured widely—"they're sentimental about their land. They don't sell unless they're backed in a corner."

Logan nodded in understanding. "I did a property search. AJ didn't donate all of the Misty Willow land to the foundation."

"That may be. I don't really know. He probably held on to acreage back by the creek, where the willow is located. Shelby's ancestors carved their initials in the trunk, so it's special to her." Amy focused on a couple of squirrels playing among the bushes between the pathways. "They spend a lot of time back there. Picnics, fishing. That kind of thing."

"He also inherited land from your grandmother," Logan said quietly, as if thinking aloud.

"That's right. I live in the cottage and he lives in the bungalow."

"Dylan wants it. All of it."

"Well, he can't have it." Indignation tightened Amy's chest. "AJ wouldn't sell Misty Willow, a property he cared nothing about till Shelby showed up. Do you really think he'd sell his inheritance from our grandmother?"

Logan ignored her question. "Do you know Tess Marshall?"

"Dylan wants her land too?"

"He's made her an offer."

"She won't sell. The stables mean too much to her."

"Maybe. But she hasn't said no. Besides, there are other ways to get land than through a sale."

"You mean by eminent domain? You can't be serious. There aren't any legitimate grounds for him to pursue that option."

"Your cousin would fight it?"

"Of course he would."

"And what about Mrs. Marshall? Are her pockets as deep as yours?"

These days, that was highly possible. Though from what Gabe said, the stables weren't in very good condition. What if Dylan made Tess an offer she couldn't refuse? Then he'd develop his project north of the cottage and across the road. What a nightmare.

"Dylan won't give up," Logan said. "There seems to be something personal about all this—about his refusal to even consider any other properties."

"He was livid when his property ended up inside the boundaries of that protected zone. Then the plan to acquire Misty Willow fell through. I filed the lawsuit to prove to Dylan I was on his side."

"It's too bad your cousin didn't have your back."

That was what she thought, but she didn't appreciate someone outside the family criticizing AJ.

"He wanted to be a hero."

"What does that mean?"

"It doesn't matter." But she couldn't keep the frustration out of her voice. AJ had chosen Shelby over Amy, and though it still stung, she couldn't dwell on old injuries. If he had leased the property to Shelby after he fell in love with her, Amy would have understood. But he hadn't even met Shelby yet. She'd written him a letter, a sappy letter, and he'd fallen head-over-heels for a stranger.

He said Gran encouraged him to circumvent Sully's will and lease Shelby the acreage. Maybe she did. Gran seemed to feel guilty about the way Shelby's grandparents had lost their farm, about their premature deaths.

It's in the past, she repeated to herself. *And the door is closed on the past.*

She needed to be thinking about today. And about tomorrow.

A tomorrow that might include houses and stores around Gran's beloved cottage.

"You'd be doing Dylan a favor," Logan said, "and me, too, if you talked to your cousin. Help us negotiate the sale." His ingratiating smile sparked her ire. "Not that you need the money, but I'll see you get a referral fee."

"Dylan needs to find someplace else to build his project. We don't want it around here." Her heart pounded against her chest, and she took a deep breath to calm her rising anger. "And I'd . . . I'd clean toilets before I accepted a dime that passed through his hands."

- 13 -

*G*abe returned to the truck so Amy wouldn't see him crossing the square, then drove to the library for Tess's books.
Afterward, on the way to the auto parts store, he spied Amy's
BMW outside a coffee shop. He immediately turned into the next
side street and parked in the first empty space. As if his mind was
on autopilot, he entered the coffee shop, ordered an iced tea and
a Danish he didn't want, and took a seat by the window.

He shouldn't be doing this. Amy wasn't his girlfriend, not now,
not ever. She was only his first crush, his first kiss. His first broken
heart.

Most men got over their first. They grew up, found the woman of
their dreams, and no longer thought about their teenage romances.

For some reason, Gabe had never done that.

Maybe because the grief over losing his mom was still so new
when Amy entered his life. Maybe because Amy lost her parents
too, and that had somehow joined them together in a way that
could not be broken.

That theory would make more sense if Amy still felt about him
the way he did about her.

He should get in the truck, finish his errands, and get back to the stables. Instead, he sipped the tea without tasting it.

~

Amy sucked on the straw and pretended to savor the chilled sweetness of her iced mocha. Concentrating on the rich flavor kept her from thinking about the calories. The icy coldness helped her focus on the drink instead of the anger she wanted to unleash on Dylan.

At least he couldn't initiate his own lawsuit. He had no standing to do so. But what hubris the man had to think, even for a minute, that Amy would try to persuade AJ to sell Gran's property in exchange for a referral fee. The land might belong to AJ, but it meant something to Amy too.

Logan sat quietly beside her, wisely not saying a word while she calmed herself.

"What exactly is your role in all this?" she finally asked.

"Same as always. Cut through any bureaucratic red tape to get the project approved. Jump through hurdles to change the agricultural zoning."

"Who on the Glade County commission is in Dylan's pocket?"

Logan pressed his lips together in a tight smile. She hadn't expected him to answer. In his shoes, she certainly wouldn't have. But his silence told her that at least one commissioner was willing to change the zoning designation. It shouldn't be too hard to find out which one.

"Maybe I should talk to Dylan," she said.

"I'd rather he didn't know I talked to you." He gave her a conspiratorial grin. "A little question of breaching client confidentiality."

"Then what was all that about offering me a referral fee?"

He leaned back on the bench, staring at the sky as if he could find the answer in the clouds.

"Logan?"

"We'd work that out in final negotiations. He wouldn't have to know."

"I can't help you, Logan. I'm not even sure why you told me any of this."

"Maybe I just wanted an excuse to see you again. It's been too long." He caressed her neck again.

"And?"

"And I wanted to see where things stood between you and your cousin. Forget about Dylan, Amy. I'll see what I can do to steer him elsewhere."

"You mean it?"

"For you? Anything."

"Be serious, Logan."

He chuckled and took her hand. "May I walk you to your car?"

Instead of answering, she let him pull her to her feet. When they reached her BMW, Logan maneuvered her between him and the door. "I meant what I said earlier. I'd like to give us a chance."

His directness scattered butterflies in her stomach and flattered her ego. The only male attention she'd had lately was from Brett and AJ. Brothers and cousins didn't count. Gabe counted, but he didn't look at her like most men did. Maybe he held a grudge because she said she didn't remember him.

Why couldn't he see through her lie?

"There's a benefit at the governor's mansion on Friday night," Logan said. "I forget the cause, but I could use a gorgeous plus-one. Come with me?"

A year ago she would have accepted any invitation to spend an evening at the mansion. Especially with someone as handsome and self-assured as Logan.

But now the thought almost made her ill.

"I can't," she murmured.

"Then how about something less formal? Dinner and a movie?"

"You'd give up going to the governor's mansion for a movie?"

"You bet I would."

For a moment she let herself get lost in his eyes, appreciative of his obvious admiration.

He leaned closer and whispered in her ear. "Just say yes."

The butterflies stirred again, and a slight smile eased the tension in her jaw. She needed this. She deserved this.

"Yes," she said softly.

~

Gabe clenched the sweating cup as he stared through the window. The man bent toward Amy, and a sweet smile curved her lips.

Forcing himself to look away, Gabe balled up a paper napkin, then gulped his drink.

He should be happy for her. If she'd found someone to make her happy . . . wasn't that what he wanted for her? Besides, he wasn't the guy for her. Not after what he'd done.

At least now he knew she had someone in her life. And he was free to do what he needed to do.

Sunday afternoon he would go see Ellen.

~

Amy set the canvas totebag on the ground and stepped onto the bottom rail of the arena's wooden fence. Tess stood in the middle of the corral, a lead rope in one hand and a training stick in the other, as a glossy black quarter horse went through his paces. He lunged, his ear cocked toward Tess, waiting for her next instruction as he circled her.

Tess acknowledged Amy's presence with a quick nod but otherwise stayed focused on the horse.

As he trotted over a series of low jumps, Amy felt herself being drawn back into this world she had once loved so much. If things had turned out differently, if she hadn't given up riding, this might be her life. Stables of her own, training a horse that belonged only to her, riding whenever she wanted.

She took a deep breath, inhaling the sun-soaked breezes as they puffed wisps of her hair across her cheek. On a day like today, when the sun played peekaboo behind giant cotton clouds, it was so easy to forget the heartaches of her past.

If only.

The saddest words in the English language.

Several more moments passed, then Tess had the horse change direction. He nodded his sleek head, whinnied, then decided to do what she asked.

To the untrained eye, it might have appeared that the horse was behaving perfectly. But Amy detected the arch of the neck, the slant of the ears that indicated he wasn't as placid as the casual onlooker might think. Even so, Tess handled him with skill and precision.

Eventually Tess halted the horse and shortened the lead. When he reached her, he lowered his head and she gave him a treat while stroking his smooth nose. After a moment of affection and praise, she led him toward the fence.

Amy stepped back.

"Hello, neighbor," Tess said cheerily, but Amy caught a wariness in her dark eyes. "How are you settling in at the hideaway?"

"I still need to paint the bathroom. Gabe helped me with the cabinet doors a couple of days ago."

"So he said."

"Who's your friend?" Amy gestured at the horse. "He's beautiful."

"This is Knight Starr. He's definitely my pride and joy."

"You handle him well. I'm guessing he can be ornery."

"You've got a good eye," Tess said approvingly. "Would you like to go through an exercise with him?"

"No, but thanks." Amy took another step backward. "It's been a long time since I've been around horses."

"That's a shame." Simple words spoken with a thin sheet of ice.

Tess removed Knight Starr's halter. He whinnied, then wandered away to graze. Meanwhile, Tess slipped through the gaps in the rails. She wore a cotton V neck over jeans and laced-up work boots. Her straight black hair, graced with dignified streaks of gray and longer even than Amy's, was pulled into one thick braid.

"Gabe isn't here," Tess said. "He's working with AJ, but I'm not sure where or what they're doing."

"I didn't come to see Gabe," Amy said with a hint of defensiveness. "I came to apologize for my accidental rudeness."

She removed a purple African violet in a ceramic pot from the canvas bag.

"When we were at the softball game Tuesday, Shelby said something about full and empty plates. I don't remember the exact phrase. Anyway, this is for you." She thrust the plant into Tess's hands. "As a thank-you for the cookies."

"You didn't have to do this." The icy tone seemed to thaw a little.

"I wanted to. I want to, I don't know, do things right. As a neighbor." She closed her mouth to stop the prattling.

"This is lovely, and I appreciate it." Tess cradled the plant, and they walked toward the house. "Would you like to come in for a cup of tea? I've got batter in the fridge, so it'll only take a few minutes to bake a dozen more cookies."

"Maybe another time, thank you. I promised to take Jonah and the girls to a matinee in town. Shelby and Dani are busy with preparations for the Heritage Celebration, so I've got to put on my cool aunt persona."

"What's that?"

"Extra patience, mostly. Especially with Tabby. Jonah and Elizabeth are close enough in age that they tend to buddy up. When Tabby feels left out, she gets boisterous."

"I suppose I should know this, but how old are the children?"

"Jonah is eight, Elizabeth is seven, and Tabby is four."

"That has to be hard on Miss Tabby," Tess said. "Just give her a little extra attention and you'll be fine."

"I'll do that."

"And feel free to bring them over here sometime if you want. They might like to pet the horses. Explore a little bit."

"I'm not sure Brett would want me to."

"Why not?"

"Jonah wants to ride. He even asked his doctor if he could. But Brett's afraid. He's so overprotective." Amy almost scoffed as she said the words but stopped herself. At least Brett was afraid for his son's well-being. Her fears were only for herself and for reasons she didn't want to think about.

"Jonah's been through a lot. It's understandable that Brett doesn't want him to injure himself."

"I suppose I could bring him over—"

"No," Tess said sharply. "Don't you dare do something like that."

"How did you know what I was going to say?"

Tess stared at her, then slightly smiled. "Because it's exactly the kind of thing I would have thought of doing."

"You?" Amy said skeptically. "That's hard for me to believe."

"Don't let the grown-up act fool you. I've had my mischievous moments. But bringing Jonah here without his dad's approval is foolhardy. You'd never forgive yourself if something happened to that child."

"You're right. I only wish Brett didn't worry so much."

"Give him time. It can't be easy to adjust to being both a new husband and a new father."

"I suppose not."

They'd reached the rear of the house, where Amy had parked her BMW beside Tess's pickup. She dug her key from her pocket and hit the unlock button on the remote. It hadn't been necessary to lock her car while it was parked here, but it was a habit she couldn't break after living all those years in the city.

They chatted a few more moments, then Amy drove to Misty Willow to pick up the kids. Before she left, Tess had invited her to come over again when she could stay longer. It had been a polite invitation, but Amy couldn't decide whether it had been sincere. When Amy had arrived at the stables, Tess had been guarded. Even wary. Though she seemed to relax while they talked, Amy wasn't sure how welcome she would be if she returned.

Maybe gossip about Amy had reached even this out-of-the-way place. Tess wouldn't approve of Amy's heavy drinking and especially not her casual affairs. Those things were in the past, but that didn't matter to most people. They would define her by how they knew her instead of giving her a chance to be different. To change.

She couldn't erase her past. So how could she make people forget about it?

- 14 -

Logan accepted the drink Dylan Tapley offered him and held it up. "Cheers," he said before taking a polite swallow. Any more than that could wait till later. Maybe he'd stop at his favorite bar on the way home for a couple rounds, see who else was hanging around. But he rarely drank during office hours. He did now to celebrate this special occasion.

Dylan was his ticket to making his dream come true. Amy didn't realize it yet, but she was part of that dream too. Despite her hiatus the past several months, he had every confidence she could be drawn back into the power limelight. The two of them together would be a formidable team. He only needed to scatter the bread crumbs, then let her figure out how profitable their partnership could be.

They both had connections. They both had influence. Combine his business acumen with Amy's sophistication, beauty, and, most important of all, her money, and within a year they'd have an elite clientele.

Though Logan had a healthy bank account of his own, he hadn't been the recipient of a single inheritance, let alone multiple ones. It was too bad about Amy's parents, but at least they'd left her more than enough to remember them by. He'd had to work, and work hard, for every penny. The past several years with Kennedy and Gaines had been a long apprenticeship, a time to make the right connections, gain an insider's look at the inner workings of state politics, and develop his own network of sources, favor seekers, and contacts.

He took another swallow of his drink.

The perfect partner. The perfect client. Everything was happening as he'd planned.

"Sit, sit," Dylan insisted as he settled his solid frame into the plush leather chair behind his immense desk. He was two or three years younger than Logan, a potential NFL linebacker who hadn't made the final cut. That setback pushed him into working with his uncle. He wasn't quite making the cut there either. At least not yet.

Logan was determined to change that dynamic.

He lowered himself into a chair.

"I want to know everything," Dylan said. "But first, did you visit our Glade County friend?"

"Yesterday morning."

"You delivered my package?"

"The commissioner sends his regards and his gratitude."

Dylan snorted. "As long as he votes his gratitude."

"He'll regret it if he doesn't."

"Is he aware of how much?"

Logan shrugged. "Blackmail is so ugly. As long as bribery works, why bother?"

"Because bribery costs me money."

"We've had this conversation before."

"I know, I know." Dylan held up his hands in surrender. "'Greed first, then fear.'"

"It's the safer strategy."

"So you keep telling me." His eyes narrowed as a leering smile spread across his face. "You saw Amy?"

"I did."

"How is our favorite long-legged blonde beauty?"

"As gorgeous as ever."

"And as high and mighty?"

Logan bent his head in silent agreement, then held Dylan's gaze. "She's not happy about your plans."

"I didn't expect her to be."

"She's living at the cottage where her cousin used to live."

Dylan gestured toward the large table near the office's back wall. "Show me."

Logan followed Dylan to the table, which was covered by a large map of northeastern Glade County. He studied it to get his bearings, using his finger to trace the route from out of the town of Madison to the cottage.

"Amy lives here." He backtracked to the bungalow. "Sullivan lives here."

"For now," Dylan said under his breath.

"One step at a time, buddy."

"If he hadn't signed that lease—"

"That dead horse has been beaten enough. Sullivan signed the lease. Amy withdrew the lawsuit. You're not getting Misty Willow."

"But I'll get this." Dylan pressed his thumb onto the part of the map where the cottage was located as if he were squashing a dead bug.

"Maybe. Probably." Logan struggled to hide his annoyance. Sometimes it seemed his biggest challenge was keeping Dylan's attention on the big picture. "Let's concentrate on the weak link first."

"Tess Marshall."

"That's right. For now, she's our priority." Logan ran his finger across the section of the map north of the cottage. Amy wouldn't appreciate a shopping center, no matter how upscale, as a neighbor. Maybe the development would drive her back to Columbus. Back to where she belonged.

"I sent Mrs. Marshall that offer three weeks ago," Dylan said. "What's taking her so long?"

"Perhaps she needs a little persuasion." Logan dragged his finger along the map, crossing the road from the cottage to the stables. A week or so ago, he'd phoned the county's animal control, anonymously of course, to accuse Tess of neglecting her horses. He had a couple other tricks up his sleeve, trifling things meant to unnerve her. To push her away.

"What are you going to do?" Dylan asked.

"Give her a little shove," Logan said quietly as he stared at the map.

"Do it soon."

"Patience, my friend."

Dylan huffed, then returned to his desk. "I almost forgot," he said as he picked up a manila envelope. "I've got something for you."

"What is it?"

"See for yourself."

Logan pulled a few photographs from the envelope. The top one showed him and Amy sitting on the bench in the town square.

He glared at Dylan. "What is this?"

"Souvenirs." Dylan's bemused gaze threatened to ignite Logan's smoldering anger at the arrogant jerk. But he forced himself to relax, to stay composed. If Dylan suspected Logan's irritation at his ridiculous cloak-and-dagger tactics, he'd only use it to his advantage. Better to let Dylan think he'd done Logan a favor.

He flipped through the remaining photos as nonchalantly as possible. In one, his arm was along the back of the bench and Amy's head was bent close to his. The last one, taken when they were at her car, showed him leaning close enough to kiss her lovely lips.

He smiled at the memory, almost regretting he'd let that opportunity slip by. But Tess Marshall wasn't the only one he wanted to unsettle.

If he came on to Amy too strong, too soon, she'd retreat. He couldn't take a chance on that happening.

"Like them?" Dylan asked as he poured another drink.

"I do," Logan said. "Mind telling me why you went to the trouble?"

Dylan shrugged. "Curiosity."

"About?"

"You're attracted to her." He reached for the photographs and selected the one of Logan and Amy standing by her car. "She's attracted to you. I approve."

"It's all part of the plan," Logan said. Dylan's and his own. As far as Dylan knew, Logan wanted to gain Amy's trust and, if possible, her help in acquiring the land they needed. After their conversation, that seemed unlikely. But Logan's own plan—the one that didn't include Dylan or his project—was his priority. Amy at his side, as his business partner, perhaps even as his wife. Her support and connections increased the likelihood of his political aspirations coming true.

"Are you seeing her again?" Dylan asked.

"Tomorrow night."

"Want some advice?"

"Not particularly."

"A warning, then," Dylan said. "Have all the fun you want but don't get so friendly with her you forget who's signing your checks."

"I've got a warning for you too. No photographing my date."

"That was all in fun." Dylan sat down at his desk and tapped a key on his laptop. "We'll meet here on Monday. Check with my receptionist for a time."

Though irked by the curt dismissal, Logan took his briefcase and left. Let Dylan think he had the upper hand. All that mattered was that he didn't.

~

Amy was flattered when Logan insisted on driving to the cottage to pick her up for their date. But then she insisted they go into town for a casual meal and a movie. He didn't need to be making two round trips to Columbus just to impress her with dinner in the city. Besides, she didn't want to spend that much time in a car with him. If the date didn't go well, it'd be a long and uncomfortable ride home.

They opted for a steakhouse at the edge of town, where Logan regaled her with the stories she had missed out on during her absence from state politics. Still the skilled conversationalist, Amy laughed at the right moments, looked appropriately wowed when he expected it, and gave the impression of having a great time.

A year ago, even a few months ago, it wouldn't have been an act. She would have been sponging up every tidbit of information, her mind whirling with how she could use each nuance for her own personal advantage. But now all the backbiting, public outbursts, and private gossip seemed meaningless.

Instead of feeling superior to the victims and jealous of the victors, she pitied all of them. It was like they were on a Ferris wheel of tracking legislation, maneuvering for position, and scrambling to the top. The wheel didn't stand still for long—not for anyone. Someone was always going down, someone else going up, but all of them were trapped in the never-ending circle.

They lingered at the restaurant, then raced to the local theater, where their two options were a nightmarish thriller and a romantic comedy. After opting for the latter, they settled in their seats moments before the opening scene.

When the movie ended, Logan shifted his weight and his chair squeaked. "This place has seen better days," he said as he stood.

"It has charm," Amy replied.

"That's code for old and run-down."

"Come on, it's not that bad." The vintage chairs might be squeaky, but the upholstery was thickly padded and probably not that old.

"Next time we'll go somewhere with reclining seats and foot-rests."

Annoyed at his put-down, Amy felt an unexpected need to defend the small-town cinema. "I think it has a coziness you don't get in the mega-theaters," she retorted.

Logan stared at her, then chuckled. "You remember that time we double-dated, went to that dine-in theater?"

"I think so."

"You threw a fit because your little flashlight didn't work and you couldn't see the menu."

"You're exaggerating." Though not by much. She'd been indignant, then rude and dismissive to the staff. Such a little thing, a burnt-out lightbulb, but she'd taken it as a personal slight. Embarrassed by the memory, she turned surly. "Besides, what does that have to do with this place?"

"The Amy Somers I know and adore isn't impressed by places like this." He paused, perhaps expecting her to admit she'd been kidding. "At least, you didn't used to be," he said. "Now you're ready to do battle for it."

"You're still exaggerating," she said. "I suppose it's about expectations. And perhaps figuring out what's really important in life."

"This theater is important?" His natural good humor lightened his skepticism. But she couldn't blame him for being surprised by her changed attitude. Not that long ago, she wouldn't have set foot inside this place.

"I've been here a couple of times with my nephew and AJ's stepdaughters. In fact, we were here yesterday afternoon. Admittedly, I felt a little outnumbered. But the movie was good, and the kids had plenty of snacks. It was fun."

"Who would have ever thought? You hanging out with kids."

"I know. Sometimes I don't believe it either." She gazed around the small auditorium, remembering how Elizabeth and Tabby both wanted to sit next to her, which was fine with Jonah as long as he got to sit in the aisle seat. "Brett once said they pull you in, one memory-making moment at a time, until they're part of your life. I didn't believe him, but now it's happening to me."

"Does that mean you're ready to settle down? Have a family of your own?"

"I want a family." She nudged him to move out of the row. Almost everyone else had already left the theater. "How about you?"

"As soon as I find the love of my life."

"I hope you do."

"So do I."

He gazed meaningfully into her eyes, then tucked her arm into his. Warm fuzzies radiated through her, and she couldn't help but smile. This was nice. Logan was nice. Easy to talk to, intelligent, ambitious.

A man with money who appreciated life's finer offerings.

He was perfect except for one thing.

They drove to the cottage, but he didn't hint to stay and she didn't invite him to.

At the door, he lightly held her hands in his. "I'm having a few friends over on July 4th. My balcony has a great view of the fireworks. Will you come?"

She wanted to give him an unequivocal yes, but she had uncertain hopes of watching fireworks with someone else.

"My family has made plans," she said, adding a touch of regret to her voice. "For most of the day. I'm sorry."

"If you're coming to Red, White, and Boom—"

"We're not. Just a family get-together. Out by that willow tree I told you about. Then we'll go to the lake in the evening for the fireworks."

"I see," he said, making no effort to hide his disappointment. "If you change your mind, give me a call."

"I will," she promised.

He kissed her softly, quickly, then smiled. "Can we do this again?"

"Do you mean see a movie in a theater with squeaky seats?" she teased. "Any time."

"I'm thinking of candlelight. Maybe dancing." He tilted his head. "Interested?"

"My social calendar fills up quickly. But I'll try to pencil you in."

He chuckled at her teasing, then squeezed her hand. "I'll call you."

She stood inside the open door until his taillights disappeared beyond the gate. Logan had been the perfect gentleman, the perfect date.

Except for that one niggling thing.

Logan Cassidy wasn't Gabe Kendall.

- 15 -

About midafternoon on Sunday, Gabe pulled up in front of the modest tract house and turned off the ignition of Tess's truck. He and Tess had gone home immediately after church and eaten a quick lunch so he could make this trip. But now that he was here, the memories he usually kept at arm's length assaulted him.

Maybe he shouldn't have come. Maybe she wouldn't want to see him.

They didn't fight the same memories, and he couldn't be sure whose were tougher. Gabe had been there. He knew what had happened. How it happened. But she could only imagine the details.

Which was worse—knowing or imagining? He couldn't decide.

"Go on, Kendall," he muttered to himself as he looked toward the house. Brown splotches appeared among the grass, and a few weeds poked up through cracks in the sidewalk leading to the front stoop. "Don't be a sissy."

He'd held his own against a bear of a man in prison and survived two tours in Afghanistan. But facing the woman inside that house took all the courage he could muster.

Before he could change his mind, he climbed out of the Dodge

and grabbed the bags from behind the driver's seat. When he got
to the porch, he took a calming breath, then rang the bell. Too
soon, the door opened. Small lines edged her brown eyes, which
widened and then narrowed with a barrage of emotions. Surprise.
Confusion. Hesitation.

She blinked and straightened her shoulders. From pride or as
some kind of strange dare. He wasn't sure.

"Hello, Ellen." His voice wavered, and he shifted the bags from
one hand to the other. "I know I should have called first, but . . ."

"You're out?"

"Earlier this month."

"It's over, then."

"Yes."

She lowered her head, whether to compose herself or to pray,
he didn't know. A moment later, she stepped through the door and
wrapped her arms around his neck. He held her awkwardly with
his free hand and inhaled the sweet fragrance of her shampoo, the
subtle scent of a flowery cologne. Warm tears moistened his neck.

"I'm sorry, Ellie," he murmured. "So sorry."

She stepped away and wiped her cheeks with both hands, but
the tears didn't stop. "He'd be home now too. If . . ."

"Maybe." Though they both knew it wasn't true. Randy had
received a life sentence for what he'd done. But then the whole
fiasco had been his fault.

Anger flared then died. Gabe's days of blaming his cousin were
done. These days he only blamed himself.

"If I'd gone into the store sooner, maybe . . ."

"We can't change what's already happened." She gave him a
watery smile, then gestured toward the door. "Why don't you
come on in?"

"You don't mind?"

"You're always welcome here."

He hefted the bags. "I bring gifts."

"You didn't need—"

"I know. But I wanted to. Besides, they're more from my aunt Tess than from me. Things she canned. Homemade preserves. That kind of stuff."

"How kind of her. Well, I'm not too proud to accept them." Ellen led the way through the neat living room to the kitchen. Gabe set the bags on a counter already cluttered with a toaster, revolving spice rack, a stack of papers, and a Bible. After drying her eyes with a tissue, Ellen stood on the other side of the counter as he pulled out the glass jars.

"It's almost like Christmas." She picked up a jar of blackberry preserves. "Umm. My favorite."

"Mine too."

"I seem to remember that about you." She set the jar on the counter and picked up one packed with slender green beans. "I thought this would be my life. Growing my own vegetables. Putting them up for the winter. But I don't even have a garden."

"It's not too late, is it? I could help you lay one out."

"Surely you have better things to do." Before he could protest, she retrieved two glasses from a nearby cupboard. "Where are my manners? I haven't offered you a thing to drink. Do you still prefer sweet tea? I hope so, because that's what I have."

"That'd be fine." He folded the empty bags while she busied herself filling the glasses with ice cubes and pouring tea from a glass pitcher.

"Where are the kids?" he asked. "I probably wouldn't even recognize them."

"They aren't babies anymore."

"How old are they now?"

"Matthew is eight and Michelle will be seven soon. They're spending part of the summer with my parents in Indiana. Gives me a bit of a break."

Gabe nodded as if he understood. But how could he? When

Randy was arrested, Ellen had to pick up the pieces caused by his impulsive recklessness. To raise their children on her own. Now that he was dead, she was even more alone.

"What are you going to do now that you're a free man?" A sliver of bitterness flattened her words. No surprise. She'd been happy to see him, but his presence dredged up questions neither of them could answer. Questions like why Randy, a decent, hardworking husband and father, had attempted something that could only end badly.

This was the price they were paying for Gabe's failure to believe his cousin could do anything so utterly stupid. Randy was dead. Ellen was a single mom. And Gabe had a prison record.

He hadn't done anything wrong, but in the eyes of the law that didn't matter. He was inside the convenience store when Randy aimed the gun at the clerk. Only a few feet away when Randy pulled the trigger.

Gabe was an accessory. Arrested and charged. Sentenced and imprisoned.

Ellen handed him the glass of tea. "Where are you living?"

"I'm staying with Tess for a while. Until I decide what I'm going to do."

"I remember her from the trial. We prayed together."

"She's been like a mom to me ever since mine died. Her horse farm has gotten run-down since she's been on her own. Seems there's never enough money to do everything that needs doing."

As soon as the words were out of his mouth, he wanted to drag them back in. Randy had said practically the same thing when the cops manhandled them into separate squad cars. *I needed the money, man. There's never enough money.*

Ellen didn't seem to notice. She looked off into the distance as if her mind was a million miles away.

"What are you thinking?" he asked.

"Just remembering," she said. "This wasn't supposed to be our story, you know. Mine and Randy's."

"I know."

"We were to raise our children together. Grow old together. We had so many dreams, so many plans."

"I failed him."

"No." She shook her head, and her eyes brimmed with fresh tears. "He failed himself. He failed us."

"If there's anything I can do. Anything at all."

She held his gaze for a moment, then looked away. "I wrote you. But you never wrote back."

"I didn't write anyone." Letters would have been a tangible reminder of those hated days. Maybe they'd get thrown away, but that didn't matter. He'd have written them, and in the writing made things real that he only wanted to forget. Besides, letters to Ellen would have drawn her deeper into that world too. He couldn't let that happen.

He sickened at the thought of Ellen, of Tess, of anyone he cared about receiving an envelope from him emblazoned with the prison's return address. He endured the shame, for Tess's sake, on special occasions. But he could do no more.

"You could have written me. Losing Randy was the hardest thing I've ever gone through. But I felt like I lost you too. And that made it even worse."

"I'm here now, Ellie. Whenever you need me." The silence between them veered into awkwardness, and he pushed away from the counter. "Where's the best place to get something to eat in this town?"

"What?"

"We had some good times together—you and Randy and me. It's time we remembered those instead of dwelling on what neither of us can change." He smiled what he hoped was an encouraging smile. "Let's go have some fun. What do you say?"

The muscles around her eyes relaxed as her lips curled upward. "I say . . . I need a few minutes to freshen up."

"Take all the time you need."

She hurried from the kitchen, and Gabe headed for the living room to wait for her. If he hadn't given his heart to Amy when he was so young, this might have been his home. His and Ellen's.

But Ellen deserved a wholehearted love, and he couldn't give that to her. Randy had, though. At least until life got the better of him, and he took the road to nowhere.

While Gabe waited for Ellen to change, he studied the photographs adorning one of the walls. A formal family photograph centered the other casual prints of birthday parties, holidays, vacations. A loving family with a hopeful future ahead of them. The nostalgia, the remembering, weighed heavy on his spirit.

If only he could have stopped Randy. Made him see sense.

Gabe had relived the nightmare thousands of times, lying on his bunk late at night, trying to find an escape in sleep. In his dreams, the scenario turned out differently. There was no gun. No bullet. No blood.

No arrest and no trial.

Ellen emerged from the hallway looking fresh as a summer day in a print dress and light cardigan. "You look nice," he said.

She slightly blushed. "Do you know how long it's been since anyone has told me that?"

"If it wasn't yesterday, then too long."

Her smile deepened. "I always liked you, Gabe Kendall."

"Then why did you throw me over for my cousin?" he teased.

She looked at him, her gaze open and direct, and her smile slightly faded. "I think you know the answer to that better than I do."

"I . . . I wanted to love you, Ellen."

"I know. And if you had, maybe"—she paused to take a deep breath—"maybe things would have been different."

"If they had been—"

"No," she interrupted. "Don't say it. I cared about you, so very much, but I fell in love with Randy. I'm still in love with him."

She clasped his arm with both of her hands and tilted her head to smile up at Gabe. "Even with all this heartache, all the hardships we've gone through because of what he did, I wouldn't trade the days I had with him for anything. Or anyone."

"You've forgiven him?"

"Yes."

What about me? Can you forgive me too?

He needed to know, but he couldn't bring himself to ask the question. At least not out loud. He held her gaze, and her expression softened.

"Oh, Gabe." She placed her palm against his cheek. "You don't need my forgiveness."

"But I do," he said softly, pleading. "If I'd believed him, if I'd . . ."

"You're carrying a burden that isn't yours to carry."

"I don't know how to let it go."

"I pray you find the way. You'll never have peace until you do."

"That sounds like something Aunt Tess would say."

"Then listen to her. And to me." Her smile broadened, crinkling the fine lines around her eyes. "Enough of this talk. I thought we were going out to have some fun."

"You ready to go?"

"I am." She hooked her arm in his, and they headed for the truck.

Gabe wanted to dispel the uneasiness in his soul, but Ellen's words, her affection and her forgiveness, stirred emotions he usually managed to keep battened beneath his chest. He was grateful Ellen didn't resent Randy, that her love hadn't turned to hate. Grateful, too, that she was with him now.

He wouldn't ruin their day together by focusing on what might have been, what should have been. The door to the past was closed, and they couldn't rewrite their stories.

They could only hope for a brighter future.

"Say," he said as he slid into the driver's seat, "what are you doing for the 4th of July?"

"I haven't given it much thought," she said as she buckled her seat belt. "The kids will still be with my parents."

"Why don't you spend it with Tess and me? We don't have big plans, but we can go to the lake for the fireworks. There's an extra bedroom so you can stay the night."

"I don't know . . ."

"Why not?"

"It's kind of an imposition, isn't it? I don't want to put Tess to any trouble."

"She's . . ." He stopped himself in time. No need for Ellen to know the invitation was Tess's idea. "She's all for it. We already talked about it."

Mischief glistened in Ellen's eyes. "You know, most men would have waited till they were leaving to extend an invitation like that. In case they changed their mind. But then again, you never were like most men."

"I hope that's a compliment."

"It is."

"I won't change my mind. I want you to come."

"Then maybe I will."

"Good." Gabe started the ignition. "Now, where are we going?"

"Your timing is perfect. The county fair is this week, and all of a sudden I have a craving for funnel cake."

"One funnel cake for the pretty lady coming right up."

Going to the fair would be just like old times. Maybe they could even ride the Ferris wheel.

127

- 16 -

*L*ogan hesitated, then hit the send button on the email. Dylan might be offended that he didn't keep the Monday-morning appointment, but he had no reason to do so.

Not once during their date did Amy bring up Dylan's designs on Whisper Lane or her cousin's property, and it suited Logan to avoid the subject. All part of his grand scheme to win Amy's trust and, if possible, her heart.

Their first date wasn't going to be ruined by discussing a topic she obviously found painful. No surprise there. Suing her cousin had to make things awkward at family gatherings.

Despite his best efforts to act natural while they were together, he'd found himself looking over his shoulder a few times to see if anyone was behaving suspiciously. But no one either at the steakhouse or the theater showed any interest in them. If Dylan had them under surveillance, his photographer was slick and clever.

Though Logan hadn't noticed anyone at the town center paying attention to them either. He'd given it a lot of thought and decided that Dylan must have arranged with the county commissioner to have someone follow Logan after their meeting.

This same commissioner would be surprised to learn he, too, had been photographed in secret. If he refused a bribe, they'd show him the photos. First greed, then fear.

With the email—short, to the point, but courteous—completed, Logan turned to other tasks. But he had a hard time concentrating when his thoughts kept returning to his date with Amy.

He was still dejected that she had refused the invitation to his July 4th party. Her reason sounded sincere, and he could understand why she wanted to spend more time with her family. Obviously she was mending fences there, which was a good thing. But part of him hoped that she would change her mind. Just in case, he wasn't going to ask anyone else.

He'd already decided they belonged together. Now he just needed to convince Amy of that too.

～

Gabe applied a thin coat of varnish to the stagecoach's body while Tess scrubbed at the rusty wheel with a square of steel wool. They had moved it from storage and parked it near the hay wagon underneath a pole barn. Though they weren't doing the full restoration Rusty had once planned, a lot of sanding and elbow grease had already improved the coach's look.

For safety reasons, Tess had decided against using it to transport guests to the creek, but Shelby still wanted to have it on display for the Heritage Celebration.

"How are you doing with that wheel?" Gabe asked.

"I've got a couple of spots that don't want to go away. But I haven't given up yet." At the sound of tires on gravel, she stepped out of the shade of the pole barn to see who had pulled into the drive.

"Who is that?" Gabe asked as he came to stand next to her. A black Mercedes stopped beside the house as if the driver was unsure where to park.

"No one I know." Tess stepped farther into the lane and waved. "Unless . . ."

"Unless what?"

She didn't answer, but her body stiffened.

The driver must have seen her because the car revved toward them.

"Does he think this is a speedway?" Gabe grumbled. He took Tess's arm and they stepped to the side.

The vehicle stopped, but the driver didn't cut the engine. The door opened, the driver stepped out, then he opened the passenger door.

A large man wearing a dark tailored suit and built like a linebacker emerged from the car. An insincere smile cut across his face, and he balanced a pungent cigar between two thick fingers.

"Mrs. Marshall," he said in a voice smoother than cream and even more insincere than his smile. "Finally we have the pleasure of meeting."

"You must be Dylan Tapley."

"I have that distinction, yes." He swept a dismissive gaze over Gabe. "Please forgive me for dropping in unannounced." He gave a strange laugh. "But that's common among country folks, isn't it?"

"We are known to be neighborly," Tess said.

"I won't take up much of your valuable time," he said with a tone that Gabe understood to mean he meant his own valuable time. Clearly he didn't see what they were doing as being at all important. "I expected to hear a yes from you before now. My offer, after all, is a generous one. If there is anything more I can say to persuade you in my favor"—he opened his arms magnanimously— "I am here to say it."

"What offer?" Gabe asked. "What's this all about?"

Tess took a deep breath and laid her hand on Gabe's arm. "Mr. Tapley wants to buy Whisper Lane."

"He wants to . . . he can't." Gabe faced Tapley. "Why would you?"

"I don't discuss my business affairs with the hired help," Tapley said.

"Hired help?" Tess said, iron in her voice. "This is my nephew. Gabe has every right to know anything that concerns these stables."

"Then why didn't he know about my offer?"

Tess's cheeks reddened, and Gabe clenched the rag in his hand, wishing it was the man's silk tie.

"Like I said, it's a good offer."

Tess turned to Gabe. "Mr. Tapley wants to raise and train horses for harness racing."

"Here?" Gabe could hardly believe what he was hearing.

"Mr. Tapley," Tess said. "I'm sorry I didn't call you sooner. But as you can see, circumstances are different now. Gabe is here, and I'm no longer interested in selling."

The smile on Tapley's face momentarily froze, and his eyes turned cold. He recovered so quickly, Gabe almost believed he'd imagined the malice. But he'd seen such flashes before in the eyes of dangerous men, and he knew they meant trouble.

"My dear Mrs. Marshall," Tapley said. "When we talked on the phone a few weeks ago, you told me the place needed more upkeep than you could provide. Can your nephew make that much difference?"

"He can." Tess smiled at Gabe with pride. "He will."

"I think you should go now," Gabe said as politely as he could but with an edge to his voice that left no mistake he wasn't asking. "Your business here seems to have ended."

Tapley took his time scanning the buildings and the pastures. He dropped his cigar to the ground and pressed his foot against the stub.

"Don't be so sure," he said. "Negotiations may be stalled, but they have not ended."

"But they have," Tess said firmly. "Now please excuse us. As you can see, we have work to do."

"I offered you a good price, Mrs. Marshall," Tapley said while staring at Gabe. "Be sure you know what you're doing before you say no."

Gabe raised his shoulders a fraction of an inch and returned Tapley's stare. He had faced more menacing enemies than this overgrown upstart. Without breaking eye contact, he pointed farther up the lane. "Your driver can turn around by the silo."

Tapley waited another beat, then directed a cold smile to Tess. "Thank you for your hospitality, Mrs. Marshall."

Except for the clenching of his jaw, Gabe didn't move a muscle. Though his stance was relaxed, his body was taut, prepared to handle any threat.

"I think you should go, Mr. Tapley," Tess said.

Despite his size, he slid easily into the Mercedes's backseat, a black tarantula encased in an ebony shell.

The tires unnecessarily spun gravel, and Gabe stared after the fender as it curved around the dirt area near the silo. Casually, as if he didn't have a care in the world, he picked up the crushed cigar stub, then held it lightly between his fingers as he took a stand in the middle of the lane.

"What are you doing?" Tess asked. "There's no need for any foolishness."

Gabe ignored her as he waited for the car to return. The driver braked only a couple feet from his legs, but Gabe didn't flinch. He motioned for the window to be rolled down and walked to the driver's side.

He leaned against the door, his head partially through the open frame. "Your boss forgot something," he said congenially.

"What would that be?" Tapley asked from the backseat.

Gabe resisted the temptation to look at him. Ignoring the man was better, a subtle means of saying Tapley wasn't worth his time.

He flipped his hand, revealing the cigar stub he held between his finger and thumb.

"Hospitality isn't our only custom around here," he drawled. "We also don't leave our trash in a neighbor's yard."

He dropped the stub in the driver's lap, then pushed away from the door. "Get on out of here."

Even as Tapley passed by him, Gabe refused to acknowledge his existence. Men like him expected position and wealth to provide them with respect they hadn't earned. And didn't deserve.

Tess joined him and stared after the departing car. "Tell me you didn't throw that cigar at Mr. Tapley."

"If I'd done that, he'd have left here thinking that's what he'd expect from someone like me. So I did the unexpected."

"You still shouldn't have."

"He shouldn't have spoken to you the way he did."

"I can handle the likes of him." She placed the steel wool in the palm of his hand. "You finish the wheel. I'll go check on supper."

She'd taken a few steps toward the house when Gabe spoke. "Would you really have done it?" he asked quietly.

She turned and faced him, her expression drawn and sad. "I never wanted to."

"But you would have?"

"I didn't think I had a choice. I'm still not sure I do."

Gabe avoided looking at her, his mind whirling with thoughts he couldn't seem to untangle. Memories and dreams and regrets and hopes.

Tess returned to stand in front of him. "I'm only sorry I didn't tell Tapley no before this. Then you wouldn't have known. And this wouldn't have happened."

Gabe removed the beaten Stetson, wiped his brow with his forearm, and rested the hat against his leg. He didn't want to upset Tess, didn't want to argue. But it hurt that she'd kept this from him. His eyes flickered, seeing everything around him except for her.

"If you didn't want me to know," he said softly, "then why did you tell Tapley what you did? Either I have a right to know or I don't."

She was silent for so long he finally looked her way. Her posture was stiff, her chin tilted upward. Tears welled in her eyes, but she'd do everything she could so they wouldn't fall.

"We bought this place for our family," she said quietly. "Red-headed boys and raven-haired girls, Rusty used to say. A whole passel of 'em."

She entered the pole barn and rested on a bale of last year's hay, as if she was wearied by a weight he couldn't see. Gabe followed her, then lowered himself to the concrete floor at her feet. He picked at the bale's thin strands.

A gentle smile curved her lips and creased the corners of her eyes. "But there was only you. We'd count the days till your arrival and dreaded every good-bye. How we missed you when you weren't here."

He'd missed them too, but he found it hard to say the words. As much as his family had moved around, Whisper Lane had been a needed constant in his life. He flicked hay across the floor. "I used to pretend this was my home," he said. "Especially after Mom died."

"We wanted it to be. Even hoped for a while that it would be. But your dad couldn't bear to give you up, not after he'd already lost so much."

"You discussed it with him?"

"We did. I even had you enrolled in school here. Then he called one morning, said he was on his way to pick you up." She gazed away, lost in memory. "That was a hard time. Letting you go when all we wanted to do was hold you close. Keep you here with us."

"I didn't know." Surprised by the revelation, he chewed on a piece of hay. So Dad had wanted him. At least for one day. "I wish he'd let me stay here."

"He missed you."

"Maybe back then."

She let the comment pass, not that there was anything for her to say. But the pity in her eyes only stoked his resentment. Dad had come to the jail shortly after his arrest but only to berate him for the mess he'd gotten himself into. Gabe didn't see him again until the sentencing hearing. As he was led away in handcuffs, he'd spotted his father in the courtroom. Their eyes met for a moment, then Dad pivoted and marched out.

When Gabe was released, he'd been handed an envelope containing the check, which Gabe had deposited in the bank, a few twenties for traveling expenses, and a brief handwritten note admonishing him not to squander his "new lease on life."

What was that even supposed to mean?

"I think he'd have been happier if I'd died in Afghanistan," Gabe said. "His son the hero instead of his son the felon."

"You can't believe that," Tess said.

"He'll never forgive me."

"There's nothing for him to forgive." She squeezed his shoulder. "You did nothing wrong."

"He obviously thinks I did."

"But you know better. And so do I."

He humphed and smiled at her. "Guess that'll have to do, won't it?"

"We've gotten sidetracked," she said. "I didn't mean to bring up painful memories."

"I know."

"What I wanted to say was that, if things had turned out differently, the stables would be yours. But now it's mortgaged to the hilt, I'm behind on the payments, and I simply don't know what to do. It's my problem, though, and I don't want you to be burdened by the mistakes I've made."

"If you sold to Tapley, would you be better off?"

"From a strictly financial standpoint, yes. But it would break my heart to leave this place."

"You'll never have to. Not while I'm here."

"You have your own life to live, Gabe. I don't expect you to stay here indefinitely. Though I'm thrilled as punch that you're here."

"There's no place I'd rather be," he said. "And I've got no other place to go."

"You say that now," she said with a teasing lilt in her voice. "But what happens when a lovely young lady catches your eye? Or am I wrong in thinking that has already happened?"

He slightly reddened. "I have no idea who you're talking about."

"You keep telling yourself that." She stood and brushed dust from her pants. "I'm headed to the house. Are you coming?"

"In a little bit. I'll work some more on that wheel first."

She walked to the edge of the barn, then turned back. "I do have a favor to ask."

"Anything."

"I'd rather no one knew about this. Mr. Tapley's offer, I mean. Rumors can get out of hand real quick around here."

She didn't have to warn him against gossip. He'd been the object of more than his fair share of fabricated stories. "Tapley who?" he teased.

She smiled her appreciation, then left him. He leaned against the bale and let his thoughts wander. He wanted his future to be here. He'd dreamed it often enough while in prison. But he didn't know if it would be possible.

Finding out that Tess considered accepting an offer for the stables had thrown him for a loop, but he had to admit she never would have done so unless she had no other choice. Then he'd shown up, and she had changed her mind. But what could he do to make the horse farm financially viable again? He hadn't a clue.

Tess needed to be thinking about her own future instead of worrying about his. He couldn't let her become financially destitute because either of them was emotionally attached to this place.

If selling was her only, her best, option for a secure future, then he couldn't stand in her way.

Noble of him to say while he was sitting alone here in the barn. But the thought of Tapley owning this place sickened him. Surely there was another solution. Something else they could do instead.

– 17 –

*A*my stepped back and eyed the placement of the stained glass art piece with a critical eye.

"This is exactly where AJ hung it." Brett held the frame against the window. "I can see the nail hole."

"No, you can't." She sidled to the left then to the right. "I spackled all the holes before I painted. Besides, AJ hung it crooked."

"Dani didn't complain when she lived here."

"I live here now, and I want it perfect."

"You need to make up your mind because this thing is heavy. If I drop it . . ."

"Don't move." She ascended the stepladder, held up the chain, and marked where to drill the holes for the anchors.

Brett set the art piece on the floor while Amy installed the two decorative hooks above the window. "That should do it," she said. "Cross your fingers."

"I suppose you want me to pick this thing up again," Brett said.

"Please." While he held the stained glass against the window, Amy settled its chain over the hooks. "All done. But be careful."

Brett lowered the frame until the chain held its weight, then released his hold. Stepping back, he admired the vibrant colors of the glass. Amy descended the ladder and joined him.

"What do you think?" he asked.

"It's perfect." Colorful wildflowers, sheltered by the branches of a large tree, grew along the bank of a broad stream. When the sun's rays gleamed through the glass, the reds, greens, yellows, and blues wavered on the cottage's painted floor. "This is where it belongs. I'm glad AJ didn't take it with him."

"He bought it because it reminded him of Glade Creek."

"Had Meghan ever been here?"

"I don't think so."

Amy dusted the frame and pretended to wipe at a speck on the glass. "I never understood why he tracked her down."

"You'll have to ask him."

Something in Brett's tone caught her attention. "That sounds mysterious."

"I thought it was odd when he told me." He slipped his hands in the pockets of his cargo shorts and rocked back on his heels. "Now I understand."

"So are you going to tell me?"

"It's his story. Not mine."

"Do you wish he hadn't? Found her, I mean."

"Maybe at first, but not anymore." His dimples deepened with the width of his smile. "I'm crazy about that kid."

"He's changed you."

"I hope so." Brett pulled out his phone, checked the screen for messages, then tapped it against his leg, rotated it, and tapped it again. "I'll tell you something if you promise not to sneer."

"I promise."

He stared at her, as if weighing her sincerity, then took a deep breath. "Once upon a time, nothing was more important to me than my business. Making deals and making money. But God has given me a second chance."

"A second chance at what?"

"To do life right." He rotated the phone again, then pocketed it. "He gave me Jonah and then he gave me Dani. We're a family, a loving and happy family. Something I never thought I'd have. Nothing else in this world is more important."

What about me? She tamped down the question and asked another one instead. "What about Meghan?"

"We'll never be best friends, if that's what you mean. But she's giving me a chance too. Besides, we both want what's best for Jonah."

Amy concentrated again on the nonexistent speck on the glass. Brett didn't need to spell it out for her. If Somers Investments, Inc., went belly up tomorrow, he'd still have what he valued most. His wife and his son.

And money. He'd still have money.

He stood beside her and slung his arm over her shoulder. "You can have a second chance too, you know. All you have to do is take it."

So easy for him to say. He'd always made his own rules. Even when his life went sideways, he stayed in control. Eventually Meghan gave in and let him see Jonah. When Dani ran away from him, he flew—actually flew on a plane, something none of them ever did—to Boise to bring her back home.

When Amy didn't say anything, Brett kissed her temple. "Anything else you need help with?"

You want to help me? You've left me.

"Not right now," she said. "Thanks."

"Like you said, that piece belongs here."

"Who knew AJ had such great taste?" she said, forcing lightness into her tone. Her thoughts had turned too gloomy, and she didn't want to spend the rest of the day in a foul mood. She wanted to imbue the cottage with cheer and light, not sadness and self-pity.

"He'd be surprised to hear you say it." As they neared the front door, Brett pointed to the room that AJ had used as an office. She'd painted the walls the palest pink she could find before adding the mirrors, lighted vanity, and portable wardrobe racks. "I just hope I'm here to see his face when he sees that."

"What did you expect me to do with all my clothes? The bedroom has one closet. One. And it's no bigger than a . . . than a . . ."

"Than a what?" The bemused tone in Brett's voice was oh so irritating.

"It was made for a hobbit."

"It couldn't be that you have too many clothes?"

"Don't even start with me. I've seen your wardrobe. All those suits and shirts and—"

"Okay, okay." Brett laughed and held up his hands in surrender. "Why don't you come over for supper? It's Tex-Mex Thursday at our house."

She hid her exasperation beneath a warm smile. "Thanks, but now that all the painting's done, I have a few more boxes to unpack."

"Sure you don't need my help?"

"I can manage."

"The offer stands in case you change your mind."

"Brett." She no longer hid her annoyance. "Leave."

He grinned, flashing those dimples that caused even sensible women to swoon. Being his sister had one advantage—she was immune to his charm.

After closing the door after him, she went through her dressing room to the cottage's only bedroom. Once she unpacked these last boxes, the cottage would be, well, maybe not home. But as close as she could get.

She settled on the bed with one of the smaller boxes, then reached inside. First she unwrapped a crystal bud vase that had belonged to Gran, then a glass box she kept on her dresser to hold odds and ends.

The next item was encased in tissue paper and bubble wrap. She carefully unwrapped the ceramic figurine and placed it in the palm of her hand. Tiny white flowers adorned the rounded body of the delicate bluebird and gave it a cheery look. Two words appeared on the wing: *Be brave.*

She'd seen it in a gift shop in Richmond. Picked it up, delighted in the whimsical touches, then returned it to the shelf. But as she turned to leave, a still voice whispered, "Take it. It's for you."

Nothing like that had ever happened to her before. Dazed by the moment, she immediately purchased the little bird. Throughout her weeks at the treatment center, it perched on her nightstand. When she returned to her apartment, it resided near her favorite books. Now she needed to find the perfect place here at the cottage. A place where she could be reminded of the message meant for her.

She carried the bird into the long room and looked around. The cabinetry beneath the windows held a few potted plants, a large porcelain bowl, and an arrangement of candles and silver-framed photos. If she put a shelf above the stained glass . . . a clear shelf so that the ceramic bird appeared to be floating. . . . Perfect.

Except then everyone who came into the cottage would see it and they'd read the two little words. What would they think of her for needing something like this? That she was a coward? Weak? That couldn't happen, so she'd have to think of something else.

She cupped the bird in one hand and traced the black lettering with her fingertip, then wrapped it again in the bubble wrap.

Be brave.

If she heeded the message, she'd have to tell Gabe the truth and face the consequences. He'd be upset that she'd lied. He'd want an explanation, one she could hardly give him since she didn't quite understand it herself.

Except he had no idea the power he had to hurt her. Because she couldn't bear his disapproval, his rejection, she couldn't let him know that she'd never loved anyone else but him. The memory pressed into her brain, and for once she couldn't hold it back.

After the memorial service and lost in her grief, Amy could only stare at the headstone engraved with her parents' names as her grandparents accepted condolences. She didn't want to talk to anyone, didn't want to hear "I'm sorry" one more time, and hardly knew how to put one foot in front of the other.

Then Gabe appeared at her side, his eyes rimmed in red. He didn't say a word, but he didn't need to. When their hands touched and she wrapped her fingers around the arrowhead he gave her, their hearts had entwined. His strength and his comfort gave her the only peace she experienced during that aching, lonely time.

～

As the nose of the black Lexus edged through the gap in the hedges, Gabe pulled back on the reins. "Whoa there, boys," he said. "Don't risk getting mauled by that beast."

The Lexus pulled out a few more feet then stopped. A car door slammed, and a couple seconds later Brett appeared on the road.

"Hey, pardner," he called up to Gabe. "If you're looking for the Oregon Trail, you've got a mighty long way to go."

"Just takin' this here stagecoach over to Misty Willow," Gabe said in the same cowboy twang. "Heard tell they're planning a shindig there on Saturday."

Brett patted Abner's sloping shoulder as he walked past, then grasped the steel rim of the wheel. "Seriously, where did you get this?"

"Tess had it in one of her barns. She mentioned it to Shelby, and I got enlisted to take it over for the Heritage Celebration."

Brett shook the wheel, then opened the door and peered inside. "Is it safe to ride in?"

"Safe enough on the road. But the pasture's too rough to take folks back to the creek. We're using the hay wagon for that."

"So you got drafted into doing the hayrides? I thought that might happen."

"Better that than docent duty. What do they have you doing?"

"Docent duty."

Gabe grimaced. "Sorry, man."

"It won't be so bad. I get to spend the day with my bride while she talks about the history of the place."

Gabe took off his Stetson and passed his forearm over his temple. "I still think I got the better job."

"Gotta say, I'm a little jealous." Brett looked admiringly at the coach. "Mind if I ride over with you?"

"Climb aboard."

Brett grabbed the rail to pull himself up, then stopped. "How about we ask Amy?"

Gabe glanced at Brett and looked toward the hedges. The cottage stood behind that thick green barrier, and inside its walls lived the woman who had haunted him since they were teens. She'd changed since then. Grown hard from devastating grief. But he had to believe that beneath her tough veneer, she was still the adventurous, vulnerable, tenderhearted girl he once knew.

"I think the horses would make her nervous."

"Amy? She loves horses. She used to take lessons from your aunt when she was a kid."

"I remember." Gabe shifted his gaze back to Brett. "When's the last time she's ridden?"

Brett thought a moment, then shook his head. "I couldn't say. Guess it's been . . ." He shrugged. "I don't know."

"She told me about that place in Richmond."

"Did she? I'm surprised."

"She's still hurting," Gabe said. "Isn't she?"

"I suppose. The last year, year-and-a-half, has been tough. On all of us."

"We rode together a few times. That summer before your parents died." Gabe slightly shook his head. "She says she doesn't remember me, but I never forgot her."

Brett stared up at him. "Do you have a thing for my sister?"

Gabe had stepped in it now. He wouldn't lie, but he didn't care to admit the truth either. "I thought it'd be fun to ride together again. She doesn't seem interested."

Apparently that wasn't enough to convince Brett. "Amy's private about the men she dates," he said. "But they're not good to her."

Brett's words caused a slow burn to wend its way through Gabe's gut. "How do you mean?"

Brett didn't answer, and his jaw tensed. Finally he focused on Gabe as if appraising him. "She's fragile. Tread carefully."

"I'd never hurt her."

"No, I don't think you would." Brett backed away and held up his hand. "Wait right there."

"Where are you going?"

"To get Amy." He turned around and jogged back toward the gap in the hedge.

"Don't." Gabe set the brake and hurriedly dismounted. "Brett, hold on a minute."

Too late. He had disappeared behind the hedge.

Gabe trudged to Abner's head and stroked the gelding's long nose. Casper nudged him, and he absentmindedly patted him too.

Hopefully Brett had enough sense not to repeat what Gabe had said. Though what did it matter? He was an ex-con without a home, without a future. He had a long road to travel before asking anyone to walk it with him.

- 18 -

*A*my emerged through the hedge and stopped in her tracks. A stagecoach, a rickety, worn-out stagecoach, harnessed to two striking Saddlebreds, stood on the road. Right outside her driveway.

And Gabe Kendall, a sheepish grin on his face, patted their noses. Almost every memory she had of Gabe included a horse.

Except the one with the arrowhead. Reliving that moment had conjured up other dark memories of grief's abyss. The night of the memorial service, and for more nights than she could number afterward, hysterical sobs had wracked her body, leaving her spent and empty. In time, she learned to release her pain by emptying her body in other ways.

Only a few minutes ago, before the dark memories could consume her, she had resorted to that same liberating, repulsive tactic. Afterward, she stood and welcomed the familiar dizziness, the sensation of numbness. She rested her hand on her empty stomach, momentarily exhilarated as she pressed toward her spine. But her initial sense of power disappeared as regret washed over her.

As soon as she heard Brett calling for her, she'd gargled with mouthwash. She didn't dare let him know of her relapse.

Standing beside the stagecoach, Brett waved his arm in a grand gesture. "What do you think?"

"This is the surprise?" Amy asked.

"Don't be rude." Taking her elbow, he nudged her forward. "Gabe is taking the stagecoach over to Misty Willow. I thought you might want to go along."

"In that thing?"

"I bet the view's better up there." Brett pointed to the driver's seat.

She looked from the seat to Gabe.

"This wasn't my idea," he said.

"Do you want me to say no?"

He glanced at Brett, then held Amy's gaze. His hazel eyes seemed to penetrate into the depths of her heart, but she didn't look away. If he could see into her soul, then he might as well see the darkness hiding there. To know she was in a prison too.

His gaze never wavering, he closed the distance between them. "I want you to be happy."

The world around them faded away. Even Brett, standing beside her, seemed to be in another dimension. Here, in this moment, only the two of them existed.

She and Gabe.

"How can I be?" she whispered.

"Ride with me." He held out his hand, steady and strong. A hand that could swing a bale of hay onto a wagon, gentle a skittish mare with a confident touch, strip the thorns from a wild rose and slip its stem into her hair.

She readied herself for the expected jolt and placed her hand in his. Longing charged through her, a longing for the innocence of first love and for the discarded dream of her own happy-ever-after.

"You're sure about this?" Gabe asked.

She eyed the dilapidated stagecoach, the harnessed horses, then drew in air. A breath of wind whispered *be brave, be brave* and she gripped his fingers. "Let's go before I change my mind."

Gabe eased into his slow smile, then supported her as she climbed onto the coach. She did her best to ignore the exhilaration caused by the warmth in his eyes and the pressure of his touch against her back. The feeling persisted even after he turned away to straighten the reins.

"I'll drive behind you." Brett jogged toward his car.

"Just don't rear-end us," Amy called after him. "And close the gate."

He waved without looking back and disappeared beyond the hedge.

Amy gingerly settled on the stiff seat. Black duct tape crisscrossed the cracked leather, but tufts of the innards stuck out near the seams. Gabe clambered aboard beside her with the easy motion of someone who drove stagecoaches every day.

"Maybe I should have worn jeans," Amy said, tugging at a bristly piece of the stuffing that had scratched her bare thigh.

Gabe glanced at her legs with an appreciative grin, and her cheeks immediately warmed. "I'll wait," he said. "If you want to change."

"You're making me blush."

"I'm sorry."

"I never blush."

His grin widened, and the lines around his eyes furrowed in amusement. "Then I'm not sorry."

She grinned back at him, her spirits suddenly lighter despite her regrettable setback. The quiet words whispered into her soul: *I am fearfully and wonderfully made; your works are wonderful.*

The golden sun shone bright in a fluffy-clouded sky. Summer scented the softest breezes with freshness. The afternoon was perfect.

Gabe was perfect.

And perhaps, for this moment at least, she could pretend to be perfect too.

~

Tess cut two of the foot-long subs into manageable portions and arranged them on a tray. "I'm going to take these on out to the kids," she announced.

"Good idea." Shelby plopped a handful of napkins onto the tray. "Maybe food will get them to stay off that stagecoach."

"We'll be out in a minute with everything else," Dani said. She stirred the pasta salad, then took a bite. "Yum, that's good. Even better than Tex-Mex."

"Save some for the rest of us." Brett took the spoon away from her. "And no double-dipping."

"I was going to get a clean one," Dani protested.

Tess smiled to herself. The newlywed bantering could have been her and Rusty once upon a time. How much she missed him on a day like today.

Gabe's arrival at Misty Willow had turned the afternoon into an impromptu party as everyone got involved in maneuvering the stagecoach into place. After about forty minutes of good-natured bickering, Gabe and Brett had it positioned "just so" between the grassy oval area and the yard behind the house. Jonah, Elizabeth, and Tabby were given the job of wiping off the dust as high as they could reach while the men spruced up the rest.

Soon after, the Owens family from the neighboring farm stopped by to help with last-minute preparations for Saturday's Heritage Celebration, and AJ had arrived with subs, sides, and drinks.

Tess called the children as she carried the sandwich platter and a pitcher of lemonade to a picnic table. Jonah and the girls, along with Austin Owens, raced toward her, followed closely by Lila, Elizabeth's Labrador retriever.

"Here you go, kids." Tess set down the platter and poured lemonade in glasses to a chorus of thank-yous.

As she handed out the sandwiches, she glanced toward the fence corner. Gabe plucked a marigold from the red wheelbarrow and handed it to Amy. She lifted it to her nose and made a face at the pungent fragrance. He grinned, said something Tess couldn't hear, and Amy smiled.

Tess squelched her misgivings with contentment, happy because Gabe was happy. Working too many hours in the day, perhaps. Rising each morning much earlier than he needed to. But never complaining. Never too tired of an evening to exercise one of the horses or tinker with that old Ford. As darkness descended, the two of them often sat together on the porch to watch the fireflies and listen to the plaintive cry of a distant whippoorwill. After those long years of confinement, he was finding his place here. With these good people.

At a nearby table, AJ scooped pasta salad onto a plate, his eyes shaded by an OSU baseball cap. Shelby chatted with Cassie Owens, whose palm rested on her swollen abdomen. In a few weeks, Austin wouldn't be an only child anymore.

Brett and Dani sauntered toward them with a jug of sweet tea, their fingers interlaced. Even Brett had grown into someone Tess was proud to know. Though admittedly it had taken him a while.

More than anything, *this* was what Tess wanted for Gabe. Friends to break bread with, to work alongside, to count on when things went wrong.

She shifted her gaze back to the red wheelbarrow. Maybe even someone to love. Her thoughts turned into a prayer. *Just let it be with the right person.*

~

All the adults pitched in to clean up, but then Gabe realized he and Amy were the only ones left in the house. "Guess I better get going," he said. "I need to get these horses home before dark."

"How are you doing that?" she asked.

"Ride one, lead the other."

"You're riding?" Amy asked. "Now?"

"I don't think we can fly."

She gave him that look, the one he'd come to think of as "Amy Annoyed." A blistering look to others, maybe, but when she directed it at him, he only felt a perverse hankering to annoy her even more.

"But you'll miss the s'mores. AJ's going to start a fire in the stone circle." Her expression changed to "Amy Coquette." He had to steel himself against that one. Those pleading blue eyes got to him every time.

"You don't want to miss that, do you?" she added.

"Don't have a choice." He narrowed the space between them and held her gaze. "You could ride with me. I'll take Abner and you can ride Casper."

"I left my saddle at home."

"I brought two."

She averted her gaze and sucked in her lower lip.

"Why are you so afraid?" he asked softly.

"It's not fear," she murmured.

"Then what is it?"

"It's a pain." She pressed her fist against her heart. "Here. I can't do it."

"We can start with a baby step."

"What do you mean?"

"Hold Abner's head while I saddle him. Can you do that?"

She hesitated, then nodded.

"My tack is in the boot of the stagecoach." He took her hand, pleased that she allowed him. Maybe she'd change her mind and ride with him after all. He glanced at her legs and decided not to push it. As good as she looked in shorts and sandals, they weren't appropriate riding attire.

151

They walked to the stagecoach, then she carried the bridle and blanket while he hefted the saddle to where the horses were tied to a fence. Though she was hesitant in her approach, she did all the right things. Abner greeted her with a sniff, and she held her hand flat for him to take the apple treat she held for him. Gabe was slipping on the bridle when Jonah joined them.

"Are you going to ride him?" Jonah asked, wonder in his voice.

"Only way to get him home," Gabe replied.

"Can I go with you?"

"I don't know about that, buddy."

"I'm not sure your dad would approve," Amy said.

"I'll go ask him." He pivoted and raced toward the picnic tables.

Gabe and Amy exchanged glances. He saddled Abner, then they joined the others.

"Can the children have a ride before you go?" Tess asked. She turned to the parents. "Abner is as gentle and steady as they come. Gabe can lead, and I'll walk beside them."

"I don't see why not," AJ said. He grabbed Tabby and lifted her onto his hip. "You want to take a ride on that there horse?"

Tabby eyed Abner and shrank into AJ. "He's awfully big."

"But very friendly," Amy said. "See?" She scratched Abner's nose. "You try it."

Tabby still looked doubtful as she placed her hand near Abner. He snuffed and she drew back, then laughed. "That felt funny."

"Me first," Jonah said. "It was my idea."

"I don't know," Brett said. "What if—"

"Oh, would you stop it!" Amy blurted. "You heard what Tess said. She'll be right beside them. And I'll walk on the other side."

"I already told you. I can't let him get hurt."

"He won't."

"You can't promise that."

She glanced at Jonah, whose light blue eyes were begging her to convince his dad to let him do this, and searched her mind for a solution. "What if, instead of being led, Gabe rides with him? Can he at least do that?"

Brett worked his jaw, then sighed heavily. "Okay. But only for a few minutes."

Amy smiled at Jonah, and he wrapped his arms around her waist in a quick hug. "Thanks, Aunt Amy. Thanks, Daddy."

She caught Gabe's eye, and he tipped the brim of his Stetson as he nodded.

"Come on, Jonah," Tess said. "Up you go."

Gabe set Jonah on the horse, then swung into the saddle. Amy gave an inward sigh. She could watch Gabe mount his horse over and over again.

After all the children had taken a turn and gone into the house to wash their hands, Gabe walked Abner close to Amy. "Do you want to take a turn?"

More than he knew. But she wasn't ready. At least not yet. "Maybe another time," she said lightly.

"Is Brett giving you a ride home?"

"He was, but I think I'm going with AJ instead."

"I didn't mean to cause an argument between you. I don't think Tess did either."

"Jonah may not be an infant, but Brett is still a new dad. He worries too much."

"About you too?"

"It's tiresome." She stroked Abner's nose. His animal scent took her to another time, another place, where she'd found contentment and peace riding horseback around the paddock and through the woods with Gabe. She didn't want to be chained to this trauma anymore, to be paralyzed by the thought of doing what she once loved more than breathing.

Baby steps, Gabe had said. She'd taken the first one, getting this close to Abner, letting him snuffle her neck and her shoulders. But it hadn't been easy.

In some strange way, her longing for a horse had gotten bound up with her dad never coming back from that plane trip. A trip he wasn't supposed to have taken in the first place. He'd left Amy to go with Mom even though they were already divorced. It had never made sense. And then she'd lost them. Lost them both. And lost her love for riding too.

The guilt she'd endured for being angry with Dad for not giving her what she wanted most, for leaving her alone, for not coming home again, was twisted with her grief. Sometimes she wondered if it was too late to ever separate them.

She didn't know if she could take that next baby step. Not even for Gabe.

– 19 –

Amy stood at the podium on top of the flatbed wagon and looked over the crowd gathered at Misty Willow for the Heritage Celebration. When the event was first planned, Brett had volunteered to be the emcee. Amy, still in her second stint at the clinic, had no plans or even any desire to attend.

But after coming back and spending more time with Brett's and AJ's families, she'd changed her mind. When Shelby suggested she take the stage, she'd been strangely flattered.

Amy took a deep breath, then smiled a dazzling smile. The murmur of voices hushed as she welcomed everyone to Misty Willow.

"This homestead has a unique history," she said, her voice clear and strong. "Even in a county where many of you can trace your roots for several generations. This land, part of the Virginia Military District, was given to Isaac Wyatt in the 1790s because of his exemplary service as a soldier in the Revolutionary War. Now, about 220 years later, his descendant has led a successful campaign to have Misty Willow listed on the National Register of Historic Places."

Amy waited for the applause to end, then continued.

"This homestead has been in the same family for almost all

those years. Then, for a short while, my grandfather owned it. I know many of you had the same reaction when you learned my cousin, AJ Sullivan, had returned the land to the Lassiter family." She grinned impishly.

"Sully Sullivan must be spinning in his grave."

The line was perfectly delivered, and chuckles rippled through the crowd.

"You're probably right," she said. "But the years Misty Willow stood here, abandoned, desolate, are only one chapter in an otherwise golden history. The house may have been empty, but it was never forgotten. And its latest chapter is a very happy one, not only for the eighth-great-granddaughter of Isaac Wyatt—yes, that's right, say 'great' eight times—who wanted nothing more than to raise her children here, but also for my family."

She gestured toward the group sitting at one end of the stage. "Ladies and gentlemen, I am honored to introduce Isaac's descendant, my cousin's wife and my friend, Shelby Lassiter Sullivan."

As Shelby made her way to the podium, Amy took a seat between Brett and AJ.

"Well done," AJ whispered.

Amy smiled her thanks and breathed a contented sigh. She may have been the pariah for suing AJ and Shelby over Misty Willow, but today marked a turning point. Sully's three grandchildren, sitting beside each other, presented a united front to anyone who might think their relationships were still fractured. Sully might be spitting nails because Shelby's dream of protecting the homestead in perpetuity was now a reality.

But Gran sure would be proud.

An unexpected tear dampened the corner of Amy's eye, and she ran a finger beneath her lashes. Brett leaned toward her. "You okay?"

"Just missing Gran."

"Me too," he whispered. "She would've loved today."

Amy gave a slight nod, then looked over the crowd as she focused on Shelby's explanation of how Rebecca Wyatt, Isaac's wife, had given Misty Willow its name.

"They were camped near Glade Creek while Isaac built their first home," Shelby said. "The willow trees were shrouded in fog. In mist."

As Shelby spoke, Amy scanned the crowd and finally found the man she most wanted to see. Gabe and Tess stood together near the stone circle. His eyes were on her, and when she looked at him, he eased into a smile.

The crowd applauded Shelby's speech, and Amy introduced the local elected officials, the chamber of commerce officers, and the Heritage Celebration committee. Dr. Wayne Kessler, the OSU history professor who spearheaded the joint archaeological project, gave an update on the team's progress, and finally the CEO of the Ohio History Foundation presented Shelby with a plaque and certificate.

After the presentation, Amy took her place behind the podium one last time. "We invite all of you to join us for a lunch catered by Boyd's BBQ. Enjoy the local bands who will appear on this stage throughout the rest of the day." She glanced at Gabe, and his smile warmed her heart. "And don't forget to take a hayride back to Glade Creek, where we have a display set up on the site of an old hunting cabin. Thanks for coming, and enjoy your day with us."

She returned to her family and hugged each one as the congratulatory euphoria lingered around them. For the first time in forever, she felt a part of the family clique.

Oh yes. Gran would be so very proud.

~

Amy sat beneath one of the old oaks with Cassie and a couple of other women she'd met at the church softball game. She smiled politely while they talked about diaper rash, temper tantrums, and

Crock-Pot meals. Things she knew nothing about. Cared nothing about. That was probably why she couldn't stop staring up the drive. It seemed like Gabe had been gone a long time with his latest group of hayride passengers. Not that she was keeping track.

Cassie tapped Amy's arm. "Shelby tells me you've redecorated the cottage."

"It's still a work-in-progress. The painting is done, but I haven't found the right dining set yet."

"What are you looking for?"

"Something with character that doesn't take up too much space. I think it's one of those 'I'll know it when I see it' kind of things." Which was true enough, though she didn't plan on "seeing it" any time soon. The paint and other supplies cost more than she had anticipated, so the table and chairs would have to wait till she had a plan for making money. Though when that time came, she'd probably leave the cottage for the next homeless waif looking for a refuge from the world. A luxurious big-city apartment was where she belonged.

"Have you ever been to an estate sale?" Cassie asked. "Sometimes you can find unusual pieces at a good one. Besides, they're fun."

"Maybe I'll try that."

Hearing a commotion, Amy glanced toward the driveway again. Gabe drove the hay wagon, returning from its latest trip to the site of the old hunting cabin, beneath an awning. A young woman—she couldn't be more than twenty—sat on the bench seat beside him. He seemed to be listening with all ears to every word—and they were many—spewing forth from her blistering red lips.

So the wrong shade for her skin tone.

Gabe laughed at whatever she said to him, then pulled back on the reins. The team halted, and the group in the back of the wagon jumped out.

Several called their thanks, and Gabe responded with a wave. After he dismounted, he reached for the girl and swung her to the ground.

Amy stood so quickly her lawn chair flipped backward.

"Are you okay?" Cassie asked, pressing her hands against the chair arms and struggling to rise.

"Fine. I just, I think I need a drink. Of water. I need a bottle of water." She set the chair on its feet. "Can I get you anything?"

"I already have a bottle, thanks." She eyed Amy with concern. "Are you sure you're okay?"

Amy nodded and strode toward the house. She refused to be jealous of a little miss thing who probably didn't even know the governor's name. Who certainly had never attended a dinner with the man.

On her way across the lawn, she glanced toward Gabe and was surprised to see he was looking at her. He tipped his Stetson in her direction and turned back to Miss "I Can't Stop Talking."

Amy scurried up the patio steps and yanked open the screen door. She entered the kitchen, letting the door *thwack* behind her.

"What's wrong?" Shelby asked. She stood at the counter, a knife poised in one hand. One half of a large watermelon rested on a wooden cutting board, the other beside it.

"Nothing," she murmured. "Do you need help?"

"You know how to cut watermelon?"

"I think I can manage."

"I'm sorry, Amy. I didn't mean it to sound like that."

She raised a hand to stop Shelby from saying any more. "I know you didn't. Besides, it's not like I'm known for my culinary skills." Only for causing trouble and making a mess of everything she touched. Her morning's success as a poised mistress of ceremonies must have been a fluke.

"I'll leave it to you, then." Shelby handed Amy the knife, then washed and dried her hands. "Cut both halves into cubes and put them in that bowl. I'll be back in a few minutes."

Amy stood at the counter, her back to the door, and waited for Shelby to leave before picking up the knife. Gripping the watermelon with one hand, she sliced through its pink meat and into the rind.

Nothing to it.

"I noticed you haven't gone on any of my rides." Startled by Gabe's voice, she practically dropped the knife. He stood beside her and placed his hand over hers. "Careful there. You don't want to cut off a finger."

"I didn't hear you come in."

"I came in when Shelby went out."

She moved her hand from beneath his and made another cut. "Having fun?"

"Tell you the truth, it's a little tedious driving back and forth." When she didn't respond, he continued. "I'm only making one more trip. Thought you might want to come along. Keep me company."

"There's nothing out there but a slab of dirt. I don't know why these people are so interested."

"Not all of them are. But a hayride is always fun." He stretched his neck and tilted his head, practically getting between her and the watermelon. "You've never been on a hayride, have you?"

"Nope."

"Don't you think it's about time?"

"Why don't you ask your little friend to go with you?"

"What little friend?" His expression shifted from puzzlement to understanding. "You mean that kid who couldn't keep her mouth shut for more than two seconds at a time? You can't possibly think . . ."

"From what I could see, you enjoyed her company." She smacked the knife blade into the slice she'd just cut, and juice squirted onto her face. She started to swipe the sticky spot with the back of her hand, but Gabe stopped her. He wet the corner of a dish towel, then gently dabbed her cheek. She relaxed her grip on the knife and turned slightly toward him. When he stood this close, she couldn't think. She could barely breathe.

"You'll mess up my makeup."

"You look beautiful when you're jealous."

"You think I'm jealous of—"

"Shh," he said, placing his fingers against her lips.

Her eyes met his, then flicked to his mouth. He touched her waist, and she rested her forehead against his chest. His shirt smelled of sunshine and horse and hay, all mingled together and surprisingly intoxicating.

"Come with me?" The question floated softly between them.

She wanted to kiss him. Knew he wanted to kiss her.

But this wasn't the right time. Nor the right place.

"Shelby will be back soon." She stepped away from him, and his hand dropped from her waist. "I need to finish this watermelon."

"I'll wait for you by the wagon." He grabbed one of the chunks and popped it in his mouth. "But if you're not out there in five minutes, I'll hunt you down."

Before she could protest, he was holding the door open for Shelby. She entered the kitchen, glanced from Amy to Gabe's departing back then to Amy again.

"What was that all about?" Shelby asked.

"He asked me to ride back to the creek with him." Amy tossed more watermelon chunks in the bowl. "It's the last trip, and I haven't gone yet."

"Then you better get out there."

"I'm not sure I want to."

"Why not?" Shelby sighed in mock exasperation. "You should at least give him a chance. He's a really great guy."

"How would you know?"

"He comes home with AJ for lunch sometimes."

Amy quartered another watermelon as she toyed with an idea she'd had. She needed to act now, while she and Shelby were alone. "If I ask you to do me a favor, will you promise not to play match-maker?"

"What favor?"

"No matchmaking. I mean it, Shelby. Promise me."

"Okay, I promise."

"Ask AJ to invite Gabe to the 4th of July cookout. Tess too. He probably wouldn't want to leave her home by herself."

"Wouldn't that be matchmaking?" Shelby teased. "Why don't you ask them?"

"It's better this way. Please. I'll cut up ten more watermelons for you."

"You need to get out to that wagon before Gabe comes back for you."

"I'll go as soon as you promise to ask AJ. But don't tell him I asked you to ask him."

"Ask me what?" AJ appeared from the utility room adjoining the kitchen.

"What were you doing in there?" Amy demanded.

"Got barbecue sauce on my shirt so I was pre-treating it."

Amy suppressed an annoyed sigh and gave Shelby a pleading glance.

"We were just wondering," Shelby said as she slipped her arm around AJ's waist, "if you'd ask Gabe and Tess to spend the 4th with us."

AJ grinned at Amy. "Be glad to."

"Just don't say anything . . . stupid." Amy scooped the remaining watermelon chunks into the bowl."

"Me?"

"You."

Shelby handed the bowl to AJ. "Do you mind taking this out?"

"Sure." He popped a cube into his mouth and headed for the door.

"You better go too," Shelby said to Amy. "Gabe's waiting."

"Thanks, Shelby." Amy quickly washed and dried her hands. "You're the best cousin-in-law ever."

– 20 –

*G*abe clicked his tongue at Abner and Casper more out of habit than a need to guide them. The team had made enough trips back to the creek today, they could probably find it without anyone holding the reins.

"How did the exhibit turn out?" Amy swayed beside Gabe on the wooden seat, their shoulders occasionally jostling each other.

"Like an old home site with invisible walls. The ground has been leveled, and there's a table, a couple of cots, that kind of thing arranged on what would have been the dirt floor."

"Can you imagine living like that? No electricity or hot showers."

"I think it might have been nice. Definitely preferable to . . ." He hesitated. "To Afghanistan."

An awkward silence followed. He searched his mind for a way to end it, considering and rejecting a dozen different lines in as many seconds. He didn't want to give Amy a line. His feelings for her ran too deep for anything that superficial.

She rescued him. "I've never been back this way before. I didn't know there was a wagon path."

"There wasn't until last week. This is where I've been laboring."

"You did this?"

"With the help of Jason Owens's tractor. Otherwise we wouldn't have gotten this wagon very far on our way back to the Civil War era."

"Brett and Dani have been out here most of the day, haven't they?"

"Since after lunch. They're telling the history, answering questions."

"It's still so hard for me to believe." Amy shook her head as if to underline her words. "Until about a year ago, Brett never gave this place a thought. Except to be glad Sully willed it to AJ instead of to him. And now he's a Misty Willow expert."

"I think Dani's the expert. She knows a lot of the family stories."

"It's her job."

"She seems to love it. She's lucky to be doing what she loves."

"Do you enjoy working with AJ?"

"I do." Definitely much more than prison life. "I like the short commute too."

"What will you do once he runs out of projects?"

"There's plenty to do at the stables." Only problem with that option was that it didn't pay anything. "How about you? Did you finish all your painting?"

"Every room."

"What's your next project?"

"The outside needs paint—"

"Wait a minute," he interrupted. "You're not doing that, are you?"

"I could if I put my mind to it," she said indignantly. "But Brett and AJ have threatened to put me in time-out if I dare try."

"Time-out, huh?" Gabe chuckled, but inwardly he sighed with relief that she wasn't going to attempt that job. What if she fell and broke her neck?

"You would think I had two older brothers instead of just one."

And one too-protective, well, whatever he was to her.

"Can't blame them for looking out for you," he said. "So what will you be doing instead?"

"I'm not sure. I feel at loose ends now."

"It all goes back to what we were talking about before," Gabe said. "Dani found a career that lets her do what she loves, and she's great at it."

"While you and I are at a crossroads. Not sure which road to take or where they might lead us."

"And not knowing what roadblocks lay ahead." Like how being a felon would affect his job prospects or whether Tess would be able to keep Whisper Lane. Driving the hay wagon back and forth from the creek had given him plenty of time to think about the future, but he still hadn't come up with a plan. Somehow he felt like God was telling him to wait. But wait for what?

~

Amy eyed Gabe behind the dark lenses of her sunglasses, wishing she could read him as easily as she read most men. Somehow he seemed able to thwart her efforts. His face was impassive, and yet she sensed the passion deep within him. He only needed to figure out how to channel it.

If only she could be the one to help him do that. She squirmed on the seat. He didn't need her assistance to integrate himself back into society. She was having enough trouble doing that herself. Besides, the people she knew, the friends she once had, weren't the kind of people who would impress Gabe. He'd probably think they were selfish and ambitious for the wrong things. Just like her.

But that wasn't who she was anymore. Was it?

She wasn't even sure.

"I wish I knew what I was passionate about," she said.

"I started to ask you what you would do if money wasn't an issue. But money isn't an issue for you, is it?"

If only you knew.

But she had to live that lie so Brett and AJ didn't find out she'd squandered her inheritances. Three of them—from her parents, from Sully, and then from Gran.

She couldn't even figure out what had happened, though reckless investments and the time spent in the eating disorder clinics had played a major role.

So had her lifestyle. Expensive vacations. New clothes on a whim. Giving to political campaigns and causes—some she believed in, some she didn't. But that was how the game was played.

"I enjoyed being a lobbyist," she said. "At least for a while."

"But not anymore?"

"No. I don't want to go back." She graced him with an engaging smile. "Your turn. Money is no object. What do you do?"

"I'm not sure I should tell you."

"Why not?"

"It might give you the wrong impression of me."

"I doubt that. Besides, how do you know what impression I have of you now?" she teased.

"Good point." He avoided answering by paying close attention to the horses' route past a fallen tree. "I'd want to do this."

"What do you mean by 'this'?"

"Own horses. Give hayrides. I don't know, I guess devote my time to something good and wholesome. Remind myself there are honest people in the world, and I can be part of their community. If they give me a chance."

"Are you finding that here?"

"Your cousin is a good man. He's welcomed me into his home, into his life. Added me to the softball team." He paused, then glanced at her before looking away. "It feels good to belong to something like that. I've been without it since leaving my unit."

The sadness, the emptiness in his voice caused her heart to ache. Without realizing what she was doing, she tucked her arm into his and leaned her head against his shoulder. He glanced at her in surprise, but he didn't seem to mind.

"AJ is a good friend," she said quietly. "I hope you'll think of me as one too."

"I'd like that, Amy."

His soft-spoken words, the gentle way he said her name, seemed to loosen a long-buried stone within her heart. Right now, she'd give all the money she had left for this ride never to end. For this feeling of comfort and acceptance to never go away.

~

As they neared the site of the old hunting cabin, Amy straightened. Gabe was sorry, but he understood. She wouldn't want her brother to see her snuggling with a former con. He pulled up beside the hitching post.

"Have you heard what they have planned for this site?" Gabe asked.

"Brett told me Dani is trying to find an old log cabin to move back here," Amy said. "I think they're planning a trip to southern Ohio to look at two or three."

"I heard that too. They also plan to rebuild the tree house that was used as a lookout."

"Where Eliza Wyatt was hiding when she first saw Jeb Lassiter."

"You know that story?"

"Elizabeth loves to tell it. She pretends to be Eliza and bribes Jonah to play Jeb."

"Bribes him how?"

"Like giving up her turn at choosing our fun outing so he can. Playing the video game he wants to play. She's a natural negotiator."

"You admire that about her." Gabe jumped from the seat, then reached for Amy. She felt light—too light—as he lifted her from the wagon. He gave her a quick smile as her feet touched the ground.

"I suppose I do."

After greeting Brett and Dani, Amy pulled Gabe to one side. "I take it you've already heard the spiel?"

"Several times."

"Then why don't we take a walk over to the creek?"

"Sounds like a fine idea to me," Gabe said, gesturing toward the overhanging willow. "Brett showed me his branch on the engagement tree earlier today. He sure is proud of it. But I guess you already know that."

"He's mentioned it a couple of times."

Gabe caught her up short. "Wait a minute. He's 'mentioned it'? Does that mean . . . surely you've seen it."

"No, I haven't." She slid a strand of hair through her fingers, then crossed her arms. "This is only the second time I've been out here."

"So when we met here that day, that was the first?"

"I came out to look at all the initials I'd heard so much about, but, well, I didn't."

"I'm sorry I interrupted you—"

"It wasn't your fault," she said quickly. "I wasn't in the best of moods, so it's probably a good thing you showed up."

"Is it because you don't like Dani?"

"Of course I like her." Amy pushed her lips into a pouty frown. "She's a very nice person."

"But?"

"She blushes easily. And she's definitely got a style like no one else's, and sometimes she sticks that tiny size-six shoe in her mouth."

Gabe sensed Amy wasn't used to being challenged. But he wasn't going to let her off that easy. "Anything else?"

"She's not the kind of woman I expected Brett to marry," she said. "He's changed, which is a good thing, but sometimes, oh, I don't know." She rubbed her arms as if to ward off a chill. But the sun-heated breezes weren't frigid. "He changed so fast. I don't know why I'm telling you all this."

"Maybe because you need someone to talk to."

"I've talked to plenty of therapists in the past few months."

"I'd rather you think of me as a friend."

"I don't have a lot of those. Not close ones, anyway."

Gabe wanted to ask her about the guy he'd seen her with. Wasn't he a close friend? Instead, he cradled her face in his palm. "You've got me."

– 21 –

At Gabe's touch, a thrill went up Amy's spine and her pulse quickened. She was definitely attracted to the man despite her efforts to keep him at arm's length. But in her world, attraction didn't equate to friendship.

Gabe was easy to talk to, though. She found herself saying things to him she'd never say to anyone else. As if she knew her words were safe with him.

But some words could never be spoken or shared. He'd never understand how she could entrust her body but not her heart to other men. She didn't understand it either, and the memories of her shallow affairs now sickened her.

"Why don't we take a look at that tree?" she said, giving him a tentative smile.

He laced his fingers with hers, and Amy's heart ached with longing for this moment to last forever.

A perfect blue sky with the rays of the sun glancing off the sparkling water in the slow-moving creek. A peaceful lull with a handsome man who cared about who she was on the inside.

With Gabe holding her hand, anything seemed possible. Even for someone like her.

They ducked under the swaying fronds of the willow tree and stood close to each other beneath its slender limbs. Within the shade of the ancient tree, the world seemed to disappear. It was almost like they had left everyone else behind, and only the two of them existed in this special place where love had been declared for generations.

Gabe examined the initials on the trunk, then pointed to a pair that had been carved a long time ago. J. L. + E. W.

"These must be the first." His voice was low, in keeping with the mystery of being enclosed within the willow's fronds.

"Jeb Lassiter and Eliza Wyatt," she said softly. Jeb, the Confederate soldier who escaped from a prison camp in Columbus. Eliza, the young woman who hid him from her family while she nursed him back to health.

Amy ran her hand along the trunk, past several of the carved sets of initials, and it was almost as if she could imagine the young couple standing on this soil, beneath these fronds, just as she and Gabe were doing. No wonder this tree meant so much to Shelby. Or that Brett wanted to be part of this legacy too, even if only through AJ.

"I'm a little jealous of old Jeb," Gabe said.

"Why?"

"He started something here." Gabe traced the initials. "Eliza's father may have built the brick house, but it's been Lassiter land since Jeb and Eliza married. He raised a family here—the two of them together. Faced the future not knowing what it would hold for them. It couldn't have been easy in the years following the war, given Jeb's Southern heritage. But a hundred and fifty years later, he's a respected family patriarch in this county's history."

"And that's what you want to be," Amy said in a teasing voice. But she wasn't really teasing.

"I want my life to count for something. It doesn't have to be anything that's important to the world. But I want it to count for something to the people I'm closest to. Like Uncle Rusty was to me."

"I remember your uncle. He used to give me peppermints."

"He used them as a substitute for smoking."

"I didn't know that."

"Like most men of his generation, smoking was what they did. After he quit, he always carried peppermints in his pocket." Gabe chuckled. "One of the horses loved them too."

"I don't really like them," Amy said. "But I always ate the ones he gave me."

"Why?"

"I'm not sure I could tell you that." She tilted her head in thought. "I guess it was so he'd keep giving them to me. It was a little thing—kind of like what you said—but it meant something to me because it was a constant. I didn't have too many of those."

"Neither did I. We moved around a lot when I was a kid." He gave a sheepish grin. "Military brat, you know."

"That must have been hard." At least she'd had Gran. The stability of living in one city.

He tapped one of the two heart-shaped metal plaques hanging on the branches, apparently wanting to change the subject. *Shelby + AJ* was engraved on one, *Dani + Brett* on the other. "Why didn't they just carve their initials too?"

"Something about not damaging the tree."

"Are you planning to add your own name someday?"

"I'm not a Lassiter. And so far I haven't been invited."

"Guess you'll have to find your own tree, then."

"I think I'd rather."

Footsteps rustled behind them, and Amy turned.

"What are you two doing in there?" Brett asked. "We've already told all the stories we know to tell. Twice."

Amy looked sheepishly at Gabe. "We're coming," she said to Brett.

They slipped between the fronds again, this time into the real world. The sun shone upon her skin, warming it. Funny, she hadn't noticed the coolness within the branches of the tree. But she'd noticed a contentment that she hadn't expected to feel. Even when Gabe pointed out AJ's and Brett's names, engraved with those of their brides, she hadn't felt the discontent she'd expected. It'd been okay.

She'd only been uneasy when he asked about her placing her own name on the tree. It wasn't Shelby's fault that the two of them weren't closer friends. She'd made every effort to include Amy in the family get-togethers and to share her life.

The problem was, Amy didn't know how to be a friend. Only a competitor, a conniver, and a conqueror. That was what her job was all about, and she'd been good at her job until the very end.

Gabe and Brett engaged in small talk while they walked back to the wagon. Then, as before, Gabe helped her up onto the bench. It may have been her imagination, but it seemed he let his hand press a little harder against her back, let it linger there a moment more than necessary.

Not that she minded.

After he climbed up beside her, she sat back and relaxed, enjoying his closeness. The way he joked with Brett, Dani, and the other passengers as they climbed into the back of the wagon among the bales of hay. His easy manner with the reins and his gentleness with the horses. The way his arm jostled hers as the wagon bounced along the pasture trail.

He was a good man.

How much she regretted that she wasn't a good woman.

~

Gabe unharnessed the horses and led them to the trailer. "No more trips today, fellas. You get to ride home."

JOHNNIE ALEXANDER

After getting Abner and Casper settled, Gabe scanned the oval area next to the house. Most of the guests had gone, and those who'd stayed were busy with cleanup. He jogged over to where Paul Norris, who owned the farm east of Misty Willow, and AJ were folding the long tables.

"Need a hand?"

"Won't say no," Paul said. "I want to get these back to the church this evening."

"I'm on it." Gabe set a table on its side, snapped shut the legs, then slid it into the back of Paul's truck. Once all the tables were loaded, Paul slammed the tailgate shut.

"Do you need help unloading?" Gabe asked.

"Seth and I can take care of it. He's around here somewhere."

"I think he's around front with Jonah," AJ said, then turned to Gabe. "Seth is Paul's son. He's an ag student at Ohio State."

"I met him on one of the hayrides. He talked about livestock genetics. Interesting young man."

"He's a great linebacker too," AJ said. "Our team had a rough season this past year without him there to lead our defense."

"They'll do better this year," Paul said. "Gabe, I'm looking to hire someone to help with the wheat harvest while Seth is on a mission trip. AJ said you might be interested."

"I told him you're a hard worker," AJ said. "You can pay me for that one later."

Gabe chuckled, then shifted to Paul. "I'd be glad for the work."

"Great. Could you start a week from Monday?"

"I sure can." Gabe extended his hand, and Paul shook it. "I really appreciate it."

"Don't mention it. Now I need to round up my family."

After he left, Gabe and AJ retrieved drinks from a galvanized tub half full of melting ice, water bottles, and soda cans. They sat in a nearby glider, facing the stone circle.

"Thanks for the recommendation," Gabe said as he popped

175

the tab. "When I came here, I didn't think anyone would give me a chance. It's nice to see I was wrong."

Truth be told, he'd dreaded being here today. Practically a stranger among people who'd known each other for years, some of them all of their lives. But driving the hay wagon had allowed him to get acquainted with only a few at a time. A handful of people, good friends of Tess's, remembered him as a boy. Those had been the best trips back and forth to the creek, the ones where his passengers told stories about Rusty.

The only trip he'd enjoyed more was the last one. With Amy sitting beside him, smiling that pretty smile that took his breath away, he hadn't wanted the ride to end.

Maybe that was how old Jeb felt—well, when he was young Jeb—and Eliza first smiled at him. The young soldier couldn't have known that one day Eliza would be his wife. Everything seemed set against them. The country was in turmoil, he was an escaped prisoner, and they were on opposite sides of the fight.

None of that seemed to matter to the young lovers. They had a bond that couldn't be broken despite their differences. And they had prevailed.

But as harsh as their differences were, they didn't hold a candle to the differences between him and Amy.

He was a disgraced Marine, a convicted felon, who only wanted to be around horses. She was a sophisticated and lovely city girl who knew her way around the state capitol's elite.

Though neither of them knew exactly what they wanted out of life, not even what they wanted tomorrow, he was sure that at the end of the day, they didn't want the same thing.

Amy would get bored with her simple cottage life long before he was ready to give up the stables. He wouldn't be enough to hold her to country living. So it was better to not let himself get too involved. Not that he could, anyway. He had other responsibilities to tend to.

"We're having a cookout," AJ said, "back at the engagement tree for the 4th. Then we're going to the lake for the fireworks. We'd like you and Tess to spend the day with us, if you want."

"Sounds fun," Gabe said. Too bad he'd already made other plans.

– 22 –

*A*my walked stealthily across the gravel from the house to the oval lawn. Not that she wanted to eavesdrop, but, well, she wanted to eavesdrop. She inwardly giggled, feeling like a naughty child, as she neared the glider. Neither Gabe nor AJ seemed aware she was sneaking up on them.

"Then we're going to the lake for the fireworks," AJ was saying. "We'd like you and Tess to spend the day with us, if you want."

Yes! This was the conversation she wanted to hear. After all, it wouldn't have done any good to ask AJ to repeat it later. She couldn't depend on him to pick up on the nuances.

"Sounds fun," Gabe said.

Another yes! With a gratified smile, Amy took another step closer.

"But we've already made plans."

Amy stopped in her tracks, her smile melting.

"Sorry I didn't ask sooner." AJ took a long drink of his soda. "Amy will be disappointed."

Oh, great. Thanks a lot, AJ.

"Amy?"

AJ took another drink. "She'd kill me if she knew I said that."

You've got that right.

"It was kind of her to think of us," Gabe said. "But I invited Ellen to come visit. She'll be alone without her kids."

Amy's mind reeled, and for a moment she thought she was going to be sick. He couldn't be in love with someone else. He couldn't. Not when he looked at her the way he did. In his eyes, she saw the boy who had touched her heart with his slow smile. And remembered the girl she'd once been.

"Bring her by if you get the chance," AJ said. "We'd like to meet her."

Amy shook her head in disbelief. How dense could AJ be?

Footsteps sounded behind her, and she made a conscious effort to relax her hands and her shoulders. With a disarming smile on her face, she looked over her shoulder. Shelby smiled back and Amy reached for her arm. At least now, AJ and Gabe wouldn't know she'd been sneaking up on them.

The men turned, then stood.

"What are you two doing out here?" Amy asked.

"Enjoying the peace and quiet," AJ said as he reached for Shelby's hand. "Before we have to bribe the girls to go home."

"Brett and Dani are giving them and Jonah the ten-minute warning," Shelby said. "They'll be around soon."

AJ gave Amy a pitying look. Did he think she cared what Gabe did? Who he spent time with when she wasn't around? She mustered as innocent a smile as she could.

"AJ, I wanted to ask you about the 4th of July plans."

"You probably know as much as I do," he said, shifting his weight from one foot to the other. He glanced at Gabe then back at Amy and gave a slight shake of his head.

"I just wanted to know if it was okay for me to bring a date."

"I . . . guess so." AJ exchanged a nervous glance with Shelby. "Anyone I know?"

"I doubt it. His name is Logan Cassidy. I know him from my lobbyist days. He recently opened his own firm."

Shelby opened her mouth as if to say something but must have thought better of it.

"I'd really like to introduce him to everyone."

"Of course he's welcome," Shelby said. "We want to meet your friends, Amy."

"He's a little bit more than a friend." Amy took Shelby by the arm and led her away. "Let's go get the girls, and I'll tell you all about him."

She knew Gabe stared after her as sure as if she had eyes in the back of her head. But she'd succeeded in completely ignoring him. As hard as it had been, she hadn't glanced at him for even a fraction of a second. She jutted her chin with pride, but the knot in her stomach only felt hollow and dull.

Maybe this hadn't been such a good plan after all.

As they came beside the jutting bay window beyond the patio, Shelby pulled Amy to a stop. "What's going on with you? Did you just make up a boyfriend?"

Unable to maintain her nonchalant air any longer, Amy bit her lip, then looked back toward the glider. AJ and Gabe stood near it as if uncertain whether or not they should have followed.

"Who is Ellen?" she hissed.

"Ellen who?"

"If I knew Ellen who, I wouldn't be asking."

"What are you talking about?"

Amy drew Shelby closer to the house. From the front yard, the sounds of the children playing some game filled the summer air.

"Gabe told AJ he invited someone named Ellen to spend the 4th with him and Tess. So she wouldn't be alone. It sounded like AJ knew who Gabe was talking about."

"Maybe AJ knows, but I've never heard of her."

Distraught, Amy pressed her hands against her stomach. But the feeling of having lost something precious only grew stronger.

"I need to go home," she said. "To be alone."

"Why don't you come over in about an hour? The girls will be bathed and ready for bed by then. You can talk to AJ. Ask him what happened."

"I know what happened. I overheard the entire conversation."

"Then tell me."

Amy recounted what she'd heard. "Doesn't it sound like AJ knew who Gabe was talking about?"

"I agree. It does," Shelby said. "But the only way to know for sure is to ask him. Do you want to come over?"

Amy considered for a moment, then shook her head. "It doesn't really matter, does it? Gabe has his plans for the 4th and now, so do I."

"With this Logan whatever-his-name-is?"

Amy took a deep, calming breath. "I think you'll like him. In fact, I'm sure you will. If he's able to come."

"So you haven't asked him yet?"

"He invited me to his place to watch the Red, White, and Boom fireworks. You can see them from his balcony."

"You said yes?"

"I told him no. But there's no reason he can't come for the cookout. I just have to invite him."

"No, you don't."

"I want to. We'll do all the picnic stuff and then . . ."

"And then you'll go to his place for the fireworks?"

"I guess so. It's not like he can just ditch a houseful of guests to go to the lakefront."

"I suppose not." Shelby frowned with disappointment. "We'll miss you coming with us. So will the kids."

"Don't do that to me, Shelby. It's not fair."

"I just hope you know what you're doing."

"I'm being realistic. And I'm facing the fact that some things just aren't meant to be."

"Why not? You like Gabe, don't you? And I'm positive he thinks the world of you."

Amy momentarily shut her eyes. This was what she got for thinking she could free her canopy memories. Instead, she had more memories to push inside—memories of Gabe painting her cabinet doors, of her riding shotgun beside him on the stagecoach, of exploring the carved initials on the engagement tree together.

"It's been a long day," she said. "I think I'll go back to the cottage and maybe curl up with a good book."

"The invitation to come over is still open if you change your mind."

She wanted to say yes, but her heart wouldn't let her. A bitter root grew there that she couldn't seem to kill. As well-intentioned as Shelby's invitation was, it galled Amy that she'd be going home with a man she loved with all her heart. To Gran's home.

While Amy once again was going home alone.

"You have everything you could possibly want, Shelby. Congratulations." Resentment poisoned her words, but she couldn't hide it.

"What does that mean?" Shelby said sharply.

"Misty Willow is officially protected. You'll never have to worry about someone like me again."

Shelby opened her mouth, closed it, then jutted out her chin. "I haven't worried about you in a long time."

"All the more reason for me to leave." Without another word, Amy rounded the front porch, entered the house, and found her bag. She was being childish. She knew it but she couldn't seem to stop herself. All she knew was that she wanted to shut herself away in the cottage without talking to anyone else. Not to Shelby or AJ. And especially not to Gabe.

Her only concern now was whether it was too late to accept Logan's invitation. She pulled out her phone and found his name.

"Hi, it's me," she said when he answered. "Plans have changed. I was wondering . . ."

~

Tess gave a contented sigh as Gabe drove her truck beneath the wrought-iron arch marking the entrance to their driveway. Home at last.

"Did you have a good time?" he asked.

"I did. What about you? It seems a shame you spent most of the day on that hay wagon."

"I didn't mind. Actually, it's a nice way to meet people, to talk to them." He pulled the truck beside the barn. "AJ invited us to spend July 4th with him and the Somers clan."

"What did you tell him?"

"That we already had plans." Gabe stared out the windshield, seemingly lost in his own thoughts.

"Do you regret asking Ellen to come visit?"

He hesitated a moment, then shook his head. "She deserves a special holiday. This is the first time I can be sure that happens."

"You don't think she'd have had a special holiday without you?"

He shrugged a little too carelessly. "I need to be there for her. However I can be."

Tess nodded agreement, though she wasn't sure Gabe was thinking clearly. Ellen was a lovely young woman, and she was probably lonely. If Gabe spent too much time "being there for her," Ellen might suspect he had deeper motives. Perhaps he did, but Tess didn't think so. She'd seen the way he looked at Amy, and she remembered how smitten he'd been with her when they were young teens.

Not in a New York minute did Tess believe that Amy had forgotten Gabe and how much he'd meant to her. Maybe it had been a mistake to encourage Gabe to invite Ellen to stay, though in all fairness Tess had only wanted to be hospitable. The fireworks display wouldn't be over until ten or so, and Ellen didn't need to be driving home so late at night.

Tess didn't want either of the young women to be hurt, but Gabe concerned her most of all. He needed to put his youthful infatuation with Amy behind him or she'd break his heart again.

"I'll get the horses settled, then carry those in." He gestured toward the totes in the backseat. They were packed with the various items, such as pans, utensils, and tablecloths, that Tess had lent to the celebration.

"I can manage."

"Nothing too heavy, though. I won't be long." He handed her the set of keys, got out of the truck, and walked to the back of the trailer.

Tess selected one of the smaller totes and headed toward the house. She stuck the key in the lock, but it didn't turn. She tried the knob and opened the door. Odd. She was sure she had locked the house that morning when they left.

She flipped on a light, then carried the tote inside and placed it on the kitchen counter. Her senses were on high alert as she scanned the room. Everything was as she remembered and yet something felt off-kilter. But what?

She wandered through the house, slowly opening doors. The one to her office creaked as she pushed it open and glanced inside. And froze.

Her desk, orderly and neat, had been searched. She couldn't tell exactly how she knew, but she was certain of it. Maybe it was the way the file folders weren't quite as neatly stacked in the holder. Or how the framed photograph of Rusty and Gabe beside that old Ford F-150 seemed slightly askew from its usual position. And her desk chair was several inches from the desk, its back angled as if someone had gotten up and left in a hurry. She always pushed it in, the back flush with the desk.

Someone had been here during their absence, a careless someone who hadn't left things exactly the way they were before. Who hadn't bothered to lock the kitchen door.

She opened her desk drawers, then opened the closet and bent down to examine the safe. The dial had been turned from the one, the number she always pointed it to after closing the door. She hurriedly rotated the knob using the correct combination, then pulled on the handle.

Everything looked the same, the papers untouched. She didn't keep money there or jewels. Even the papers weren't that important—those she kept in a safety-deposit box in town. She riffled through them. The rejected offer from Dylan Tapley, still in its envelope, was on top.

She closed the safe, pointed the dial to one, then wandered back into the kitchen.

Someone had been in her home. But why?

Nothing had been taken—not the computer or the TV. Her jewelry was still in her bedroom. Her revolver was still locked in the box in her nightstand.

What did she have that anyone would be interested in? She couldn't even imagine.

She shook her head, not wanting to believe her intuition. She must have set the dial wrong last time she was in the safe. That was the only explanation. Still . . . she went through the rooms again with an even more critical eye, then sat at her desk and tried to remember if she'd left anything out that was no longer there. But she couldn't think of a thing.

She accidentally touched her mouse, and the computer monitor lit up. An Excel worksheet filled the screen, and surprised shock raced up her spine. The display showed her financial records—the register she'd designed to track her monthly income and expenses. She hadn't been in this particular file since recording her monthly income from the pasture lease last Thursday.

Now she knew for certain someone had been in the house. Not to steal but to snoop.

But she still couldn't imagine why. No one would benefit from knowing her personal financial information. Or knowing how close she was to bankruptcy.

Except maybe for Tapley. But surely he wouldn't do anything so stupid.

Anyone careless enough to leave the door unlocked and the worksheet open may have left fingerprints. Maybe she should call the police.

She returned to the kitchen to unpack the tote, her thoughts in a whirl of indecision.

The unlocked door. The photograph and the desk chair. The opened worksheet.

It wasn't carelessness but something more sinister.

A shiver ran up her spine as the certainty of her thoughts assailed her.

The actions had been deliberate. Whoever had entered her home while she was gone had wanted her to know.

She was vulnerable. She wasn't safe.

Was Tapley—or someone else—deliberately trying to frighten her? And what should she do about it?

- 23 -

*A*my ended the call with Shelby and tossed her phone on the bed. After apologizing for what she'd said, Shelby had again invited Amy to the bungalow. She apologized too but decided to stay home. The day had been long, hot, and, at the end, stingingly disappointing.

When she and Gabe were at the engagement tree, it had felt as if they were at the Hearth again. Their relationship was easy, unassuming, yet connected at a deeper level than she had ever been with anyone else.

To hear him say he was spending Independence Day with this Ellen hurt her more than she could have imagined. This was what she got for allowing her heart to override her sense. For assuming he cared about her because he had made a point of asking her to go on the hayride. How many times did she have to remind herself that Gabe would never understand why she had done the things she did? And that she was tarnished beyond what a man like him could accept.

The knock at the door startled her, and she quickly pulled a loose sweatshirt on over her camisole. Maybe it was Gabe coming to tell her it was all a big mistake. That he'd be spending the holiday with her after all.

More likely it was Shelby, come to offer platitudes and well-meaning advice. Or even worse, AJ. What if it was both of them? Horrors!

"Amy, answer the door."

Brett. Him, she hadn't expected.

"I didn't hear your car," she said as he entered. "You startled me."

"I left it on the other side of the gate and walked up."

"Do you want something to drink? I was about to make a cup of tea."

"No, I'm fine." He followed her to the kitchen and hoisted himself onto a stool.

Amy emptied her bone china teapot of the water she'd added to preheat it. "You're out late. Why are you here?"

"I've been meaning to talk to you for a couple days, but with everything going on, we just didn't seem to have a chance."

She added specially selected fair trade leaves to a tea ball and placed it in the pot with boiling water. "Talk to me about what?"

"Something Gabe said."

"Oh," she said carelessly, though the mere mention of Gabe's name quickened her heart rate.

"Remember that day he drove the stagecoach over?"

"You mean two days ago? Yeah, I think I remember that."

"Don't be snarky." He rested his arms on the counter and toyed with the broad leaves of a nearby philodendron. "When I stopped him out on the road, he asked me how long it had been since you rode a horse. I couldn't tell him."

"It's been a long time. That's no big deal."

"I didn't think much about it at the time, but since then it's been nagging me. You rode whenever you could when you were a kid. I even suggested that clinic in Richmond because it offered equine therapy, but I've been thinking about that, and you've never said anything about riding."

As Brett talked, she placed a silver spoon in her teacup, then added cream and lemon. The routine motions steadied her hands so he didn't see how upset he was making her.

"So what? I didn't ride because I didn't want to ride. Believe me, there were plenty of other therapies."

"You haven't ridden since Mom and Dad died. Have you?"

"I didn't really have a chance. Surely you remember how chaotic it was." She poured boiling water into her cup and breathed in the fragrant aroma. "Moving in with Gran and Sully. Adjusting to a different life."

"Why won't you go riding now? Gabe said he asked and you refused."

This had gone on long enough.

"How long did you and Gabe talk about me?" she said sharply and slammed the kettle onto the stove. "What else did he have to say?"

"It wasn't like that."

"Oh, really? And they say women are gossips."

"Then you'll go riding with him?"

"Why does that matter to you?"

"I think it would be good for you. You spend too much time cooped up in this cottage. You need to get out more."

"In case you haven't noticed, I've been very busy repainting this place. It needed sprucing up."

Brett pressed his lips together. He obviously had more to say, so why didn't he just come out and say it?

"Is there something else?" Amy finally asked.

The words spilled out, as if all he'd needed was an invitation to berate her. "You don't ride, you don't fly, you don't watch Cary Grant movies. Sometimes I think all you do is 'don't this' and 'don't that.'"

"That sounded really stupid."

"Maybe so. But you know it's true."

"I don't ride horses because I've outgrown that hobby. You know why I don't fly, and except for that cross-country trip to bring Dani back, neither do you. Have you been on a plane since then?"

"No."

"Then don't criticize me for that. Or for not having the same Cary Grant obsession that you and AJ have. It's ridiculous how you spout all those lines and watch the same movies over and over again."

"We watch those movies because they bring back memories of Gran."

"I don't need to watch some slap-happy black-and-white movie to remember Gran. It's pathetic that you do."

"The word is *slapstick*. Besides, those movies aren't his best. As you'd know if you ever watched one of them."

"I am done with this conversation."

Brett braced himself against the counter and took a few deep breaths. Was he . . . praying?

He met her gaze and frowned. "I didn't mean for this to become an argument," he said. "But after Gabe and I talked, I felt bad that I hadn't realized you'd stopped riding. I wish I had noticed when we were kids. Maybe I could have helped somehow."

"You couldn't have."

"How do you know?"

Amy avoided his gaze by staring at the stained glass piece. The dim lighting in the cottage suppressed the colors so it was almost impossible to distinguish the greens from the blues, the reds from the purples. Somehow her spirit reflected the same subdued dullness, as if all the colors of her life had puddled together into an indistinguishable mess. Maybe Brett was right about her *don't's*.

"I couldn't go to the stables anymore. Not without Dad. It didn't seem right somehow."

"I get that. But, you know, it wouldn't hurt you to change your mind about going with Gabe."

"Are you trying to set me up with him?" she snapped.

"You could do worse," Brett retorted. "You *have* done worse."

"You did not just say that."

Brett remained silent and Amy took a deep breath. She didn't want an argument either, but he was driving her mad. A dull ache tensed the back of her neck. "It's late," she said. "It's been a long day, we're both tired, and I just want to curl up with my tea and my Kindle."

"I'll be going, then." Brett flashed a halfhearted smile. "You want to come to church with us tomorrow?"

"No."

He dug his keys from his pocket but seemed reluctant to leave. "I guess we'll see you on the 4th if not before. Are you bringing anything good?"

"I haven't decided yet."

"Do you have lawn chairs to take to the lakefront? If not, I can bring an extra one."

Amy hesitated. He wasn't going to like this, but she might as well get it out. "I won't be going to the lakefront."

"Why not?" His surprised tone sounded almost like an accusation. He should have left when he said he was instead of hanging around to ask her stupid questions.

"Because I got a better offer," she responded. Even to her own ears, the words sounded haughty and dismissive.

"A better offer?" Brett appeared stunned, and his eyes widened with hurt.

Amy wanted to take back what she'd said, to say she was sorry. But he didn't give her a chance.

"This is our first, our very first, time to see fireworks with Jonah and with the girls. Do you have any idea how excited those kids are? How much this means to me?"

The fire burned in Amy's gut, sparked by guilt and fanned by

Brett's outburst. "Perhaps I prefer to spend the holiday with adults instead of children."

He stared at her, speechless.

"While you're stuck with your cute little wife," she continued, "and all those adorable kids, I'll be sipping champagne on a high-rise balcony as the colors light up the sky." She softened her eyes and sighed dreamily. "Doesn't it sound romantic?"

Brett's eyes narrowed, and his jaw hardened. Amy braced herself for his defensive comeback.

One slow second passed, followed by another and another. Brett's shoulders relaxed and a dimple flashed in a smug smile.

"Is he married?" His conversational tone made the question sound innocent, but the coldness in his eyes cut deep.

"I wish they'd never called you," she said.

"Who?"

She wrapped her arms across her stomach and didn't answer.

"You mean the ER people?"

If they hadn't called Brett, he wouldn't have known about her collapse at the nightclub. He wouldn't know the humiliation she endured when she came out of her stupor to learn no one had stayed with her. When she was most vulnerable and most needed him, her married senator had fled. Avoiding a possible scandal had meant more to him than Amy's well-being.

Brett jangled his keychain, then tapped his fist against his leg. "Don't come to the lakefront. Don't go riding with Gabe, don't watch the classics with us. Don't, don't, don't do anything because that's what you're best at."

He walked to the door and placed his hand on the knob. "And most of all, don't eat. Maybe then you'll end up in the hospital again, and when the ER calls, maybe I won't answer."

His words hammered into Amy's heart, beating her to a pulp. Stunned, her mind was momentarily blank before she seized one of his mandates.

"I eat," she declared.

"I never see you."

"Because I don't eat in front of you. Because you're always watching. Always taking notes. I can't stand it."

He opened his mouth then closed it again as his posture slumped, and his demeanor changed from anger to regret. But she didn't want his pity any more than she wanted him monitoring everything she did. Long seconds widened the gulf between them.

"I don't want to leave you like this," he finally said.

"Everybody leaves me. Why should you be any different?"

"I'm always here for you. Always have been."

She curled up in a chair, her knees close to her chest, and refused to look at him.

"You know that, don't you?"

She nodded, not because she believed it, but so he would leave her alone. Give him the reassurance he wanted and he'd return to his new family.

"I know," she murmured.

"We'll miss you at the fireworks." He sounded contrite and also a little sad. "I suppose you're spending the day in Columbus."

"We're coming to the family cookout first. I already cleared it with AJ."

"Is he anyone I know?"

"You've probably run into him a couple of times. Logan Cassidy. He was a lobbyist with Kennedy and Gaines but now he's gone out on his own."

"The name sounds familiar. Is he the reason you won't go riding with Gabe?"

"He's just a friend. An *unmarried* friend."

"Yeah, I shouldn't have said that. Forgive me?"

"Just don't embarrass me in front of Logan. Or talk about Gabe."

"I'll behave myself." He knelt by the chair and peered into her eyes. "And I'll do my best to not watch you eat."

She stared at him, but her fiery anger had ebbed enough for her to recognize his clumsy attempt at an apology.

"Great. Now I'll be conscious of you not watching."

He gently tugged her hair. "It'll be a fun day, Amy. You'll see."

After he left, Amy locked the doors and closed all the blinds. After changing into pajamas, she tugged a storage tote from the tiny closet that held a few of her childhood belongings. And one keepsake from her college days.

She lifted the stuffed teddy bear from the tote and crawled into bed. During her first flirtation with anorexia, the one no one knew about, the teddy bear had been her ally. She slipped her fingers into its secret pouch, where she'd once hidden laxatives and diet pills. Now it held a note she'd written to herself after the ER visit. She unfolded the slip of paper and read its words.

If you want to live, you have to change. If you want to change, you have to grow. If you want to grow, you have to live.

After tucking the note back in its secret pouch, she clutched the bear and cried herself to sleep.

- 24 -

*L*ogan stood by the grill, laughing at the right times, saying the right things, and counting the hours until he and Amy could leave. By accepting Amy's invitation, he'd broken his own rule about not meeting the family too early in the relationship. He shouldn't have.

Even though he'd known Amy for years, and it turned out he and Brett had a few mutual friends, he had little in common with her brother and almost nothing at all with her cousin. Being an alumnus of The Ohio State University wasn't a requirement for working at the state capitol, but people outside of the city seemed to expect it. Brett and AJ were no exception to that parochial misconception, expressing amazement that Logan had graduated from Dayton's Wright State University. Still, both men had money. That excused a great many shortcomings.

Logan prided himself on being a good sport by wading in the creek and enduring the splashing of three kids skilled at using their outdoor voices and their barking dog. Though Amy had explained the family relationships as they hiked to the spot from her rustic cottage, he wasn't as interested in understanding them as he made her believe.

Amy's eventual introduction to his family would be quite different. While AJ talked about his high school football team's prospects for the upcoming season, Logan listened politely. But his mind was occupied with possible venues for such an auspicious occasion as showing off his sophisticated girlfriend to his parents. A fine restaurant, perhaps. Or maybe a catered dinner at his apartment. What about a river cruise on the Ohio River? Better yet, on Lake Erie. He made a mental note to check into those possibilities.

After they ate the grilled assortment of meats and usual sides, AJ unpacked several fishing poles. He gave one to each kid, then held one out to Logan.

"Want to try your luck?" he asked.

"I think I'll pass," Logan said. He caught Amy's eye and made a silent plea for escape.

"Give it a try," she said, apparently amused by his discomfort. "If you catch something, you'll have a story to tell at tonight's party."

"As fun as that sounds, don't you think it's time we go?" He looked pointedly at the time on his cell phone. "We have a lot to do before our guests arrive."

Amy mulled it over then nodded. "I suppose you're right."

"If you go now," Dani piped up, "you'll miss the anniversary cake. One year ago today, AJ asked Shelby to marry him."

AJ placed his arm around Shelby's waist and drew her close. "Best thing I ever did."

"Reenact the moment for us," Brett urged. "Did you get down on one knee?"

"No," Shelby said.

"He didn't? And you still said yes?"

"No, he did." Shelby's cheeks flushed. "I meant, no reenactments."

"That's a memory just for us," AJ added.

Logan hoped that was the end of such silliness, but apparently it wasn't for Brett.

"You could at least give her a kiss, cuz," he said.

AJ responded with a mischievous smile. He removed his ball cap and blocked everyone's view from what Logan considered an unnecessarily long kiss. But he played along, clapping and whooping it up with the others.

Dani unveiled the cake, which mixed patriotic colors with a heart and the names of the couple. Shelby cut it into slices and Logan dutifully accepted one with a polite smile. He ate it quickly and, relieved to see Amy appeared finished with her sliver, announced once again that they should leave.

"Before you do," Brett said to Amy, "could I talk to you a minute?"

"Must you?" Her tone was half-resigned, half-teasing.

"I must." He led her several yards away from the others.

Logan feigned interest in the fishing activities while keeping an eye on Amy. The conversation appeared serious, but then Brett smiled and Amy punched his shoulder. Logan's consternation grew as Brett wrapped both his arms around her neck in a playful headlock and she kicked at his shins.

"Ow!" he said loudly, then released her.

"Serves you right," Amy called over her shoulder as she walked away. Brett jogged to catch up with her.

"Sure you don't want to hang around with us instead of going to some stuffy party?" Brett asked softly, though not softly enough.

The glazed chicken breast Logan had eaten turned into stone as he strained to hear Amy's response.

"I promised I'd go," she said. "Anyway, you'll have more fun without me."

"Not true."

"That's a sweet fib. You're forgiven for being an overbearing and obnoxious brother."

"And I forgive you for being you."

197

"Ha-ha."

Logan swallowed his annoyance at their banter, then walked toward them with a broad smile. "I hate to be the one to break up the party, but Amy, honey, we should go. Traffic in Columbus will be a nightmare."

"You're right," she said. "Give me a minute to say good-bye to the kids."

She took at least ten while Logan quietly fumed.

~

Gabe brought up the rear as he, Ellen, and Tess rode single file in front of the hedges hiding the cottage. Once they reached the bridge, they planned to follow Whisper Lane, the narrow hard-packed path that gave the horse farm its name, to an open pasture that lay southeast of the stables. Glade Creek flowed through it, and Tess thought it would be a fine place to gallop the horses.

From Gabe's perspective, the pasture's prime benefit was its location in the opposite direction of Misty Willow. He had no interest in riding anywhere close to the engagement tree and seeing Amy with her date.

As they neared the bridge, Tess reined Knight Starr to a stop and Gabe urged Daisy next to her. Amy walked toward them from the other end. Striding next to her was the man Gabe had seen in town. Clean-cut, impeccably dressed even in casual clothes, and with the confident posture of someone who expected to get what he wanted from life. Naturally, Amy looked gorgeous in a spaghetti-strapped top and denim shorts. Her hair was pulled into a ponytail, and huge sunglasses hid her eyes.

Amy veered toward the bridge's guardrail as the horses neared. Gabe didn't understand her irrational fear, but he respected it. When he dismounted, Tess and Ellen did the same.

"Nice day for a ride," Amy said with an awkward smile.

"And for a walk," Gabe replied.

"We're taking the long way back from the willow tree," she explained, "past the bungalow. The ground is flatter."

"The picnic's already over?"

"Only for us." She introduced Gabe and Tess to Logan, then gazed at Ellen. "I'm Amy Somers."

"This is Ellen Barnes," Gabe said quickly, before Ellen could respond. "She's spending a couple of days with us."

"It's nice to meet you." Amy's polite smile seemed to lack warmth. Probably another jealous snit, though that was unlikely considering she stood next to her boyfriend. Where had she found this guy? One punch and he'd be flat on his back.

"I hope you enjoy your stay," Amy added.

"I'm sure I will," Ellen said.

"Where are you riding to?"

"Toward Whisper Lane," Tess answered. "Back toward the springs."

Where we used to ride. Gabe willed Amy to read his thoughts in his eyes. *Where we found the arrowhead.*

Amy's polite smile clouded, then broadened as she glanced from Logan back to him. "Enjoy yourselves," she said. "Logan is having guests this evening so we need to go. It wouldn't be very polite for us not to be there when they arrive, and we can't go looking like this." She fanned her hands to her sides.

"I hope you have a pleasant evening," Gabe lied.

"I hope you do too." Amy took hold of Logan's arm. "Ta-ta."

A smile, both proprietary and smug, crossed Logan's face. "Pleasure meeting all of you," he said as he led Amy away. "Happy 4th."

Tess and Ellen remounted, but Gabe waited a moment. Amy and Logan strolled along the country road as if they didn't have a care in the world, and Amy's musical laugh floated back to him. As much as he hated to admit it, they made an attractive couple. Both cut from the same cloth.

But where Amy's sophistication and polish deepened her natural attractiveness, Gabe didn't think the same of Logan's. Not because he was jealous but because the guy seemed a little too slick. He might hold his own in a boardroom, but set him down in a war zone and see how he fared. That smug, self-satisfied smile would be gone in an instant.

Better yet, see how he handled himself in a prison yard.

"Gabe," Tess called. "Are you coming?"

At the sound of Tess's voice, Amy looked over her shoulder. Gabe immediately turned away and mounted Daisy. He tapped her sides with his heels, and she trotted toward the others.

Maybe he should have written Amy after he'd read her letter. But too much time had passed between the time she wrote it, just before she left home for college, and when he read it. By then, their lives were going in separate directions, and the gap between them was too wide to cross.

ood of you to squeeze me into your busy schedule."
Logan made no attempt to hide his sarcasm. Meeting
with Dylan on a Sunday wasn't his idea of a good time. Not that
he had anything better to do. Amy had declined to spend the
day with him because her family planned to spend the afternoon
canoeing. He'd been relieved but also disappointed she didn't ask
him to join them.

"Had to be today," Dylan said. "Uncle Joe is sending me to
Arizona tomorrow. Not a good sign."

"What's in Arizona?"

"It's a scouting trip. I'm supposed to 'investigate and evaluate
potential opportunities.' In other words, go look at a bunch of
run-down strip malls and apartment complexes."

"Isn't that how he made his millions?" Logan asked, though
he already knew the answer. He'd read everything he could find
about the Tapleys before purposely cultivating a friendship with
Dylan. "Revitalizing properties everyone else ignored?"

Dylan grunted. "The point is, these trips are his way of sending
a message. He's making me go because I'm expendable."

"That won't be true once you break ground at Whisper Lane."

"How much longer is that going to take? It's been over a week since I saw Tess Marshall, and you haven't done anything to change her mind."

Logan slowed his breathing to ease the growing tension from his body. Amazing how much of a lobbyist's job involved soothing clients who behaved like petulant children. When Dylan called him after his visit to the stables, Logan had wanted to reach through the phone and shake him by his thick neck.

"That's not true," Logan said. "I paid Mrs. Marshall a visit too."

"When?"

Logan slid a folder across the desk toward Dylan. "When no one was home. That's a rundown of her finances. She can't hold out much longer."

"Maybe I should make her another offer."

"You will. But not yet."

Dylan opened the folder and concentrated on the financial worksheets. "You stole these from her computer?"

"Sat at her desk and printed them out."

"Lucky her cowboy nephew didn't catch you."

"I met him."

Dylan looked up from the folder in surprise. "When?"

"On the 4th. He's a nobody. An ex-con." Logan leaned forward and lowered his voice. Dylan unconsciously mirrored Logan's posture as he strained to listen.

"Here's the thing about ex-cons," Logan said conspiratorially. "It's not that hard to send them right back to prison. If Kendall stands in our way, we'll make sure that happens to him."

"How will you do that?"

"Leave it to me. In the meantime, you stay away from him. And from Tess Marshall."

Dylan sat back with a wide smile. "Glad you're on my side."

"As long as it's profitable." Logan said the words lightly, but they both understood the underlying message. They were partners because they each had what the other wanted. Logan needed Dylan's money and connections. Dylan needed Logan's expertise and know-how.

Dylan clapped his hands on his desk and rose. "How about a drink and a cigar?"

"Neither for me, thanks. And no cigar for you until I leave."

"You're ruining all my fun, Cassidy."

"Just looking out for my lungs." Logan stood and retrieved the folder. It was the only copy, and he intended to hang on to it.

"Don't go yet. I've got something to show you." Dylan went to the map table, pulled an overlay from a shallow drawer, and placed it on top of the map.

The property with the house and stables, located west of the road, was unmarked. But the Whisper Lane property across the road, north of Amy's cottage, was clearly labeled Phase One. It encompassed land from the road to the area north of Glade Creek. Logan had seen that property with his own eyes at Amy's family picnic.

In a few years, the houses and condominiums wouldn't be lines on an overlay but actual residences.

"I'm impressed," Logan said.

Dylan placed another overlay on the map. "Phase Two."

The planned community sprawled on both sides of the road, which, in this version, had been widened. The extra width cut into the cottage property. Just another slap to Amy and AJ, and one they'd find difficult to stop once Dylan's development was approved. The county could show just cause for taking that swath of land.

"Do you have a Phase Three?" Logan asked.

With a satisfied grin, Dylan pulled out a third overlay and placed it on top of the others. He pointed to where the cottage was located. "This hill will be leveled. Along with the current dwellings."

"Amy won't like it. Neither will Sullivan."

"She should have done more to look after my interests." Dylan's voice turned surly. "It's what I paid her to do."

Logan had no interest in pursuing a conversation they'd already had too many times. Personally, he didn't care whether Phase Three ever became a reality. Only Phase One needed to be a success. By that time, Dylan's uncle would recognize Logan as someone who could get things done. He'd have other influential clients, too, who'd become willing donors. Then he'd make his move from lobbyist to politician.

The only wild card was Amy. Last year a certain state senator, poised to run for Congress, had unexpectedly changed his mind. He said he wanted to spend more time with his family, retired from public life when his term ended, then moved to Florida. Though the gossip mill had been eerily quiet, Logan believed Amy was involved. She'd had a mysterious boyfriend who seemed to disappear at the same time the senator closed his congressional campaign. It wasn't much to go on, but combined with a few whispers he'd heard here and there, Logan was certain she'd used her influence to end a political career.

That same influence could ignite his.

– 26 –

The dark clouds and sunless sky of the dreary mid-July day diminished the usually vibrant colors of the stained glass piece. The rain had started yesterday afternoon and pounded the cottage's roof throughout the night. Thunderous claps woke Amy in the wee morning hours, and she'd had trouble falling back asleep.

At least the drapes on the bedroom window had hidden the flashes of lightning, but now the streaks pulsed through the sky past the row of long windows.

Amy curled in her chair, a blue-and-cream afghan wrapped around her legs. She'd tried to concentrate on her online bank statements, but it was too hard to focus on the numbers with so much noise and bother going on outside. Besides, she was disheartened by how quickly her spending added up. She thought she was being careful, but the balance indicated otherwise.

The hair salon, maintenance on her BMW, weekly mani-pedis, and groceries. The paint for all the cottage's interior rooms, the mirrors, the portable wardrobe racks. An impromptu trip to the zoo with Shelby, Dani, and the three children, her treat of course. The Cary Grant DVD collection she'd bought, not because of what

Brett had said but because she missed Gran so much the day of the Heritage Celebration. And countless other impulse purchases that didn't seem like much but added up to a great deal.

Was she ever going to learn?

Another thunderclap practically shook the cottage from its foundation.

No wonder the Greeks and Romans believed in the gods of Mount Olympus. It certainly seemed like a giant mythological being was having a major temper tantrum above the clouds. This was the worst storm she'd experienced since moving into the cottage, and she was not enjoying it.

In fact, she wouldn't mind hurling a few lightning bolts from a tall mountain herself. One at Brett for not calling to see if she was okay. Another at AJ for the same reason. Didn't they realize how scary a storm like this could be? Whose idea had it been to install a whole wall of windows in this place anyway?

Another bolt for Logan, though she wasn't sure why. Perhaps for drawing her back into a world she wanted to escape. His 4th of July fireworks party had overflowed with interesting people, entertaining conversation, and an elaborate buffet. She'd nibbled on several delicacies while fighting the urge to calculate calories.

Watching the fireworks from his balcony had been a delightful experience despite the tendency of her thoughts to skitter other places. Shelby and Dani both posted photos of the children ooh-ing and aah-ing as the fireworks broke the black of the night sky. For several minutes, until she caught Logan frowning at her, she'd had a hard time staying off the social media site.

She wanted to be with the kids, with Brett and Dani, with AJ and Shelby. But she enjoyed the evening with Logan. His attentiveness stroked her ego, and she could imagine herself falling in love with him. Of course she could. If she wanted to.

They'd gone out a couple more times since then. The candlelight dinner he'd mentioned. A movie at a giant Cineplex. If they were in a relationship, perhaps she'd be at his place today. Lounging in the comfort of his high-rise apartment. Spending her days shopping and their nights dining at the finest restaurants. All at Logan's expense.

She'd once planned such a life for herself, but she had miscalculated the senator's survival instincts. He'd enjoyed her company, her intelligence, her shrewdness, and she'd relished her role as the influential woman behind his dream of running for Congress. Her plan had been to stay with him until he settled in Washington, then find another man who could offer her even more prestige. Preferably someone with his sights on the White House and the wherewithal to get there with her as his hidden muse. The one who really had his ear, a not-so-secret secret known only to the Beltway insiders. They'd curry her favor to get to him, this mythical man of her dreams.

A dream that seemed more like a sick fantasy now that she'd spent time away from the machinations of politics. She still hated the senator for abandoning her, but the trip to the emergency room had been the wake-up call she needed to seek help for her eating issues. She had been on a downward spiral without any hope of escaping until that night.

She leaned her head back on the cushioned chair and closed her eyes. Thinking about that nightmare caused her body to tense and her stomach to heave. But she refused to give in to the impulse to empty her stomach. She'd done that by allowing her childhood memories of Gabe to lead her to darker places. She wouldn't do it again. Not today. Not ever.

If she couldn't be strong, she'd have to go back to treatment. Or she'd simply curl up and die a slow, lingering death. Perhaps that was the best she could ever hope for in this life.

Neither alternative appealed to her.

She hadn't wanted to face the truth, but it stared her in the face. She could tell herself the reason she came to the cottage was because of her messed-up finances or because she didn't have anywhere else to go. But the truth was, she wanted to, needed to, hide herself away from the world she'd known and build a life without either treatment or illness.

She needed her family.

Brett hadn't meant to hurt her when he moved out of the city and settled so easily into the community's rural rhythms. But she felt the pain of his leaving anyway. Yet the move had been good for him. He was more relaxed, a truer version of his best self than she'd ever known. Despite their recent argument, a strange peace seemed to emanate from him. A peace she desperately wanted but didn't know how to find on her own.

At the Heritage Celebration, she had, now that she thought back on it, enjoyed being with Cassie and a few of the other women. True, she had little in common with them, but they'd been open and friendly. No one seemed to have a hidden agenda. A couple may have been a little nosy, but there'd been no malice.

Even when she felt unsure of what Cassie and the others would think of her—telling herself she didn't care while knowing deep down she did—she hadn't put on the mask. And they seemed to like her anyway.

Another flash of lightning split the sky, and Amy sighed heavily. Enough soul-searching and philosophy. She opened her book, *The Silmarillion*, and prepared to enter a world she'd visited several times before. Tolkien's creation story, with its musical motifs and imaginative beauty, never failed to calm her restless mind.

Thunder sounded, ended, then the pounding continued. Except it didn't come from the sky but from her front door.

She jumped from her chair and peered through the window. Gabe stood on the porch, huddled within an ugly brown slicker. His beat-up Stetson covered his bent head. She hadn't seen him since the 4th of July, and that had been almost two weeks ago.

Unexpected warmth flowed from her toes and spread through her entire body until she glowed.

In the depths of her mind, a little thought took shape. Perhaps the peace Brett had found wasn't because of where he lived but who he was living with. His love for Dani, her love for him, had made him whole. Just as Shelby's love for AJ had healed the heartache he'd carried for so long.

"Amy?" Gabe's voice carried through the storm.

She opened the door only wide enough for him to squeeze through. "Wait there," she ordered, pointing to the small square of tile right inside the door. "I'll get you a towel." Before he could reply, she hurried to the tiny bathroom, grabbed two plush towels, and rushed back to the door.

"What are you doing here?" She tried hiding her giddiness, but it was no use. "I'm so glad to see you." Embarrassed by her gushing, she laughed too loudly. "I mean, I didn't expect to see you."

"I told you I'd bring over my famous chili when it stormed." He placed the box on the floor, then shrugged out of the slicker. She traded him the towels for it and the hat. "Or did you forget?"

"I guess I didn't think you really meant it. Especially since . . ."

"Since what?"

"I haven't seen you around lately."

"Been working long hours. What about you?"

"Oh, keeping busy." She folded the slicker into itself to keep the dripping to a minimum. "I'm going to hang this from the shower. I'll be right back. Make yourself at home."

"Okay if I take over the kitchen?" he asked as he dried his hair with one of the towels.

"You know where it is."

She quickly hung the slicker over the shower rod to dry it out and placed the soaked hat on a towel on the pedestal sink. After examining her face and hair in the mirror, she dusted on powder and blush, stroked mascara on her lashes, and brushed her hair.

Her rainy-day clothes—a cozy old sweatshirt of Brett's, yoga pants, and heavy socks—were fine when she was alone. But not now. Though if she changed, he'd know she'd changed.

What to do, what to do?

– 27 –

*G*abe slipped off his boots, then carried the box to the kitchen. By the time Amy appeared, he had plugged in the Crock-Pot and was chopping scallions on the wooden cutting board he'd brought with him.

She wore dark jeans that skimmed her long legs topped by a royal blue sweater.

"You didn't have to change." In fact, he was kind of sorry she had. She looked beautiful, of course. The blue of the sweater deepened the blue of her eyes. But he'd enjoyed seeing what she wore when she wasn't expecting company. Though she'd be even more appealing in one of his old sweatshirts than the large OSU-emblazoned one she'd been wearing.

"This is supposed to be a lazy, kick-back, stay inside to stay dry kinda day," he said.

"I can change back if you want me to."

"How about helping me with the mise en place instead?"

"Oh, wow. That's impressive."

"I bet you didn't think I knew that phrase."

"Just tell me what you want me to do."

He handed her a block of cheddar cheese and a grater. She eyed it suspiciously. "Good thing you came prepared. All I have is a pot for boiling water. And an egg pan."

"Hopefully I didn't forget anything." He put the scallions in a glass dish, then opened a bag of corn chips, which he poured in another bowl. "I made the chili yesterday so the ingredients have had plenty of time to get acquainted. I hope you're hungry."

Her face clouded and he broadened his smile. He didn't want to nag her like Brett too often did. But it was hard to ignore what she'd told him.

Her one word—food.

He lifted the Crock-Pot lid, speared a piece of the Conecuh sausage on a fork, and held it out to her. "Try this and tell me what you think."

She daintily placed the meat in her mouth, and her eyes widened as she savored the flavor. "Delicious," she said.

"Isn't it? I had to send for it all the way from Alabama."

"You're kidding."

"No, I'm not."

"When did you do that?"

"The day after we talked about my chili and your lemon meringue pie." He made a point of looking around the kitchen. "Where is it?"

Her lips stretched into a straight line so she looked apologetic, guilty, and teasing all at the same time. "I meant to pick up the ingredients so I'd have them, but then, well, I didn't."

"I see how it is," he said.

"I doubt that you do." There was a slight challenge in her voice, but he chose to ignore it. At least for now.

"Then we go to Plan B." He reached into the box and drew out a brownie mix. "But you have to bake them."

"My favorite brand." Amy took the mix from him and opened it. "Is there room for me in that kitchen?"

"I'll make room," Gabe said.

With both of them in the tiny space, they couldn't help but bump into each other. Amy's sophisticated fragrance mingled with the tantalizing aroma of the chili and the sweet chocolate of the brownie mix. They teased and bantered while he took over grating the cheese and she got the brownies into the oven. Once the kitchen was tidied up, they carried bowls of steaming chili to the living area along with a tray of the toppings.

Amy settled on the couch, and Gabe placed the tray on the coffee table, then sat in a nearby chair. Though he couldn't explain why he didn't sit next to her. Maybe he just didn't want to push his luck.

"I miss my fireplace on days like today," Amy said as she added scallions to her bowl. "Even though it's summer, a fire would be nice on a day like this."

"The rain doesn't seem to be slacking off any."

"I guess the farmers around here are thankful for it."

"I know I am. Otherwise I'd be out on a tractor." *Instead of with you.*

"What does AJ have you doing these days?"

"I'm working for Paul Norris now. Jason Owens too."

"I met their wives at the Misty Willow celebration. They're both very nice."

"Good cooks too. One of the perks of the job is all the home-cooking I can put away. Between them and Tess, I'll turn into a medicine ball with legs if I'm not careful."

She playfully gave him the once-over, a teasing grin brightening her features. A little of the same light she'd had as a girl and that he'd missed seeing in her as a woman.

"You're looking fine to me," she finally said with a hint of suggestiveness.

"Flatter me all you want, little darlin'," he said. "I'll never tell you my chili recipe."

"Then I guess I'll have to hope for more rainy days."

"Not too many. If I don't work, I don't get paid."

"How long have you been working for them?"

"A week or so. We've been putting in some long hours though."

"Is that why I haven't seen you lately?"

"That. And I wasn't sure you'd want to see me." He had another reason too, though it was harder to put into words. Long days on the tractor gave him too much time to think. He was having a hard time understanding what AJ had said about Amy being disappointed that Gabe already had plans for the holiday when she already had a date of her own. But he didn't think he could talk to her about it. At least not today, when all he wanted was a few hours alone with the woman he adored. Snug in the cottage, he could pretend his troubles didn't exist. That Logan Cassidy didn't exist.

"So you dropped by without any warning today?"

"I gave you warning when I said I'd come. Now here I am, along with my chili fixin's," he added in an exaggerated drawl. "I knew you wouldn't turn that away."

"Guess I owe you a pie."

"I'll expect you to keep that promise."

"Don't worry, I will."

A comfortable silence followed, the humming sounds of the cottage drowned out by the raging storm outside.

"Now you know what I've been doing with my days," he said. "What have you been doing with yours?"

"This and that. Nothing too exciting."

"I've missed seeing you at the church softball games."

"I heard you were the hero the other night, hitting a homer with bases loaded in the ninth inning."

He gave what he hoped was a humble grin. "We won the game. That's all that matters."

"Jonah was very impressed. He couldn't stop talking about it."

"It's nice to have a fan."

"It's nice for him to have a role model."

"I'd think he had as many as he needed. Brett, AJ. Jason too, as much time as the families spend together."

"I'm not sure a young boy can have too many. Especially when . . . well, let's just say Meghan's ex-husband certainly wasn't someone to look up to. We're all glad he's no longer a part of Jonah's life."

"Any chance he'll pop back in again?"

"I doubt it. Last I heard, he'd been in another automobile accident. This time he was charged with vehicular homicide. So he'll be in prison for a very long time."

Prison. His one word. He couldn't keep himself from making a face, though he tried not to let his emotion show. She was too perceptive not to have caught it—he could tell by the look in her eyes—but she didn't say anything.

"You never said why you haven't been at the games," he said to change the subject.

The timer on the oven sounded, and Amy gave him a mischievous smile. "Saved by the bell."

Carrying his chili bowl, Gabe followed her to the kitchen. "Looks like we'll be rained out tonight. Think you could come next week?"

She tested the brownies for doneness, then set the pan on a rack to cool. "Brett told me you play better when I'm not there."

Gabe pulled his head back in surprise. "I don't think . . ."

"You did get that game-winning homer—"

"That was a fluke."

"Brett said I'm a distraction." Her smile dared him to contradict. And distracted his thoughts.

"I don't mind."

"But the rest of the team does."

"You have a mighty high opinion of yourself, don't you?"

"If I don't, who will?"

"Me."

"Only because you don't know me that well."

"Maybe it's time we did something about that."

A cloud crossed Amy's face, but she chased it away with one of her dazzling smiles. "I'd rather know more about you."

"I'm not sure where to start." The contents of his bowl suddenly needed his attention. "Besides, you've probably heard the story by now."

"No one's told me anything."

"I find that hard to believe."

"I wouldn't let them tell me." She headed back to the couch, then added more cheese to her chili. "I wanted to hear it from you."

This time Gabe sat beside her and placed his bowl on the coffee table. "You're not kidding, are you?"

"It's your story. No one else's."

"That means something, that you . . ." He wasn't sure how to finish the sentence. "Thank you for that."

"What happened, Gabe?"

"My cousin Randy, he's my dad's nephew, needed money. He'd been laid off and was having trouble finding work. Then his son broke his arm so there were medical bills. He was a fairly good poker player so he made a bit of money doing that. But then, no surprise, he got involved with the wrong people."

The nightmare went through Gabe's mind again, as it had so many times since that day he and Amy painted the cabinet doors. He'd been rehearsing how to tell her what had happened until the 4th of July holiday. After seeing her with Logan, Gabe was no longer sure she wanted to hear it.

"I'm surprised you waited to hear this from me," he said. "Several people around here already know."

He had voluntarily shared his story with Jason and Paul. The last thing he wanted was a veil of mystery surrounding him. For people to question his honesty, his ethics. As long as he stayed with Tess, he hoped to be part of this community, and he wanted the families to trust him. Amy was probably the last one to be told the details.

"I told you I only wanted to hear it from you," she said. "I take it he gambled more than he should have."

"Yeah." Gabe sighed heavily. "At first he didn't want to tell me how bad it was, but I wouldn't let up. I wanted him to go to the police. Told him I'd go with him. But he said he had a different plan."

"What happened?"

"We stopped at a convenience store, and he went inside to get a six-pack while I filled the tank. I waited for him but when he didn't come back, I went in after him."

Gabe paused, needing a moment to collect his thoughts before he could tell the rest of the story. He sat forward, resting his elbows on his thighs with his hands clasped in front of him. It hadn't been this difficult to tell the others, but he found himself giving more details to Amy than he had to them.

She leaned close to him and tucked her arm through his. Her fragrance, so beguiling and sensuous, pulled him to her while her touch electrified his entire being. He couldn't live without her, couldn't breathe without her. Except he had no choice. Any relationship, with her or anybody else, couldn't be permanent until he found his place in the world.

He took a deep breath, unable to disengage himself from her presence. No man would have had the strength. He put his arms around her, and when she didn't resist, he held her close. He breathed in her perfume as she nestled within his arms.

Before his stint in prison, he wouldn't have hesitated to cover her welcoming mouth with his, to kiss the hollow of her gorgeous throat. How easy it would be to stretch out with her on the couch, for their bodies to press against one another in their longing for intimacy. Two lonely people in a secluded cottage in the midst of a raging storm. It was perfect.

Except . . .

He'd have never made it through those long monotonous days of his sentence if God had not been with him. If again and again he hadn't sensed God's promise of provision for his future. He believed in that promise. He trusted in it even when he faltered and couldn't see beyond the next day's sunrise.

"What did your cousin do?" she asked softly.

"He had a gun." His voice caught in his throat, and he gave a jagged cough. "He threatened the cashier."

She didn't say anything. It was as if she realized his need to tell the story in his own way. In his own time. Her hand rested on his chest, upon his heart, soothing his pain with her touch.

"I tried to stop him. He panicked and the gun went off. The clerk died." He sucked in another breath.

He felt her stifled gasp, the heave of her sigh. "Oh, Gabe," she whispered. "It wasn't your fault."

"But it was. Don't you see?" This was the hardest part, the part he'd left out when he told the story to the others. The part he could barely face himself but that he needed Amy to understand. "He panicked because of me."

She pushed against him to look into his eyes. "He made his choice."

"I should have stopped him."

"You tried."

"And someone died. If I had handled things differently, if I'd gone inside the store with him . . ."

"A thousand ifs. But not one of them changes the facts. Your cousin had a gun with him."

"That doesn't change the guilt I carry around with me every day."

"Why did they arrest you?"

"The DA was smarter than my public defender. I was charged as an accessory."

"What about your cousin?"

"He got life."

"Do you visit him?"

Gabe's vision blurred and he worked his jaw.

"I can understand why that would be hard for you."

"He's dead, Amy. He died in prison."

Her eyes rounded with shock. He could almost see the horrific scenes she must be imagining racing through her mind. "Not because of . . . it was natural causes. He died of appendicitis, of all things. A couple of years ago."

She pressed her palm against his jaw, her touch feather-light and warm. "I'm sorry, Gabe. I'm so very sorry." She rested her cheek against his and buried her face in his neck. He wrapped his arms around her again, holding her tight and feeling the give-and-take of grief between them.

And again, the urge to kiss her overwhelmed him.

He shifted so he could stare at her eyes, her lips. He slid his finger along her fine cheekbone and rested his thumb against her jaw.

Her expression told him that her longing matched his, but he refused to give in to the temptation. In his mood, in this place, one kiss would lead to another and another and he—they—wouldn't be able to stop.

Their second kiss, if it ever happened, wouldn't stem from sympathy or pity or loneliness but from something as real and genuine as their first.

– 28 –

*A*my closed her eyes, expecting Gabe's lips to touch her own. Instead, he loosened his hold and leaned into the soft cushions of the couch. She shifted and rested her head against his shoulder. If only he had kissed her, maybe she could have told him how much she had missed him. How much she loved him.

But fairy-tale romances only came true in fairy tales. In real life, people made a mess of their lives, and then, when Prince Charming finally showed up, it was too late to be his princess.

At least now she'd heard his story from his own enticing lips. Unfortunate as it was, the sad tale seemed the safest topic of conversation as long as she was nestled in his arms.

"I'm sorry your cousin died," she said. "But I don't believe it was your fault. None of it."

"Maybe not. But I carry the guilt."

"I understand that. But nothing you do now will change what happened."

"Isn't that true for you too?"

She sighed heavily. "I suppose so. But somehow I keep hoping for . . . "

"What?"

"A different story."

"What would you want to be different?"

"Almost everything."

"Even this?" He pressed his jaw against her temple. "I like sitting here with you."

She liked it too. But she didn't believe they could begin again, that they had a chance for a different story.

Things might have been different if they had stayed in touch with one another. Maybe even if she'd come home for Rusty's funeral.

If their paths had crossed then, perhaps both their stories would be different.

Now it was too late. She couldn't tell him she'd lied about not remembering him. It had been such a stupid lie, but she was stuck with it. She couldn't tell him she'd arranged the date with Logan because she was mad he had other plans for the 4th. That said nothing good about her.

She didn't even want to ask him about this Ellen anymore. Not when he was here with her. Maybe Ellen was simply an old friend. After all, he'd said something about her having kids. Maybe she was Tess's friend instead of Gabe's.

She was clutching at straws, but at least she recognized that was what she was doing. She should have simply asked AJ. But then he'd know she was interested in Gabe. Though he obviously already knew that.

Her mind seemed to go around in circles. Couldn't she put all the craziness away for a little while and just enjoy cuddling with Gabe while the lightning flashed and the thunder crashed outside? They were cozy together on the couch with the warm aroma of simmering chili wafting from the kitchen.

The hours would pass quickly enough. Gabe would go home, and their lives would continue on their separate paths.

"How long do you plan to stay with Tess?" she asked.

"I guess until I find a steady job."

"Maybe I can help. I know a lot of people. What do you want to do?"

"Nothing that involves a desk. Or eight hours within the same four walls."

"That's the life of most of the people I know."

"I'm sorry for them."

"Don't be. They certainly aren't. Besides, they don't necessarily stay in their offices all day. They go to meetings. Out to lunch. Things like that."

"Meetings." Gabe made a disgruntled sound. "I bet you thrived on them."

"Depends on who else was involved," she said with a teasing haughty air. "Once in a while we even accomplished something worthwhile."

"And other times?"

"Maybe not so much." They were silent for a moment, then she asked, "Don't you like working with Paul and Jason?"

"Actually, I do. But neither of them need anyone full-time. And while the pay is adequate for now, it's less than what I need if I'm going to make a life for myself."

"Do you want to stay around here?"

"Maybe. It's nice being with Tess, and everyone else has made me feel welcome. I've appreciated that."

"You do seem to fit right in. Better than I do."

"What makes you say that?"

"I'm just not sure the country life is for me. I don't want to garden or raise chickens. Even Brett is talking about getting hens for the eggs. It's unbelievable."

Gabe laughed. "I don't think you have to do either of those things if you don't want to. Don't you like it here in your hideaway?"

"I love it here. But that's different."

"Why?"

"This was Gran's place. And then AJ's. It's familiar and it's safe."

"Safe?"

"Shut away from the world the way it is, hardly anyone even knows it's here. But it's more than that. It has a spirit about it, don't you think? As if all the times Gran stayed here and all the time AJ lived here, most of the memories are happy ones. So the cottage is happy."

She laughed at her rare fancifulness. Maybe she'd spent too much time in *The Silmarillion* lately. "I'm not explaining it very well, and I don't mean to sound mystical. But the cottage has a personality, and I love it for that."

"I agree. Places do have personalities, feelings about them. Think about going into a prison. It's an institution with metal doors, harsh lighting. The cells are small, but there's nothing cozy about them." He snorted. "Sorry. I didn't mean to talk about that again."

"What you've gone through isn't fair. Not when you didn't do anything."

"At least it's over now."

She sat up and gazed into his eyes. "It *is* over, Gabe. You're free now, and you can do anything you want."

"Except that I can't. I can't go back into the military. In some states I can't vote. I can't even apply for a job without admitting I'm a felon. Right now, my options don't seem like much."

"Are you worried?"

"Sometimes." Gabe squirmed. "I think we've talked enough about me. What about you? Are you planning on going back to a desk and an office and meetings and lunches?"

"I don't know what I'm going to do. Not anymore."

"What changed?"

"I guess I did. At least, I'm trying to."

"Because of your eating"—he hesitated—"issues?"

He'd told her his story. She might as well tell him at least a little bit more of hers.

"Before I went to the clinic, I ended up in the hospital. At first, I didn't want to face the truth about what happened. But I was scared. I knew girls in college who slid too far into that abyss. Who almost died because they couldn't bear to swallow even one calorie."

She pulled her knees close to her body and slid a strand of hair through her fingers. "I didn't want to end up like that, so I sought help."

"That took a lot of courage."

"I don't know about that. Brett gave me all these pamphlets and brochures to look through. I finally admitted myself into a place so he'd leave me alone."

"He loves you," Gabe said. "It must have been hard for him to see you hurting and not be able to help."

"It was," she admitted. "And you're right. He does love me." He and AJ were probably the only ones who really did. "Brett was going through a hard time then too. Last summer wasn't the easiest year of our lives, though I guess good things came from it."

"How's that?"

"AJ found Jonah. Brett met Dani." She smiled broadly. "And look at them now. A couldn't-be-happier family." The same with AJ, Shelby, and their girls. Amy was the only one left out. The only one without someone to call her own.

Ironically, the man she wanted was right beside her. Despite his own past struggles, he was an honorable man, a loyal man. He'd be so disappointed if he knew all the things she'd done, the kind of life she'd been living before she'd gone into treatment.

This Ellen, who wasn't afraid of horses, who would ride with him back to the springs, was probably more his type. At his age, he might be happy with his own ready-made family. No wonder he needed more than a couple of part-time farming jobs to make his way in the world. He needed money to support a wife and her children. If Amy felt anything for him at all, any lingering affection or respect, she needed to let him go.

As hard as it was, she couldn't hold on to him for her own selfish purposes.

Not this time. Not with Gabe.

An ache settled into her heart just thinking about how much he could be hurt by someone with her cavalier attitude. She had to be sure this relationship stayed in the "just friends" category no matter how much she might want it to become something else. The hurt expanded, pressing against her chest.

Was this what it meant to love someone? To really, truly love someone?

"You are so beautiful," he said. "I can't believe you aren't married."

Startled by his unexpected change of subject, Amy said the first words that popped into her head. "I don't think I'll ever marry."

"Never?" His fingers trailed along her arm. "Don't you want to fall in love with someone? Have a family?"

She studied his face, then shifted to gaze out the long row of windows at the relentless storm. "I loved someone once. A long time ago. But our lives went in different directions."

Gabe was silent for a moment, then he cleared his throat. "What if your paths crossed again?"

His question, laden with unspoken meaning, pressed against Amy's heart. He knew she meant him, that she had lied about not remembering him. But it was too late for them.

"Too many years have passed. Too many things have gone wrong."

She avoided his gaze as all the words she couldn't say tightened her quivering stomach.

Don't you see, Gabe? I've lived my life so differently than you would have wanted me to. I'm not worthy of your love, your respect. How could you possibly love me now? If you knew even half the things I've done, you'd leave here and never come back.

Her heart ached with longing, but she knew he wouldn't kiss her now. If he'd wanted her, he'd have already kissed her. Something had stopped him—something had changed his mind. If only the past could be changed. But that was a vain wish. Do-overs only happened in children's games.

– 29 –

At the sound of tires crunching on gravel, Gabe slid out from beneath the Ford F-150. He sure would be glad to get the heap running. Tess didn't mind it when he borrowed her truck, but he didn't like being dependent on someone else for transportation. Most mornings he rode Daisy to whichever field he'd be working in. No better way to start the day than in the saddle.

A sedan from the Glade County Sheriff's Office parked near the Ford. Gabe wiped his hands on a rag, then greeted the deputy.

"What brings you here?" he asked while a million possibilities raced through his mind. If his parole had been revoked—but it couldn't have been. And a sheriff's deputy wouldn't handle something like that. Would he?

I can't go back. Please, God. No.

The prayer was short, fervent. And he hoped for an immediate answer.

"I'm Deputy Hank Hood. And you are?"

"Gabriel Kendall."

"Are you working for Mrs. Marshall?"

"I'm her nephew." Gabe refrained from asking any questions

of his own, though he wished the deputy would forego the pleasantries and state his business.

"Her nephew? Is that right? You're not from around here, are you?"

"No, I'm not."

"You planning to stay long?"

Gabe tamped down his impatience. This deputy wasn't about to be rushed. "As long as Tess will have me."

"That's real nice. Would she be home, your aunt Tess?"

Gabe gestured toward the stables. "She's tending one of her horses."

"Is there something wrong with it?"

"He's off his feed."

"Is that so?" Deputy Hood pressed his lips together and nodded knowingly. "Think I'll go take a look-see. You don't have any objection, do you?"

"I'll go with you."

Gabe led the deputy down the stable's wide passageway to where Tess sat on a camp stool outside an open stall. The lines around her mouth and eyes were creased with tension. She stood as they drew near, her eyes registering surprise.

"Hank," she said, glancing at Gabe. "What brings you here?"

"I wish it was a social call, Mrs. Marshall. I really do."

"Gabe?" The worry lines deepened. "Is everything okay?"

"He didn't tell me."

Tess folded her arms and glared at the deputy. "Whatever you have to say, Hank, just spit it out."

"It's like this, ma'am." He averted his gaze, then cleared his throat. "It's like this. Someone called in a neglect complaint."

Tess's eyes practically popped out of her head. "Again? Who's doing this?"

"Well, ma'am, they're unanimous complaints."

"You mean anonymous?"

"Yes, ma'am, that's what I mean." The deputy shrugged, but he obviously wasn't happy about Tess correcting him. He looked as if he would be happier for the floor to open up and swallow him whole than continue the conversation. "The caller said some of these horses aren't getting proper care."

"I don't understand this," Tess said. "You know it's not true."

"Still have to investigate." Hood shrugged again, then gestured toward the stall.

Knight Starr lay on his side, his head pillowed on an old blanket. His labored breathing disturbed the quiet of the stables. "What ails him?"

"I'm not sure. Flint Addison was here earlier. He took the usual samples—blood, hair, feces."

"He's not looking good."

"He seemed fine this morning," Gabe said before Tess could lash out at the deputy for stating the obvious. "I don't see how anyone except us could even know he was sick."

"The complaint's not about any one animal," Hood said, shifting his weight from one foot to the other. "I need to look at all of 'em."

"You do know, don't you," Gabe said, letting his exasperation show, "that Tess takes care of neglected horses for Animal Control? Most of the ones she has here are because of someone else's neglect. Not hers."

"I'm aware of that," Hood said stubbornly. "But I still have to take a look."

"Fine." Tess strode from the barn, leaving the deputy and Gabe to follow in her wake. Despite the dire situation, Gabe found the deputy's nervous jitters amusing. Tess had seized control, and she was angry.

They went to a set of pens, where four county horses recuperated from the neglect they'd endured under their former owners. In a nearby pasture, Daisy, Abner, Casper, and three other rescue horses who'd been with Tess for several months grazed along the tree line.

"Access to water. Good grazing. Do you see any neglect, Deputy Hood?" Tess emphasized his title.

"No, ma'am. Can't say that I do."

"I want you to take pictures of these." She pointed to the penned horses. "Compare them with the photos taken when they were brought here."

"That won't be necessary."

"I insist."

"There's no need for you to get all riled up now. We get a complaint, someone has to look into it. You know that, Tess."

"So now it's 'Tess'? I don't think so."

"Don't be mad at me. I told the sheriff this was rubbish. All the horses you've taken in over the years—I know you'd never do anything to hurt one of them."

Tess wrapped her arms around her body and averted her gaze. Her chiseled profile was as unmoving as a statue.

Not in anger, Gabe realized. But hurt.

"What are you going to do now, Deputy?" Gabe asked.

"Got no choice. Sheriff said to write up a formal report."

Tess pivoted toward them and pulled her phone from her back pocket. "You'll please excuse me. I'm going to give Sheriff Foster a call."

"Now don't be bothering the sheriff," Hood said.

Tess rested her hand on Gabe's arm. "Will you please help Hank with his report?" She glared at the deputy. "One of my horses needs me more than he does."

"Of course," Gabe said.

"Thank you." She headed back for the barn, her eyes straight ahead, her posture stiff.

"She's mad," Hood said, "ain't she?"

"More hurt than mad. Can you blame her?"

"I'm only following orders."

"My guess is that the sheriff just lost himself a supporter."

"Maybe two," Hood mumbled.

Gabe answered the deputy's questions and made sure he took the pictures Tess had requested. Just to be on the safe side, Gabe took photos with his own phone too. After the deputy left, he returned to the barn. Tess knelt beside Knight Starr.

"How is he?"

"I don't know." Her voice cracked. "Flint called a few minutes ago. It'll take about a week to get results back, but he said one possibility is that it's poison."

"Poison? But how?"

"I can't imagine."

Gabe entered the stall and knelt beside her. "Could he have gotten into something lethal? I mean a weed of some kind?"

"I don't see how." She rubbed the gelding's neck, then sat back on her heels. "There's something else I need to tell you."

"What is it?"

"I haven't wanted to worry you. Not when you've already got so much on your mind."

"Tess," he said emphatically, "you can tell me anything."

"I think someone was in the house when we were at the Heritage Celebration."

Gabe rocked back on his heels in surprise. "What makes you think that?"

"The back door was unlocked. Of course, I thought maybe we'd just been in such a hurry, we'd forgotten. And it doesn't really matter. It's not like criminals hang around out here."

"But . . . ?"

"There were other things, little things. Taken alone, I wouldn't have thought much of any of them. But taken together?" She shook her head. "The clincher, though, was my computer. I bumped the mouse, and an Excel worksheet appeared on the screen. I know I didn't have it open when I left here that morning."

"What kind of worksheet?"

"Financial information. Personal information." She gasped as if trying to catch her breath. "I know someone was snooping around my office."

"Why didn't you tell me before now?"

"What could you have done? Only worry, and there's no need for that."

"I'm a big boy, Tess. I'm allowed to worry, especially about something like this. About anything that concerns you." He bit his lip, knowing he had to tell her now of his own suspicions. If he'd told her before, she would have told him what she knew. Maybe they should have called the sheriff's office then. "Besides, I think someone was snooping in the barn that day too."

"Why do you say that?"

"It was like you said—nothing definite. The door wasn't latched, even though I hadn't gone out that way and I didn't think you had either. A couple of other things seemed out of place. But I dismissed it as paranoia."

"So you didn't tell me and I didn't tell you."

"Did you tell the sheriff when you called him?"

"I did. He's coming out later, but it's been almost three weeks." She pressed her lips together and focused on the ailing horse. "Maybe we made a mistake. Not taking Tapley's offer, I mean."

Gabe wasn't sure how she had jumped from a possible break-in to Tapley. But with her thoughts consumed by Knight Starr's health, he guessed it made sense.

"How could you ever think of selling to that man?" he asked.

"He made a good offer. Certainly more than market value."

Gabe exhaled heavily, trying to expel the rock settling in his gut. He couldn't imagine someone else running this place. Someone who didn't love it the way Tess did. Someone who didn't know about the Hearth and its secrets.

"Seems to me he'd want someplace closer to the racetrack."

"Maybe land is cheaper here."

"But why does it have to be this land?"

"The stables are already here. We have a good setup. Though I don't really know." She swiped at her cheeks. "Rusty and I dreamed of leaving this place to you. It seemed like you loved it as much as we did. Maybe more. I'm sorry I won't be able to do that."

"It sounds like you've already made up your mind."

"I don't have a choice."

"But you do." He pressed his hand against his chest. "I'm here now. We'll do this together."

"Gabe, you don't want to take on this responsibility. You need to find something that will support you."

"I have. And it's here."

"Gabe . . ."

"Why not? Right now, I'm floundering. But if I could make a go, if we could make a go of this place, why not? If you and Rusty wanted me to have it anyway, why can't I put in the sweat equity to make that possible?"

"It has to earn money. And it's not."

"Then we'll figure out a way to make that happen."

"How?"

"If Tapley can raise racing stock here, then why can't we?"

"He's got the money to get started. We don't."

"Then we do something else. I can talk to Paul, to Jason. See what they think. Please don't sell to Tapley. Give me a chance to try."

"I think you're asking for heartbreak."

"My heart's been broken before. It'll heal."

She slowly shook her head while stroking Knight Starr's neck. "I don't know, Gabe."

"If I have to, I'll ask Dad for a loan. If I put together a strong proposal, he might see it as an investment."

"The last thing I want is for you to be indebted to your father on my account. I don't want you to even ask him."

"It won't kill me to swallow my pride a bit."

"It kills me."

He smiled at how serious she was, and she smiled in return. "None of this solves our other problem," he said. "Who was snooping around here? And why?"

"My guess is Tapley sent someone to be his snoop."

Gabe nodded agreement. "Maybe I should have another talk with him."

"Don't you dare."

He gripped the iron bar of the horse stall with both hands, tightening the muscles in his arms. Tess was right—staying away from Tapley was the wise thing to do—but he had to do something to keep any more snoops from invading their privacy.

"Think I'll clean up and go into town for new locks," he said. "Maybe we should think about a security system."

"Another expense."

"I know."

Tess stroked Knight Starr's neck, then looked at Gabe. "The strange thing is, whoever it was wanted me to know he was here."

"Why do you say that?"

"Because of the way things were out of place. Almost as if they were done on purpose."

He thought back to the day in the barn when he'd felt that things were somehow off without really being able to pinpoint how or why. "That doesn't make sense."

"Think about it. Nothing was taken, at least not that I can tell. But the door was unlocked, the worksheet left open. It wasn't like someone had left in a hurry."

"Tapley would have had to know we were at Misty Willow."

"If it was Tapley. We can't be 100 percent sure."

"I'm sure."

Tess rose, stretched the kinks from her back, and continued as if she were thinking out loud. "If we'd passed a strange vehicle on the way home, I would have remembered. It's almost second nature out here."

A skill Gabe had picked up quickly. He might not know the names of all the people who lived around here, but he knew what they drove.

"Though I haven't been very observant lately," Tess said. "How long did you say Amy was living here before I knew she was at the cottage? And that's just across the road."

"I have a feeling Amy wasn't getting out much. I still don't think she is."

"Then why don't you see if she wants to drive into town with you? You could even get a hamburger from the Dixie. I don't think you've been there since you've been back. And as skinny as Amy is, she could use one."

The thought of a Dixie Deluxe burger made Gabe's mouth water, but he didn't know if he should take the time. The locks needed to be changed and pronto.

As if she read his mind, Tess said, "Whoever was here may have been brazen enough to leave evidence of his snooping, but he's too cowardly to stop by when anyone is home."

"You can't be sure of that."

"He's not been back since."

"That we know of."

"Don't be a smart aleck." She patted his cheek. "Go to town if you're going. But call Amy first."

"Why do I feel like a teenager all of a sudden?"

"Do you?" Her laugh was shaky, but Gabe was glad to hear it. "Good. You carry the weight of the world around on your shoulders, and it's too big a burden for anyone."

"Why don't you go into town with me?"

"I can't leave Knight Starr."

"I'm not leaving you here alone."

"I won't be alone."

"Oh?"

"If you must know, Flint is coming back out after the clinic closes."

"You weren't going to tell me this?"

"I didn't want you to get the wrong idea. Just like you're doing now."

"He is a widower, isn't he? Seems the two of you spent a lot of time together at the Heritage Celebration." He leaned over and kissed her cheek. "For what it's worth, you have my blessing."

She blushed beneath her olive skin, and for a moment he saw the beauty of the young woman she'd once been. No wonder Rusty had been so taken with her. "It's nothing serious. He's just a good friend. A dear friend."

"That's the best place to start, isn't it?"

It was where he wanted to start. With Amy. Maybe he would give her a call, though he doubted she'd say yes. This late in the day, she was either out already, had plans to go out, or planned to stay home.

"You'll have to let me take your truck."

"You know where to find the keys."

He walked toward the house and pulled his phone from his pocket. Gathering his courage, he dialed Amy's number.

Please say yes.

- 30 -

*A*my totally disregarded her own rule about accepting a last-minute date and hurriedly changed into a sleeveless crocheted top over tailored jeans and added turquoise and silver accessories. She spent a few more minutes touching up her makeup and curling the ends of her hair. Only moments after she closed her gate, Gabe stopped in front of the drive, his elbow resting on the open window frame.

"Need a ride, purty lady?" he asked in an exaggerated drawl.

"Depends on where you're going," she said coyly.

"With you?" He flipped on his flashers, then stepped out of the truck. "Anywhere your little heart desires."

"Be careful with your promises. I might hold you to that someday."

"Don't think I wouldn't let you."

What about Ellen?

Amy dismissed the thought as soon as it appeared. At least for the next few hours, she had Gabe to herself.

He escorted her around the truck to the passenger door. She paused before climbing in to revel in his closeness. The ends of his hair were slightly damp, which meant he'd taken a quick shower

237

since he called to invite her to town. She didn't mind that he hadn't shaved. The scruffiness looked good on him, and his elusive cologne invited her even closer.

Gabe was such a man, and his masculinity electrified her.

She imagined Logan with a five-o'clock shadow, but it didn't work for him. Too much of an affectation.

A car appeared behind them, and Gabe waved them on by.

"Any idea who that was?" he asked.

"None at all. Why?"

"Hadn't seen that car before, that's all. Probably somebody just passing through." His lips smiled but not his eyes as he shut her door.

She tracked him as he rounded the front of the truck, his gait sure and confident but also alert and wary. Even out here where nothing ever happened.

Unless something had happened.

"What's got your rope in a tangle?" she asked after he settled into his seat and engaged the clutch.

His eyes relaxed as he smiled his lazy smile. "Tess thinks someone was in the house while we were at the Heritage Celebration."

"Someone broke in? But why?"

"No idea. Nothing was taken, but whoever it was got on her computer. I think they were in the stables too."

"What could they want in the stables?"

"Again, no idea. But that's why I'm going to town. To get new locks for the house."

"You know how to change locks?"

"I think I can figure it out."

"I wonder if I need new locks too. They probably haven't been changed since the cottage was built."

"I'll change them for you if you want."

Such a simple offer, and yet it warmed her all the way through. Logan would have offered to call a locksmith, and she would have appreciated his thoughtfulness. That's what Brett would have done too.

But now—this was something new, and she liked it. Gabe, competent and capable, could do what needed to be done himself. He probably had no idea how appealing that quality was to a woman. She hadn't known herself until just that moment.

"I'd like that," she said. "Thank you."

They drove to Grange Station first. Once they got inside, Amy roamed the aisles in awe. Fifty-pound bags of feed were stacked on shelves and pallets. Animal troughs, fencing materials, and rows of tools and strange metal doodads lined the outer walls. Every aisle seemed to hold something that fascinated her.

"This is amazing," she said. "I've never seen anything like it."

"Then you've been hanging with the wrong crowd." Gabe chuckled and steered her toward the locks. He picked out what they needed, then Amy insisted on exploring the aisles she had missed.

"Do you know what all this stuff is for?" she asked.

"You have led a sheltered life, haven't you?"

"I never would have said so. But I do find all this strangely fascinating. I have no idea why." She gasped and reached for a headlamp. "Oh, look at this. It's got a green light and a red light and a regular light. Do you think Jonah would like it?"

"It'd be fun for exploring after dark."

"I'm going to get it for him. Though now I need to find something for Shelby's girls. I'm trying to be a thoughtful 'aunt,'" she said, making air quotes. Brett had once told her she was responsible for how AJ's stepdaughters would remember her. At the time, she closed her ears to his lecturing. But during her time in the clinic, she had realized she wanted their memories of her to be good ones.

"I'm not sure you'll find anything for a little girl in here."

"I don't know. They like outdoorsy things." She wandered along another aisle and found the clothing section. One rack displayed pink-and-white-checked bibbed overalls in a variety of children's sizes.

"These are adorable." She grabbed one hanger then another, checking sizes and lengths. After making selections, she discovered another display of assorted caps with the Grange Station logo and selected a brown one and two pink ones. On an impulse, she grabbed a larger pink one for herself.

"Look," she said, placing the cap on her head. "The girls and I can be triplets."

Gabe tugged at the cap's bill. "Did you buy yourself bibbed overalls too?"

"I don't think I'm ready for those. At least not yet."

"Now I know what to get you for Christmas."

"Christmas is months away. But if you're thinking what I think you're thinking, I'm happy to wait."

"What do you think I'm thinking?"

"That maybe you'll still be at Whisper Lane and I'll still be at the cottage and maybe we can exchange presents."

"I hate to disappoint you, but I wasn't thinking that at all."

She smiled impishly and whispered in his ear. "But now you are."

He eased into another smile. "You got that right."

As the clerk scanned the gifts for the children, Amy tried to ignore the growing dollar amount.

"Sure adds up fast, doesn't it?" she said with as much flippancy as she could. She had to learn to economize but not at the expense of those three little kids.

"Too fast," Gabe agreed.

As he paid for the locks, Amy checked her phone and saw a couple missed calls from Logan. He probably wanted to make plans for the weekend, but she preferred to keep her options open. If Gabe asked her out, she wanted to be free to say yes.

They left the store, then opted to eat at the nearby Italian café instead of the Dixie Diner.

"I've never been here," Gabe said as the hostess led them to a table. Seemingly by instinct, he arranged their seating so he didn't have his back to the door. "Have you?"

"It's been awhile," Amy said as she placed her napkin in her lap. "Brett, AJ, and I came here—it's been over a year ago now—after meeting with Gran's lawyer about her will."

"If this brings up bad memories for you, we can go somewhere else."

"That's not necessary. The three of us didn't spend much time together back then, so it was kind of nice. We talked about happier childhood days."

Which wasn't a topic she wanted to get into with him—not when her lie still hung between them.

"But then something happened. I laughed about it back then, but actually it wasn't funny."

"I'm all ears."

"I'm not sure I should tell you. It doesn't put me in the most flattering light."

"There's nothing you can't tell me."

She wasn't sure about that. She hoped he never found out about her disastrous fling with the state senator or her lack of ethics in dealing with a few clients. Okay, several clients. This story she might as well tell him.

"I won't go into all the details, but last summer Shelby didn't like AJ very much because he'd let her beloved house fall into ruin. Brett was courting her, but he neglected to tell her that he and AJ are cousins."

"Wait a minute. Brett was courting Shelby?"

"Not because he liked her. Though he ended up liking her." She heaved a giant sigh. "It's all part of the details I don't want to get into."

"Maybe we can talk about those another time."

"Maybe. Anyway, Shelby didn't know Brett and AJ were cousins.

We're here"—she looked around the dining area—"sitting at that table, all done eating when Shelby and her girls come in. Elizabeth and Tabby race to AJ, and that's when it all came out."

"What did?"

Amy hesitated, not sure how to end the story. For the first time, she saw herself as Shelby must have seen her—petty, spiteful, even vindictive. But she didn't want to be those things anymore, and she didn't want Gabe to see her that way either. She should never have started this stupid story.

"We were unkind to Shelby, Brett and me," she finally said. "Especially me."

Gabe reached for her hand, and she entwined her fingers with his. "I've seen you and Shelby together," he said. "I don't think she's holding a grudge. And she must not be mad at AJ anymore or she wouldn't have married him."

"You're right. But I'm still sorry for . . . for being who I am."

"You mean for who you were."

"I'm not so sure."

"The Amy who sat over there," he said, pointing to the table she had indicated, "she's not the same person who's sitting across from me now."

"How can you know?"

"Because that Amy wouldn't have bought presents for Elizabeth and Tabby. Maybe not even for Jonah." He paused a moment. "I'm not sure that Amy would be here with me right now."

"Sometimes it seems everyone else can change. Brett certainly has. But I'm not sure I can."

"I believe you have."

"You don't really know me, Gabe."

"Maybe I know you better than you think."

Only the girl you remember. Not the nasty person I became.

Their food arrived, saving Amy from having to respond.

"Do you mind if I say grace?" Gabe asked.

"No," Amy said slowly.

His prayer was simple, brief, but heartfelt. She didn't remember him as being religious when they were teens.

"Have you always prayed?" she asked.

"I didn't used to. But you know what they say. 'There are no atheists in foxholes.' There aren't any in prison either. What about you?"

"Gran tried to instill some holiness in us. It didn't stick, though AJ eventually went back to church with her." She speared pasta with her fork. "That was after the mess with Meghan."

"After a mess is a good time to get reacquainted with God."

"Do you think God minds?"

"I think he's always waiting for us. Arms outstretched and watching for us to come home."

"Like in the story of the prodigal son?"

"Exactly."

"You don't blame God for what happened to your cousin? For all those years you spent in prison?"

"I ask why."

"How does he answer?"

"I'll let you know when he does."

"What if he never does?"

Gabe took a moment to answer. "You know who Job is?"

Amy nodded.

"He didn't know why, either, but he never wavered in his trust. I've wavered, but I have to keep coming back to God having a purpose for my life. I may not be able to see it. I may never see it this side of heaven. But I know it's there as surely as I know anything."

"What purpose could there be in going to prison for something you didn't do?"

"It's where I found God again. If that's what it took to get my life straightened out, then I'm glad for it."

"You're thankful for prison?"

His slow smile slid across his face. "Because I went to prison, I came to stay with Aunt Tess. And because I'm staying with Tess, I live across the road from the most beautiful woman I've ever known. Hard not to be thankful for that."

An uncharacteristic warmth flushed Amy's cheeks. Men's compliments and flatteries rarely fazed her. But Gabe was different. Perhaps it was because she sensed he didn't hand out compliments with any more looseness than he did his kisses. And he certainly wasn't being free with those.

Gabe was a man who meant what he said, and she could believe she was beautiful to him in a different way than she was to anyone else.

Other men were taken by her height, her sweeping blonde hair, the clear blue of her eyes, and her model-like cheekbones.

Gabe saw more than her outer appearance. Where she knew there was ugliness, he still saw beauty.

How much she regretted lying to him that first day. But maybe it wasn't too late to make up for that.

He had once asked her to ride to the Hearth with him. That was the perfect place to tell him the truth and try to explain why she'd lied. If she could figure that out for herself.

Only one problem with that plan. She hadn't been on a horse in ages.

Maybe she could persuade Tess to give her refresher lessons while Gabe was in the fields. When she was comfortable riding again, she'd plan a special date for the two of them. A date that would take them back to that long-ago summer when an innocent kiss joined their hearts in a love that might still have a chance to grow.

She realized now she had compared every man she ever dated to an ideal set by Gabe. None of them could attain it.

Perhaps Gabe had done the same thing. Despite the life she'd led for the past several years, he still saw the girl she'd been before her parents' tragic deaths had torn her world completely apart. Having lost his own mother, he understood her grief as few others did.

He'd tried to comfort her. But the pain had been too much for her then. All the changes in her life too excruciating.

She'd make it up to him though. She wouldn't tell him she remembered. She'd show him.

Delighted by the plan, she made up her mind to talk to Tess that very evening. If she could get her alone. And then she would ride again.

With an adult's sudden perception, she realized this was what her father would have wanted. How disappointed he would be, how sad for her, to know she'd given up riding because it made her miss him too much.

But now, because of Gabe, she'd find the courage she needed.

Someday soon, she and Gabe would ride to the Hearth.

~

Logan left the county commissioner's office, then paused on the sidewalk to see if Amy had returned his calls. She hadn't.

He frowned in frustration and debated whether to try again. Instead of inviting her to dinner at one of the local restaurants, like he had originally planned, he could get carryout. A casual but intimate dinner at her cottage might lead to an invitation to stay over. No reason to pass up an opportunity like that. He started to tap her name, then hesitated.

Why give her a chance to say no?

"Why indeed?" he murmured. He'd surprise her. If she wasn't home, no harm done. But if she was . . . this could be a pivotal evening for both of them.

Whistling softly to himself, he opened an app for nearby restaurants and found an Italian place around the corner. As good a choice as any, he decided as he walked along the block.

As he turned the corner, he suddenly stopped and stepped into a nearby doorway. Amy, sophisticated and beautiful in jeans and turquoise heels, stood outside the restaurant. Kendall joined her carrying a to-go bag. They laughed about something, then Amy took Kendall's arm. He bent his head close to hers and she leaned into his shoulder.

A smoldering fire burned in Logan's gut as the couple strolled along the sidewalk away from him, pausing occasionally to window-shop. As they stopped beside a Dodge Ram pickup, Kendall placed the bag inside, then turned to assist Amy. Before she climbed in, her eyes focused on his.

At this distance, Logan couldn't be sure of Amy's expression. But given Kendall's relaxed stance and the smile that cut across his bristled face, Logan guessed her look was one few men could resist.

The fire in his gut erupted, and he rushed to his car. Once inside, he took a few deep breaths to compose himself, then gave in to anger again as the pickup turned on to the street and headed away from him. Without thinking, he followed it out of town. He expected Kendall to turn in to Amy's drive, but instead the Dodge passed the hedges and turned in at the Whispering Lane driveway.

Logan drove farther up the road, made a U-turn, and parked on the shoulder. Not that it did him any good. He couldn't see inside the house, couldn't listen in on their conversation. He couldn't do anything but fume while Kendall—the good-for-nothing felon—romanced *his* girl.

Kendall needed to go.

Logan got Dylan on the phone as he drove to Columbus. "It's time to send another offer to Tess Marshall," he said.

"How much higher?"

"Not higher. Lower."

"Where's the sense in that?"

"Trust me. She knows your first offer was generous. If this one's lower, she'll get nervous. Afraid that if she doesn't sell now, she'll regret it later."

"You really think that will work?" Dylan asked.

"I do." Especially once Logan implemented his second plan. Tess's financial worries were about to take a backseat to much more pressing concerns. And she'd want all the money she could get to help her nephew.

~

While Gabe and Flint changed the locks on the front door, Tess retrieved her china dessert plates from the dining room hutch and set them on the table. "This was so sweet of you, Amy," she said. "Bringing us this lovely dessert platter."

"I hoped it would cheer you up. Gabe told me about Knight Starr. Is he doing any better?"

Tess eyed her sharply, but there didn't seem to be any deceit in Amy's words or her tone.

"Not really," Tess said. "Flint and I will go back to the barn after we eat."

She wanted to ask about Amy's eating issues, but she didn't like to pry. At least now she knew to pray for her health. And for more than that. Gabe seemed so taken with her, and as much as he denied wanting a relationship with Amy, this young woman held his heart. She always had.

If he was ever going to be happy with Ellen or anyone else, he needed to get Amy out of his system. The more time he spent with her, the sooner he would see she wasn't the girl he dreamed of.

I'm sorry, Father, she prayed. Her thoughts weren't kind, but she didn't wish Amy ill. In fact, she hoped Amy could find the spiritual peace Brett and AJ had found.

But she wasn't right for Gabe, and his welfare was foremost in Tess's mind.

"Before they come in," Amy said, "could I ask you something?"

"Sure. What is it?"

Amy gripped the back of one of the dining room chairs as if her life depended on it.

"Is something wrong?" Tess asked.

"Not really." Amy's face paled, then the words spilled out. "I was wondering if you'd give me riding lessons. I'd pay you, of course."

"You want to take riding lessons? After all this time?"

"Gabe has asked me to ride with him, but it's been a long time since I've been on a horse." The appeal for help in Amy's eyes caught Tess off guard.

"I don't want to make a fool of myself," Amy continued. "As much as I hate to admit it, I'm scared."

"Why don't you ask Gabe to—"

"I don't want him to know. Maybe," she said, her expression now guarded but hopeful, "I could come over while he's out plowing."

Tess hid a smile. "I think they're harvesting."

"Whatever. Will you, would you mind, helping me feel comfortable in a saddle again?"

Tess laid a cloth napkin at each place on the table while she thought about Amy's request. This wasn't how she wanted God to answer her prayer. Amy and Gabe riding together would draw them closer. But how could she refuse Amy's pleading hopefulness?

"On one condition," she said.

"Name it."

"Tell me why you quit."

Amy's face clouded over. "It's hard to explain."

"Try," Tess said gently.

Amy slipped a strand of hair between her fingers, a habit Tess remembered from when she was a girl. Strange how one gesture transformed Tess's impression of Amy from a self-centered snob to the young teen who only wanted a horse of her own. Who now wanted to ride again.

"After Dad died," Amy said, "I just couldn't be here anymore. When I was little, Mom wanted me to take piano and singing lessons. But I wanted to ride more than anything else. Dad insisted on letting me choose, and this became our thing. Without him . . . it just hurt too much."

"But now you think you're ready?"

"Earlier tonight, I realized Dad wouldn't have wanted me to give up something I loved because he couldn't be with me. And I very much want to ride with Gabe." A slight dimple appeared in her cheek as she smiled. "I have a surprise for him."

"What kind of surprise?"

Amy averted her gaze, and her cheeks turned slightly pink. Apparently she wasn't going to tell Tess everything she had planned.

"Nothing indecent, I hope."

"No." She appeared appropriately shocked. "No, nothing like that."

"Okay, then. Why don't you come over in the morning and we'll get started?"

Amy rounded the table and embraced Tess. Surprised by the spontaneous hug, she stiffened a moment, then relaxed and patted Amy's shoulder.

"Thank you," Amy said. "I am so excited, I'll never sleep tonight."

Masculine voices sounded in the hall and Amy placed her finger against her lips. "Our secret."

"I won't tell," Tess said with a smile. She wouldn't revise her opinion about Amy based on one conversation, but she hoped she was fair-minded enough to give the girl a chance.

As long as Gabe didn't get hurt.

Because if he did, Amy would have to answer to Tess.

– 31 –

About midmorning on Monday, FedEx delivered an envelope to Tess from Dylan Tapley. She carried it, unopened, to the front porch of the house. Gabe was working with Jason today, putting in long hours harvesting wheat. She doubted Gabe would drop by, but one could never be certain. She didn't want to be surprised if he decided to come by the house while on a quick trip to Bryant's, a small market halfway between here and town, for drinks and snacks. Despite what she had said about him having a right to know everything having to do with the stables, she hadn't been totally forthcoming with the shameful financial losses she'd suffered over the past few years.

Pride had taken her down that road, and in recent months she had swallowed huge helpings of the nasty dish.

Money hadn't been Tess's motive for agreeing to Amy's request for riding lessons, but the extra cash would be a godsend. Jonah and the Sullivan girls had loved riding on Abner the evening Gabe took the stagecoach over to Misty Willow. Maybe Amy would bring them for lessons too. This could be just the boost Tess needed to revive the stables.

She closed her eyes and allowed the indulgence of her daydream to refresh her spirit. If Jonah did well at his lessons, Brett could easily be persuaded to buy his son a horse, which he would naturally board at Whisper Lane. AJ and Shelby might do the same for their girls. Two boarders would lead to more, and Tess's days would be filled once again with the work she loved most.

A honk stirred her from her dreams, and she automatically waved at the neighbor driving by.

Lost in her hopes, she'd almost forgotten about the envelope. Despite Tapley's behavior during his earlier visit, she guessed he was renewing his offer. Letting go of her pie-in-the-sky daydreams, she turned her thoughts to the present. Hopefully Tapley's new offer would be a generous one.

As hard as it would be to sell this place, she didn't have a choice. Not really. Tapley had already offered more than the appraised value, so she was certain no one else would match his price. She might not like the man, but that didn't mean she couldn't take his money.

Perhaps she could find a small house in town. Gabe could live with her while he figured out what to do with his life. It wouldn't be what either of them wanted, but it would be a fresh start for them both.

She slid the documents from the envelope and skimmed the first page. Tapley still wanted the stables—she'd been right about that—but his offer was less than it had been before. Starting at the beginning, she read the page more carefully while her throat tightened in an odd sensation of embarrassment and hopelessness.

By the time she reached the end, her heart was palpitating. How could this be? Why would he think she'd say yes to this new offer when she'd refused a higher one?

"He's punishing me," she said aloud. Most likely for telling him no, since he was obviously a man who didn't like to be thwarted. Or perhaps it was because Gabe dropped the cigar stub in his driver's lap. He shouldn't have done it, though they'd both laughed about it later that evening. Still, it had been an insult. And one thing you could say about a man who didn't like to be thwarted—he despised being insulted.

Whatever the reason, now Tess would pay the price, losing out on tens of thousands of dollars because she'd allowed sentiment and pipe dreams to cloud her judgment. As much as she hated the idea, she knew what she had to do. The time had come to let go of the past and figure out a new future.

She'd counter with the amount Tapley had originally proposed, then see how the negotiations played out. But she wouldn't tell Gabe until the price was settled. Then it would be too late for him to talk her out of the deal.

This was the best thing for both of them. He might not see it now, but in time he would. Her mind made up, she returned the documents to the envelope and locked it in her safe. As she set the dial to one, her hand froze. She gazed from the safe to her computer.

If Tapley was behind the break-in, then the information on her Excel worksheet had told him all he needed to know about her financial situation. How desperate she was despite her bravado. He only needed to wait. She'd either sell to him or lose everything in foreclosure.

She slid to the floor and laid her head upon her knees. Her heart pounded an unsteady rhythm, and for a moment she couldn't catch her breath.

"I failed you, Rusty," she murmured. She yearned to feel her husband's work-hardened arms around her, to hear him whisper words of comfort. "I failed us all."

~

Amy stroked Daisy's long nose and held out a handful of treats. Now that she was here, the long-forsaken scents of horse, leather, and saddle soap returned her to summer days of riding around this paddock on Marigold, Daisy's mother. Perhaps it would be like riding a bike. They said you never forgot how. Still, Amy was nervous as she stood beside the buckskin mare.

"I remember your mama," she murmured as Daisy snuffed her, testing her scent and confidence. "We used to ride all over this farm. You and I can do the same in a week or two. If we get along okay. And I think we will."

Daisy nodded as if she agreed, and Amy laughed.

Tess went over a few basics, and Amy felt her confidence soar. She could do this. The saddle creaked as she mounted, then pressed the balls of her feet against the stirrups. Her thigh muscles ached slightly as she touched Daisy's side with her heels. The mare quickly settled into a steady walk around the training arena.

"Heels down, keep them back," Tess called. "Now relax your shoulders. Give through your elbows."

Amy paid close attention to Tess's infrequent instructions as she maneuvered Daisy around various obstacles and over low jumps.

"I'm not sure why you thought you needed lessons," Tess said when Amy dismounted. "You're still a natural. How did it feel?"

"Like . . ." Amy paused a moment. "Coming home."

"I understand that." Tess averted her gaze, staring out over the land. "This isn't much of a place, really. But I sure do love it."

The tone in her voice caught Amy's attention. Maybe she should have said something before now. What would Tess, or even worse, what would Gabe say, if they knew she knew someone wanted to buy this property?

But what good would it have done? Dylan needed to find other land, that was all there was to it. Tess's acreage wasn't enough for what he had planned, and nothing he could do would persuade AJ to sell the cottage property. She just needed to come up with a way for Logan to direct Dylan into a different project. Maybe Brett would have a couple of ideas.

"Do you think Gabe will stay?" Amy asked, surprising herself with the question. It was one she often pondered, but she hadn't meant to ask.

"I'd like him to. And he knows he can as long as . . ." Tess set her jaw and avoided Amy's gaze.

"As long as what?"

"Nothing to bother you with."

Amy's senses went on full alert. Dylan must have already approached Tess. But surely she wasn't considering his offer. "Tess, please, tell me what's wrong. I might be able to help."

"I don't think so."

"You don't think much of me. Do you?"

Tess pressed her lips together but didn't answer. Amy inwardly sighed. She knew better than to ask a question when she didn't want to know the answer. But Tess's feelings about her weren't an issue she wanted to pursue right now. It was more important to find out if Dylan had contacted her. Puzzle pieces clicked in her brain, presenting a despicable but plausible picture.

"Gabe told me about the break-in. Do you have any idea who it was?"

"No. Maybe. I don't know." Tess scratched Daisy's ear, then rubbed her neck. "Let's head back to the barn. You remember the rule. You ride, you groom. Besides, I need to check on Knight Starr."

"How is he?"

"Back on his feet, thanks to the transfusion Flint gave him over the weekend."

"I'm glad."

"Me too."

Amy led Daisy across the lane toward the stable entry. She meant what she said about Knight Starr, but Tess couldn't distract Amy by talking about the horse. Obviously Tess wasn't going to voluntarily admit to anything. Amy might as well take the direct approach.

"May I ask you something?"

"Of course. But I reserve the right not to answer."

"Fair enough." Amy halted by the gate and faced Tess. "Do you know a man named Dylan Tapley?"

Tess's surprised reaction gave Amy the answer she needed.

"He's offered to buy Whisper Lane. Hasn't he?"

"Did Gabe tell you?"

"No. Logan Cassidy did."

"That young man you were with at the bridge?"

Amy nodded. "Please tell me you aren't going to sell this place to Dylan. He'll only ruin it."

"It's not that I want to." Tess leaned an arm against the top rail of the fence. "But unless I can figure out a way for it to make money again, I don't have a choice."

"But you can't sell to Dylan. He'll destroy everything that's important to you." *And to me.*

"How do you know Tapley?"

"He was my client once." Amy took a deep breath. "He considered buying Misty Willow."

"Is that when you sued AJ?"

"Yes." Amy sighed in frustration. That lawsuit was like an albatross around her neck, and everyone seemed to know about it. "If I could take that back . . ."

Tess gave her a sympathetic look. "I'd say in that case everything worked out for the best."

"At least AJ and Shelby are happy," Amy spouted, then held her gaze steady. Tess wasn't going to distract her with any rabbit trails. "Tell me about your conversations with Dylan."

"He made an offer," Tess said. "I was seriously considering it but then Gabe contacted me about coming here after his release. So I didn't give Tapley an answer until he showed up a few weeks ago. Gabe didn't like his attitude and he sent him away."

"I wish I could have seen that."

"Tell you the truth, it was funny."

"I'm so glad you're not selling," Amy said as relief eased the tension that had been building inside her. "Without Whisper Lane, there's no need for him to go after the cottage."

"Wait a minute," Tess said. "Tapley wants the cottage? Why?"

"Not just the cottage. He wants all the land Gran owned plus any of the Misty Willow acres that aren't protected by the foundation."

"How do you know this?"

"Logan told me the entire plan. It's ridiculous, of course, but Dylan's stubborn. And vindictive."

"Maybe you should know . . ." Tess hesitated, took a deep breath, then continued. "He sent me a second offer. I received it this morning."

"But you won't take it." At Tess's hesitation, Amy widened her eyes. "You're not going to, are you?"

"I need to think about my future, Amy. And Gabe needs to think about his. Neither of us have the capital to turn things around here." Tess flung out her arm, encompassing the entire property in one large swoop. "But Tapley does. He'll make it a showcase. A horse in every stall, whitewashed fences, a seeded pasture. He's even talking about building a small grandstand near the paddock. Whisper Lane will become the stables Rusty and I always dreamed of, even if we're not the ones making the dream come true."

Amy shook her head in exasperation. This could not be happening. "I'm surprised he's keeping the stables. Though I guess it could be a draw for some of the residents."

"What residents?"

"The residents who build here."

"No one's going to build here," Tess said. "Tapley wants a working horse farm. To raise and train racing stock."

"No he doesn't."

"I saw the plans."

More puzzle pieces attached to the picture in Amy's head. It was brilliant, really.

"Dylan wants to build a mixed-use development here," she said. "Houses, condos, retail shops, and restaurants. He knew you wouldn't sell to a developer—"

"Of course I wouldn't."

"So he lied to you. Once all the documents are signed and the deal is done, he'll revert to his original plan. Believe me, he has absolutely no interest in training horses."

"But the county would never let him build something like that here. This land is zoned agriculture. It's protected."

"Until someone gets a variance. He's got the clout and the money to do that. In fact, I'm pretty sure he already has at least one county commissioner on his payroll."

"Who?"

"I don't know. At least not for certain." Amy had made a point of chatting with each of the commissioners at the Heritage Celebration and was researching their voting records and campaign donations. But she didn't want to make premature accusations.

"That seems farfetched. Even for Tapley."

"Why would I lie to you, Tess? He'll get Whisper Lane, and then he'll go after AJ's property."

"Are you sure this Logan knows what he's talking about?"

"I'm positive."

Tess scrutinized her expression, then nodded knowingly. "Of course, you do. You're dating him."

"We've gone out a few times."

"What about Gabe?"

Amy squirmed under Tess's harsh gaze. But she could hardly tell Tess she was in love with her nephew.

"And here I thought . . ." Tess made a disgusted sound. "Does Gabe know you're seeing someone else?"

"Gabe is seeing someone else too."

"No," Tess said firmly, "he's not. He loves you." She clammed up, apparently horrified by what she'd just said.

"Then who is Ellen?"

"Ellen is his cousin's widow."

Then why didn't he say so? Why didn't I ask?

Holding on to her exasperation, Amy fired up a retort. "He seems to be fond of her."

"He is. But not like that."

Not trusting herself to speak, Amy grasped Daisy's halter and led her to the stables. Tess hadn't meant to say that Gabe loved her, but that didn't mean it wasn't true. But if he did, why hadn't he told her?

The answer was plain—he might love her, but he didn't like the person she'd become. His love was based on a childhood crush. That was all. Perhaps she should forget her crazy plan.

As she brushed Daisy's soft beige coat, she imagined how it would be. The two of them riding back to the Hearth as they had as teens. Pulling out the loose stone and removing the tin box they'd hidden there. Opening it up to reveal its secret contents.

She'd give him the arrowhead, slipping it into his hand as he had slipped it into hers at her parents' memorial service. He'd be surprised to find it in their keepsake box. She'd tell him how she'd come back here before leaving for college. That the Hearth was the safest place she knew to keep the most precious thing she owned.

The arrowhead he had given to her on the saddest day of her life. A strange gift, but nothing could have been more meaningful.

She'd ask him if he remembered when they found it. And of course he would say yes. And then, there at the Hearth, he would kiss her like he had all those years ago.

She slightly smiled. No, not quite like that. They were adults now, and the kiss would be more than the tentative touch of two adolescents.

How she cherished the memory of that first kiss.

How she longed for the second.

If he kissed her again, she'd never kiss anyone else as long as she lived. First and last—that would be their story.

If he truly loved her.

And if he would have her again.

～

Tess stood by the fence, reluctant to follow Amy into the barn. All the things Amy had said about Tapley's plans—they couldn't be true. Could they?

The misgivings Tess felt toward the man made it easier to trust Amy than to trust him. Especially since she hadn't been able to shake her suspicion that he'd been behind the break-in.

Besides, Amy was obviously concerned that Tapley intended to acquire more than just Whisper Lane. Though he must be exceedingly deluded if he expected to snatch the Sullivan property from under AJ's nose. The Somers/Sullivan clan weren't divided anymore—not like they were last year over the Misty Willow homestead. Tess had no doubt that AJ, Amy, and Brett would pool their resources to protect the land that had belonged to their grandmother from Tapley's development designs.

She seldom yearned for riches, but in this moment, she wished money didn't have to be a factor in her decisions. Leaning against the fence, she prayed for guidance. At least she intended to. Instead, her thoughts mingled with her prayer, centering on Gabe then Amy and finally her own need to trust in God's protection from the unscrupulous and deceitful.

A year ago, that was Amy.

But that was not who Amy was now.

The young woman had been stunned speechless when Tess blurted out that Gabe loved her. Had she really believed he was in love with Ellen?

If only.

Tess wishing it were so would never make it happen. Perhaps

if Amy wasn't living across the road, if she and Gabe hadn't become reacquainted, he could have found happiness with Ellen. But it would have been a second-place kind of happiness. Both of them—all three of them—deserved better.

Feeling a heavenly push, Tess entered the stables and found Amy in the stall, brushing Daisy's buckskin coat.

Tess leaned over the half-door.

"Gabe and Ellen went to high school together. They dated a few times, but she fell in love with Randy."

"Poor Gabe," Amy said dismissively.

Tess ignored Amy's childish tone. "He moped around for a while, but it wasn't all that serious. She didn't break his heart."

"Why are you telling me this?"

"I shouldn't have said what I did out there. But since I did, and since you asked about Ellen, I thought you should know."

Amy finally faced her, as if testing Tess's expression for honesty. "Thank you."

"I want to thank you too. For telling me about Tapley's plans."

"What are you going to do?"

"I won't sell to him." She'd have to do something, but it wouldn't be that.

"Will you sell to someone else?"

Tess hesitated, wishing God would tell her what to do. Whom to trust. But she knew that wasn't the way things usually worked. God speaks through our circumstances, Oswald Chambers had said. Something like that, anyway. What was God saying to her?

Through Gabe, God had given her hope. Through Amy, God had given her a warning.

But a definitive answer still lay outside her grasp.

"I don't know what I'll do. Except wait for God to guide me."

Amy gave her a strange look, which changed to determination. "While you're waiting, I'm going to pay a little visit to Mr. Dylan Tapley."

"Why?"

"I want him to know that I know what he's up to." Anger fueled her words. "And that he can take his development project somewhere else. No one around here wants that kind of traffic, that kind of disruption to our lives."

Tess stood back, amazed at the outburst, then laughed. "*Our* lives?"

"That's right," Amy said, obviously annoyed at Tess's laughter.

"Amy. Have you truly become one of us?"

She paused, grew thoughtful, then smiled. "I suppose I have. Though I never realized I wanted to be until now."

"I'm not so sure of that," Tess said. "I remember times when your dad had to bribe you to get you to leave here. Though he had a difficult time coming up with something you wanted more than being on Marigold."

"Whatever happened to her?"

"I sold her a couple of years ago. It wasn't easy, but she went to a good home. The family had a teenage girl who adored her. That girl reminded me a lot of you."

Amy slowly brushed Daisy's mane, and for a moment, Tess was in the past. A day much like today when Amy, a much younger Amy, brushed Marigold's mane. Daisy was the spitting image of her mother, and though Amy had matured, her long blonde hair still flowed past her shoulders. Tess blinked, and the younger Amy disappeared.

"I wanted my dad to buy Marigold for my birthday. I thought he was going to, but . . ." She sighed heavily.

"I didn't know," Tess said. "Though I suppose I should have suspected." All these years later, there was no need to tell her that Tess wouldn't have sold Marigold back then.

"Rusty didn't tell you?"

Tess arched her eyebrows. "Did Rusty know?"

"He and my dad talked a long time the last time we were here.

Before the crash." Amy gave a small laugh. "I remember sitting on the paddock fence waiting and waiting. It was so hard to be patient, but I didn't want to interrupt. They were walking beneath the apple trees at the side of the house. All the way home, I wanted to ask Dad what they had talked about, but I didn't want him to suspect I already knew."

Tess's heart jarred inside her chest as the memory came rushing back. She remembered it clearly now, the conversation Rusty had with Mr. Somers, the last conversation they'd had before the plane crash.

It had nothing to do with Marigold.

– 32 –

*A*my waved as Tess stopped her truck in front of the cottage gate the next day. Ignoring her aching back and leg muscles, she hurried around to the passenger's side, set her picnic basket on the floor, and climbed in.

"This is so much fun," she said as she fastened her seat belt. "Thanks for asking me."

"Glad you could come along," Tess said. "But I didn't mean for you to bring anything. I only thought you'd like to see what goes on in the fields."

"I do." Amy wanted to bounce up and down on the seat, she felt so giddy. The feeling was strange, especially given its reason. Even a month ago, she couldn't have cared less what the farmers were doing, let alone want to have lunch with them. Strange things were happening to her, as if she were being drawn into a warm and comfortable place and away from darkness.

"What did you bring?" Tess asked.

"I know what you're thinking," Amy said mischievously. "And of course you're right. I don't often cook. But I promised Gabe I'd make him a lemon meringue pie. Gran's recipe. So that's what I made."

Tess looked impressed. "I remember Joyanna's pie. It took all kinds of ribbons at the county fair. Are you going to enter this year?"

The question took Amy by surprise. "I never thought about it. I wouldn't even know how."

"Easy-peasy. You just fill out an entry form."

"I guess I can do that," she said doubtfully.

Tess chuckled. "The fair is still a couple of weeks away. You've got time to decide."

"I don't know. It's Gran's recipe, but . . ."

"But what?"

"I'm not Gran."

Tess shot her an amused glance. "As lovely a person as Joyanna was, God didn't need for there to be two of her. So he only made one."

"I suppose you and Gran visited a lot. Living as close as you did."

"We did sometimes. Though of course we were both busy with our own lives. I had the stables, and she had a fairly active social life until she took that turn."

"Did she ever talk about me?"

Tess didn't answer at first, and Amy stared out the passenger window. It was a question she shouldn't have asked, but something had compelled her.

"She was very proud of you," Tess finally said. "Proud of your accomplishments—graduating from that prestigious college with all those honors, how you got to rub elbows with all those important people you've met."

"Gran didn't really care about those people. She thought they were too full of themselves."

"Was she right?"

"I suppose so." Amy studied her fingernails. The French manicure needed professional attention, but she'd canceled her appointment after Tess invited her to go to the fields. "Did she ever say she was disappointed in me?"

"She worried about you. About all three of you. But that's what grandparents do. They worry."

"We gave her enough reasons."

They rode in silence for a moment, then Tess spoke. "I think she's smiling down on you, Amy. She would want you to be happy and to be healthy. I've seen a difference in you just in the short time you've been at the cottage."

"Do you mean that?"

"You have a glow and a sparkle instead of a surly frown. It's good to see."

"Maybe I have more reason to smile these days."

"Gabe?"

"I so hope he likes the pie."

Tess laughed. "I'm sure he will." She maneuvered the truck down the long lane leading to the field where Gabe and AJ were helping Jason harvest his wheat. As she parked beside Cassie's van, the men headed their way. Amy helped arrange the food on the tailgate of Tess's pickup—fried chicken, green beans kept warm in a penguin pot, and homemade rolls.

"Looks like you're about to pop," Tess said to Cassie. "Shouldn't you be at home with your feet up?"

"I feel great except for the cramps and the heat and the swollen ankles," Cassie said. "I'm ready whenever she is."

Amy felt a touch of envy when Jason arrived and greeted Cassie with a kiss. His love for her shone in his eyes, and he obviously thought she was beautiful despite her bulge and awkward posture.

After handing Jason a plastic cup filled with sweet tea, Amy gazed toward the field, shading her eyes against the glare of the sun. Gabe walked toward her. Dusty. Sweaty. And more attractive than anyone she'd ever seen.

~

Gabe took the basket Amy held out to him. "What do you have in there?" he asked.

"What have I been promising you?"

He gave her a knowing look and licked his lips. "The elusive lemon meringue pie."

Amy nodded and laughed.

"Sorry, guys," Gabe said over his shoulder. "The dessert is all mine."

"I don't think so," AJ said. "I've been craving Gran's lemon meringue for months now."

"You'll get a slice," Amy said. "I made one pie for Gabe and one for the rest of you."

"Oh, I see how it is," AJ said. "Better a little than none, I guess."

Gabe removed his Stetson and wiped sweat from his forehead. "Did you really bake me a pie all my own?"

"I did," she said. "The catch is, you have to eat it all—whether you like it or not."

"That's not going to be a problem." Gabe set the basket on the tailgate with the rest of the spread. They filled their plates, and he and Amy sat a little off to themselves.

"I was surprised to see you arrive with Tess," he said. "Even more surprised about the pie."

"She called me this morning to see if I wanted to tag along. And then I scurried into the kitchen and got busy."

"I'm glad you did."

Amy bent her head and slightly lifted the brim of his Stetson so their eyes met. "Me too," she said quietly.

If he'd been used to kissing her, he would have kissed her now. But he was still holding out for that special moment. Him sweaty from the fields while she was fresh as a daisy after a spring rain—

this wasn't that moment. As the hopeful gleam in her eyes dimmed, he wished he could tell her that. But he didn't know the words.

~

On the drive home, Tess unconsciously gripped the steering wheel as she neared the cottage. She'd been up late last night and early this morning since two more horses had taken ill. While she tended them, her thoughts had been troubled by what Amy had said about her dad's last conversation with Rusty. Once Tess had returned to the house, she'd written about what she should do in her prayer journal. Now she prayed for wisdom.

"Would you mind coming in for a few minutes?" Amy asked as Tess slowed before the cottage. "I want to talk to you about something."

Guess that's a sign.

"Great minds," Tess said. "I have something I want to talk to you about too."

"Is it okay if I go first? I have a great idea," Amy said mysteriously. "And I wanted to see what you thought about it."

Tess couldn't get anything else out of Amy until they were inside the cottage with tall glasses of chilled blackberry lemonade.

"I'm not sure where to begin," Amy said. "All I know is that I can't have Dylan building a subdivision north of this property."

Tess wasn't sure what she'd expected, but this wasn't it. "Believe me, Amy. I don't want to sell. But I have to think of the future."

"So do I." Amy's tone was firm. "Gran's great-grandchildren should be able to enjoy this cottage as much as Brett and AJ and I did when we were kids. Elizabeth and Tabby should have their names on the engagement tree without staring at a bunch of backyard fences."

"What are you saying?"

"I want to buy your property on this side of the road."

"You can't be serious."

"But I am. It's the only way to protect the cottage and what AJ and Shelby still own of the Misty Willow property."

"Have you talked to AJ about this?"

"I plan to. Actually, it would be helpful if he bought the land back near the creek. Then I'd only have to purchase the frontage."

Tess inwardly sighed as she considered Amy's idea. At first glance, it seemed a win-win for both of them. But in reality, for Tess, it was only a short-term solution. Tapley might not buy the property on the west side of the road if he couldn't have the property on the east side too. She needed his money to have enough for a fresh start after the mortgage was paid.

Feeling Amy staring at her, Tess met the young woman's gaze. A light shone in her eyes that Tess hadn't seen since she was a girl. "I didn't know you were sentimental about the land."

"Neither did I until Logan told me about Dylan's plans." She momentarily lowered her eyes. "I know now why Shelby feels the way she does about her grandparents' legacy. I feel that way about Gran's. This cottage may not have the same sense of history and grandeur as Misty Willow. But Gran loved it here. I'll sacrifice anything to keep Dylan or anyone else from spoiling it."

"I wish I could say yes, Amy. I really do. But—"

"There's more." Amy retrieved a folder from the kitchen counter, pulled out a brochure, and handed it to Tess.

"Is this the clinic you went to?" Tess asked.

"Mmm-hmm." Amy took the brochure and opened it. "Look at this. They offer equine therapy."

"Did you participate in this?" Tess asked in surprise.

"No. I couldn't . . . not then." She sat on the edge of her chair and leaned close to Tess. "Don't you see? There are all kinds of equine therapy these days. For eating disorders, for kids with autism, for speech problems. And it's all great. But what about the kids who just want to ride but never have a chance? Kids from the city whose parents can't afford lessons and boarding fees. Wouldn't it be great if they had opportunities to ride too?"

"I'm not sure what you're suggesting. To start anything like that would take money I don't have. And it wouldn't generate any income."

"Don't you see? A foundation protected Misty Willow. Why can't a nonprofit save Whisper Lane?"

"But I don't know anything about running a nonprofit."

"You wouldn't have to. I would."

"Amy, you can't be serious."

"Why not? I have connections. I know how to raise money." She gave an embarrassed laugh. "True, I didn't help much with the Heritage Celebration, but that's only because I was still being a brat. But I've planned major events before. I'm organized and—"

Tess laughed and held up her hands. "Enough already. I get the picture," she said gently. "And I saw you handling the crowd at the Heritage Celebration. You're a poised, sophisticated, and intelligent woman."

"Then you agree we can do this?"

Tess shook her head in resignation. "A group wanting to do something like this would look for donated land. I can't do that."

"This would not be a shoestring operation," Amy said, her voice pleading. "Even if we couldn't outright buy your property, we could lease it. You'd stay at the house, help train the horses, oversee the activities. And get a steady salary. Please tell me you'll think about it."

"Have you talked to Gabe about this?"

"I haven't discussed it with anyone. There's too much to do, too many details to work out. I want to be able to answer every single question, address every single objection, before we go public. So for now, it's just between us."

"I'd like it to stay that way till I make a decision. And I promise. I will consider it."

"That's all I ask." Amy's gleeful expression lit up her face. "I know we can do this, Tess. I just know it."

She sat back in her chair, tucking her feet beneath her. "Your turn. What did you want to talk about?"

Tess gazed out the long row of windows, whether for guidance or inspiration or assurance she was doing the right thing, she couldn't say. Puffs of clouds accented a brilliant blue sky and the trio of silver birches gracefully swayed in the gentlest of breezes. "Something that might seem difficult to hear at first. But I hope you'll be glad to know."

"You've got my attention. What is it?"

"Yesterday you mentioned a conversation your dad had with Rusty."

"You mean about Marigold?"

Tess barely nodded as she prayed for the right words. "I'm sorry, Amy. That's not what they were talking about."

"They had to be. What else could it have been?"

"They were talking about forgiveness. And about grace."

"I don't understand."

"Your dad was tired and broken, both emotionally and spiritually. He didn't want to fight with your mom anymore, but he felt like they were trapped on some strange kind of merry-go-round. Having the same arguments again and again."

"You're telling me Dad was asking Rusty for marital advice?" Amy's tone bordered on skepticism. "They'd gone to counseling and it never helped."

"He wanted to try again." Tess bit her lip, then glanced out the window. The day's quiet serenity soothed her spirit and gave her the courage to go on. "That's why he was on that plane, Amy. He and your mom were taking the first tentative steps toward a reconciliation."

As Tess spoke, Amy's expression lost its skepticism. Now she was aloof, almost detached.

"Why didn't he say anything?" she asked, her voice so quiet that Tess could barely hear her.

"You and Brett had already been hurt so much by their animosity. They didn't want you to get your hopes up in case they couldn't work things out."

"But what about Gran? They would have told her, and she never said anything." Her voice rose an octave, and she pressed her lips together.

"To the best of my knowledge, the only people who knew were Rusty and me. And their counselors."

"So," Amy said haltingly as her eyes reddened, "if they had come back, we might have been a family?"

"I'd like to think so."

Neither of them spoke for several moments. Tess listened for God's voice in the silence as she prayed for Amy's heart to find comfort in what might have been.

~

In the dusk of the evening, as fireflies flitted around the sloping yard, Amy told Brett what Tess had told her earlier that day.

"Do you think it's true?" she asked him.

He sat in a lawn chair, elbows on knees and hands clasped in front of him. "Yeah," he finally said. "I do."

"Why?"

"It's the only thing that makes sense. Otherwise, why did he go?" Brett leaned back in frustration and tapped the chair arm with his thumb. "Why fly to New York with your ex-wife, her brother, and his wife? I never understood it."

"I've been thinking about it all afternoon," Amy said. "I finally admitted to myself how mad I was at him for not coming back." More than that. She practically hated him for breaking his promise, and his death had been a final rejection. Irrational thoughts,

271

yes, but she couldn't get past them. They were so strong, so real, that she scarcely tried.

Those weren't thoughts she could share with Brett or anyone else. Instead she had kept them buried, even during therapy sessions at the clinic.

"Are you glad Tess told you?" Brett asked.

"Yes. I think I am." Dad's effort to make amends with Mom gave Amy a reason to forgive him. Perhaps she should have forgiven him anyway, without a reason except that she loved him, but that had proven too hard when grief threatened to swallow her whole. As the months passed, her lack of forgiveness had become so deeply ingrained, she no longer recognized it for what it was.

Dusk turned to twilight while they talked. In the dim light, Brett's features weren't as discernible as they had been, and the blinking lights of the fireflies were even more noticeable.

"What about you?" she asked.

"It matters," he said. "The pain. It seems a little less heavy."

"I know what you mean."

Even in the darkness, she could tell the instant he flashed his dimples at her. "Get packed. You're spending the night with us."

"You don't have to worry about me. I'm fine."

"Come on, Amy. Let's have a game night. Celebrate the family we have instead of mourning the one we didn't."

The invitation did sound more appealing than being alone with thoughts that wouldn't settle down. She absolutely didn't want a repeat of the last time Brett had left her after a serious conversation.

"Can we play Settlers of Catan?"

"If we must."

"Then I'll come."

"Great. I'll call Dani and let her know."

Amy started to rise but shifted toward him as she ran a strand of hair through her fingers. "I want to believe that Mom and Dad would have married again. That they would have been happy."

"I want to believe that too."

"Do you think *I'll* ever be happy? The way you are?"

"I think you could be." He purposefully gazed across the road toward the stables. "That's up to you."

Not only up to her. But maybe, if her plan worked out, she'd find happiness again at the Hearth.

- 33 -

*L*ate the next afternoon, Gabe tightened the spark plugs on the Ford F-150 and signaled for Amy to turn the ignition. The engine sputtered, cranked, then ignited and held. He made an adjustment, then stepped back with a smile. "What do you say? Shall we take her for a spin?"

"Are you sure this thing will hold together?" Amy said through the open door.

"Nope. That's why it's fun."

She gave an exaggerated sigh and scooted across the bench seat to the passenger side. "Let's go."

With a smile, he slammed shut the hood, stored his toolbox behind the seat, and climbed in.

"I'm still not sure how I got roped into this," Amy said. "I only came over to talk to Tess."

"Lucky for me she went to town and I was here."

"I expected you to be out on a tractor somewhere."

"Usually I would be. But Jason wanted to go with Cassie to her OB appointment. So I got time to spend with *my* baby." He patted the rotting dashboard.

"You really love this heap, don't you?"

"Rusty taught me to drive in this thing. We took it camping a few times. Hauled hay and feed, even a pig once."

"I'm glad I missed that experience."

Gabe stopped at the end of the drive, then glanced her way. Never would he have thought she'd be in this truck with him the first time he drove it. This was a day he'd never forget, and he wanted to tuck each moment of it deep into his soul.

"Where should we go?" he asked.

"Surprise me."

He drummed for a moment on the steering wheel, then caught her gaze. "I've worked up a bit of an appetite getting this thing to run." He let the rest go unspoken, watching closely for her reaction.

"I was hoping you'd say that."

"You serious?"

"I am," she said. "Believe it or not, I'm starving."

He checked the gas gauge. "Not sure we can make it all the way to town, but Boyd's isn't that far, is it? Rusty and Tess took me there a few times when I was a kid. Great idea having them cater the Heritage Celebration. I think I gained ten pounds."

"You can thank AJ and Brett for that. It's one of their favorite places."

"Best pulled pork this side of the Ohio River," they said in unison, then laughed.

"My dad liked to go there." Amy stared out the windshield, her expression pensive. "We used to stop in sometimes after riding lessons. I loved their bread pudding. It's all I wanted to eat."

"I don't want to bring up sad memories," Gabe said. "Maybe we should think of somewhere else."

Amy slowly shook her head. "I'm tired of coloring my happy memories sad and hiding them away. Besides, it seems right somehow. To go there in Rusty's old truck. Remember the people we loved."

"Boyd's BBQ, here we come."

"I know you need to drive past Misty Willow to get there. I'll find the rest of the directions on my phone." She tapped at the screen while Gabe fiddled with the radio until he found a country classics station. With the windows rolled down and the music turned up loud, they could be a country song.

Rusty's truck. Pretty girl.

What more could a man want?

Amy fussed with her windblown hair, and Gabe finally stuck his Stetson on top of her head. She laughed, gathered up her loose strands, and tucked them beneath the hat. They blared the horn when they passed the bungalow and Brett's ranch house, even though no one was outside to see them, sang along with the songs they knew, and threw their worries to the wind.

To think, only a few weeks ago, he knew little about his neighbors. Now they were his employers and, even better, his friends. Tess still worried about the future—and to tell the truth, so did he—but she no longer talked about selling to Tapley. Gabe prayed daily for guidance, for an answer. God hadn't given him one, not yet. But he wouldn't give up hope.

They arrived at Boyd's and discovered it was classic car night. Since they were early, most of the owners were still setting up. Gabe and Amy wandered the lot, chatting with the owners about their treasured autos. A couple of them teased Gabe about his broken-down Ford, but he assured them he wouldn't trade it for anything—not even one of their expensive restored vehicles.

After they went inside, the hostess appeared to show them to a table.

"Would you mind if we ate outside?" Amy asked. "It's such a lovely evening."

"Great idea," Gabe said. "That way I can keep an eye on my truck. One of those guys out there might want to steal it."

"I don't think you have anything to worry about. Now, if it was my baby . . ."

"You mean that little blue bucket you drive around in?" He pretended to sneer. "That's a sissy car."

"I love that car," Amy said. "But it is an indulgence."

"What do you mean?"

"All I need is something to get me from Point A to Point B and back again."

He tapped her temple. "What's going on in that head of yours?"

"Just thinking about stuff. Like what's really important and what isn't." She gave him an endearing smile that caused his heart to swell. "Strange as it sounds, your Ford is more valuable than my BMW."

"What makes you say that?"

"Because of its memories." She reached for his hand. "We're making a memory now."

"One I'll always remember," he said. Seemed like memories were all he had to offer her.

~

Amy refused to calculate any calories as she savored her last bite of bread pudding, then ordered two servings to go, one for her and one for Tess.

"Must be as good as you remembered," Gabe said.

"Even better. Sure you don't want one for later?"

"I'm still waiting for another one of your famous lemon meringue pies. You did promise."

Her stomach did a flip-flop. If she was ever going to do this, now was the moment.

"How late are you working on Saturday?"

"As late as Jason wants me to. Why?"

Immediately Amy's planning wheels went into motion. She'd talk to Cassie, ask her to talk to Jason.

"I thought, I mean I wondered, if you'd like to go on a picnic with me. When you're free."

Gabe leaned back and stared at her. "Are you asking me on a date?"

"I am."

"Will there be lemon meringue pie at this picnic?"

"Maybe." Definitely. Though she had no idea how well a pie would travel in saddlebags. Maybe Tess could suggest something.

He made her wait a second or two, then his lazy smile spread across his face. "I'm honored."

"Great. Let me know when you're done for the day, and I'll come over."

"So you're going to chauffeur me around in your fancy baby?"

"You'll see." She could hardly hide her excitement. How surprised Gabe would be when she led him to the stable and saddled Daisy. Once they were at the Hearth, she'd retrieve the tin and ask him to open it.

"What are you up to?" he asked, playfully suspicious.

"You'll find out on Saturday."

"It can't get here soon enough."

Once Amy had her to-go order, Gabe escorted her to the truck and slammed her door twice to get it shut. "Maybe you should sit in the middle," he suggested. "I wouldn't want you falling out."

"That's original," she said. "I bet you broke that door on purpose."

"If I had thought of it, I might have."

She sat beside him, breathing in the mingled aromas of baking bread and roasted meat while the band's golden oldies were piped through loudspeakers hung on the light poles. She'd probably been on hundreds of dates in her life, ranging from the movies at the old theater in town with Logan to more than one inaugural ball at the state capitol. But this might be her favorite.

Thinking of Logan shot a twinge of guilt through her conscience. It wasn't kind to keep him hanging. But if things didn't work out like she hoped on Saturday, if Gabe still meant to keep her at arm's length—well, Logan had always been her back-up date. He never had to know he was also her back-up love.

She stared out the window, ashamed of her own thoughts. Deep inside, she knew she couldn't do that to Logan no matter how lonely she was or how much she longed for a family of her own. Her heart belonged only to Gabe. Nobody else.

Tomorrow. Much as she dreaded doing it, she'd call Logan tomorrow. Ask him to meet her in the city. Pray he wouldn't be too hurt.

"Everything okay?" Gabe asked. "You're suddenly quiet."

She mentally shook away her gloomy thoughts and smiled her most dazzling smile. "Just making plans."

"Which you aren't going to tell me."

"Nope."

"You want to listen to some music?"

"Let's just listen to the country sounds. The real country sounds."

"Fine by me."

They drove past the Norris farm, past Misty Willow, past the Owenses'. After making the turn, they passed Brett's sprawling ranch house and then the bungalow. As soon as they crossed the bridge, the engine conked and sputtered. Gabe applied slow pressure to the brake and steered the truck to the shoulder of the road.

"What's going on?" Amy asked.

"Not sure."

The engine groaned, choked, then died.

"Good thing I brought along the toolbox," Gabe said. "And just for the record, I didn't plan this either."

"But you would have if you'd thought of it?"

"Maybe," he teased. "At least we're close enough to the house to walk if we have to."

"Do you want me to call Brett? Not that he would be much help. Or I can call AJ."

"Give me a chance to fix it on my own first."

"As long as you don't expect me to help." She stood on the step by the door and looked out over the cab of the truck. The sun hung low in the sky, though it wouldn't set for another hour or so. Breezes, scented with warmth and green and at least a hint of cow manure, wafted around her. But not even the animal odor offended her. Not anymore.

No matter what happened between her and Gabe, she no longer wanted to return to apartment life in the big city. Though if Gabe didn't love her after all, she wouldn't be able to stay at the cottage if he stayed with Tess.

Again she pressed down the gloomy thoughts. She was going to live in the present and be thankful for this moment when she and Gabe were together, even if together meant being stranded on the side of the road in a broken-down Ford.

"Looks like we're going to need a tow or a push." Gabe grinned up at her. "Think your baby could handle the job?"

"Um . . . no," she said emphatically.

"I'll call Tess and see if she's home yet."

"Don't do that. If she's not, she'll feel like she has to hurry back." Amy pulled out her cell phone. "I'll call AJ."

While the phone rang, she climbed into the truck's bed. A wave of euphoria swept through her. This was what it was like to be a country girl, and she loved it.

"What's up?" AJ said when he answered her call.

"I'm with Gabe, and his truck broke down. We need help."

"Where are you?"

"Just past your place, across the bridge." She breathed in the sunshine-soaked air, then wrinkled her nose. An acrid odor mingled with the expected scents. "You aren't grilling out, are you?"

"No, why?"

She took another deep breath. The odor was stronger, even more pungent. She scanned the nearby fields, beyond the hedgerow, then toward the stables. Smoke rose into the sky, gentle threads of it one moment followed by a mass of black.

"Fire." Her voice held unbelief. It couldn't be.

"What?" AJ demanded.

"Gabe!" she shouted. "Look. It's a fire."

"Amy," AJ said in her ear. "Where's the fire?"

At the same time, Gabe appeared at the side of the truck. "What's going on?"

"At Tess's." Her voice choked, and Gabe looked around wildly, then momentarily froze.

"Stay here. And call 911," he ordered, then sprinted up the road toward the stables.

"Gabe, wait!"

"Amy, stay where you are," AJ said. "I'm on my way."

Amy ended the call and dialed 911 while debating whether to run after Gabe or wait for AJ. But her feet seemed to make the decision for her. While she answered the operator's questions, begging for immediate help, she awkwardly climbed from the truck bed and half jogged, half stumbled along the road.

A few moments later, AJ caught up with her and she climbed into his Jeep. She barely had the door shut when he pressed down on the accelerator and sped toward the stables. Gabe had climbed the fence and was racing toward the burning barn.

Tears poured down Amy's cheeks, but she barely noticed them.

"Shelby is calling Brett, a few others," AJ said. He glanced at Amy, then focused on the road.

They sped past the hedges hiding the cottage and then past the stables. The entire structure appeared to be on fire.

Amy craned her neck to see if she could locate the horses in the pasture, but she didn't see any of them. AJ drove past the house, and the Jeep's wheels squealed as he slowed only enough to make the left-hand turn into the drive.

Amy smacked into the door.

"Sorry," AJ said.

"Doesn't matter."

The instant he braked between the house and the garage, she opened the door and leaped out, on a run for the stables. AJ quickly caught up to her, grabbed her arm, and pulled her to a stop.

"Stay here," he ordered. "Wait for the others."

"I can't." Her voice broke, and she swiped at the tears. One part of her brain realized she'd dropped her phone, but she didn't know where. Nor did she care. "The horses," she said, almost in a whimper. "Gabe. He'll . . ." She couldn't even say the words that gripped her heart like an iron fist, but she didn't have to.

AJ nodded understanding, then gave her a slight push and pointed his finger at her. "Stay here." He ran toward the stables while she tried to breathe. But she couldn't stay. Not when her imagination raced with horrific images.

The sky grew blacker with each passing second, and the smell of the smoke descended around her. She couldn't wait any longer. Her sandals weren't made for running, but she didn't notice the thistles scratching her feet and ankles as she scurried past Tess's truck after AJ.

- 34 -

Gabe ran harder than he ever had in his life, shutting his mind to everything around him except the fire blazing out of control ahead of him. As if on autopilot, his mind calculated where to jump the ditch beside the road and where to clamber over the white wooden fence and the best angle for running across the pasture to the burning stables.

He had to save the horses. Nothing else mattered.

The billowing smoke choked him. He quickly splashed water from a nearby trough onto his shirt and wet the rag he'd stuck in his back pocket while fiddling with the truck. As he tied the rag around his nose and mouth, the terrified screams from inside the barn confirmed his worst fear. Taking a deep breath, he ducked his head and made his way to the first stall. Daisy stamped and whinnied.

Gabe grabbed a lead rope, then opened the door. Talking softly, he placed the rope around her neck as quickly as he could and led her along the central aisle to the outer door. He hurried her into a pen, then ran back to the stables. By the time he came out with Casper, AJ was directing a hose used to fill the water trough toward the base of the fire. But the small stream of water wasn't powerful enough to slow the raging inferno.

"Take Casper," Gabe called. "Get him and Daisy to the field."

AJ dropped the hose and reached for the rope, placing his hand close to Casper's neck so the horse couldn't slip it.

"You can't go back in there," AJ shouted above the roar of the flames. "It's too far gone."

"I've got no choice." Gabe wet his shirt and the rag again with the hose.

"Help is on the way."

"It'll be too late."

As Gabe took a deep breath, readying himself to enter the stables again, Amy appeared. She ran to him, coughing and stumbling, grabbing at his arms.

"The horses?"

"I'll save them," he said with more bravado than he felt.

"You can't." She looked one direction and then another. "Where's Tess?"

Gabe's heart plummeted to his stomach. "What?"

"Her truck's in the driveway." Amy's eyes widened in horror and she stared at the stables. "Oh no."

Gabe raced into the barn with the sound of Amy screeching his name ringing in his ears. Tess would have gone in after the horses. Which meant she had to be in here.

"Tess!" he called, trying to shout above the creaking and groaning of the burning wood. "Tess, where are you?"

Since Daisy and Casper had still been in their stalls, Tess must have started at the other end of the barn. Fire blazed there, strong and steady. Gabe's eyes stung and watered, and mucus dripped from his nose. But love for his aunt spurred him through the gray smoke and rising inferno.

"Gabe!" Amy shouted. "Gabe, don't!"

As he disappeared into the barn, ducking beneath the burning doorframe, her legs turned to jelly. She stumbled forward, her arms in front of her face, bracing against the intense heat. "Gabe! Come back!"

He wouldn't. Not if Tess was inside.

She forced herself to move forward as tears streamed down her face. The beam above the entrance burned with a feverish glow. Gabe had ducked beneath it. So could she.

She closed her eyes, took a deep breath, and felt herself being pulled backward. She fought the pressure against her stomach as strong arms held her tight.

"You can't," AJ said behind her. His grip tightened as he pulled her away from the barn. "Amy, you can't."

"I have to," she cried, kicking at his legs. "Let me go. Let me go."

Instead, he dragged her farther from the fire as the flames blazed before them. "This won't help him. It won't help Tess."

She fought to calm down, knowing he was right but hating the helplessness she felt.

"Breathe," AJ said. "Just take a moment and breathe."

She did what he'd said, but the air was heavy with smoke and reeked of burning odors. "What can I do?" she said, her voice sounding pitiful and small.

"Find blankets. I'll hose down the doorway. Maybe that will at least give him a chance."

"AJ," she said, then bit at her lip. "If he . . ."

"Go," AJ ordered. "Just go."

She nodded, then ran toward the house.

~

Gabe staggered along the aisle, opening each stall door as he went in a futile attempt to free the horses. But they wouldn't leave on their own. A stall, even a burning one, represented safety to them. There was nothing he could do for them until he found Tess.

He was more than halfway down the aisle when he saw her lying on the concrete floor beside the open door next to Knight Starr's stall.

Gabe paused as a wooden beam fell before him, then he maneuvered around it. His single focus now was getting Tess out of the barn. Sweat poured down his face, his ears and neck felt as if they had been attacked by a swarm of stinging hornets, and his lungs ached to draw breath. But still he struggled to get to her.

He dropped to his knees, ignoring the heat of the concrete floor through his jeans and on the palms of his hands. He crawled to her, turned her over. Blood oozed from her forehead, and she wasn't breathing.

Reacting in fear, Knight Starr reared, striking out at Gabe. He quickly pulled Tess into the aisle.

He started to administer CPR, but the fire loomed closer. He glanced behind him. The aisle wasn't as clear as it had been, and the sickeningly sweet smell of burning plastic and burnt horseflesh was making him gag. He wouldn't have much longer to escape.

Standing, he heaved her into his arms and staggered toward the door. He was almost there when he stumbled and fell. He grabbed both of Tess's wrists and walked backward, crouching as low as possible while he dragged her along the floor. As the fire blazed around him, he emerged from the flames.

AJ met him at the door, his expression showing relief followed quickly by concern. He dropped the hose, then helped Gabe pick up Tess and carry her a safe distance from the fire. Brett had arrived, and he and Amy rushed to help. Part of Gabe's brain registered the sound of sirens. They were close. But were they too late?

He bent over, hands to knees, sputtering and coughing. "She's not breathing."

"I can do it," AJ said. He tilted Tess's head backward, blew air into her lungs, then compressed her chest with the heels of his hand.

Gabe staggered, then fell to the ground as he gulped in air. Ghost-like images appeared and disappeared in the smoke. Amy beat at the fire around the door with a blanket. Brett, Paul Norris and his son Seth, and a few other people Gabe had met since moving to the stables were also doing their best to put out the fire.

But one look at the barn, and he knew it was a lost cause. The wood burned too fast. A scream echoed above the roar of the flames, and he hung his head, knowing that the sound would haunt him as long as he lived.

He had to give it one more try. To save at least one more horse.

He stood, lurched toward the door, and glared at the flames shooting from inside. They couldn't beat him. Not after what he'd been through in the past six years. He'd endured that long prison term and was only now finding his way in the outside world. It couldn't come crashing down—not without a fight.

~

Amy hit at the flames as they sparked from the building and ignited the nearby grass and fencing. Her arms ached, her lungs felt clogged with carbon, and her mouth tasted like ash. The air stank, but she couldn't let herself think of the dying horses right now.

More than anything, she wanted to run to Gabe, to hold him, but she was like a robot caught in some kind of mechanical loop. All she could do was hit at the ground, the fence, the barn itself with the water-soaked blanket.

The fire trucks appeared, and men came running toward them.

Brett directed the EMT personnel to where AJ was still giving CPR to Tess.

Amy hit at another spark, smacking the ground again and again until a fireman stilled her motion. "We've got this," he said firmly. "We need you to get back."

"The horses," she said, holding tight to the blanket, unwilling to let it go. "You have to save the horses."

He glanced at the stables, his expression grim. "We'll save what we can."

She released the blanket as she turned to where the EMTs were surrounding Tess. AJ stood nearby, hands on his hips, head bent. Praying. As if she could hear his thoughts, she knew he was praying.

He raised his eyes, stared toward the barn, then sprinted toward it. Amy followed his gaze to where Gabe struggled to get past two of the firemen. Somehow he found the strength to push through them, and he rushed toward the barn.

"Noooo!" The scream clawed at her throat.

Without missing a beat, AJ ran inside the barn after Gabe.

Amy stumbled forward, tripped, and fell to her knees. Exhaustion pressed her to the ground, and she struggled to get back to her feet. But instead she stumbled again. Rolling to her side, she lost the fight in a heart-wrenching groan. The firefighter who'd taken the blanket from her knelt beside her, and a couple of paramedics immediately joined him. She fought against them, thinking only of getting to the barn. Shouting at them to help Gabe and AJ. To save the horses.

The paramedics tried to quiet her, but sobs wracked her body. She descended into momentary blackness, and when she opened her eyes, Brett was beside her, pushing her hair from her forehead. Grimy smoke streaked his face, and his eyes were rimmed in red.

"Sir, we need to check you out too," one of the EMTs said. "We'll take care of her, just give us a chance."

"I'm not leaving you, Amy," Brett said.

She tried but failed to smile. Her mouth seemed frozen. She swallowed hard, blinked, and held his gaze. "Gabe?" Her eyes closed before he could answer, and she was lost in darkness.

- 35 -

Amy picked at the tape holding the IV in her hand. A tube surrounded her head and released oxygen into her nostrils from a nearby tank. A monitor rhythmically tracked her vital signs, but her heart rate didn't register the ache she felt inside.

The door opened and Brett appeared, dressed in a hospital gown and cheap robe. He pulled an IV stand with him as he sat down in the bedside chair. "How're you doing?" he asked.

"Okay," she murmured. "Should you be up?"

"I escaped when no one was watching." He gestured toward the IV flowing into his arm. "This is all an unnecessary precaution."

"AJ ran into the barn." She felt torn between her fear of the questions piercing her heart and her need to know the answers. "After Gabe."

"The firefighters got them out."

"Are they all right?"

Brett released a pent-up breath, and he passed his hand over his eyes. "Emergency Services called a helicopter to transfer them to the burn center in Columbus."

Amy closed her eyes against the tears welling inside of her. Her breath caught and she cleared her throat. "Will they be okay?"

"They're alive. I don't know any more than that." He twisted the IV stand so the bag swung from its hook. "They couldn't save any more of the horses."

Conflicting emotions warred within her. Sorrow for the lost animals. Gratefulness that Gabe and AJ were alive. Fear for what they were going through.

"Where's Shelby?" she asked.

"With AJ. The Norrises drove her to the center."

"What about Gabe? He doesn't have anyone . . ."

"They'll stay with him. If they're allowed."

A new fear, irrational and sudden, gripped her chest and she clutched her blanket. "The kids?"

"Cassie watched them till Dani got home from fussing over me."

An anxious dread smothered Amy, as painful as the last time it descended upon her. "They must be so afraid."

"They probably are." His expression told her he felt it too. That shock of learning something awful has happened to your family. The vain hope that everything will turn out all right when everything has already turned out so wrong.

"But I talked to them, and Dani will take good care of them." He blinked a couple of times, then twisted the IV stand again. "Jonah said he's praying extra hard. And Tabby ordered me to pick up pizza on my way home. It's tradition."

A small smile emerged before Amy could stop it. "You spoil her."

"Nah, just buying her affection."

"Quit making jokes." She rubbed the tape on her hand, then stared at him. "Admit that you're as scared as I am."

"I'm as scared as you are. But we will get through this."

"When can we go home?"

"Probably tomorrow. We both inhaled a lot of smoke."

"Is that why my throat hurts?"

He nodded. "Mine does too."

She leaned her head back on the pillow and stared at the ceiling. One question still remained. She'd avoided asking it as long as she could, but she had to know. Her body trembled beneath the blanket, and she suddenly felt cold.

"Tess?"

Brett covered her hands with his and bowed his head. "AJ tried. The EMTs tried. But she didn't . . ."

The tears fell, a stinging stream along Amy's cheeks. Her heart, pressed thin by hurt and sorrow, no longer seemed to beat. "Gabe needs to hear it from me." She gulped. "No one else."

"I'll make sure no one tells him."

"Tess and I were becoming friends. We were making plans."

"What kind of plans?"

"To protect Whisper Lane."

"Protect it from what?"

"Gabe's going to be all right, isn't he?" She stared into her brother's eyes, needing his strength to hold herself in one piece. "I can't lose him."

As soon as the words were spoken, she bent her head in despair. The weight bowing her down was more than she could stand, and she sank into the mattress, curling up into a fetal position as the sobs wracked her body.

Tears for AJ and Gabe. Tears for Tess and burned horses. Tears for losses she'd never healed from.

Brett bent near and tucked the blanket around her. "Cry it out," he said, his own voice breaking. "Cry it out."

~

Amy awoke the next morning when a nurse came to check her vital signs. Brett stirred in the nearby chair, then flashed his dimples at her when she looked at him.

"How're you doing, sis?"

"Were you there all night?"

He grinned at the nurse. "They chased me back to my own room, but I snuck back in here this morning."

The nurse pretended to glare at him. "He's not a very obedient patient."

"He's not used to following rules," Amy said.

"Did you sleep well?" the nurse asked.

"Well enough. When can I leave?"

"That's for the doctor to say. She'll be here soon."

Amy endured the pokes and prods, then sighed heavily when the nurse closed the door behind her.

"Hungry?" Brett asked. "I know where they hide the orange sherbet."

"No thanks." After what they'd been through, she wasn't sure she ever wanted to eat again. The physical pain of gnawing hunger was preferable to the death grip squeezing her heart. "It's about control," a therapist had said in one of their group sessions at the clinic. But knowing that, understanding that, didn't alleviate the anguish eating her up inside.

"They've got those little cups of vanilla ice cream too." Though his voice was upbeat, worry lines etched his mouth and eyes.

"How many have you eaten?" Amy said.

"Two or three."

"Before breakfast?"

"Midnight snack."

"Have you heard from Dani?"

"We talked a few minutes ago. AJ has a few burns but nothing too serious. He'll be home in a couple of days."

"That's good." She bit her lip, then attempted a smile. "Do you remember what the media called us? After the plane . . ." Her throat caught on the painful words.

Brett snorted. "The Tragic Trio."

The media outlets had sensationalized the story of the three orphaned rich kids when all they had wanted was to grieve in private.

"A reporter cornered me outside of school. AJ was there to pick me up, and he told the reporter to leave me alone, but the guy wouldn't quit."

"I'm surprised AJ didn't hit him." Brett unconsciously rubbed his jaw, and Amy couldn't help a small smile. She hadn't been present when AJ decked Brett, but she'd seen the bruise.

"AJ took my arm and stood between us. He just stared at that reporter, not saying a word. The reporter tried to goad us both into making a comment, and he said some awful things. But AJ just stared at him, and so I just stared at him too. Finally he left us alone."

"AJ's a good guy." Brett clasped Amy's hand. "He'll get through this."

She nodded, then swallowed the lump that threatened to choke her. "What about Gabe?"

"He's, um . . ." Brett sighed heavily. "His recovery is going to take awhile."

"I love him."

"I know you do."

"Tess said he loved me too. But he doesn't know me. Not the real me." Her voice grew in vehemence, and she squeezed Brett's hand until her fingers ached. "I lie. I manipulate people. I exploit their weaknesses. Gabe would never do any of that."

"That's not you, Amy. Maybe it was once, but it's not now. It's definitely not who you have to be."

"Just because you changed doesn't mean I can."

"You don't have to let the past define you. Especially not when someone you love loves you back."

"Like you and Dani?"

"Believe me, I wouldn't have stepped foot in a plane for anyone else." He rose and brushed his lips against her temple. "I need coffee. You want a cup?"

She shook her head, unsure whether she could trust her voice. "Everything is going to be okay. You'll see."

She sniffed and wiped at her eyes. "Can you promise me that?"

He gave her a sheepish look, then took a deep breath. "'I trusted in the Lord when I said, "I am greatly afflicted."'"

"Huh?"

"Psalm 116:10. The first Scripture I ever memorized."

"Shelby tell you that?"

"Elizabeth. Out of the mouth of babes." He tweaked her foot as he walked by the bed, then headed out the door.

Little Elizabeth who had lost her dad when she was only five. He'd died a hero's death, but that couldn't have been much comfort for a grieving little girl.

Haven't we had enough sorrow? Amy's heart cried. *We've lost so much—Shelby and her girls, Brett, AJ, and me. Even Dani. Please don't take Gabe from us too. Please, God. Please don't.*

~

Amy sat up as the attending physician entered her room followed closely by Brett. After a few preliminary questions and scowling at the information on her electronic tablet, the doctor smiled at Amy.

"I don't feel comfortable discharging you, Ms. Somers," she said. "Your body needs rest, and I want to be sure your heart rate is stable before you leave here."

"Something's wrong with my heart?"

"Just a little arrhythmia. Given your past health history, another day of observation is advisable."

"You mean because of my eating problems." Amy's gaze bored into the doctor's gray eyes. "Euphemisms aren't necessary."

"Then I too will be direct. Until you eat, I won't sign the discharge papers."

"You haven't eaten?" Brett said. "You mean nothing?"

The doctor pursed her lips and waited for Amy to answer.

"I'm not hungry," she said, sounding like a petulant child. She waved her hand toward the untouched breakfast tray. "The scrambled eggs are soggy, and the toast . . . I can't eat that stuff."

Brett flashed a smile at the doctor. "She does have a point."

The doctor lifted the cloche to reveal a bowl of oatmeal and looked pointedly at Amy.

"So I guessed wrong," Amy said.

"I meant what I said. You must eat or we'll have to ensure your nourishment with other methods."

"A feeding tube?" Amy stared in disbelief. "You can't do that."

The doctor leaned closer. "Watch me."

"I don't think she's bluffing," Brett said. "Tell me what you want and I'll ask Dani to get it. She'll be here soon. That would be okay, wouldn't it, Doc?"

"That's an excellent idea. Are we agreed?"

Amy turned away from them, then gave a curt nod.

The doctor left and Brett frowned at the tray. "It's not too bad if you put a lot of sugar in it."

"You eat it, then."

"I might." Instead, he slurped his coffee.

The burns on Amy's feet increasingly ached as the pain medicine wore off. She pressed the button for another dose and felt her body relax as it immediately took effect. Perhaps this was reason enough to stay another day.

"I left my bag in Gabe's truck," she said.

"Paul and Jason towed it into AJ's driveway. They probably locked it up."

"Gabe has had that truck since he was twelve. He's so proud of it."

"Where were you going, before it broke down, I mean?" Brett asked.

"We were at Boyd's. I bought bread pudding for Tess." Her

voice faded as she succumbed to drowsiness. "I guess it's still in the truck."

"I'll take care of it."

Amy scooted down into the bed and pulled the flimsy cotton blanket up to her chin. Her lids grew heavy and she closed her eyes. Her body yearned for sleep, but her thoughts relived yesterday's events as if she were watching a movie.

They'd had such a great time, she and Gabe. It was the first time she'd ever been around a man fixing his truck, and as uncomfortable and rough as the truck was to ride in, she couldn't imagine Gabe driving anything else.

He held on to the things he loved. She prayed he'd hold on to life. On to her.

- 36 -

*L*ogan rapped on the door, took a deep breath, and stepped inside. Amy lay on the bed, an oxygen tube around her pale face, an IV tube snaking along her arm and into her hand.

Her eyes blinked open, and she gave him a faint smile. "What are you doing here?"

"I came to see you. And to bring you these." He placed a vase of pink roses on a nearby table. "I seem to remember you like pink."

"They're lovely." Her voice was soft, almost ragged. "Thank you."

He pulled a chair close to the bed and leaned as close to her as he could. "I still can't believe you were involved in that fire. Are you okay?"

"I'm fine. At least I'm alive."

"But what were you doing there? What happened?"

"I don't know. We saw the smoke and . . ." She turned her face away.

"It's okay," Logan said. "We don't have to talk about it."

Except he needed her to talk about it. Since she had been there, on the scene, she could give him the details the news reports left out.

"It's nice that you came," Amy said sleepily.

"Of course I came." He gently stroked her arm. "Can I get you anything? Do anything for you? All you have to do is ask."

"Can you make it yesterday again? Make it so the fire doesn't happen?"

"I wish I could," he said with as much sincerity as he could muster.

They sat in silence for several minutes as Amy dozed. Logan watched over her, his thoughts a mishmash of guilt and satisfaction. He hadn't intended for anyone to get hurt. Somehow his best-laid plans had gone awry when it came to the timing of the fire. But at least Amy would recover. If Kendall didn't, well, so much the better for Logan.

For now, he needed to prove to Amy how much she needed him, that they belonged together. And to be sure no one linked him to the arson.

~

Late that afternoon, Amy leaned against the chilled window of her hospital room as windswept rain cascaded from dark clouds. No lightning. No thunder. Only drenching, dousing rain. If the torrent had come yesterday instead of today, scorching flames couldn't have destroyed the stables. AJ would be home with Shelby and their girls. Gabe might have dropped by the cottage with a Crock-Pot of chili made with Conecuh sausage.

Tess would still be alive.

A knock sounded on the door, and she heaved a heavy sigh. She'd had enough visitors traipsing through her room today. Dani had brought a hearty to-go breakfast from the Dixie Diner, which Amy dutifully ate. She'd eaten nothing since.

Well-meaning neighbors, friends of AJ's who Amy hardly knew, had dropped in throughout the afternoon, and so did a couple of the paramedics who'd treated her yesterday. Just checking to see how she was, they said.

Cassie Owens came too, bringing garden flowers and homemade cards from Jonah, Elizabeth, and Tabby. Jason had kept the kids so Brett and Dani could visit AJ.

The knock sounded again. Heavier this time.

"Come in," Amy said rudely.

"Ms. Somers?" The man who entered wore a black polo shirt tucked into pressed jeans. "I'm Ken Abbott, a fire investigator with local law enforcement. I don't want to take up too much of your time, but I'd like to talk to you if you think you're up to it."

"I'm not."

"I only need a few minutes." He joined her at the window. "My daughter goes to Glade County High School. Coach Sullivan is one of her favorite teachers. Do you know how he's doing?"

"He's been better."

"What about you?"

"I'll survive."

"How long are they keeping you?"

She glared at him. "Why are you here?"

"Like I said, I need to ask you a few questions."

"Can't this wait until I get home?" She eased into a nearby chair. "My mind's a little fuzzy from the drugs."

"Usually, I'd say yes." He stuck his hands in his pockets, leaned against the windowsill, and crossed his ankles. His relaxed stance exuded friendly confidence, and he clearly didn't want her to feel intimidated. But his posture was a little too deliberate, too practiced. "But because of the circumstances surrounding this fire, it's vital that we don't delay our investigation."

"You mean because Tess died."

"Were you and she close?"

"I think we could have been. Given more time."

"I am sorry."

Amy nodded but said nothing. Too late she had realized that spending time with Tess was the next best thing to being with Gran. If she hadn't shut Tess out of her life as a teenager, she'd have had the older woman's wisdom and strength to rely on when Gran died. In the few short days they'd had, Tess shared stories about the neighborly things they'd done together. Now those memories were lost, and Amy hadn't heard enough of them.

"Ms. Somers, were you the first one to arrive at the scene?"

"I saw it first, but Gabe got there before I did."

"That's Gabe Kendall, right? Mrs. Marshall's nephew."

"Yes. No." She shook her head to clear her muddled thoughts. "Yes, Gabe is Tess's nephew, but he wasn't there first. Tess was already there. She was inside the horse barn."

"Where were you when you saw the fire?"

"Gabe and I were on our way back from Boyd's." She explained how the truck had conked out, about climbing into the truck bed and calling AJ. How Gabe had raced across the pasture toward the stables.

"When AJ and I got there, Gabe was coming out with Casper. One of the horses. That's when . . ." She leaned forward, sucked in air, and felt her chest tighten like a vise. "It was my fault," she gasped. "My fault that he . . ."

She could not go on. The room tilted, and she swayed as the blood rushed to her feet. Abbott caught her by the shoulders and gently pushed her back into the chair.

After hitting the call button, he handed her a cup of water. "Drink this."

She obeyed, sucking the cold water through the straw and into her parched throat.

"I don't want to talk about this anymore." The words came

out in short gasps, as if the smoke were once again clogging her lungs, preventing her from breathing. "No more."

Her legs burned, her feet and ankles sizzled in pain, and a heavy weight pressed against her chest.

If she hadn't asked about Tess, Gabe might not have gone back into the stables. She was to blame for his injuries.

– 37 –

The following morning, Amy was sitting on the bed, fully clothed and anxious to leave, when Jonah popped in the door and jumped on the bed beside her.

"I've got a plan," he said.

"Careful there, buddy," Brett gently admonished him. "Don't bounce your aunt. She might go flying to the ceiling and bump her head."

"That's not gonna happen." His expression clearly read, "Dads are so embarrassing."

Amy laughed, her spirits light for the first time since this ordeal had begun. "I've missed you," she said.

"You've only been gone a couple of days."

"Do you always have to be so practical?" She tousled his hair, then squeezed his shoulder. "I'm glad you came. Especially when I know how much you hate hospitals."

"That's why I made my plan."

"What plan?"

"No more hospitals. We'll make a pact to never go to a hospital again."

"I'm all for that." She pulled him close and rested her chin on his head. "What do you say we get out of here?"

He jumped from the bed. "And fast."

When they reached the cottage, Amy allowed Brett and Jonah to settle her on the couch with the TV remote, a glass of juice, and her Kindle within easy reach.

"Dani picked up a few groceries," Brett said, "but if there's anything you need, just let me know."

"I'm not an invalid."

"Maybe not. But you've been through a horrific experience, and you need to take care of yourself."

"I don't see you lying on the couch being waited on hand and foot."

"I didn't breathe in as much smoke as you." He handed her a knitted throw, and she tossed it to the other end of the couch. "Do you need anything else?"

"Only to thank you both for your gallantry and to bid you farewell. I'm tired."

"Maybe we should stay. Just to keep watch."

"Jonah, would you please do something for me?"

"Sure."

"Take your dad to his car and let the door smack him on the way out."

"You heard her, Daddy." Jonah pulled Brett to his feet and gave him a push. "Can we come back later, Aunt Amy?"

She wanted to say no, but how could she resist the quiet plea in those crystal blue eyes? Eyes just like hers. Just like Brett's.

Just like Dad's.

"Come here," she said.

"Are you going to hug me?"

"You bet I am."

He hesitated only a moment before flinging himself into her open arms. She hugged him tight, grateful that he was still young

enough to accept an embrace. She glanced up to see Brett's gaze—
love mingled with pride—upon them.

"You're a blessing, Jonah," she whispered. "Do you have any
idea how much I love you?"

As she released him, he gave a sheepish shrug. "I'm glad you're
home."

"Me too, buddy. Me too."

"See ya later, gator," he chimed.

"After while, 'dile," she answered.

As soon as the gate closed behind them, Amy took a quick
shower, dressed, and sank to the bed to regain her strength. She'd
felt fine at the hospital, restless and eager to get home. But the
drive had wearied her more than she'd expected.

After taking several deep breaths, she pushed herself from the
mattress and slipped on a pair of sandals. The burns on her feet
ached, but she didn't care.

All she wanted was to see Gabe.

~

Amy pressed her hands against the window separating her
from Gabe's room. The drive to the burn center had been excruciating, and she had stopped a few times on the way to catch
her breath and renew her resolve. Only sheer willpower, intense
concentration, and perhaps a well-timed prayer or two had gotten her here safely. But the ordeal had been worth it just to see
him.

If only she could hold his hand, talk to him so he would know
he wasn't alone. But she wasn't allowed inside his room. Hospital
policy.

She hated rules.

"Excuse me," said a voice behind her. The man wore a military
uniform, and his distinguished gray hair was cut short. "Colonel
Steve Kendall. Are you a friend of Gabe's?"

She studied him, then extended her hand. "I'm Amy Somers."

"Amy?" He looked her over, concern—not appraisal—in his eyes. "Should you be here? I thought you were in the hospital."

"Who have you been talking to?"

"I've spent a few anxious hours with Shelby. If I have the family relations straight, her husband is your cousin."

"It sounds like Shelby has told you all about us."

"I think we both needed someone to talk to." He sighed heavily and peered through the window. "Is it true what they're saying? Gabe ran into the stables to save Tess?"

Amy nodded, afraid to trust her voice. Once again the guilt assailed her.

"It was a foolhardy thing for him to do," Colonel Kendall said gently. "But I'm not surprised. Tess filled a void in his life. Rusty too."

"Does he know about Tess?"

"Not yet. He's heavily sedated."

"Would you mind?" She paused, closing her eyes to garner the strength she needed. "Will you let me tell him?"

The colonel gazed at her, studying her as she had studied him. "Would I be right in assuming you and my son are more than just friends?"

"I don't know the answer to that."

"I see." He locked his hands behind his back and stared through the glass again. After a few moments, he strode to the door and held it open. "Are you coming?"

"They said I couldn't. I'm not family."

A slight smile lifted his lips. "I'll vouch for you."

"Thank you," she gushed while resisting the urge to hug him. "Thank you with all my heart."

Gabe's eyes fluttered in a dim world. His arms and legs were leaden weights holding him against a hard surface. His mind drifted from one nebulous dream-like place to another without rhyme or reason. Screams echoed from far away, and tendrils of smoke crept around him.

He blinked a couple of times and opened his eyes. The screams and the smoke disappeared, and his mind cleared. But he wasn't sure where he was or why he couldn't move his limbs. He focused first on the window, a rectangle of soft light from a distant sun. It was a fairly new day, or one that would end in a few hours. He couldn't tell which.

Either way, he shouldn't be in bed.

He never slept past 5:45. Never went to bed before 11:00.

"Gabe."

The sweet voice of an angel caressed his ear, and he turned his head despite the pain.

"You're awake," she said.

"Amy." The effort to speak scratched his clogged throat.

"Don't talk." She put her fingers on his lips, and he hoped she'd hold them there forever.

Can't move. He tried again to say something, but the words were only thoughts caught inside his head.

"I'll call the nurse."

Stay with me.

He strained to lift his hand, to move his fingers so he could catch hers when she touched him again. Distant voices faded in and out as he drifted between worlds.

When he woke again, the room was filled with sunlight. He blinked a couple of times and shook away the drowsiness. His limbs still felt heavy, but his fingers moved and he could raise his hand. White gauze surrounded each one of his fingers.

He could do this.

"Hello, Gabe."

He smiled at the angel's voice and forced his head to turn her way. "Amy." His voice was hoarse and it hurt to talk, but her name felt good on his lips.

"How are you?" she asked. "I've been so worried."

The memories came back again. The burning stable. Taking Daisy and Casper from their stalls then going back in again. His mind stopped.

"Are you . . ." The hoarseness forced him to pause.

"Drink this," Amy said. She held a straw to his lips. The cool liquid, flavored like lemons, soothed his mouth and throat.

"Are you hurt?" he asked.

"Not really," she said. "Not like you."

"The horses?"

"You rescued Casper and Daisy, remember?"

"I meant Abner and Knight Starr. All the others. Did they get out?"

"We can talk about that later. For now, you need to rest. To get better."

He strained to reach for her hand. She must have noticed, because her fingers gently touched his arm. The touch gave him strength to press on.

"Tell me," he said.

"Only Daisy and Casper survived. I'm sorry, Gabe. I know it hurts, but if you hadn't gone in, they'd have died too. The news media are calling you a hero."

He didn't want to be a hero. He only wanted to wake up from this nightmare.

Another memory floated into his consciousness, and he closed his eyes. He dreaded this one most of all, but he had to face it. He had to know the worst.

Heat forced him back, smoke filled his lungs. But he had to push his way into the barn. He had to find . . .

"Tess? Did I get her out in time?"

"You tried, Gabe. You tried so hard." Amy's voice caught. "But she didn't make it."

No, God. Please no. He had only one escape from the crushing pain. When the darkness came, he didn't fight it.

- 38 -

On Sunday morning, Amy went to church with Brett, Dani, and the three children while Shelby stayed home with AJ. His burns were healing, but he tired easily. Shelby confided in Amy that he wasn't ready to go out in public. He didn't want to answer questions or repeat the details of what had happened. But most of all, he was having trouble alleviating the guilt he felt because he hadn't been able to save Tess.

As Amy entered the sanctuary, Cassie welcomed her like a long-lost friend and stood close while others greeted her. Strengthened by Cassie's presence, Amy smiled and shook hands and even endured a few hugs from strangers without falling apart.

Before the sermon, the elders prayed specifically for healing for AJ and Gabe. Though Tess had attended a different church, they honored her memory. Many of these people knew her as a loving friend and a good neighbor.

Amy sat stoically between Dani and Cassie, determined not to join the quiet sobbing that could be heard throughout the sanctuary. She'd cried too many tears over the past few days.

Then the elders prayed for Amy and Brett. As their words surrounded her, a peace unlike anything she'd ever felt before nestled in her heart. Gabe once said that God's arms were always outstretched, like the father welcoming the return of his prodigal son. He'd also said that after a mess was a great time to get reacquainted with God.

Perhaps that time had come for her.

She bowed her head in a private prayer and heard those whispered words.

Be brave.

If only she knew how to be in the face of so much pain and tragedy. She knew she couldn't unless God was with her.

~

The familiar voice murmured near Gabe's ear, and he strained to decipher the words, to give a name to the speaker.

"... hear me, Gabe?" A long pause while Gabe blinked several times. "Come back to me, son."

Dad.

Gabe stretched his dried lips, struggled to form the word past the ache in his throat. A moist sponge dampened his mouth, and he forced his eyes to stay open despite their heaviness.

"Hello, son." Steve held the pink lollipop-sponge by its stick as if he wasn't sure what to do with it.

His father was never ill-at-ease, never unsure of anything. This must be part of the same nightmare where Tess couldn't breathe and horses screamed as flames scorched their flesh. Burnt his ears and his hands and . . .

"Dad," he whispered, closing his eyes against the pain of remembering. Amy had come. She'd told him about the horses, about Tess. They had talked, but now he could barely say a word. His swollen throat, his drug-addled brain made it almost impossible to concentrate. To think.

"I'm here, son."

Gabe's eyes flickered open again as his dad's fingers rested on his arm.

"I'm here. And I'm not going to leave you. I'm not going to—" His voice cracked.

"I didn't save her." The words emerged as separate breaths that took all of Gabe's effort. "I failed you, sir."

"No, Gabe. I'm the one who failed. I failed you and Tess both." A heavy sigh filled the space between them. "If I'd been a better man, maybe this wouldn't have happened. I don't expect you to forgive me. All I ask is that you don't give up. I can't lose you, son."

The pleading warmth of his dad's words eased the clog in Gabe's throat and somehow lessened the pain that tensed his body.

"You won't, sir," he whispered as he once again drifted to the place where pain couldn't follow.

~

After the church service, the family gathered at AJ's bungalow for a buffet lunch. The kitchen counter was filled with casseroles and other food provided by the neighbors. Amy put together a grilled chicken salad, joined the children at an outside table, and choked down each bite.

Despite the tremendous urge pulling her to the brink of her horrible abyss, she did not throw up.

Later that afternoon, she stood outside the ruins of the burnt-out stables and closed her eyes as the memory of the heat and the smells and the smoke assailed her. Ken Abbott, the fire investigator, had requested that she, Brett, and AJ meet with him to answer more questions.

"I didn't even know you were here," Amy said to Dani. "I don't think I was aware of much that was going on around me except beating that blanket against the flames."

"Shelby and I came as soon as we could," Dani said. "But by then they were putting you in the ambulance and trying to get Brett to let them give him oxygen. He didn't want to leave you."

"That's my big brother. Always overdoing it in the too-protective department." Amy walked along the stable's foundation, then stopped and kicked at a loose board. "Someone said Dr. Addison took Casper and Daisy to his place. How are they doing?"

"Both had a few burns, but they'll be okay. He's taking good care of them."

"Tess would have appreciated that. I think she had a crush on him."

"Jason said he's pretty broken up."

"Aren't we all?"

When Abbott arrived with the county sheriff, they stood around him in a loose circle.

"We've read all your statements," Abbott said. "But we thought it might be helpful to walk through what happened here at the scene."

"Are all fires given this level of scrutiny?" Brett asked. "It's not like any of us are responsible for what happened."

"We like to be thorough," Abbott replied, then turned to Amy. "Would you mind going first?"

"I suppose not."

Brett touched her arm. "Are you sure you're up for this?"

"Do I have a choice?"

"We do appreciate your cooperation," Abbott said. "I know how hard this must be."

She glared at him, then answered his questions as he slowly, painstakingly, took her through everything that had happened that day. Once they'd finished, she retreated to the paddock while he did the same with AJ and Brett. Abbott even questioned Shelby and Dani.

Amy had a hard enough time telling her own story. She couldn't abide listening to their versions of the same horrid event.

As the men prepared to leave, Brett stopped them. "We've cooperated with you, answered all your questions," he said. "I think it's time you told us what's really going on here."

Abbott exchanged glances with the sheriff.

"How did the fire start?" Brett asked.

"I'm not at liberty to say."

"But it wasn't an accident," Brett clarified.

"No." Abbott looked from Brett to Amy. "It wasn't."

Amy gasped, barely able to comprehend the horrific ramifications of what Abbott was saying.

"Someone did this on purpose?" she finally sputtered.

Hot tears stung her eyes as seething anger bubbled inside her. Images of Gabe emerging from the barn, of AJ praying over Tess, of the screaming horses ricocheted around her brain. Her body felt about to explode into a multitude of individual particles—each one overflowing with raging sorrow.

Brett drew her into an embrace, and she hid her face in his shoulder while her body knit itself back together. For as long as she could remember, this had been her safe place. Her refuge from fighting parents, from chaos, from pain that made her want to shrivel away into nothingness.

She took deep calming breaths, willing the heat of her anger to cool enough for her to regain control.

Horses had died.

Tess had died.

Gabe and AJ could have died.

But why? Why would anyone do this awful, horrible thing?

- 39 -

*B*efore her follow-up appointment with her physician, Amy met Logan at the bakery. She didn't want to, but his frequent calls asking to see her were driving her mad. Better to meet him here with an end time than invite him to the cottage. Once he got there, she was afraid he'd never leave.

Logan had ordered iced mochas before Amy arrived. He stood as she joined him and assisted with her chair. "I know I said it before, but I can't help saying it again. You don't know how glad I am you're out of that hospital."

"You're not nearly as glad as I am."

"You know, I would have come out to your place. Been your chauffeur to the doctor's office. Should you even be driving?"

"I'm fine, Logan. And I don't like being treated like a baby."

He gently took her arm and caressed the unblemished skin around a burned circle about the size of a quarter. The result of one of the many sparks that had assailed her while she beat at the flame.

~

Logan stared regretfully at Amy's marred skin. If only he could have kept her away without raising her suspicion. In the end, he had left her well-being to chance, and now he was paying the price for his negligence.

"You're too beautiful to have something like this happen to you," he said. "It won't scar, will it?"

"Probably not. But it might take a few weeks to heal."

"I suppose you can wear long sleeves."

"Why would I do that?"

Was she serious?

"You're trying to be strong. I get it." He leaned close, his voice soft and intimate. "But you're Amy Somers. Flawless. Perfect. Your vanity is one of the many things I admire about you."

"I'm also smart. Some might say cunning."

Not exactly the response he expected. Apparently she wasn't in the mood for flirting, but he wouldn't give up yet. After everything he'd done, she had to see they belonged together. "Also very attractive qualities."

He allowed his eyes to slowly follow the cascade of her gorgeous blonde hair past the curve of her cheek and the length of her slender throat.

Amy sipped her drink, then pushed it away. "We had to meet with the sheriff and the fire investigator yesterday. At the stables."

Her words gripped his chest like a vise, though he pretended they meant nothing. Instead, he focused on the pendant of her necklace and wished her neckline was cut a few inches lower.

"Are you listening to me?" she asked.

"I'm sure it's routine. Prominent citizens are injured in a fire. Of course the sheriff is going to do everything he can to demonstrate his concern. Prominent citizens then donate to his re-election campaign."

"The fire wasn't an accident."

He leaned back as if shocked by the news. "What do you mean?"

"Arson."

"But who would do something like that?"

316

She hesitated a moment as if the words choked her. "I think they suspect Gabe."

Yes! The news Logan wanted to hear. About time too. He squelched his desire to shout for joy and instead looked puzzled. "Why him?"

"I don't know." She ran a strand of her hair through her fingers. Such an annoying habit. "Probably because he already has a record."

Logan feigned ignorance. "What kind of record?"

"His cousin robbed a convenience store, and Gabe was with him when it happened."

"Maybe they're right."

Amy stared at him, as stunned as if he'd slapped her. "They're not."

"But if not him, who? Surely not Tess Marshall. She wouldn't have set a fire then died in it. Who else had motive?"

"What motive did Gabe have?" Her tone was angry, indignant even.

"Maybe for the insurance money. Maybe because he didn't want Tess to sell the stables. Maybe—"

"I have a different theory," she said. "Dylan Tapley."

"You think Dylan set that fire?"

"More likely he hired someone."

"I don't believe it."

She leaned forward and smacked the table. "He wants that land. I'm beginning to believe he'd do anything to get it."

"Dylan's desperate to prove to his uncle he can be successful, I'll give you that. But you can't seriously believe he'd stoop to murder just to get a land deal."

"He probably didn't mean for anyone to die. But I'm convinced he's behind this."

"I don't know, Amy. You don't want to hear this, I get it, but if the authorities think it was Gabe, then they must have evidence."

She straightened her shoulders and stared at him. The cold light of her eyes practically dared him to blink. "Did you know Dylan planned this?"

"It wasn't him."

"If I find out you knew . . . that you allowed this to happen . . ."

"Are you kidding me? Of course I didn't."

She only stared, her jaw set like stone. "I can't believe you. I want to, but I can't." He reached for her hand, but she jerked away. "Don't call me. Don't text me. Never even think my name."

"Amy, please."

She grabbed her bag and walked out. The splotched burns on her calves and ankles tore at his heart, but he couldn't look away. Her misguided attempt to save the stables had marred her beauty. But that didn't change his desire for her. He'd have to give her more time, that was all. Time to mourn Tess Marshall. Time to get over Kendall.

Eventually she'd see that they belonged together. Then all his dreams of wealth and prestige would come true.

~

Gabe could take the physical pain. No matter how bad it got, he'd cope. The treatments, the therapies, were excruciating, but he fought through the agony.

However, the pain of losing Tess, of not saving her, was different. He could never forgive himself for not saving her first. If only he'd known she was in the stables, he'd have searched for her. Gotten her to safety.

"Mr. Kendall," Ken Abbott said. "This doesn't look good for you."

"How can you think . . ."

"Amy Somers said that your aunt wasn't home when the two of you went to Boyd's. Obviously you didn't expect her to be there."

"She'd gone into town, so no, I didn't. I didn't expect someone to set the stables on fire either."

"Was Ms. Somers in on the plan?"

"There was no plan." Gabe emphasized each word.

"Somebody went to a great deal of effort. Setting the timers, hooking them up to the heating rods. We did our homework. Your aunt was near bankruptcy. About to lose the property. You have to admit this is all very suspicious."

"It is," Gabe said, no longer able to hide his anger. "And instead of suspecting me, suspecting Amy, you should be finding out who did this. Because if I find out who's responsible, I'll—"

"Don't finish that sentence, son." Steve Kendall stepped forward to face Abbott. Gabe hadn't realized his dad had come back into the room. "You will not question Gabe again unless his attorney is present."

"If he's innocent, he doesn't need an attorney."

"If only that were true. I think you can find your way out."

After Abbott left, Steve took his stance in front of the window, his posture military-straight, his hands clasped behind his back.

"They're going to arrest me, aren't they?" Gabe said. "I can't do this again."

"The evidence is circumstantial. They have no proof."

"Who would do such a thing?" He didn't know why he bothered to ask the question. If Tapley was behind the break-in, he could be responsible for this too.

His dad shifted his weight uncomfortably. "Did you know Tess was about to lose the property?"

"I knew she was in trouble." He looked down, examining his burnt fingers. "She could have sold the place, but I talked her out of it. This is all my fault."

"I know you don't want to hear this, son. But it's possible Tess did this. Maybe it was her only way out."

"No," Gabe said harshly. "She would never have endangered the horses. Or got caught in the fire herself. That doesn't even make

319

sense. Someone else did this. And as soon as I get out of here, I'm going to find out who."

"Make me one promise."

"If I can."

"Don't talk to anyone again without a lawyer present. If they charge you, they will find you guilty."

"How can you be so certain?"

"You claimed innocence before and the jury didn't believe you. Do you think a jury will believe you a second time?"

"I don't have a motive."

"Abbott thinks you do. The same motive Tess had."

"So now you think Tess and I planned this together?" Gabe shook his head in disbelief. "And here I thought you believed me."

"I do, Gabe. But you can't shut your eyes to their accusations."

Gabe leaned back into his pillows and stared at the ceiling. "I can't believe this is happening all over again."

"It won't. I won't let it."

"What can you do?"

"First? Get you an attorney. Then later, when your name is cleared, we'll talk about your future."

His future? He didn't have one.

- 40 -

*A*my woke early the next morning after a restless night's sleep with one steadying thought. She needed to get the arrowhead from the Hearth, and she needed to give it to Gabe. As soon as she dressed, she drove over to Tess's. The graveled driveway gave way to packed dirt, which eventually turned into a barely discernible lane along the edges of the wood. Her BMW bounced and jerked, but she maneuvered it around and through the ruts and weeds until she could go no farther.

She walked across the long, weathered boards bridging the stream and entered the woods with a brief prayer she could find the Hearth. The path was obscure in places, and a couple of times she had to double back, but eventually she found the split-trunked tree that sheltered the ruined fireplace.

Its stone remains were caught in a tangle of vines and fragrant wild roses. Over the years, more of the stones had fallen, but the interior corner was still intact.

When Amy and Gabe had found this place, they imagined stories about the people who had built the fireplace and about the house that must have stood there at one time. Sometimes the stories were realistic, plausible. Other times they pretended the fireplace was a portal into another world.

It had been their secret place and hallowed by love's first kiss.

Amy carefully parted the long grass, keeping a wary eye out for snakes, then knelt before the ruins.

"I should have brought gloves," she muttered as she brushed away cobwebs with a squeamish gesture. She reached within the stones of the crumbling chimney. Relief flooded through her as her fingers touched the tin canister hiding within the recess.

She carried the box to the split-trunked tree and perched in a nook created by two of its lower branches. Breathing a prayer of thanks, she ran her fingers across the dirt-encrusted lid. About ten years had passed since she'd last held this box, but she remembered the moment as if it had just happened.

She'd come here shortly before moving to a private liberal arts college in Pennsylvania. On that day, she had placed the arrowhead inside the box for safekeeping. It was only an artifact from a long-ago civilization, not that rare in these central Ohio fields and pastures. But this one was special because she and Gabe had found it together while watering their horses in the springs branching off the southern branch of Glade Creek.

The arrowhead symbolized the summer of their youth, their token of future dreams. She never wanted to lose it, never wanted anyone else to find it. So she'd left it here.

She'd also left a letter for Gabe, though she was sure he would never read it.

Another moment passed and another while Amy relived her memories of that sad and glorious summer. Sad because Gabe was mourning the loss of his mom. Glorious because the two of them together had made it so.

And because it was the last happy summer Amy ever had.

She pressed her palm against the lid, then gripped an edge with her fingernails and pried it off.

Instead of her letter to Gabe, the box contained two envelopes. Her name, written in Gabe's distinctive handwriting, appeared on each. The arrowhead lay beneath them.

Gabe had been back. He'd taken her letter and left the arrowhead behind.

She paused to remember what she had written.

Only a short note saying she needed to leave, that she wanted to find her own way instead of following AJ and Brett to OSU. She told him the box was the safest place she knew to keep their arrowhead. Someday, when the time was right, she'd come back for it.

She tucked the arrowhead into her hand, holding it like she had the day Gabe slipped it to her, the day when neither of them could speak for the emotion clogging their throats.

The day of her parents' memorial.

The last time she'd seen him until he found her at the engagement tree.

While holding on to the arrowhead, Amy opened both of Gabe's envelopes, scanned the dates, and read the earlier one first. It had been typed and printed, probably so he could revise as he wrote. The message was brief, a spilling of his heart.

Dear Amy,

I ship out next week to an undisclosed location. Hint: it's hot there.

So why am I writing to you? Because I have to write to someone, and who better than the girl who took away my heart on a hot summer day? We rode out here to the Hearth, you and me, and we placed our summer finds in a tin and hid it within a chimney. A kind of time capsule of a year bookmarked by grief. First the loss of my mom, and then the loss of your parents.

The last time I was here I came for the arrowhead. It was

stupid, but I wanted to give you something to hold on to. That's why I handed it to you at the memorial.

I'll never forget your face—so sad, so broken. You have no idea how much I wanted to kiss away all your tears right there in front of everybody.

What a scandal that would have been. Your grandfather would have tanned my hide, but I like to think your gran would have found it secretly funny.

I just want you to know, my sweet Amy, that no matter where in the world I am, no matter where you are, I will always love you.

> *My heart is yours,*
> *Gabe*

Beneath the signature were handwritten lines.

Come back for the arrowhead, Amy. Come back for it soon. When the time is right, place it in my hand. I'll be waiting.

Amy sat in the tree nook, her back against a rough branch, and let Gabe's words flow through her. He'd written the letter years ago. Could he still be waiting for her to place the arrowhead in his hand?

It was as if their minds were in sync with one another, that his plan had somehow, all these years later, become her plan.

Or was this God's plan? Did he care enough about two broken people to use an arrowhead—a lost relic from another time—to bring them together again? To help them become whole?

She read the second letter, penned in ink.

My dearest Amy,

I don't know what I hoped to find when I pulled out our box. Until I opened it and found my last letter to you. Un-

324

touched. Unopened. The disappointment was so keen that then I knew. I had hoped to find you had been here. I had hoped to find a letter from you.

I need you, Amy. I need you now, today, when the finest man I've ever known has been laid to rest. Rusty's gone, and I feel lost.

Where are you, Amy? Why aren't you here?

I think I'd rather have found a letter telling me to get lost, that anything I thought we had was puppy love, a first crush, a summer fling. I'd rather have had that than nothing at all.

Maybe that's all it was to you. But not to me.

When I saw the arrowhead, I wanted to throw it as far away from here as I could. But something stopped me. As strange as it sounds, I felt like God stayed my hand.

If you ever come back, I want you to find our arrowhead here. So I'm leaving it in the box. I'm leaving the box in the chimney. And I'm praying that someday you'll come here again. And you'll know that, wherever I am, I'm still waiting for you.

> *With all my love,*
> *Gabe*

Amy read the letters again, hearing Gabe's voice whispering his words in her ear.

She wished he had said something about the letters. About how he felt. Why hadn't he?

The answer was hurtful but plain.

He didn't say anything because all along he knew she was lying about not remembering him. He knew she had returned to the Hearth and hidden the arrowhead in the only place that mattered.

That was one reason, but the ugly voices in her head gave her another. After they'd met again, someone must have told Gabe

325

what kind of person she'd become. He was content to be friends, to hang out together, go on a date now and then. But he was no longer waiting.

He no longer wanted her.

How could she blame him?

"Is it too late?" she whispered. "God, please don't let it be too late for Gabe and me."

- 41 -

Amy paused outside the elevator and took a deep breath. Then she dug the arrowhead from her bag and slipped it into her pocket. She'd chosen her outfit with special care for this afternoon's visit. The dark blue of the textured dress deepened the clear blue of her eyes while the gold belt and matching cuff bracelet added glamor.

If things went well, it'd be a memory she and Gabe would always treasure, and she wanted him to remember her as looking beautiful. If things didn't go well . . . She shook her head. She didn't even want to think about that possibility.

She smoothed her skirt, applied a fresh coat of lip gloss, and strode confidently toward Gabe's room. The blind on his window was open, and she peeked inside, then drew back. Steve Kendall and Ellen were in the room along with one of the specialists. The conversation appeared intense, and a wave of jealousy swept over Amy that Ellen was included.

Amy backed away from the window and slipped into a nearby alcove. It held a few chairs, a couple of tables with magazines, and a coffee station. She busied herself pouring a cup of coffee she didn't want, adding sugar and cream, going through the motions while scarcely aware of what she was doing.

She took a sip of the coffee and made a face. Definitely not worth the calories, and that had nothing to do with eating issues. How did anyone stomach this stuff?

Voices sounded in the hall, and she peeked around the corner. The conversation was now taking place in the hall. She pulled a strand of hair through her fingers, took a deep breath, and walked confidently toward the small group.

"Colonel Kendall, Ellen," she said cheerily, then extended her hand to the doctor. She held the practiced smile that revealed her single dimple. Brett wasn't the only one blessed with charm. "Hello, I'm Amy Somers, Gabe's friend. And you are?"

"Dr. Grant," he replied. She let him hold her hand a second longer than necessary. "My pleasure."

"And mine. How is Gabe?"

"Restless." Steve smiled at Amy. "As soon as the paperwork is complete, he can leave."

"Gabe's being released?" Amy said. "Isn't it too soon?"

"We're arranging at-home care," the doctor said. "His bandages need to be changed a couple of times a day, and we'll be keeping an eye on his pain management. But he's free to go."

"The question is where," Ellen said. "Steve and I believe he shouldn't be alone, so I've offered my home."

"I see," Amy said warily. "What does Gabe want to do?"

"He wants to go to Tess's," Steve said.

"Of course he does. That's where his friends are. Me, my brother, my cousin. We'll take care of him."

"Ellen is also his friend," Steve said. "Please don't take offense, but she's known him longer than any of you."

I wouldn't be so sure about that. Amy fingered the arrowhead in her pocket, feeling its rough edges beneath her fingers. Arguing about who knew Gabe first and best was a waste of breath. She needed a more persuasive argument.

"We're only thinking of Gabe," Ellen said. "You must see that."

"So am I." Amy straightened her shoulders and lifted her chin. "But it really doesn't matter what you or I think or what we want. All that matters is what Gabe wants. He loved Tess." She looked pointedly at the colonel. "Please don't take offense, sir, but she opened her home to him when no one else did."

The colonel's chest swelled, and Amy feared he was going to blow. But after a moment, he sighed. "A decision I will always regret."

"Then don't make another."

He held Amy's gaze for a long moment, then nodded. "Ellen and I will see to the paperwork. Why don't you have a few words with Gabe? Let him know he's going home."

Overcome with joy, Amy whispered a quick thank-you, then entered Gabe's room. His eyes lit up when he saw her.

"Hi," he said.

"How are you?"

"Anxious to get out of here. Except . . ."

"I just talked to your dad. He agreed that it was your decision. Where you wanted to go, I mean."

"Are you telling me that you talked my dad into changing his mind about something?"

"Guess I did."

"You are a sweet talker, aren't you?"

Warmed by his teasing, Amy smiled. The arrowhead weighed heavy in her pocket, but this wasn't the time to give it to him. Not when Colonel Kendall or Ellen could walk in at any moment.

"Please come back to Whisper Lane. If the memories aren't too painful."

"There's nowhere else I'd rather be," he said.

"I won't let you lose it. Not after all you've been through."

"Then you might have to use those sweet-talking skills on Abbott."

"Has he been here?"

"He thinks I set the fire. That I would do something like that."

"I think it was Dylan Tapley."

"You know Tapley?"

"I've worked with him before. He knew Tess didn't want to sell so he's been trying to ruin her. Think about it. The break-in. The poisoning. Then arson." Her eyes grew round. "He's framing you."

Gabe's jaw worked, and his eyes narrowed. "I'm calling Abbott. He left his card here."

"I'm going to see Dylan. I should have confronted him days ago. Then maybe this wouldn't have happened." Amy stood, breathing deeply to calm her angry nerves. Dylan had the upper hand during their last argument. This time it was her turn.

~

"Amy," Gabe called after her. But she didn't stop. "Oh, great," he muttered. The only thing he could do was go after her. Now.

He pressed the call button and pulled out his IV. "Find my dad. And hurry. It's an emergency—it's important."

His dad had bought him new clothes, a light cotton shirt that wouldn't irritate the burns on the back of his neck and khakis. By the time his dad arrived, Gabe was slipping his bare feet into boat shoes.

"What's going on?" Steve asked.

"It's Amy. She's convinced Tapley set the fire and went to confront him."

"Who's Tapley?"

"I'll explain on the way. We need to get there pronto."

"You still have papers to sign."

"For once in your life, Dad, will you forget the rules? I'm going after Amy. Are you going to help me or stand there and cite regulations?"

A slow easy smile crossed his dad's face. "I'm going with you."

His dad drove while Gabe used the car's GPS to navigate to Tapley's office. They illegally parked in front of the building, then Steve helped Gabe into the spacious lobby. Amy stood in front of the bank of elevators, obviously impatient as she waited for the doors to open.

"Amy," Gabe called.

She turned and hurried toward him. "Why are you here?"

"You didn't think I'd let you have all the fun, did you?"

"Just don't pass out on me."

The elevator door opened, and they ascended to Tapley's floor. As they approached his office suite, Amy hesitated. "We'll have to walk past the admins as if we know what we're doing. Remember, appear confident. In charge."

Gabe and his dad exchanged amused glances, and Amy gave an exaggerated sigh.

"Right. You're military. You don't need my coaching."

As she led them toward the office doors, Steve whispered to Gabe, "She's a keeper, son."

"Don't I know it."

~

Logan stood at Tapley's table in disbelief. The map and overlays he'd seen a few days before had been replaced by another one, a more detailed version of the Whisper Lane property. It showed a few of the current structures, including the horse barn that had burned, plus proposed new ones.

"What is this?" Logan said.

"My plans for Whisper Lane," Dylan replied. "Just like I told Mrs. Marshall before she died."

"That was a ruse, Dylan. We both know it."

"Perhaps at first. But I'd enjoy raising horses."

"What happened to turning Sullivan's land into a shopping mall? To making Amy pay for ruining your previous deal? Your uncle isn't going to like it if you fail again."

Dylan stuck his hands in his pockets and ambled to a nearby

window. He stared at the street, three stories below him, then flashed a humorless smile. "My uncle has bigger problems. Apparently, he's to be arrested for tax fraud any day now. Lucky for me, I was his least favorite nephew. Or I might be headed to prison too."

Logan's mind whirled. After everything he had done, all the planning and scheming, it couldn't all fall apart. Not now.

Dylan returned to his desk but didn't sit down. "We're about to have company," he said as he pulled an envelope from a drawer.

Logan faced the door as it opened.

Amy, his beautiful Amy, strode in, followed closely by Kendall and an older version of the ex-con. With false bravado, Logan glared at the men. With his bandaged fingers and slumped posture, Gabe didn't seem much of a threat. But the other man, despite his age, looked formidable in his pressed Air Force uniform.

"Logan?" Amy said. "I didn't expect to see you here."

Before he could respond, Dylan gestured toward the chairs. "I saw you arrive from the window," he said. "Please sit down."

"I'd rather not," Amy answered.

"You think I'm responsible for that fire." Dylan focused on Amy, his voice quiet but firm. "It's true I wanted Mrs. Marshall's land, your cousin's land. And I'm not above a little bribery when it's worth my while. But I'd never resort to arson." He faced Logan, and his eyes filled with loathing.

A cold chill ran up Logan's spine, and his feet seemed frozen to the floor. He hadn't confided this part of the plan to Dylan, so he could have no proof. Unless . . . he stared at the envelope on Dylan's desk.

~

Amy pressed her hand against her stomach as she stared at Logan, trying to see beyond her handsome plus-one to the fiend who had caused such misery. "You?"

"No," he said quickly.

But guilt filled his eyes with panic.

She took a step toward him, though she didn't know why. Gabe's bandaged fingers reached for her hand, giving her strength as hot tears stung her eyes.

"We should call the fire investigator," he said.

Dylan spread his hand on the envelope. "The evidence he needs is in here. If I'd known what Logan was up to sooner, I'd have stopped him."

"Stop me?" Logan huffed. "We're partners. If I go down for this, so will you."

"I wanted property. You're the one who wanted Gabe back in prison."

Amy startled, then her mind clicked the puzzle pieces into place as Logan's intentions became clear. Hatred flared then inexplicably disappeared. The stories Gabe had told her—about Job surviving his miseries and the open arms of the prodigal son's father—filled her heart instead. She refused to be consumed by anger. Not when Gabe's strength could be hers.

"How could you, Logan?" She bit her lip and struggled to control her shaking voice. "How could you be so heartless? So cruel?"

"I'm cruel?" The hurt in his eyes pinched his features into a sad caricature. "It was our time, Amy. Yours and mine." He glared at Gabe. "He was ruining everything. Don't you see? I had to get rid of him."

"So you set the fire," Gabe said quietly. "Tried to make it look like I did it."

"Yeah," Logan retorted, his hurt replaced by hatred. "I did."

Immediately, a man and woman entered from an anteroom and flashed their badges. After introducing themselves as homicide detectives, the man cuffed Logan and charged him with Tess's murder and the arson. Dylan removed the wire he was wearing and handed it to the woman.

After they left, taking Logan with them, Amy turned to Dylan. "What just happened?"

"It's simple," he said. "I helped the police solve a crime."

"But why?"

"My lawyer advised me to. Otherwise I might have been charged as an accessory."

"Did you know—"

"I didn't. I promise you I didn't." Dylan eased his large frame into his desk chair. "But I knew other things. My testimony will keep Logan behind bars for a very long time."

"What kind of things?"

"Logan broke into Mrs. Marshall's home. Printed copies of her financial information. He also made anonymous calls to animal welfare."

"What's in the envelope?" Gabe's voice shook with controlled anger.

"Oh, that." The hint of a smile flashed across Dylan's features. He upended the envelope, and several photos spilled out. "A run-down strip mall and a derelict apartment complex in Tucson."

"But Logan thought . . ." Amy suppressed a sudden urge to giggle.

"'The wicked flee,'" Steve quoted, "'when no one pursues.'" He rested his hand on Gabe's shoulder. "'But the righteous are as bold as a lion.' Proverbs 28:1."

"Thanks, Dad. But that isn't me." Gabe's voice sounded ragged, and his shoulders slumped as if losing the fight to stay upright.

"We'll talk about it later, son. Are you ready to go?"

"As ready as I'll ever be."

Amy turned to Dylan. "Thank you," she said. "But you still can't have Whisper Lane. Or any part of Misty Willow."

"Didn't expect I could."

"There's one more thing."

"You want to know whose strings I'm pulling on the county commission."

"I want his resignation."

"You'll make sure people know—Logan's the murderer. Not me."

"I'll do what I can." Amy flashed him a dimpled smile. "Unless you try to cheat me or my family or anyone else I care about ever again."

Dylan gave a tight smile. "I wouldn't dare."

– 42 –

Gabe sat beside his father in the second pew at Tess's church. The seat was cushioned but still uncomfortable. Throughout the service, a celebration of Tess's life that honored her commitment to her faith, her community, and the horses that were placed in her care, Gabe sat as erect as his dad. His face was stoic, emotionless. He could not show vulnerability in front of these people who cared about his aunt or he would fall apart.

After singing the last song, Gabe and his father were escorted from the sanctuary by an usher. They stood in the foyer, the only relatives Tess had, and accepted the condolences of those who had been touched by her generous spirit.

Amy approached Gabe, gave him a watery smile, then gently hugged him. He returned the embrace, finding the comfort he desperately needed in her arms.

"You look so tired," she said.

"I guess I'm not sleeping very well."

"The pain?"

He bit the inside of his lip for a moment before answering. The physical pain he could handle. But the ache in his heart? He doubted it would ever go away. He wasn't even sure he wanted it to.

He only wanted to return to Whisper Lane and mourn the aunt he loved in private.

"It hurts," he said simply, trusting Amy to understand.

~

Hearing tires on gravel and the blare of a horn, Gabe stepped outside to greet Dr. Addison. He was bringing Casper and Daisy home, and Gabe was looking forward to a ride.

In the weeks since the fire, Gabe's neighbors had devoted their spare time to cleaning out the barn where the stagecoach had been stored and building horse stalls. Gabe wasn't able to do much at first, and he still wasn't at 100 percent. But he'd returned to his routine, up at 5:45, in bed no earlier than 11:00, in hopes of calming the restlessness that had eaten at him since his discharge from the hospital.

Once he got in the saddle, he hoped that would change.

Flint parked his truck and got out. "Hey, Gabe," he said. "How're you doing?"

"I'll be better now that Daisy and Casper are home."

"I'm sure you will." They walked to the end of the long trailer, and Flint opened the door. He entered the trailer, led Daisy down the ramp, and handed Gabe the reins.

"You've already got her saddled?"

"Thought you might want to take a ride once she got here." Flint disappeared back into the trailer.

Gabe buried his face against her neck. She snuffed his shoulder and his hair.

"Hello to you too," he said. "Ready to gallop?"

Flint reappeared leading another saddled buckskin. She could almost be Daisy's twin except for their slightly different black markings.

"Who's this?" Gabe asked in surprise.

"Her name is Wild Rose."

Another flower name.

"Where did you get her?"

Doc glanced into the trailer, and Amy stepped to its edge.

"She belongs to me."

"Same question," Gabe said with a chuckle. Her unexpected appearance added another sparkle to the day. "Where did *you* get her?"

"She's a daughter of a daughter of Marigold. Once I found her, I did a little wheeling and dealing, and now she's mine." Amy jumped off the trailer and tugged on the brim of Gabe's beat-up Stetson. "You wanna go for a ride?"

"To the Hearth?"

She nodded slowly. "To the Hearth."

Gabe tried not to read too much into her answer. But his heart raced faster the closer they got to the stone chimney.

When the woods got dense, they tied the horses to a low branch and followed the path on foot.

Gabe took her hand, thankful the bandages had finally been removed from his fingers. "When did you start riding again?" he asked.

"Tess gave me a lesson or two. I wanted it to be a surprise."

"That it was."

They reached the chimney, and Gabe knelt in front of it. "Do you remember what's hidden in here?"

"What?" she asked with a glint of mischief in her cool blue eyes.

Instead of answering, he reached behind the stone and retrieved the tin box. He sat on a nearby log and held it toward Amy. "Would you like to do the honors?"

He eyed her closely, but her poker face gave no indication of having seen the box before.

"You open it," she urged.

He pulled off the lid and blinked. It couldn't be.

The box was empty.

Amy reached into her pocket and sat beside him. She placed his hand on his knee, palm up, then opened her palm against his. Something hard and rough pressed against his skin.

"Is this what you were looking for?"

He stared at the arrowhead then at her. "I knew you couldn't have forgotten."

"I'm sorry I lied to you, Gabe. I was so surprised to see you, and my life seemed such a mess that day. Then having told the lie, I felt like I was stuck with it."

"The last time I saw this," he said, hefting the arrowhead, "it was in the box. When did you take it out?"

"I hiked back here after the fire." She wrapped her arms around her knees and swayed on the log. "I read your letters, Gabe."

"Where are they?"

"At the cottage. Tucked away in a safe place."

He pulled out his wallet and retrieved a folded piece of paper. "Recognize this?"

Her gaze darted from the paper to him. "My letter to you? You still have it."

"You know me, Amy. I hold on to the things I care about. Whether it's a pickup truck I can't get running or this old beat-up Stetson. I held on to this too, because it was the last connection I had with you."

She placed her hand against his jaw and gazed into his eyes. "In your letters, you said you would always wait for me. Did you mean it?"

"I meant it. But now isn't the right time for us, Amy. I have nothing. No idea what's going to happen tomorrow. No plan for the future."

"Why can't we make one together? Tess and I had an idea about what to do with the stables. It's not too late."

"You mean the nonprofit for kids?"

"She told you?"

"I found a folder in her office where she'd been making notes, writing down questions and so forth. It looked like something she wanted to pursue."

"We can do it, Gabe. You and me in Tess's memory."

She sounded so hopeful, confident and assured. But to him the idea seemed too risky. He needed something more permanent than a struggling nonprofit could offer. He needed a career he could count on to support a family someday.

He took her hand in both of his. "If I asked you to, how long would you wait for me?"

"A lifetime. But please don't make me."

"I need to get a job and I need to try to hold on to Whisper Lane before it goes into foreclosure. If I can't do it, I won't even have a place to live." His shoulders sagged. "I've got nothing to offer you."

"My 'home' belongs to my cousin."

Gabe made a harrumphing noise. "You're used to a different life, Amy. We can pretend it's not true or that it doesn't matter. But we both know our circumstances aren't the same."

"I don't know that."

"Come on. You drive around in a BMW. I've got a broken-down old Ford. My checking account is in the three-figure range. I can't even imagine what you must have squirreled away. It may be old-fashioned or prideful, but I'm not going to live off my wife."

"Let me set you straight on a few things, Gabriel Kendall." Her eyes sparkled with pretend outrage. "You have a few hundred in the bank? I'm a little ahead of you there since I have a few thousand. But that's it. And I traded my BMW for Wild Rose so we'd have three horses instead of just two. Our herd may be small, but it's a start."

"Back up a minute. You traded your baby?"

"And I have a job. At least a temporary one."

"Doing what?"

"Didn't you hear? Dylan's commissioner friend resigned."

"Guess I've been busy with other things." Like sorting through Tess's belongings. Trying to figure out how he was going to keep the place without taking a handout from his dad.

"I'm campaign manager for the man who's going to take his place."

Gabe took a moment to let that sink in. "Who are you working for? AJ?"

Amy snorted. "I didn't even try to talk him into running."

"I give up. Whose arm did you twist?"

"Paul Norris. Though I didn't have to twist very hard. He'll protect this county. Its ag industry. And I'm going to help him do it."

Determination shone in her eyes, and its light filled Gabe's heart with renewed hope that maybe the future wasn't so grim after all. "Who'd have believed it? City gal Amy Somers all enthusiastic about country folk," he drawled.

"I'm serious, Gabe." Her eyes shifted away, she took a deep breath, then stared at him. "I did something else. Now don't get mad."

"You definitely woke up my curiosity with that line. What did you do?"

"Made it so you're all caught up on the mortgage." She placed her hand against his lips before he could respond. "I know what you're thinking, but I also know we can do this."

Gabe rose, then paced in the small space in front of the log. "I don't believe it." Though he shouldn't be surprised. If anyone could succeed at such a venture, it was his Amy.

"Now we're partners. I know the property has to go through probate and all that, but you can keep living in your house. Or you can move into the cottage with me. Or I can move in with you."

He widened his eyes in mock horror. "What exactly are you suggesting?"

She gave him an impish grin. "I do expect there to be a wedding first."

"Hold it right there, little lady. If anyone is going to do any proposing around here, it's me."

"Just make it soon."

Gabe reached for her hands, pulled her to her feet, then clasped his arms around her waist. "You said you'd wait a lifetime."

She removed his hat and gazed into his eyes. "I doubt I'll have to."

He shook his head as he bent closer. "Do you remember the last time we were here?"

"Every moment."

He gently pressed his lips against hers, and tasted again the innocence of their youth.

A breeze quickened, rustling the leaves surrounding them and whispering long-ago echoes of their first kiss.

I love you, Amy.

I love you too, Gabe.

– 43 –

ONE YEAR LATER

Gabe stirred from a restful night's sleep and checked the glowing red numbers on the old clock radio.

6:52 a.m.

He breathed a contented sigh as Amy nestled into him. His eyes closed and his hand rested on the swelling curve of her abdomen. A tiny yet firm movement pushed back.

In the house at Whisper Lane, where children rode horses on warm summer days and ate snickerdoodles made from Aunt Tess's recipe, Gabe and Amy slept.

Acknowledgments

You might say this is an unexpected story. For years I dreamed of telling Shelby and AJ's story, and I hoped to tell Brett's too. But I never expected, never thought, never ever considered telling Amy's.

But friends insisted. So thank you to Carol Anne Giaquinto, Joy Van Tassel, and Mandy Zema for caring about Amy during her dark times and pushing me into listening to her tale. I hope you love her love story.

My deepest gratitude also goes to these fine people who answered a multitude of questions on a wide range of topics: Tina Yeager, therapist and life coach; Mark Mynheir, novelist and law enforcement investigator; Leanna Lindsay Hollis for farming and gardening info; Cathy Gambill for farming info and for sharing her personal story of a barn fire; Alan Hale, Ft. Worth firefighter; Teresa McDanel, who's married to a cowboy and also the mom of one; Dr. Stephen Galloway, my favorite veterinarian; Gayelynn Oyler, my equine expert; Natalie Snodgrass and Jennifer Zarifeh Major, my tea-brewing experts; and to everyone on Facebook who took time to answer my odd and crazy questions. (Any details I got wrong are on me.)

My special thanks to novelist Naomi Rawlings for her invaluable feedback when this series was a one-story draft; fashion whiz Mandy Zema for creating Pinterest wardrobe boards for each of the series' heroines; novelist Patricia Bradley for asking the right questions when I got stuck in a corner; author (and daughter) Bethany Jett for listening to me read the final draft as we drove to a writers conference; and to my sister Hebe Alexander, who courageously endured my writerly angst as the deadline grew closer and a resolution was nowhere in sight.

As always, I am so appreciative of my lovely agent, Tamela Hancock Murray, and my amazing team at Revell: Vicki Crumpton, Kristin Kornoelje, Michele Misiak, Karen Steele, Hannah Brinks, and Cheryl Van Andel. Each of you holds a special place in my heart.

Huge thanks and a heartfelt hug to each person on my Misty Willow Team. You are invaluable in your support, encouragement, and resourcefulness. Thank you so much.

My deepest love as always to Bethany, Jillian, Nate, and their families.

And thanks to my heavenly Father for the gift of unexpected stories.

Johnnie Alexander imagines stories—contemporaries, historicals, and cozy mysteries—whether she's at home in Florida or on the road. Sharing her vagabond life are Griff, her happy-go-lucky collie, and Rugby, her raccoon-treeing papillon. Join Johnnie at www.johnnie-alexander.com to experience the love of random travel and the joy of treasured moments.

MEET
Johnnie Alexander

AT JOHNNIE-ALEXANDER.COM

Can love redeem
A BROKEN PAST?

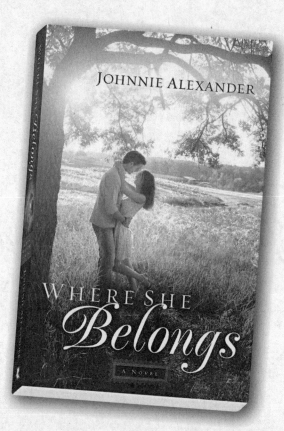

JOHNNIE ALEXANDER

WHERE SHE
Belongs

A NOVEL

In this emotionally rich contemporary romance, a young widow
determined to reclaim her cherished family home clashes with the
handsome yet infuriating current owner who has let it fall into ruin.

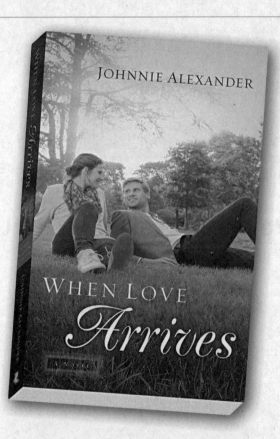